Flight o

The Saga of Bjorn Halfdanson

Peter Richards

For John, much loved and greatly missed

NORTHERN
EUROPE
c. 1000 AD

Trondheim

Bergen

Haugesund

Stavanger

Earldom of ORKNEY

Kingdom of SCOTLAND

Bamburgh

IRISH

Dublin

Kingdom
of
ENGLAND

WELSH

Maldon

Lundenburgh

GER
EMP

Pirou

Kingdom of
FRANCE

Kingdom of NORWAY

Uppsala

Poseboen Oslo

Kingdom of SWEDEN

Laeso

DENMARK

Klaipeda

Trelleborg

Jelling

Truso

Jomsborg

POLAND

MAN
I RE

Range of the
Jomsvikings

Introduction

The golden age of the Vikings took only three centuries to rise and fall. Their ascendency in Dark Age 8th-century Europe, following the cultural and economic decline brought on by the demise of the Roman Empire, was dramatic. The Vikings (never a term they used to describe themselves) came largely from Scandinavia, and their effect on the history of the world cannot be underestimated. Although they are widely known for their destructive prowess, they were a little more balanced than popular fiction would have us believe. Their story is one of epic proportions, and their leaders – with names like Eric Blood-Axe, Bjorn Ironside and Cnut the Great – have stirred the blood, and the imagination, for over a millennium since their deaths.

The Vikings were farmers, fishermen, traders, storytellers and raiders. Their men and women sailed all over the known (and unknown) world in search of wealth and reputation. On a whim they set sail and literally went where the wind blew their longboats, taking their traditions, language and skills with them. They left Scandinavia for many reasons: overcrowding, opportunity or, perhaps, just to find out what lay on the other side of the ocean. They reached America, Africa, Asia and all over Europe, penetrating huge land masses via thousands of miles of river systems, carrying their longboats with them overland whenever they needed to. Death through war, pestilence or famine seldom slowed their progress, and their relentless thirst for land and silver remained unquenched throughout three hundred years of seaborne dominance. The Norse travellers took their gods with them wherever they settled until Paganism was engulfed by Christianity which ultimately gained widespread adoption all over their Scandinavian homelands. Thor and *Odin* were eventually assimilated into a less violent religion although their stories and artefacts still have a popular place in historical fact and fiction to this day.

It is beyond doubt that the Vikings were fierce people, but their story is not only one of delivering death, destruction and pillage to the unlucky victims of their invasions. They also brought culture, technology and trade to many of the places where they settled and assimilated. Their colonies, from the west to the east, took root, endured and prospered, from Greenland to far beyond the Caspian Sea. The effect of the Vikings on the British Isles was equally dramatic, and their people settled large swathes of the Anglo-Saxon kingdoms and never left. After an active campaign against the Franks, King Charles the Simple gave the great sea king, Rollo, much of the Duchy of Normandy in return for peace, fealty and conversion to Christianity. A little later, in 1066, two armies of Viking descent faced each other at the pivotal Battle of Hastings, shortly after one had defeated a third army of Norsemen in the north of England en route to the battlefield.

The main protagonists of our story, Bjorn Halfdanson and Torstein the Warrior Skald, demonstrate and articulate many of the characteristics expected of the sons of Odin. They are fictitious characters on a journey through a factual landscape set against a backdrop of real events. They are not perfect human beings by any stretch of the imagination and are prone to the foibles of their type. However, they are probably more authentic than many of the Vikings described in the millions of fictional words written about their people since they faded from history.

> "Keep away Christians,
> We're are busy inside,
> Sacrificing to elves and spirits,
> Keeping the old faith
> In fear of Odin's fury"
> - Pagan prayer

Chapter 1: Leaving Home

Our town of Haugesund lies at the feet of the great Norse mountain range and has been home to my people for five hundred years or more. Looking out to sea, I can see the rocky outcrop of the rough and barely habitable islands of Røvær rising out of the mists. They have, for centuries, offered us some shelter from the great North Sea. It is late summer and there are few signs of life in the early morning. The sun is a pale-yellow orb, burning away through the fog of another morning that is slowly coming to life. The waves from a sluggish ocean break lazily on the sandy beach blowing salty flecks of foam that catch in my hair and beard. I wait for my cousin, Torstein. I have important news for him.

My name is Bjorn Halfdanson, and I have lived here for eighteen years with my family. Until recently my father was the local *jarl*, the head of his clan of two hundred and sixty folk, ruler of his *aett* and the *ring-giver* to his people. He was killed on the eve of his fiftieth birthday by an axe wound to the belly sustained confronting raiders who came to attack us. It was a lucky blow that took the life of such a famous warrior as Halfdan Strong Arm, but he died in the manner of ordinary men. Our town mourned his passing greatly, and the loss to my mother, my siblings and me was bitterly felt.

We are now under the protection of his brother, Rollo, who has taken my father's place. We are a community of farmers, traders, fisherman and sometimes raiders who supplement an ample subsistence by taking what we need by force when needs must. We are a sea-going people and will sail thousands of miles of relentless ocean in search of reputation and plunder. Our folk are the direct descendants of Ragnar Lodbrok and Halfdan Gunnerson, famous Norsemen who have taken their place in the story of our people. Our

3

warriors have always been keen to go a-viking from whence they can return home with longboats full of gold, silver and slaves.

For over six years I have been a warrior and since boyhood, I learned to fight with the axe, the sword and the spear. My father took me on my first raid on my twelfth birthday where I learned the virtues of discipline and training. I took my place in the shield wall at the age of fifteen and I was quickly put to the test. The smell of fear and impending death as men stood shoulder-to-shoulder, braced behind locked shields was a brutal and lasting memory. It was a pitiless, savage existence – raiding and fighting – but I was never happier than when I went out with my father in search of treasure and tribute bringing death and destruction to those who would stand against us.

I am tall, muscular and yellow-haired – the image of my father when he was my age, I am told. When he was a young man my father and his war band roamed with impunity and raided wherever they wished. To the east, the lands of the Slavs were easy pickings and silver and slaves were plentiful. To the west, England and Ireland would give him a good bounty; their churches and monasteries were full of treasure and their priests were easily taken. These days the eastern silver mines are exhausted, and the Slavs are poorer than ever. The Saxons of England, however, are well organised now into defensive armies and can react quickly whenever our people attack them. They will strike back from behind strong fortresses at the first sign of invasion. Our old ways of attacking in loose warbands have lost their impact over time and the traditions of raiding and plundering will one day become only memories. I yearn for the freedom of our old way of life for we range and raid less and less as the days go by.

Our world is changing fast – a change that began a hundred years ago or more. The destruction of the old, independent small states of Norway started in my grandfather's day. The King, Harald Finehair, inherited a small kingdom from his father from where he controlled the trade routes to Southern Norway. Harald set about defeating each of the petty kingdoms surrounding him, swallowing their land and people, before moving onto the next. After that, he held the whole country in an iron grip and the last of the old kings were forced to bend the knee to him. Worse was to follow when his son, the Grey Cloak, tried to force Christianity on his people that threatened our very pagan roots. Many folk left the country looking for new land and opportunity; like them, my time here in Rogaland will soon be at an end.

One evening in Rollo's hall I discussed my fears and concerns with my uncle. As the flames on the hearth were dying and his men and dogs were snoring Rollo turned to me and put his hand on my shoulder.

"Bjorn, you now have a choice. You can accept the new ways, or you can search for a different path. Our people have always left and searched for new opportunities when they have needed to. We are no longer able to raid at will and must obey the King's every whim or face the consequences. However, in Wendland on the Baltic shores there is a citadel called Jomsborg. Within this fortress, there is a new, powerful band of warriors that are like nothing we have seen before. They are organised and determined and led by Styrbjorn the Strong – a prince of Sweden. You may find what you are looking for there. The rest is up to you. But enough now, it is time to retire."

That night I could not sleep, and I knew that I must find the Jomsvikings. After a couple of restless *eyktir*, my new plans took shape, and I was up and out of my bed before the cock crowed that morning. I still lived in the same house as my family and had to creep out to avoid waking anyone. Neither of our two wolfhounds stirred and I passed them dreaming and fidgeting in their sleep beside the dying embers of the open fire in the centre of the main room. I needed to speak with my cousin Torstein, so I walked to the house he shared with five other bachelors and hammered on his door.

"Torstein, wake up," I shouted. "Meet me at the old rock on the shoreline as soon as you can."

Our town is still and silent at that time of day but there is always the pounding of the waves, the calling gulls and a wind that constantly whistles along the shoreline. Haugesund lies on a sandy shore that slopes steeply down to the sea and is surrounded by a double wooden palisade on all the other sides. Most of the cooking fires in our dwellings had not yet been made from the previous night although a few smoke trails curled through one or two roofs as the town woke up. About a hundred paces from the last of these houses I waited for my cousin on the beach next to an old standing stone covered in ancient runes. A huge black raven landed on top of the stone and peered down at me for a moment before taking off again.

Lost in my thoughts I barely noticed the large, shambling bear of a man coming towards me. My cousin is at least a head taller than me, very broad, with heavily tattooed arms, prominent beneath a sleeveless tunic. His long red hair and bushy beard are normally immaculately combed and plaited but at this time of the morning he was unusually dishevelled. Torstein is a year older than me and we grew up together in a very close-knit family group. My father had a favourite saying, "Bjorn, it takes two men to make a single brother." In Torstein, I understood the meaning of these words.

Unlike me, Torstein could take very little seriously and had a huge appetite for raiding, women and drinking. He could raise the dampest spirits after the most bitter of disappointments and was a good man to have on your side. A formidable fighter with axe or sword, my cousin feared nothing and had little respect for reputations.

"Góðan dag, cousin," he shouted when he got close enough. "Whatever you have to tell me must be important for that raven watching you is a good omen. Was it *Hugin* or *Munin*?"

"Hello, Torstein," I replied. "I hope I wasn't interrupting you."

"Just humping some of the new slave girls – nothing that can't wait… and they are very eager to please. What is it?"

"This could take a while," I told him.

"Then we had better sit down, cousin," he said.

He sat down on a piece of driftwood, and I babbled away like an idiot for some time. I talked about the future, the overcrowding and the increasing number of mouths to feed. I talked about the demands of the new King for taxation, fealty and burdensome service. Our enemies were growing in strength, and there were few opportunities to raid as we became part of the new kingdom of Norway. To make matters worse the creeping curse of Christianity that swept through Ireland and England was now spinning its dark web across Scandinavia. Both of us desired to retain our Norse heritage and to live as generations had done for centuries before us. I told him what his father, Rollo, said to me about the Jomsvikings last night and the great opportunity that, I believed, awaited us.

"I have also heard of them," said Torstein. Then, after considering the proposition for an age he added, "It is true they are not without reputation, and I would like nothing better than to raid England again and this time with an unbeatable force. But I have also heard they are very selective about who they take into their brotherhood and there are many rules by which they live. I have heard that they do not even allow women into their fortress – on pain of death."

"Well, cousin, I think that the gold and the land we might be able to take under their colours would be ample compensation for leaving the women aside for a night or two. What do you think?"

As is Torstein's wont, he prevaricated and wandered this way and that, but finally he agreed with me that it might be time for us to seek wealth and reputation in foreign fields once more. He sat and finally nodded his great shaggy head and laughed.

"We shall not become heroes of the kitchen nor be celebrated only in the memories of old folk alone. I am with you and we shall go together. All men are mortal, but only a noble name can live forever – we are as one mind. Come, Bjorn, I am starving. Let's eat then and make a plan before I wilt away to almost nothing."

We agreed that we were both of singular purpose and that we should leave our homeland and travel across the sea. We would travel by ship to Wendland; it would take us about ten days to get there if the winds and tides were good to us. The voyage would take us down the coast towards the south and then sail between Denmark and Sweden to reach the Baltic shores in a small longship, the Raven, with thirteen other men who would wait for us in Jomsborg where we would try to get an audience with Styrbjorn. If our application was successful, the men would leave us to our fate. Our voyage was not one of war, so the ship's carved figurehead was to be stowed below decks – denoting our peaceful intentions. As always, we would be fully armed to dissuade any attack.

A week after talking with my uncle we stood, in bright morning light, on the dock in front of the town and prepared to take our leave, but for how long I could not say. My father had been a wealthy man in Haugesund and left me with gold and silver, now stowed in my sea chest with my weapons and armour. Dressed in my best clothes and replete with father's *Ulfberht* sword, *Gunnlogi* – Heat of Battle – I was ready for fame and fortune.

I waited on the quayside on that late summer morning and bade goodbye to my friends and family, and one by one we said our farewells. My mother was one of the last, and she hugged and kissed me. When she finally released me, she looked up at me.

"I have watched you grow from a tiny seed to a man these eighteen years, and I must now let you go to your fate.

We will think of you often and may Aegir watch over you until you come back to us," she said.

With that, she thrust a drawstring leather bag into my hand containing something small and heavy. I put it inside my tunic and struggled for some words, but before I could say anything the silence was broken as Torstein came into view ahead of a noisy little procession. Following in his wake as quickly as possible were two slave girls struggling to carry his sea chest. Above the commotion, I could hear him cajoling them for greater speed.

"Come on you two be quick and don't drop that chest again or we shall miss the morning tide."

We finally said our goodbyes to the rest of the town who waited patiently and then boarded our ship to take our places at the oars. The helmsman took the tiller and steered us out to the North Sea where we headed south. The lump in my throat grew, and I watched my family become smaller and smaller figures on the shoreline until I lost sight of them altogether.

We reached the other side of the rocky islands and were into the open sea. Oars were shipped and a blue-striped woollen sail was hoisted for the winds to blow us towards Wendland. I remembered the bag my mother had given me and retrieved its contents from inside my tunic. It was my father's gold amulet – Thor's Hammer. Our saga had begun.

Chapter 2: Setting Sail

Jomsborg lies on the Baltic Coast – a voyage of almost one thousand miles ahead of us. If the winds blew in the right direction, we could sail without the backbreaking labour of rowing against the currents. The Raven was a small longboat made of oak and pine. It had been used to range from Haugesund and only needed a crew of sixteen men. Although similar in shape to some of the larger warships that prevailed along the coastline, it had also been used as a merchant ship. The Raven had been used to carry high valued goods like gold or silver, and she was agile and quick if we needed to manoeuvre away from any attackers. On this voyage, our crew of fifteen was about half the men the Raven would carry for war, but hopefully we would avoid any trouble to or from Jomsborg. If we were attacked on our journey, we could defend ourselves or at least be able to out-run any enemy. She was of a classic Scandinavian design – a *skeid* – and about half the size of a regular warship. Like all Scandinavian longships, she owed her speed to her design. The shipwrights always laid the planed timbers on the outer hull to form a pocket of bubbles on the planking when she moved, allowing her to glide quickly over the waves. The Raven sat high in the water and had a shallow draught allowing her to navigate in shallow waters and rivers.

The Raven had two small, raised platforms at bow and stern and between them was a rough deck made up of loose planks that could be lifted to allow baling when we needed it. During rough weather this was a continuous process, so if the crewmen were neither rowing nor baling, they were able to get some rest. Each oarsman sat at his oar on his sea chest in which he kept his weapons and armour. At night we would attempt to find shelter either ashore or anchored off the coast where a large awning would be rigged which would afford us some shelter. The captain of the Raven was a middle-aged man called Helge – one of Rollo's men and a mariner of many years' experience in sailing the Baltic and beyond. He was neither tall nor short and wore both his greying hair and beard loose. His bright green eyes were as sharp as a man half his age and he was a veteran of many seaborne war parties. The rest of the crew were family and friends, all a similar age to Torstein and me – and all seasoned warriors apart from two armed slaves who carried out the chores. We were on a peaceful mission, but we were well-equipped to fight if it became necessary.

That day we made good headway under sail and travelled within five or six miles from the coastline. This was familiar territory to all of us and we passed only a few merchant ships plying their trade along the coast. We enjoyed good sea breezes on our first day, and the white horses scattered in front of us as we cut through the waves. After an *eykt*, I took the tiller from Helge and at once felt the familiar exhilaration as the boat responded to my touch. Feeling the wind and salt spray in my face that day signified the beginning of a voyage that would take many twists and turns before we arrived at journey's end.

We had supplied our ship with about two weeks' vittles of hard bread, cheese and some salted fish and meat, along with three hogsheads of ale. We were well provisioned. Our journey took us through numerous points where unprepared ships were often prey for pirates, and it was essential we were ready for trouble. Each member of the crew carried his armour – a mail shirt, a protective jerkin and a helmet – and additionally a shield, a spear and an axe or a sword. There were also at least eight hunting bows between us, each with dozens of arrows. We could fight off anyone but a large band, and each man was a seasoned fighter. Our slaves too were armed, willing and able to fight.

We made good time after running in front of the wind all day, and the captain decided that we would spend that night in the lee of an island called Rott. It was deserted but for a few goats and the occasional clump of stunted trees. Helge steered us into a quiet little bay he knew. The waters were flat, and each man sat down at his oars and rowed us into the beach. As we got closer, oars were shipped and the familiar crunch of the shale meeting the bow signalled to the men to get into the surf and pull the Raven up to the high watermark on the shoreline. We camped on the beach that night.

There was enough driftwood along the shoreline to make a decent fire above which an iron cooking pot was suspended. One of our two slaves, a Saxon called Athelstan, prepared food for us. He had been captured two years before during a raid in Northumbria with his brother Godwin. They had proved their loyalty, and we treated them well – affording them such respect as they earned during their captivity. They were allowed arms and would be expected to fight should the need arise. They were strong oarsmen, good workers and valued members of our crew – but never our equals. That night we sat around the fire and – after we ate and drank ale – settled down under a clear star-filled night sky. Like he had done a great many times before, Torstein told a story – the Old Norse saga of the Curse of Andvari's Ring. He was a natural storyteller and a gifted skaldic poet who needed no second invitation to entertain his listeners with stories, which he accompanied with dramatic action. The more ribald the story the more he indulged himself and his audience. That night was no different and Torstein was in his element retelling the popular folktale to rapt and eager listeners. After an *eykt* or so the ale and fatigue took their toll, and the first snores echoed under the cliffs of our home for the night.

The next morning, I woke to the familiar sound of seabirds and breaking waves. The men began to stir for a new day emerging from beneath their cloaks and *hudfat* bags. After a cold breakfast of hard bread and cheese, we were ready for another day's voyage and hauled the Raven back through the surf and rowed out into the open sea. The wind was slightly brisker than the previous day, and we shipped oars and watched the sail flutter and fill. Then I joined Helge at the tiller, and we scanned the horizon for a hint of the day's weather.

"Looks like another decent day's wind," he shouted, but I knew he could see what I could see; storm clouds on the horizon heading our way from the south.

If we had been expecting a storm, we were very much mistaken. The wind dropped suddenly, and the choppy sea was becalmed – resembling soup – and barely a ripple disturbed the water's surface. If the day was clear we could navigate using a 'sun compass' – a simple wooden circle with a pin in the middle, which we used to find direction according to the height of the sun and time of day. The sky, however, was darkening, and a thickening fog was rolling in. In the absence of the sun, Helge was using crystals, kept in a bag around his neck, to navigate. Turned in a certain direction, they either darkened or lightened according to the amount of available sunlight. Even on a foggy day like this, these crystals enabled the navigator to know where the sun was beyond the clouds, and Helge was still able to plot our course.

The order was given to lower the sail, and as quickly as it had gone up – so it came down. The pivoted shutters that covered each oar to prevent water coming in were opened again and the oars threaded through. Each man took his position and we rowed in unison whilst Helge stood at the tiller studying his navigating crystal and took us south. The fog was getting so thick that you could barely see the man two 'benches' in front of you. It muffled any noise about us, and we could not even hear the sound of the sea which had died to a whimper. The normally breaking waves that would have warned us of our proximity to the shore were silent, and I spent an anxious time praying for the sea mists to lift. We were rowing blind and all we had to keep us from disaster was Helge's memory of the shoreline and the faintly glowing crystal in his hand.

Norsemen are sea-going people who trust both in their destiny and experience. For hundreds of years, we have gone where the winds and tides have carried us, marking our journey so we could return home the same way and allowing others to follow our path. We trusted in the Raven and ourselves, and once the day passed into the evening the fog lifted completely, the winds freshened, and we could see where we were going once more. We were still a couple of thousand paces off the coast and Helge moved the tiller to take us to the leeward side of an island called Eigeroya. We could not beach the Raven that evening as the coastline was extremely rocky and we found no point where we could go ashore. Instead, we anchored in shallow water and erected the awning over the ship, which afforded us cover for the night. Our crew was a little quieter this evening than the previous night, and even Torstein was not his normal enthusiastic self. Perhaps we were both reflecting on our forthcoming journey into unknown waters and what might lie ahead of us.

All the same, I gave thanks to the goddess Frigg for providing us with safe winds so far and for the secure berth she had blown us to tonight.

There is an old Norse saying: Cattle die, kindred die, we ourselves also die; but the fair fame never dies of him who has earned it. Would I earn my longed-for place in the memories of men for gaining importance, wealth and fame as well? Time would tell, and I took a final look at the clear night sky with its constellations of stars gleaming down on us and thanked the gods once again. I went to take my place under the awning with Torstein and the rest of them as we gathered our strength for whatever was thrown at us on the morrow.

Chapter 3: Lost at Sea

The next day of our journey was the complete opposite of the previous one. After less than a single *eykt* of being back in the open water, the weather turned on us. The heavens opened, and we sailed into one of the most savage storms I have ever encountered. The gods had decided to test us and they did so with increasing venom, hurling down thunder, lightning and storms that tossed our small vessel about like a piece of cork. The fierce offshore winds were dragging the Raven out into the open ocean, and we could not fight against it. All we could do was drop the sail and pray that we would not be driven onto any rocks should the winds change. I joined Helge at the tiller, and between us we fought the elements. Our intended course had been to hug the coast of Norway as far as Scalevik and then head across to Denmark, but this storm had thrown everything into confusion. I glanced over my shoulder and saw the coastline disappearing as our small vessel was tossed about like so much flotsam and jetsam.

"What now?" I bellowed in Helge's ear as another wave broke over the stern, drenching us again.

"I need six oarsmen to row and the rest of you to bale," he shouted back.

I hurried forward and shouted the order to the crew. Torstein and five of our best oarsmen rowed as the rest of us baled with everything we had. Helmets, cups and buckets were all put into action as we fought against the incoming water that endangered our survival. Helge lashed himself to the tiller as breakers crashed against and into the Raven threatening to engulf us. Hands and fingers quickly became numb as we battled against the great North Sea, scooping out the swirling water in the boat with whatever came to hand. After each wave broke over us and filled the boat up with water, sometimes to the gunwales, we would bale like men possessed and brace ourselves for the impact of the next attack from the sea.

Wave after wave, time after time, the process repeated itself. We would row into and up the swell (and then hopefully down) until the next breaker hit us. With each impact, the boat filled up with water again. As soon as they had recovered from the impact, men would scramble about in the bilges baling water over the side. So it went on, and after an *eykt* we changed tasks as rowers became balers. Helge steered us into the unremitting maelstrom. Many *eyktir* passed and the skies began to darken even more. I realised that day was turning into night. There was no moon or stars now only the thundering of the crashing waves and the inevitable confusion when a big one crashed over us again. Still, we baled.

This was no ordinary gale, and the noise was deafening. It numbed my senses, changing pitch and direction as Aegir's music hammered through the boat making the timbers judder and the shrouds shriek, and I could not imagine escaping his wrath. The noise was terrifying, but the windswept sea was worse. It was as if the sea gods, in a drunken rage, were stirring the waters into a confusion of water and air, whipping the foam into a frenzy of fury that flayed men's skin. As the night wore on, we staggered blindly up the sides of mountains of water which then hurled the Raven down into the deep voids of the ocean. Somehow, we were not swamped, and I felt that if the waves did not kill us then the freezing cold would.

I struggled to the back of the boat to relieve Helge who was now slumped over the tiller to which his arm was still tied.

"What now?" I shouted to him.

"Just keep steering into the wind," he shouted back.

I called for Godwin, who was trying to hand out food to the men, to come and help me get Helge down. We carried our helmsman onto one of the rowing benches where he lay drenched and exhausted. I stepped up to take the helm. That night was the longest night I can remember. I was freezing cold, soaked and could barely see my hand in front of my face, but I would not relinquish my grip on the tiller until dawn. I draped myself across it and refused to budge – until the next wave hit us. Then the next, then the next.

Morning came. Not with any visible rising sun, but with just a little light spreading amongst the squally gloom. The sea gave us a temporary respite as the winds dropped and the swell became a little less oppressive. I was able to survey the crew. The rowers were still moving but at a vastly reduced speed. The balers continued their actions but were moving stiffly and slowly. Helge had fallen off his bench in exhaustion and was lying on his back in the bottom of the boat. Godwin was dispensing food and ale again, and we had made it through another awful night. The Saxon came up to me at the tiller.

"Lord?" he said, holding out some dried meat and a mug of ale.

I took it from him and looked into his face. He was approximately my age, and his long, brown, wet hair clung to his face. Like the rest of us, he was drenched. His pallor was grey, and he stood on unsteady legs. One side of his face was heavily bruised.

"What happened to you, Godwin?" I asked.

Two of the hogsheads of ale had broken their bindings and gone overboard in the night as well as another one containing the salted pork. He tried to save them but only suffered injury for his efforts. The loss of supplies was not good news, neither were the tidings that saltwater had also found its way into the rations of hard bread in their supposedly waterproof sealskin bags. We all ate, regaining a little strength, and the boat slowly came to life again.

I watched Torstein throw back the remnants of his mug of ale and call to the others.

"Come on you bastards! Keep baling. There are fish nibbling at my balls!"

17

He laughed like a madman. The rowers started rowing, and the balers baled. So the day continued. Helge roused himself from where he had been lying in the belly of the Raven and joined me at the stern of the ship.

"Any idea where we are?" I asked him. I looked all around for a sign of landfall.

Helge withdrew his vital navigating aid once more from its sodden pouch. "According to the crystal, we're still heading south. But where we are, I cannot tell."

"We must take on new supplies as soon as we can," I said. "We lost half of them last night, and all the bread is ruined."

As we both contemplated that sobering fact, we watched in horror as the black storm clouds headed straight for us again. We were once more in the teeth of the great storm, and the Raven was pulled and dragged this way and that. Up and down the massive waves we went – catapulted to their peaks and then hurled down again. They crashed over us repeatedly and endlessly filled the ship with water. The oarsmen and the tiller man kept us on as straight a path as they could while the rest of us baled as quick as our weary bodies would allow. Should any man fail on this vital task then we would surely sink.

For two more days and nights we suffered at the hands of the sea gods, and I took turns with Helge in trying to keep the course, but it was like fighting the army of Hel. With every lurch forward or sideways the storm sapped a little more of the crew's remaining strength. Then on the morning of the storm's third day, I woke up sore, stiff and hungry and tied to the tiller by some rope. Helge was lying underneath the tiller with his arm also secured with the same piece of rope. The six oarsmen were all in place, but their exhausted bodies were still and rocking with the now gentle swell of the ocean. I untied myself and looked into the bilges and counted seven more comrades. First one began to move and then the rest followed suit. The crew had all made it through the storm alive, but we were now hungry, and we had lost even more supplies, leaving us with only a handful of salted fish to see us through. It was time to take stock.

The storm lasted for three days and nights and now seemingly left us. We had lost most of our food and drink but still had all our original crew. It was early morning and the sun was rising from the East on a sea empty of any sign of land. We needed to find a port soon to resupply but without knowing where we were it was difficult to make an adequate plan. Whilst Helge was the captain of our ship, I was the leader of our group, and I knew that I needed a little luck to get to somewhere safe quickly. We had to stop at the first available opportunity whether the locals were friendly or not.

I dragged Helge off the deck as gently as possible and shook him awake. I gave him a minute to gather his senses and then pressed him: "Where are we?" I asked repeatedly. The Raven's captain was a good man and an experienced navigator, and after a few mental calculations and a check on the rising sun's position he looked me in the face and said:

"Bjorn, I believe we are in the middle of the Skagerak Sea. We will sail east, and as soon as we get our bearings, we will turn south again towards the Island of Laeso where *Jarl* Eric is Lord. I know him well, and he was a friend of your father. He is a Dane but still a good man, and his people will resupply us. That is if your sea chest hasn't joined our food and ale in the sea," he added with a faint smile.

I told the men our plan and they cheered weakly. Our spirits were further lifted at the sight of our sodden sail which, once hoisted, caught the wind and propelled us towards the rising sun and the east. After a while, the hazy sun climbed high in the sky and shone a few of its early autumn rays upon the boat. The wind maintained a constant level and blew us east towards the coast of Sweden. Our clothes started to dry for the first time in three days, and the baling finally slowed to a manageable pace. Although it was difficult to forget recent events – and being at the mercy of the sea gods – things started to feel lighter. I no longer felt we were on an impossible mission and most, if not all, of the feelings of guilt for what I was putting the men through started to recede. Faces that had once been grey with fatigue and cold started smiling again through salt-encrusted hair and beards. Everything became possible again, and Torstein in a large booming voice struck up a song. The subject was his favourite pastime – women and drinking – and he boomed out a popular refrain. The others, who were slowly gathering their strength after the ordeal, joined him. They sat exhausted on their benches as the Raven carved her way through the light swell.

After a while, we ate the last of the salt fish, and sensing a meal the gulls hovered on the sea breezes around us. The number of gulls increased – a sign that land was not too far away. Without a word, Helge moved the tiller and the Raven veered south and towards Laeso. I went to stand beside him, and without waiting for me to ask the question he said, "We should reach Laeso in a day. They should have plenty of food at this time of year and will have plenty to trade for silver."

"I have plenty to spare," I said. "Aegir spared my sea chest so there will be no need to go raiding."

"Good, because Laesoins have a reputation for meanness and driving a hard bargain," replied Helge.

Torstein, now basking in the sun's weak rays like a bull walrus saw us talking and shouted to us, "I am not proud and am quite prepared to ride a Danish woman. What are the whorehouses like in Laeso?"

Not getting any reply he stood up and gave full voice – this time treating us to a few verses of skaldic poetry:

She-wolves they were, and scarcely women.
They crushed my ship, which with props I had secured,
With iron, clubs threatened me and drove away Thiâlfi.
What meanwhile didst thou, Harbard?

He went on like this for a while but noticing that no one was listening he stopped and sulked. For centuries we Norsemen would go raiding when food onboard became low. This was known as a *strandhogg* – a raid ashore where sheep and cattle would be rounded up and either slaughtered or taken aboard to provide fresh meat. People were also captured and taken back as slaves as well as any goods or valuables that were found. We believed that we were able to help ourselves to these bounties and this practice had once been customary even in Scandinavia against other Norse people. In recent years the practice had been outlawed unless at the express consent of the King. Like many others, I believed that *strandhewing* was our right and I longed for the day when we would be out of reach of these laws when we could go a-viking once more. However, Laeso was Danish and the Danes were our confederates, and there was – mostly – peace between us. Besides we were too few to make up a powerful war band, although we were certainly large enough to put off any random attack by outlaws or pirates.

Helge told me that we would sail to the south side of the island to the town of Byrum where we could moor in the harbour before going ashore. It would be good manners to pay our respects to *Jarl* Eric before we started to buy our supplies. After a quiet day-and-night's sailing, we woke up hungry and looking forward to finding Laeso. I had been at the tiller for much of the night, and as the sun came up behind us, I strained my eyes for any sight of land. I was to be disappointed, but I told myself that we must surely be close now – judging by the number of seabirds flying around us. Godwin was the first one to spot it about an *eyktir's* sail away. For the second time in a day, the men cheered as they looked forward to standing on solid ground for the first time in a while. Judging from the look of all our crew, the storm had taken a great toll on our appearance, and we all looked dishevelled and dirty – not a trait often found amongst vain Norsemen. We took turns sharing combs, and beards and hair were groomed as well as possible. Good time had been made, and we passed the rocky headland of the island and made our way to the harbour on the other side. The sun was behind us, a fresh breeze was kicking up salt spray in our faces, and I stood on firm legs at the tiller. Spirits were high.

According to Helge, who was the only one of us to have visited Laeso, the island was the biggest rock in the North Sea and was very close to Jutland and therefore part of the new Kingdom of Denmark. It was famed for its salt and honey, and in the old stories it was the home of Aegir the *Sea Jotun* and his wife Ran. These were the very gods who had caused us such an uncomfortable few days, which were now becoming just a memory. We would also be able to get some of the damage to our vessel repaired whilst we were there. I agreed with Helge that we should stay no longer than two days, for it was still quite a way to Jomsborg; as we knew, an Autumn storm could be a capricious mistress.

So far, we had not encountered a single Danish vessel – neither merchant nor fishing boat nor longboat – not that I thought it strange at the time. We soon spotted the entrance to the harbour – a small ingress in between two towering cliffs leading up a small fjord and then to the port. As we got closer, we dropped the sail and made ready to row towards the harbour. We rowed slowly through the gap in the cliffs, which formed a natural wall for the town against the elements. Then we steered to port and rowed for about a quarter of a mile, and inside the inlet lay the town of Byrum. We moved forward slowly so as not to unnerve the locals even though we had no carved figurehead on our bows and were obviously visiting in peace. We were also exhausted, and I stood on the bow forecastle anticipating how good it would be to feel solid ground beneath my feet. It would not take long for this forlorn hope to desert me.

Chapter 4: The Raid on Byrum

The Raven glided through flat water, but as we approached there were no signs of life – not a single dog barking, a child playing nor any movement on the shoreline. Nothing. Neither were there any boats in the harbour. More ominous still was the spiraling smoke coming from some of the burned-out shells of a number of the houses on the shore. The town itself comprised of thirty-or-so wooden dwellings on a gentle upward slope including a large hall, which I took to be *Jarl* Eric's longhouse. At this time of day and season, I would have expected the quayside to be busy, but this one was deserted; save for the gulls there was no movement. Torstein joined me in the bows to survey the scene.

"Looks like they might have been attacked and everyone has gone," he said.

"Back down oars," I ordered the crew, and the boat stopped moving while the two of us looked on and considered the fate of the town. As I was trying to make a plan, I saw movement near some of the houses and a boy and a girl – I guessed about twelve or thirteen years old – ran between the buildings towards the jetty. Not far behind them, two men were in rapid pursuit – both armed with spears. The girl was slower than the boy and her skirts prevented her from running quickly. She tripped and fell before reaching the wooden jetty. Her pursuer caught up with her and kicked her on the ground. He lifted his spear and brought it down driving its point through her back. She screamed in pain as he stabbed her several times, two-handed until she stopped moving.

By now the boy had made it to the jetty and he ran down its length – although the man chasing him was catching him fast. Before he could do so, his quarry had reached the end

23

and dove into the sea – swimming towards our stationary boat perhaps two hundred *fot* away. As he swam, we watched the spearman stop, steady himself and hurl his spear into the water. The boy sank beneath the surface for a moment and disappeared, only to reappear and continue his escape. As he swam towards us, the rest of our crew were now on their feet shouting encouragement to him. He appeared to tire but finally reached our oars where he was dragged out by strong arms. The two men on the jetty were joined by about twenty others who glared at us silently while we all took stock of the situation.

I gave the order to row a little closer to the quay where the waiting men stood there watching us. I told Torstein to string his bow and prepare himself and three other bowmen to be ready to shoot if I gave the order. We came within a distance where we could make our shouted words audible to the men on the quay and close enough for me to make out how many were armed. They carried swords and axes but bore no shields, only a few wore mail and were not ready for a confrontation just yet.

"I think we surprised them," said Torstein.

"Where is *Jarl* Eric," I shouted in the common tongue, *Donsk tunga*.

Just then, a large man wearing a grey wolfskin cloak pushed to the front of the stationary throng. He was about my height, dark-haired and had a long, plaited beard. Underneath his cloak, he wore a long mail coat and was bareheaded. He shouted something unintelligible back, and his words caught on the wind. I signalled to the crew to move us closer, and we gently eased forward until we were but a few boat lengths from them with our bow pointing directly at the jetty.

"Frisian pirates," said Torstein to me, "I can smell them from here."

I shouted again, this time in Frisian and I asked the big man again:

"Where is *Jarl* Eric, the lord of this island."

"He is not here," he responded. "Neither are his men, but his wife and daughters have been very welcoming. You are also very welcome to come ashore and avail yourselves of their hospitality. There is plenty to be found here and you and your men look like you need some food and rest." All his men laughed as if sharing a private joke.

"Thank you for the invitation" I replied and gave him a mocking half-bow. "But I do not think it is in your gift to invite us here, and by the way, you just killed that young girl for no reason, other than she was just trying to escape your filthy clutches. I do not think you would make a good host. I just don't think we would all get on."

The big man bridled at this and all pretence of civility left the conversation when he shouted back:

"Listen to me, Norseman, why don't you fuck off back to whatever frozen piece of rock you have just come from and you might live. If not, just come ashore and take your chances. There are lots of us here, and I would love to take that pretty little boat of yours."

I was close enough to see the flecks of spittle spraying from his mouth. He became angrier and continued his tirade.

"There are plenty of swords and axes here if you would like to come and try your luck," he added, and as he did so a number of his men split off and ran back to the houses, presumably to retrieve their arms.

He was right; we were outnumbered. We had already seen twenty of them standing in front of us, and there were probably many more that we could not see. We were very vulnerable until we got ashore and even then, we would find ourselves confronted by many times our number. There was only one course of action, and I signalled to 'back oars' again as we slowly retreated our vessel the way we had come in. The standing group were now joined by more armed men whilst others started laughing and cursing us in their native language. At least two of them decided to drop their breeches and show us their bare arses as a further insult. I could hear Torstein behind me muttering curses with increasing volume. I paid him no attention and just kept my eyes on the group in front of me, which suddenly parted. A man ran straight through the gap to the edge of the quay and hurled a spear at me. I watched it sail straight towards me as it travelled the hundred-or-so *fot* to reach its target. I moved quickly within the narrow confines of the ship's bows and caught it cleanly in my left hand, transferring it to my right, and pivoting on my right foot I returned it in a single fluid action. It did not hit the thrower, but instead it went through the throat of the man standing next to him, breeks still down in insult. The dying man dropped to the floor, spraying the onlookers with gouts of blood. It caused much confusion onshore during which time we turned the Raven around and made our way back to the mouth of the fjord. Our crew whooped and howled at the misfortune of the fallen man and insults were returned.

I jumped down from the forecastle and went to the bench where the escaped boy was sitting wet and shaking. He was recovering from his swim to freedom and doing his best to hold back tears. His name was Ulf and he was twelve years old. He lived in Byrum with his family who farmed a smallholding on the outskirts of the town. His father had gone with Jarl Eric who was answering the call of the King of Denmark who had summoned all his *Jarls* to a meeting in Hedeby to join the rest of the Danish army there. The town had been left in the care of a few armed retainers, old men and boys. Two days earlier, Frisian merchant ships had entered the fjord and docked at Byrum – seemingly looking to trade their cargo. The crews of the ships came ashore – about fifty of them – and finding the town in the care of a flimsy group of defenders decided to take their chance. They killed what resistance there was namely murdering twelve men and boys and started on a two-day campaign of looting, raping and killing. During that time, they ill-treated the town's inhabitants and stripped them of all their valuables which were now in a pile on the floor of Eric's longhouse – together with the *Jarl's* now unhidden horde of gold and silver. Some of the women of the town had also been taken there where they suffered (and were still suffering) a good deal of mistreatment at the hands of the raiders. The leader of their group, the big man in a wolf-skin cloak was named Duko. Feared by his own men, he had been particularly harsh in his treatment of the captives.

Putting aside all thoughts of going ashore at Byrum I looked at Ulf and said, "We need food and a place to repair our boat. Is there anywhere on the island where we could do this in safety?"

The boy replied, "I will take you to the far side of the island where my grandfather lives in a small community of farmers who will sell you food and ale, and you can repair your boat in safety." Then he added timidly "Will you help us?"

"I don't know," I said. "I will decide by tonight, but right now you must guide us to this place."

With that, we joined Helge at the helm. Ulf gave him some instructions while the men pulled at their oars, and we went back into the open sea. Very soon the wind picked up and we were under sail again. I told the men where we were heading and that we hoped to be there before nón on the windward side of the island. The men were now resting in the belly of the ship and I went to join them.

"Hell of a throw," called Torstein to me, and I nodded with a grin. "Teach those Frisian goatfuckers a bit of respect,' he added.

I smiled again, but secretly I was elated with my throw that day. I tried unsuccessfully to be modest, but Torstein knew me much better. Should we meet the Frisians again they would not treat us quite so lightly, but that decision was completely in my hands.

Chapter 5: The Raid of the Raven

After an *eykt* of fighting the offshore winds, Ulf pointed out the small cove on the other side of the island where his grandfather's community could be found. There were tall white cliffs that towered above a sandy beach, and I strained my eyes to see the path that ran up to the top of the cliffs where we might climb. The atmosphere on board was one of excitement after the confrontation in Byrum, and we were all thinking the same thing: should we stay and attack the Frisians? They were pirates and there might be plunder. They had already discovered Eric's hoard, and by rights we should not take it. But still…. However, we needed new supplies, and if Ulf's grandfather did not have everything we needed then we would definitely have to return to Byrum. What I needed was a meeting with our group. Although our party had started out on a peaceful mission it had every possibility of turning into a raiding party very quickly. I had just killed a man, albeit in self-defence, and if we were to go into battle every man needed to have his say. I was paying these men to deliver Torstein and me across the seas, and we needed to decide whether we were to change our mission from being defenders to attackers.

We beached the Raven and hauled her up the beach. Our Saxon slaves went to collect firewood and the rest of us huddled together on the windy shoreline to decide what our next actions should be as Ulf sat watching us. I spoke first:

"I asked you all to deliver me and Torstein to Jomsborg. We are only your cargo and you are not in a war party – yet! However, we have been attacked by these pirates who will take the town's gold, silver and many slaves and depart with them when they are ready. There are at least two-score of them and although they are lowly Frisians, we would still be heavily outnumbered. This boy's grandfather lives on top of the cliffs

28

and may or may not have enough food for us for the next part of our journey. But we know that there is plenty in Byrum."

Rolf, one of a pair of identical twins, stepped forward and spoke.

"I have been trapped on that boat for days, and I would like to stay awhile – particularly with a Frisian head on my spear."

To this pronouncement, most, if not all, guffawed their approval. His brother Svein also nodded in agreement.

Leif, another of Rollo's nephews, was next.

"I am not one to take insult easily, and we have been sorely tested. It would be a terrible slight on Haugesund and the rest of Norway if word got out that we had retreated in front of these goat fuckers."

Had there still been any waverers, Torstein dispelled any doubt when he got up and delivered his speech. Having sensed a certain drama of the situation – he spoke with not a little passion.

"Every summer our fathers and their fathers and their fathers before them went plundering across the oceans to look for great riches. Not just gold and silver but for great fame, which would be earned through their deeds in conquering all before them. They were considered great warriors that few could equal, and their names were spoken in the longhalls with reverence down through the generations. Now, these days, our raiding and taking war to our enemies have been curtailed by our new king who tells us when to pay our taxes and when we should bend the knee to him. I for one am no longer willing to kiss his arse. I vote we stay and kill these Frisian scum."

All now nodded in agreement and the die was cast.

"We are agreed then," I said. "Get your armour and weapons from the boat and make yourselves ready."

We made a great fire on the beach using the Raven to shelter us from the wind. I took Ulf and Torstein to look for the grandfather, and we made our way up the cliffs. We left

Helge to oversee the repairs to the boat, for the hull needed re-caulking with pitch, and the sail needed some patching. We were fully armed for we knew neither who nor what waited for us at the top.

It took a short hike for all three of us to climb up the cliff, and Torstein was the last to reach the top. He arrived perspiring and cursing in full armour with his wooden shield and his huge double-bladed axe in hand. However, there was no fierce war band to meet us, only three shepherds dressed in ragged sheepskins, carrying nothing more offensive than their crooks. They stood in silence and apprehension not knowing whether to stand or run. In the end, they stood their ground, albeit humbly. When we got closer to them Ulf ran towards the oldest of the trio, and they hugged one another fiercely. The shepherds nodded to us deferentially as the boy's story tumbled out about the attack on the town and his escape. His grandfather was named Ragnar and was a spare man of about fifty years old with long, tangled grey hair and beard. He listened carefully, and I could see the look of grave concern shadow his face as Ulf continued. When the boy had finally completed his story, Ulf looked around to us and said:

"Grandfather, these men rescued me from the town. They are great lords from Norway and they have already killed one of the raiders – they will help us."

"And what of your sister, Hild?" he asked. The boy looked at the ground. His shoulders started to shake, and he began to cry noisily.

I held up my hand to end the caterwauling and to get their attention.

"No, we cannot help you, Ragnar, but we will clear Byrum of these filthy Frisians for they have dented our pride, and we would like to relieve them of their meaningless existence."

I did not add that we were also in search of booty and that we suspected the Frisians of having plenty.

"But first and foremost, we have not eaten for a day or

more and have been lost at sea for many more days than that."

"Please, come to our camp," said Ragnar. "We are poor shepherds, but we will share with you what we have."

"We will buy what you can spare," I said, "for we are not beggars".

They all three turned and bade us follow them. By and by, we came to a group of six wooden hovels that were arranged in a circle in the middle of which burned a fire with a large cauldron suspended over it. This little community was poorer than I had hoped for, and I doubted that they would have much spare food. Women and children came from the huts to stare at us inquisitively. We must have made a curious pair as we stood before them – two heavily armed warriors from a foreign land looking hungrily at their cooking pot. One of the women pulled up some logs for us to sit on, and once seated she brought us over some bowls of stew which we quickly devoured. I could see Torstein eyeing the cooking pot for another helping, but before he could reach for it, I said to Ragnar:

"We will need two goats, some bread and ale."

I pulled out six pieces of hack silver and put them in Ragnar's hands – which was about ten times the price of any food he might provide us with.

"Yes, Lord of course. I am sorry, but I wish we could provide you with more. You can see we are very poor."

"No matter," I said, "as long as we have enough energy to kill those bloody Frisians it will suffice. Now tell me of the land between here and Byrum. We are going to need to set a trap for these men to even the odds a little."

I told him what I had in mind.

"I think I know a place that will suit your purposes," he said.

For some time, Ragnar described the height, contours and landscape that lay across the island. It was a rocky little outcrop of a place that included a great deal of grazing land for sheep and goats. A band of hills, growing into mountains, rose up steeply right across the middle of the island and beyond. To get to Byrum there would be a lot of marching up and down these hills. I knew from first-hand experience that the town was built on a rising slope. Apparently, this slope rose steeply into the first of two mountains, between which ran a narrow pass. The trail, by which we would return to Byrum, narrowed into this pass, and was wide enough for two men at a time. Beyond the mountains were green uplands – home to some very small farming communities. It was about a day's march to Byrum, and I started to make our plans for the attack. Three of the men of this community would be coming with us, both as guides and to bolster our numbers.

Before long, we were back in our makeshift camp. Ragnar, Ulf and two of the shepherds carried the slaughtered goats, bread and ale with them. They also brought two of their women and while one of them cooked the other one took our two slaves onto the shoreline to collect shellfish. It was getting dark now, and our hungry men stopped grumbling and began to eat.

We sat around our fire in the lee of the Raven – each man harbouring thoughts of the action ahead and no doubt imagining the size of the Frisian booty.

"Is the boat repaired?" I asked Helge who nodded, his mouth full of goat flesh.

"Good," I said.

After waiting until the meal was finished, I began to relate my plan of attack.

"We leave at first light for Byrum…"

Chapter 6: Bjorn's First War Party

I slept fitfully again that night and woke up on the sandy beach to the sound of the surf breaking. My bearskin cloak was damp with salty dew, and I got up and stretched my limbs. The rest of the men were still deep in sleep, and I walked to the water's edge and went over our plan in my head again. I was eighteen years old and commanding my first war band. Excitement and trepidation were in equal measure, and I was well aware of the responsibility I owed to this small group of family and friends. We were still going to be outnumbered three-to-one, but if our luck was good, I knew that we would triumph.

I clutched my father's golden amulet in both hands and gave thanks to Thor and Aiger for bringing us this far. To Loki, the trickster, I prayed for good luck in the forthcoming deception. I had no doubt about our fierceness and bravery as warriors, and I promised the gods that if we all returned to our boat safely, I would sacrifice the Frisians in their honour.

One group would take the Raven, manned by five men and the two slaves, and sail back to Byrum and up the inlet in full view of the invaders. They would anchor within a few hundred yards of the shore. When the Frisian guards saw the Raven, which they would surely do, they would alert the others and wait for us at the place where they expected our attack. They would be engaged with a fusillade of arrows, and while their attention was drawn, I would take two men in from the other side of town and burn their boats. As soon as they saw the conflagration, their men would run towards it and, hopefully, pursue us into the mountains, then on towards our ambush. The success of the raid needed some good timing and even more luck, and we would still be greatly outnumbered.

A hand on my shoulder brought me back to the present –

it was Helge's.

"Nearly time to fix the Raven's head in position," he said, smiling broadly and nodding towards our beached craft.

Two of the men had taken the carved figurehead from under the forecastle and were fixing it onto the bows of the boat. Carved out of a single piece of wood it was an effigy of an angry raven with a sharp, horny beak ready to strike. Once installed on board, our boat would be transformed into a warship, and our enemies would be under no illusion as to our intent.

By the time the Frisians discovered what was going on, they would withdraw from the beach and hopefully give chase. Helge and his crew would then up-anchor and sail away to where we would meet them later in an inlet a little way out of Byrum. If our plan was successful, we would all return to the town and finish off what they had started.

We walked back to the boat and once the figurehead was in place all the men hauled the ship back down the beach and through the surf. Helge took Rolf, Svein, the two Saxons and Ulf – together with some of the bows and most of the arrows – and rowed away from the shore while the rest of us got ready. Each of the remaining men donned armour, weaponry and shields. We were warriors once again. I put on my knee-length mail shirt under a bearskin cloak, and my fine battle helmet – made of steel with a nasal guard and decorated with silver and bronze. At my waist hung my sword, *Gunnlogi*, and my *seax* – a short single edged Saxon blade that was very effective in close quarters combat. We all carried spears and were ready – full of expectation and menace and without a care in the world.

"How do I look, Torstein?" I called across to my cousin – himself looking even bigger and more menacing in his own battle gear.

"Well, you scare the shit out of me," he replied, "so the Frisians will probably give up without a fight."

Each man carried a round shield over his back decorated

with a black raven – our herkubl or war-mark. Fully armed, we marched up the cliff to meet some of the locals who were to be our guides. Ragnar greeted us at the top and introduced us to three other shepherds - young wiry men of about sixteen or seventeen years old who knew each mountain pass and hillside cave.

"I will not come with you myself, Lord," he said "for I will not be able to keep up with you. But these men are trusted members of my family and will not let you down. They carry enough food and drink for you and your men for a day or so and have armed themselves as best they can. I wish you the speed of the gods to take you to Byrum and rescue our people." Then, with head bowed, he added, "My daughter, Ulf's mother, is in Byrum and I pray that she still lives."

The three shepherds stood before us shuffling about nervously. They were each dressed in skins and carried two daggers and a rusty axe between them. Each man also carried some puny looking hunting bows, and I heard some of the men unkindly snorting their derision at our poorly prepared allies. With that, we were off, marching towards Byrum and looking forward to delivering some Norse justice. Making ourselves a little richer in the process seemed only fair. Our column moved swiftly enough with the shepherds at our head. I had a sneaking respect for them, for they were clearly not warriors and must be travelling with some fear of what might befall them. However, they never showed any sign of weakness as we marched on.

We travelled quickly enough and made good progress, up through the foothills stopping only once at another small community to eat and rest for a while. This community looked just the same as the one we'd left earlier – a small collection of hovels, housing raggedly dressed families eking out a living in the wind-swept hills. We marched into their camp and gratefully took their poor hospitality, which they gave us willingly. The headman also had relatives in Byrum, and he asked if two of their men could join us. I accepted. I knew that the source of this generosity lay in their fear that if we failed there was not much to stop the invaders should they start to explore the rest of the island.

We marched on, climbing higher, with our new comrades, both similarly armed as the first group of shepherds. The day was fair, and a slight breeze blew one or two high clouds scurrying across the sky. Around mid-afternoon, the landscape had changed from lush, green pastureland to rocks and boulders. After that our path became a single track. Less than an *eykt* later we reached our goal as the pathway went off to the right and the ground levelled into something of a barren, stony plateau.

One of Ragnar's men turned around to me and spoke.

"We are nearly there, Lord. A few hundred paces and we will have arrived."

I looked on intently but failed to notice any changes in the rocky surface. And then I saw it; the pathway dropped sharply where men would have to climb down clinging to the rock face. The last five hundred yards dropped vertically to the bottom, and walls of rock flanked each side. The track then widened slightly at the bottom to a point where it could take two men walking side by side. I discovered that it was an ancient riverbed that had long since dried up, and this had once been the path of a river on its route towards the sea. We would have to climb down the path of an old waterfall and then return the same way. It looked like a perfect place for an ambush. I flashed a look at Torstein who murmured his approval.

"A great place to kill a Frisian!" he roared.

Each man dropped whatever he was carrying, and we worked at building up piles of rock – each about the size of a man's head – which were piled up along either side of the cliffs overlooking the gorge. By the time the light began to die we managed to build up some decent sized mounds of rock along the edges of both cliffs for about two hundred paces along the lip. I peered over the edge close to the last pile and saw that the path flattened out at the bottom and looked to be a tough climb. If we could set the trap and lure the prey into it, we would stand a good chance of doing plenty of damage.

I walked a little further with my cousin along the plateau until we saw light coming from Byrum in the far distance. It looked to be about five miles away. In the late of the evening, we could clearly see the town, the inlet that we had approached in the Raven and, importantly, the two Frisian ships that were beached almost out of sight of the seaward entrance. They could be reached by coming down from our mountain and following the shoreline around to the town where they lay. We would hide close by until the Raven arrived through the inlet with the crew making plenty of noise to get our enemy's attention. The Frisians would hopefully be massing on the beach expecting the crew of the Raven to engage them there. While this diversion was going on I would get to their ships and set fire to them. Hopefully, the pirates would pursue us back to the rocky pass where the rest of the men could assail them.

"I will be at your side tomorrow, Bjorn," said Torstein.

I shook my head. "We'll be moving fast and light on the return journey."

At this he looked a little crestfallen, and so I added, "And besides I need you and the rest of them to save your strength for attacking these bastards when they take the bait."

We made our camp for the night at the head of the gorge, high in the cliffs. I got little sleep again as I tried to ponder all the possible outcomes. The rest of the men seemed unmoved by what might happen the next day. A little before daybreak, I slipped out of our camp with Leif and one of the shepherds. We stripped off our heavy cloaks, armour and weapons and were armed with only long daggers to protect ourselves with. We also carried flint and steel to ignite the pitch which we would use to set fire to the Frisian ships. The shepherd would guide us to Byrum, to the boats that lay there and then back again. We moved off together trying to follow in the shepherd's sure-footed steps and then down into the gulley. Before long the track turned into a sharp drop straight down and we started our downward climb.

It was a decent plan but there was one detail that I had neglected to include in my reckonings.

Chapter 7: The Attack on the Pirates

Tostig had been a shepherd for as long as he could remember. He was seventeen or eighteen years old but did not know exactly. Pirates had taken his father and mother as slaves when he was a baby, leaving him to his fate in their burning village. He had been found by shepherds who came to investigate the source of the smoke and was taken in by their community who brought him up as one of their own. He was small and wiry and moved lightly among the rocks on tireless legs and appeared to me to be half-man and half-goat. He wore a long-sleeved plain woollen shirt under a sleeveless leather tunic that was belted by a thick piece of rope in which he kept a rusty knife. Leif nodded at it and asked him if he had ever used it against anyone in anger. Tostig shook his head.

Leif and I had grown up together in Haugesund where we had been close friends. When we were boys of ten and eleven, our fathers took us east on a raid and we attacked a Slavic town where our party met more resistance than expected. The village's desperate defenders killed two of our men and both of us had unexpectedly been forced to fight side by side with the other raiders. Ultimately our war band overcame some stiff resistance and we took many slaves, which we sold further along the coast. The town was quite poor, but we got a good price for the captives which made the ranging a success. More importantly for us boys, we had both been blooded in battle – an important milestone for any warrior to pass.

At the height of this action, Leif and I were confronted by one of the wounded defenders who charged towards us with a spear. The man had been running blind, as a wound in his head was gushing blood into his eyes. Leif sidestepped the man while I tripped him, and he fell to the ground. We had both fallen on him stabbing him with our spears until he stopped moving. It had been the first time I killed anyone and made me realise that sending a man to his death was harder than I thought. Men do not often die from a single spear thrust, and it takes a good deal of strength and courage to overpower a warrior and take his life. This man was no different and took some time before he breathed his last after our frenzied attack. Ever since then, I had been even closer friends with Leif and trusted him completely. He was quiet but always thinking as if considering his next move in a game of Hnefatafl. I was glad Leif was coming with me today – he was quick, brave and skilled as a fighter. Today he would need all those attributes and more.

It took us a little under an *eykt* to follow the horseshoe-shaped coastline until we were within sights of the Frisian boats. It was low tide and the stubby vessels were lying some way out of the water on their sides. We hid behind some tall rocks about two hundred paces away from the boats at the top of the beach where we waited and watched for the Raven to come sailing through the gap in the cliffs. She was to approach the town and engage with the Frisians – at least, at a relatively safe distance. We planned for her arrival to be around nón – which was fast approaching. As soon as the action started, we would set fire to the beached vessels. When – and if – the pirates followed us, we would keep a safe distance and lead them back into the mountains where Torstein and his crew would attack them from the clifftops. It had sounded so simple when we talked it through last night.

From where we were hidden the two ships appeared at first to be easy targets – until we spotted the man guarding the boats. He was one of the biggest men I had ever seen – about the size of Torstein. He was three or four heads taller than me and this giant strode directly towards the rocks we were hiding behind. He was shaven-headed and wore long moustaches on a large-boned, heavily scarred face. Fully armed with a waist-length mail shirt, he carried a sword and dagger on a belt around his girth. From his ambling gait, he showed little sign of being alert to the impending danger, and his oblong shield and spear had been left, absent-mindedly, leaning against the hull of one of the ships.

By the speed of his approach, I was convinced that he had not seen us, and I whispered to Leif, "He's just taking a piss. Wait until he has started, and we will catch him and kill him. You take the left – I'll take the right."

Leif nodded his agreement. We moved in opposite directions, and I peered around the rock as the huge Frisian untied the cord tying up his breeches and let them drop to his ankles. He started to piss against our rock, and I stepped out and walked towards him with my *seax* unsheathed and ready to strike. Still, he did not see or hear me approaching, the damp sand and sound of him splashing the rocks muffling my footsteps. I was now close enough to smell him – a rank mixture of rotten fish, sour ale and sweat.

"For a big man you have a woefully small cock," I said, close enough to whisper it in his ear.

He looked over his shoulder at me and span around quickly – surprisingly quick for such a big man – and reached for his sword. But my *seax* was stabbing upward up into his unprotected groin where it met soft, unprotected flesh. Leif was already at the man's throat with his blade. With his free hand he covered the Frisian's mouth to stifle his groans. It was too late for the man, but it was not over yet, and even in his death throes he was still powerful enough to do us damage. I stabbed and Leif hacked, and between us we brought him down like a slaughtered bull until he lay between us pulsing blood and piss on the sand. The shepherd joined us and all three of us dragged the dead beast behind the rock, leaving a trail in the bloody sand.

"He was a monster," said Leif, breathing heavily as we watched Tostig make short work of rifling the man's pockets.

"Take the dagger as well," I told him. "It will be much more useful than the rusty shell opener you have been carrying with you." The shepherd looked pleased with himself as he strapped his trophy around his waist in its bejeweled sheath.

"What now?" said Leif.

"We wait," I said.

We did not have to wait for long because the Raven shortly appeared through the gap in the cliffs around noon. As we agreed she was under sail, for the small number of rowers would give away the fact that there were so few men on board. Helge had arranged shields along the gunwales, and he and his small crew had done an excellent job of burnishing the brass bosses on each. They shone in the bright noonday sun and glinted their arrival to those onshore. The Raven's crew rowed slowly past the quay and approached the beach in front of the town's houses, dropping the anchor from the stern, and bringing the ship to an abrupt halt. Her sail was dropped immediately. She now lay motionless in deep water about two hundred feet away from land, bows pointed towards the shore.

"Now we need to do our part," I said to the other two, and we ran across the sand to the two boats. The first one was empty, but lying against the second one was another guard, this one asleep on the sand. He was younger and smaller than the man we had just killed and looked to me to be about fifteen years old. Leif drew his dagger for the second time that day holding it to the boy's throat while I roused him with a few kicks to his out-stretched legs. He woke with a start and tried to get up. As he did so Leif moved behind him and locked his free arm across the Frisian's throat in a vice-like grip. Our prisoner, realising the desperation of his situation, stopped struggling and stared up at me. He looked me in the face with pleading eyes and blurted out, "Please don't kill me, please don't kill me."

I held my hand up to signal him to be quiet.

"Tell me how many there are of you," I said, giving him a moment to compose himself.

"Forty-nine when we came here," he said, "but one died yesterday."

"Well, I have just killed your big friend, and we are now going to kill the rest of you," I said.

He then began to snivel wretchedly, pleading for his life again. Alarmed by the noise of the boy's wailing, Tostig moved towards him, dagger drawn, with some intent.

"Wait," I said. "Let him live for the time being. Just make sure he doesn't move for the moment."

Tostig, obviously keen to test his new weapon, looked a little disappointed but pushed the Frisian onto his back and knelt heavily on his chest, pinning him to the floor.

"Right, Leif, let's get these fires lit," I said, and we moved quickly to the boats, taking one each.

The boats had been out of the sea for a few days and the wind and sun had started to dry them inside and out. Hopefully, they would burn well. We collected some dried driftwood, and I placed it against the inside of the hull. I then took my tinderbox from my tunic, removed its contents and sparked the flint against the steel, into the dry flax beneath the piled-up firewood. Soon I had the making of a decent fire. I could see Leif working feverishly in the second boat and was about to call to him when I heard a commotion coming from the Raven. I looked towards the scene where Helge was on the forecastle in her bows haranguing the growing number of men on the shore who were now forming up. From within the ship, the crew were making all manner of noise and beating weapons on shields while Helge shouted curses at the rapidly assembling Frisians on the beach in front of him. The noise stopped as those on board started to shoot arrows towards the group onshore. I saw one man fall but the others quickly organised themselves with their shields held up to protect themselves from our arrows. I saw a large man, who looked to be their leader, Duco, shouting at his men as they formed into a shield wall – presumably against the expected attack from

43

the sea. It never came – just more arrows from the Raven, although by now they were easy to defend against from behind the shield wall.

"How is your fire?" I called across to Leif in the other boat.

"It is catching well," he replied.

The fire had now caught successfully in my boat, and I added some of the pitch we had brought with us from the other side of the island. The boat's sail had been furled and tucked away in the stern of the vessel, and I pulled it free and added it to the conflagration. Satisfied with my work, I went to join Leif in the other vessel to lend a hand. He did not need it, and I found him standing watching the flames making rapid progress through the second boat.

I looked over to the beach again where the Frisians had by now guessed that an attack from the Raven was not going to happen. Our crew had ceased their firing, lifted the anchor and were now back-rowing away from the beach. They were soon out of arrow-range from anyone onshore.

I shouted to Tostig to release the boy. Our prisoner took his chance of freedom and scampered away to join his enraged comrades about a mile away along the shoreline. For now, anyway, he lived to fight another day.

"Time we were going too," I said.

With one last look at the flames, which were now engulfing both vessels, we turned and retraced our footsteps from earlier in the day. We walked away from the burning boats without haste. It was important that we did not get away from the pirates too quickly lest they should not pursue us. We needed to be visible to them all the while to lure them into chasing us into the trap. At the point where the beach ended and the mountains began, we stopped and waited. It was an anxious wait. If they failed to take the bait our ruse would have been for nothing and we would still have no supplies – and definitely no booty. I was counting on the anger of the Frisians to ensure that a chase ensued. Their boats were now ruined and would soon be no more than cinders on the beach. By then they would have no means of escaping Byrum. *Jarl* Eric would return sooner or later, and they would face his wrath unless they were able to find another boat.

We could see where we had been from the huge plume of smoke coming from the burning ships, which were only about a mile away. A band of about forty armed men were standing around the blaze and they were highly animated. I estimated that the gap between us was perhaps a ten minutes march – far less at a run. They would be carrying arms so we should be able to move faster, and I was relieved to see them turn towards us and begin their pursuit.

It was then that I heard the sound that chilled me to the bone. It was the sound of hunting dogs barking and howling as they picked up our scent. The chase would be different from the one I had planned, and men and dogs were now hunting us.

Chapter 8: The Ambush

In Norway, we used dogs to hunt elk, wolves and bears. Dogs were also used to attack raiders and were sometimes used in war to spread fear in the enemy. Against a disciplined shield wall of armoured warriors, they were not effective, but against a rabble of running soldiers they would cause panic in an instant. I have seen dogs catch and kill men, and they are very good at it. A pack of dogs can find and run down a man very quickly, and they will tear their prey to pieces in minutes. It is a very painful way to die.

We now faced the same fate and would need to stay far enough ahead of our hunters for safety but without completely eluding them. I looked at my companions and they both knew our next course of action. We ran, and the hunt was on. Tostig took the lead and led the way back. He was light and fast, and his years in the mountains had made him nimble and quick, and we had nothing to carry but the daggers at our waists. The first few miles were easy going, and we could keep up a good pace. I followed Tostig and Leif ran after me. From my freind's laboured breathing I knew he was struggling to keep up with us. I stole a look over my shoulder and saw that he was now falling further behind. "Wait," I called to Tostig and we stopped to let Leif catch up with us. The terrain changed from sandy scrubland to rocks as we climbed into the mountains and the going was getting harder.

Leif caught up with us and stood, hands on knees, gulping in the air as I looked past him to the chasing pack of dogs and Frisians. They were a still a good league or so behind, but we could see them now. There were about forty men and they had eight or nine dogs who were barking and howling away as they clambered up after us. I had every expectation of keeping away from them as we fled, but now Leif was in obvious trouble. The giant on the beach had fallen on him before he died, and now Leif was holding his ribs in pain.

"Have we much further to go?" I said to the shepherd.

"Run like this and we will be there very soon," said Tostig.

I looked at Leif.

"Let's go," he said, and we continued up.

The rocky slopes soon gave way to a small plateau that I recognised from our earlier journey, and I knew we were not far away from the others. Leif was breathing very hard now and was causing us to slow and wait for him to catch up. The gap between the Frisians and us was lessening and the hunters must have sensed we could soon be caught. I knew they would release the dogs when they got close enough and that moment would shortly arrive. We ran on.

The path over the plateau narrowed as the mountain walls on each side of us rose up. Tostig pointed to the route of the dried waterfall leading to where we had climbed down from our camp. If we could reach that point and climb, we would be safe. The sound of the howling dogs was much nearer as they closed in. I ran back to Leif who had stumbled to the ground again and dragged him to his feet. There was blood in his beard, and he brought up more of it as he coughed. The Frisians must have thought they had us, and we could hear them screaming insults as they grew ever closer. Suddenly the howling stopped as the dogs were released, and now every second would bring them nearer. I had my arm around Leif, and we approached the foot of our escape up the sheer cliff face climb. The path was narrowing, and as it did so the mountain walls rose up sharply on each side. Tostig dropped his pace and we both carried our comrade along the pathway that was just wide enough for all of us to drag ourselves forward.

Finally, we were there, and I pushed Leif ahead of me and began to clamber up following Tostig's nimble ascent. The dogs reached the point where we had started our climb and could do no more than bark up at us only ten *fot* above their heads. A spear was thrown, hit the rock to my left and fell harmlessly away. Another one came a little closer and grazed my leg. We climbed away as yet another spear came from below.

"You will have to do better than that if you want to kill a Norseman," Torstein was shouting from his lofty position about five hundred *fot* or so above me. With that came down the first of several hefty rocks landing amongst the dogs and men below. As the other two continued to climb out of harm's way to join our comrades on the top, I exhorted them to greater haste. Looking up, I could see several bearded faces willing us to climb faster.

"Come on you lazy bastards or there won't be anyone left to kill," shouted Torstein.

Shortly after that, another huge piece of rock whistled down close to my head and crunched into the pack of men and animals below. From the triumphal whoop above I guessed that it had reached its target successfully. The forty or so Frisians below me were now comprehending the full extent of their folly and the trap they had been led into.

I watched the drama unfolding beneath me. Rocks, arrows and spears were raining from above, and men and dogs were being stabbed and crushed. Their howls of triumph changed to screams of pain as the fusillade from above began to take its toll. Men and dogs were now lying dead or dying. The deluge continued, and those struck staggered drunkenly as more carnage poured down from the cliff tops. Some of the dogs were still barking away at us in ignorant fury, and missiles of all sorts were hitting the men. I turned back to the cliff face and shouted encouragement to Leif to keep moving. We had climbed over halfway now, and I could see that Tostig was almost there ahead of us. My hands and fingers were skinned in the upward scramble.

"Nearly there now, Leif," I shouted.

We forged on for what seemed like an eternity and

suddenly I felt powerful arms grab me and pull me up and over the lip of the cliff to safety. I looked around and saw our crew and the shepherds standing along the cliff top by their piles of rocks, hurling them downwards as quickly as they could. I peered down into the chaos below.

The forty or so Frisians, thinking they had caught us, had rushed forward to finish the job, letting their dogs loose, to run ahead of them. In their efforts to reach us they ran up the narrow gully from where we had just escaped and were caught by a torrent of missiles from several hundred *fot* up. The gully's path was not much wider than two men standing abreast. By the time the first of the dogs fell, the rest of the pack turned and ran back the way they had come. Our companions had left it late and had started by attacking the hind-most of the Frisians – killing or disabling those at the back of the column. They carried no shields, as they had assumed they would not need them during the pursuit. Those dead and dying at the back now blocked the escape route and formed a human barrier hindering the retreat of the rest. The fleeing dogs were going berserk and turning on their masters in an effort to escape. Still more rocks rained down, killing and maiming. The sounds of men and animals being crushed to death echoed upward from the confined space. I looked down at a scene of complete confusion, as our rock piles grew smaller. Below, men were having to tread on their fallen comrades to escape the death trap. They, in turn, were struck down, and then more men and dogs climbed over them in panic.

"Not much of a competition," chuckled Torstein, casting yet another head-size piece of granite over the side and waiting for the sound of impact. When the rock piles were exhausted the bowmen took over seeking out the remaining targets. It had been a highly effective action and out of the forty or so Frisians only five escaped with their lives, and they were sure to have received injuries. I saw them disappear out of range as they ran for their lives and back to Byrum. Our crew, now joined by Helge and his party, were cheering heartily as the last pirate disappeared from view, limping heavily and with a couple of arrows bristling from his back. The action cost us no men and the only injury was, seemingly, Leif's broken ribs.

Svein led six of our number down to the gully floor to finish off the wounded, loot the bodies and retrieve our spent arrows. They returned with a bag full of hack silver and jewellery. They had also found a couple of swords and daggers of good quality and a beautiful helmet of steel, bronze and silver. We shared the captured booty and Torstein was delighted that his giant head was the only one big enough to fit the helmet.

I gathered the men around me and after much backslapping and laughter I finally managed to speak.

"We'll camp here tonight and go back to the Raven in the morning. There are still a few of them left but not many to put up much of a fight. We will go back to Byrum to finish the job and collect their booty as they obviously didn't bring much of it with them."

The men cheered again, and after much talk of who did what in the day's action we settled down for the evening with our meagre rations and made a plan for the following day.

Torstein was in an unusually quiet mood as we sat looking into the fire's embers a little later.

"What's the matter with you?" I asked him.

"Nothing. But it is not the most satisfactory way for a warrior to kill a man. I would rather look them in the eyes first. Warriors should kill with a sword or an axe rather than throwing stones," he said.

"There will be plenty of time for such manly pastimes. Tomorrow we shall finish the job, and you can kill as many pirates as you can get up close to. However, for me, I am quite glad to have made it back here losing only the skin from my hands. Those dogs were so close I thought it might have been my balls," I said.

"Then I shall look forward to finishing what we have started today. A few women and some booty would also be very welcome. I feel sure *Jarl* Eric would like to reward us for saving his people." he said.

With that last utterance, he lay down to sleep and started to snore. The events of the next few days would change my life forever.

Chapter 9: The Relief of the Townsfolk

The next day we made our way back to the Raven, which had been beached in a sandy cove a few miles march away. We would sail back to Byrum, but this time we would land there and kill the remaining Frisians. The men were in high spirits after dispatching the pirates with such ease the day before and we were all heavily armed. Even the shepherds were dressed for war with arms taken from the dead men. I wore my bearskin cloak over a mail shirt – thick enough to absorb all but the fiercest of blade strikes. Each of us had taken some care of his appearance that morning, and beards and hair had been combed and plaited. Torstein, in particular, had taken great care in preparing himself and looked clean and kempt. I surmised that this was mostly for the benefit of any rescued women he saved rather than inciting fear in enemy hearts. Blades had been whetted and shields cleaned with sand. We were ready to go.

We counted forty-one dead men in the gully after we dispatched their wounded, and we had already killed two at the boats. There should be nine still alive, and the survivors staggered away so pitifully from our ambush that I had little expectation of them putting up much of a fight in the town. Still, a wounded bear could be a dangerous opponent.

We pushed the Raven through the surf and boarded her once more. The men took their seats at the oars – including the armed shepherds. They looked ill at ease at their stations but rowed as manfully as they could after receiving a rudimentary education on our march to the boat. I am not sure how much went in, but they deserved to be part of this little victory however small it was to be. I took my place in the bows whilst Helge took the tiller. Standing close to him was Ulf, dressed in a leather jerkin that was far too big for him and a long, sheathed dagger strapped to his waist – both looted from dead Frisians. He stood as straight as he could, feigning bravery, and Helge went through some final instructions with him. In truth he looked as frightened as any twelve-year-old boy might be on his first confrontation with an enemy but did his best to pretend that this was not the case

The sail was hoisted, and a steady breeze pushed the Raven forward. With a weak autumnal sun at our backs and a fine sea spray in our faces, this part of our journey felt very good. Doing what we were born to do – finding and killing our enemies and relieving them of their booty. Our plan was simple. We would drive the Raven onto Byrum's sandy beach and engage with what was left of Duko's pirates. According to the boy, they had carried their booty to the town's longhall for safekeeping. What was theirs would now be ours. They had also taken many of the women and girls there including Ulf's mother. Once we liberated the town we could resupply and be on our way to Jomsborg – none the worse for this little adventure.

The Raven rounded the next line of cliffs and there it was; the gateway to Byrum. The sail was dropped, and we rowed at speed onto the beach in front of the town. As soon as I felt the familiar crunch of shale against the ship's bow, I jumped into the shallow water and up the beach. Ulf was pointing to the longhouse from where he had run not two days before and where we were now heading. We passed several houses, and as we did so I heard their doors slowly opening. Women, children and old folk gathered behind us and followed cautiously in our wake. Ulf, trying to look every inch the avenging warrior called for them not to be frightened and that their deliverance was at hand. We soon reached our destination and I raised my hand, stopping our crew and those following. Ulf shuffled up to my side.

"The men you seek are all inside, Lord. Their captain lives - wounded but was still able to kill some of the women and children last night. They are still very frightened of him here."

I walked forward until I was about fifty paces from the

longhouse. It was about the size of the one we had in Haugesund – but this one was made of oak and had a large door strengthened with brass straps.

"Come out here you murdering bastards!" I shouted. "You've shown us how to kill children – see how you manage against grown men."

The door opened slowly, and nine men filed out and formed up in front us locking their shields together to form an untidy shield wall.

"They seem to want to make a fight out of it," said Helge at my shoulder.

Their men shuffled into position in a quite wretched manner. They were the survivors of the rock shower, and each one carried a reminder of yesterday. Some limped, some dragged broken bones whilst others still had blood dried on their faces and in their hair. They were a sorry-looking band, but desperate men have nothing to lose in a fight. Another figure followed them – it was Duco. In one hand he carried his shield whilst in the other, he led six women, ropes tied around their necks. They were in an even worse state than their captors and had obviously been badly mistreated during their captivity. They were all in bare feet and their clothes hung about them in rags. Their faces were bruised and bloodied, and they held themselves in abject silence looking only at the ground.

Duko pulled the women roughly after him as one might do to a rebellious herd of goats going to their slaughter. He walked around the side of his men dragging his burden with him. I heard Ulf whimper and cry out "Mor" as he recognised one of the captives as his mother.

Duko looked straight at me. "If you want to save these women just give us your boat," he said, adding "and we will let you live." I felt my men behind me bracing themselves for the assault on this desperate band, and I could hear Torstein cursing and snorting threats of his own.

"These women mean nothing to us – do what you want

with them. As for your offer I reject it," I said and spat on the ground. His men moved closer together and braced themselves for our inevitable assault. There were about fifty townsfolk now standing behind us, and their voices were growing in anger and not a little excitement as they watched the scene unfold.

In one swift movement, Duko took his dagger to the nearest shackled woman and slit her throat. Before she hit the ground, he turned back to me.

"Just fuck off back to your home in the ice, puppy," he said, spitting in my direction.

I hurled my spear at him. He caught it easily on his shield, and I moved forward to engage with him. He moved to meet me, let go of the ropes and unsheathed his sword.

The rest of our crew hurled their spears at the shield wall which buckled from the impact – moving slightly backwards. Torstein covered the ground between them very quickly for such a big man. He smashed into them, splintering the first shield he met with a huge downward slash of his double-bladed axe. His comrades closely followed him, and they were amongst the Frisians, causing carnage.

Meanwhile, I had my own enemy to defeat, and I hurried forward to close with Duko. Although he was clearly limping from a leg wound, he moved quickly towards me, shield and sword in either hand. My spear was still stuck in his shield, and he had been unable to dislodge it. I caught his first blow on my shield, and he repeated the movement twice more. He was a lot bigger and heavier than me, and despite his wounds, there was still strength in his blows. The fourth time I took a downward slash onto my shield, crouching low. I swept at his leading leg with my sword catching him high on the thigh. The razor-sharp Ulfbert cut through the muscle of his leg effortlessly. I moved in and hacked at him with a flurry of blows and felt the strength ebbing out of him as he staggered backwards. With a final display of brute strength, he slammed back into me with his shield causing me to check my advance.

But he was now spent, badly wounded in both legs, gasping for air and no longer able to hold up his shield. I aimed another slash at his sword arm. He could not raise his arm quickly enough to parry the blow, and my blade cut through the bicep of his right arm to the bone. With both his arms lying limply down I swung my shield at him catching him hard with the brass boss on the side of his head. Duko fell to the floor.

I looked over to my left. We had killed five of the enemy after Torstein had shattered their resistance with his first charge. He and his comrades were hacking away at those left standing. He was in the process of dispatching the sixth man with a series of downward axe blows shattering shield and bone as the broken man lay at his feet. The remaining Frisians, seeing their leader fallen and their comrades dying around them, threw down their weapons and asked for mercy. I always found these moments quite strange, when all the fight was gone from the enemy and they were at your mercy, like beaten dogs awaiting their fate.

Ulf stepped forward with tears running down his face and ran to his mother, gently removing the rope around her neck and hugging her. The woman kissed him and hugged him back. Their ordeal was over.

"What should we do with the rest of these cowards," asked Torstein, and our men looked towards me.

"Give them to the women here. They will know what to do with them," I said. The women who had been standing behind now came forward to release their sisters who had so recently been hostage to those now kneeling passively at our feet.

"They're yours," I said to them. Without a word, they armed themselves with whatever lay to hand – sticks, stones, spear shafts, broken shields and proceeded to beat the captives without mercy.

I stepped over Duco's prone body and led the other men into the longhouse. It stank of blood, sweat and shit.

"Whatever went on here took much time," said Helge. "They have been busy."

We poked around the big open room looking for what we had come for. We found two dead women – naked, bound and lying where they fell. There were also the bodies of several old people, their limbs blackened by fire. The rank smell of burnt flesh hung in the air. In a few days, the Frisian pirates had turned this room into a place of torture and death, and the air was heavy with the fruit of their labours.

We searched for a while and finally found what we sought. The pirate's booty was in the corner of the room in a large brass cauldron hidden by an elk skin. We gathered around in some excitement. It did not look like a king's ransom but was enough to make our visit to the island a profitable one. There were silver rings and brooches, combs, buckle loops and arm rings. There were also gold jewellery, neck rings and coins. Beside the cauldron stood a large chest, which was full of valuables too.

"A decent haul," I said to the men. "And after all we only came to get food and water," I added, which drew a little laughter. "Bring it outside – we can share it out later. Leave the chest for I don't think it belongs to us."

The twins picked up the cauldron and took it outside, and we all left the reeking longhouse and sat down in the fading light. There was still a great commotion going on, and we sat and watched. The women (and Ulf) were wreaking their revenge on the men who had tormented them. They had stripped all the captives, bound them and beaten them all to a bloody pulp where they lay in front of us in an untidy heap. The men that remained alive were held down and gelded by an old woman with a knife. Then the bodies of the fallen – dead and alive – were dragged off by the angry mob. I saw Duco being dragged away to meet his fate, naked and bloody yet still alive.

I lost sight of the mob as it disappeared into one of the narrow town streets and turned back to the men. As I did so I felt a hand on my shoulder. It was a woman's hand, and I looked up at her before getting to my feet.

"My name is Frida," she said. "I am *Jarl* Eric's wife".

"And I am Bjorn, let me help you," I said.

She was about twenty-five years old, yellow-haired, and one of her eyes had been closed where she had obviously received a beating. Her clothes had been ripped and torn and she was covered in dried blood. She was in some discomfort, and I put my arm around her and guided her to sit down on a bench outside the longhall. She sat down and began to shake. I took off my cloak and wrapped it around her bare shoulders and saw the deep bruising she had suffered to her skin and neck. When she stopped shaking, she turned and looked up at me with her one good eye.

"Thank you," she said. "Another day or so and they would have killed a lot more of us."

"What happened here?" I said.

"They came about a week ago," she said slowly through bloodied lips. "My husband is away with the men, and they caught us off guard. They killed about a dozen of the old men and boys who defended us as best they could. Then they killed all those who remained standing and imprisoned many of the women in the longhall and tortured them for many days. They wanted the *Jarl*'s gold and threatened to kill the children if I did not reveal where it was hidden. I gave it to them to prevent any more deaths to my people, but they refused to stop. They killed and abused many of us for days, and I feared we would all die. They were the cruellest of men and would not stop finding new ways to hurt us. Then you arrived in your ship." She stopped talking, her shoulders slumped, and she started to sob.

"I am sorry for your pain," I said. "We are on our way to the Baltic Coast and stopped here for supplies and came across the pirates."

I did not tell her that we were also very keen to take any bounty that we might find on them. Frida composed herself and found her voice again.

"However, you came – for whatever purpose, I am very grateful to you. We have much to thank you for, and you are welcome to stay for as long as you like, although we are normally better placed to provide some decent hospitality."

"Thank you, Frida," I said. "We'll be happy to stay for a while."

Today we will rid the town of the last vestiges of this scum, and tomorrow we shall show you some Danish hospitality."

She shuffled off to join a group of women and children standing close by. I went to look for Ulf and found him skulking close to where our men were sitting or lying in front of the longhall. I called to him, and he came over to me, head down and covered in blood.

"I hope that is not yours,' I said to him, pointing at his shirt which looked like it had been soaked in a bucket of blood.

"No," he replied, "it came from that bastard, Duko. He was the last to die. After the women took his balls, he screamed for quite a while. Then I slit his throat."

He said no more and then started to clean his knife on some nearby glass.

"You did well, Ulf," I said. "I hope *Jarl* Eric rewards you for your services when he returns. But for now, your shipmates are hungry and thirsty, and we need you to find us some sustenance. We will be down on the beach by the Raven, and when you have found something suitable for warriors to eat and drink – bring it to us. And of course, you must take your share of the booty."

That was when I first saw her.

Chapter 10: Bjorn and Turid

I led the men back to the beach close to where the Raven lay on the drying sand. The evening was unseasonably warm – almost like early summer. We had lost no one in the brief fight in town, and the six men that we had killed had not put up much of a fight. Torstein managed to carry the cauldron full of Frisian booty by himself, and we sauntered back in high spirits to where we made our camp on the shale. The Saxons went along the beach in search of driftwood to make a fire while the rest of us, including the shepherds, looked greedily at the contents of the cauldron.

"Let's see what these kind Frisians had left behind for us," I said, tipping the booty onto my cloak on the ground.

In the sunlight, I saw that the haul was more valuable than it seemed when we found it in the gloom of the longhouse. What I originally took for silver coins were actually made of gold as was much of the jewellery.

Torstein whistled.

"Well, that was a good day's work," he said, and looked around at the others with a huge grin across his face.

We split the booty and shared it in the normal fashion with each man making his choice. Some of the silver pieces were too big for one man, and I cut up some of the candlesticks and cups into hack-silver. I did not like doing this as it destroyed the beauty of the actual pieces, but it was preferable to keep the peace. In the end, each man – Norwegian, Saxon and Dane – was more than satisfied with what he received. We all agreed that Ulf should take some of the pickings for his part in our successful venture. At the mention of his name, I looked up and saw the boy directing some of the town's women towards the Raven, heavily burdened with food and drink for all of us.

"To the victor the spoils of war are plentiful," guffawed Torstein.

The other men's heads turned to the procession of about ten young women. As they came closer, most of us got to our feet to greet the new arrivals. A young woman whose face looked familiar led the procession. I stood and brushed the sand off my clothes as she approached. She looked much like *Jarl* Eric's wife, but younger, perhaps sixteen or seventeen years old. She strode straight up to us and looked at me confidently with piercing blue eyes.

"My sister Frida sent us with food and drink and the thanks of all of us. She apologises that it is only simple fayre, but there is much damage to repair in our town," she said and smiled.

She had long yellow hair like her sister but had a much slighter frame and was very striking to look at.

"My name is Turid," she continued, not taking her eyes from mine, "and we have brought you plenty to eat and drink, for you must be very hungry after your fighting."

"Thank you, Turid," I replied. "I hope you and your friends did not suffer too badly from these pirates?" I noticed that none of these girls had much in the way of cuts and bruises like the women we had seen earlier.

"My sister hid us from them in a cellar for several days where we remained until you arrived. The raiders attacked us without much warning, and Frida and some of the others got us to safety. We waited in the dark for five days underground while all we could hear were the screams of our friends and family being killed and tortured." She halted reflectively and added, "but the raiders got what they deserved – eventually." Then she laughed.

Was she scolding me for arriving late to the fight? I stumbled around thinking of something wise to say but failed awkwardly. Torstein who, suffering none of my clumsiness, noisily introduced himself to the rest of the women thus saving my embarrassment.

"The town is having a feast in your honour tomorrow, and we will show you some proper Danish hospitality and our deepest gratitude," continued Turid.

She smiled a dazzling smile at me and turned and led her group away. They went away chattering and giggling, and I watched their progress along the beach and back to the town. Torstein, clapping me on the back and bellowing in my ear, broke the spell.

"Bjorn, you look like you have caught Thor's hammer – in your mouth!"

The rest of the men joined in the laughter. We sat back around the fire and settled down for the evening. The women had brought us ale, roast chickens, bread, cheese and some smoked fish and left as quickly as they had arrived. Ulf stayed with us for he was now part of our crew, if only for the next few days and nights. I called him over to join me.

"Ulf, you have been very brave and deserve your share of the booty."

I reached into my tunic and drew out a fine gold Frankish necklace and a silver and brass sword scabbard. "The necklace might just help your mother with her pain, and of course you will need something to carry that new Frisian blade you have acquired. Now tell me what you did to the pirates?"

After stripping and gelding the invaders, the people of Byrum, mostly women, dragged them outside the town. They built a pile of wood and heaped up all the bodies – dead and alive – and set it ablaze. Ulf lit the fire himself. The town had suffered greatly for many days at the hands of the raiders, and the people had been badly mistreated. They left thirty people dead and many cruelly tortured. Children had seen their mothers abused in front of them, and many houses had been razed to the ground. After hearing Ulf's story, I pressed a silver arm ring into his hands.

"Here you are – this is your first warrior's arm ring. I can see you winning many more in your lifetime," I said, helping to fix it to one of his skinny arms and having to bend it to make it fit. Our actions had not strictly been to rescue the people of Byrum, but it was pleasing that we had brought them some sort of justice. The booty we captured was also pleasing but most importantly we were acquiring a new reputation. The Saviours of Byrum seemed a fitting name under which to continue our saga.

After plenty of ale and much telling and retelling of "how we killed the mighty Frisian Pirate Army", the men drifted off to sleep one by one. All but me – I could not get the image of Turid's piercing blue eyes from my mind. Eventually, my weary body succumbed to sleep, although she continued to invade my dreams until morning.

The next morning the sun rose on another fine day although a stiff onshore breeze was causing the breakers to crash noisily onto the beach. I walked down to the edge of the sea and gave thanks to the gods who had delivered us safely. I thanked Thor and Aiger for our safe journey and Loki for his help in the deception that gave us victory in the 'rock storm', dedicating the deaths of the raiders to all of them. Finally, eyes closed in silent prayer, I thanked the *Norns*, those goddesses of all our fates who controlled our destinies of where and when we should live or die.

The men were now stirring and the volume of noise in our camp grew. We ate the remains of the food brought to us on the previous night then made our preparation for the feast. It seemed like a long time since we had been in the company of women, although it was only two weeks since we had left Haugesund. We carried our shields and armour back to the Raven and stowed them aboard. The treasure was put into individual sea chests and bags and secured by each man's oar.

Helge spoke. "As the Raven's helmsman I would like to make a complaint. You men smell worse than those stinking bastards we killed yesterday, so I refuse to take you any further until you bathe."

The men started to sniff at themselves and each other self-consciously whilst I just stripped off and ran headlong into the sea. Soon, we were all in the water trying to remove the caked-on filth we had accumulated over the past two weeks.

Eventually, the Saviours of Byrum were clean and the layers of dried blood and dirt had been removed. I have always been surprised how people of other races did not take care of their appearance. The Franks, the Irish and the Gauls take little time with their personal appearance and the Saxons are quite filthy. The Norse people tend to keep their bodies and clothes clean, and bathe regularly with most men carrying a comb for personal grooming. This often made us popular with the women in foreign ports when we visited as traders. After the visit of the Danish women yesterday, it soon became clear that each man was making a special effort to appear clean and well turned-out. Torstein was no exception, and after spending much time in the sea he continued to groom himself until his long hair and beard had neither a single knot, nor a louse living within them. He spent an eternity plaiting both before standing resplendently on the beach challenging the others to be quite as "dazzling" as he.

I watched a woman coming towards us from the town. It was Turid, and I promised myself that I would not be tongue-tied this time. She wore a simple woollen dress the colour of the sky, and her hair was tied in plaits which had small blue flowers woven into it. All conversation stopped as she approached, and I fought to stop myself from staring.

"Come, men of the north," she said in a loud, assured voice. Then, turning, as if to walk back to the town, she added, "We are ready for you."

I hurried to step in beside her, and we walked together with the rest of our crew falling in behind us.

"You have recovered after your exertions of yesterday?" she asked me. I nodded and mumbled a few words back, then silently cursed myself for being so awkward. "We hope we can repay your kindness," she said, "everyone has been busy preparing this feast for you."

The town had indeed been very busy, and Frida met us in front of the longhouse. All evidence of the fighting had been removed, and now tables and benches stood where the Frisians had made their last stand. She looked much better than she did yesterday. Her eye was still swollen, and her bruised arms and legs were now covered with a long-sleeved dress of autumnal colours. She came forward and embraced me. Then, in front of the rest of the townspeople and our crew, she spoke in a loud voice.

"People of Byrum! Today we welcome these brave men of Norway who have rescued us from the yoke of our unwelcome visitors. They have delivered us from enslavement and worse – and we bid them welcome. I ask you to give these men thanks and to afford them your gratitude for this deliverance. We shall honour them today with a feast and give thanks to the gods. The *Norns* have fixed the fate of all of us here and brought these men to our shores, and for that we thank them and give this sacrifice."

She raised her hand and a large black bull was brought out in front of the crowd, led by the nose by a young boy. Frida approached the animal with a long knife with which she slit its throat, the boy catching the spurting blood in a bowl as the beast fell. Frida dipped her fingers in the blood and daubed each one of us on the forehead.

"We give thanks to Thor and his brothers and sisters who have made us face our fears and defend our family and kindred," she said, to which the townsfolk murmured their thanks. The dead bull was then dragged away by a group of people to be butchered and roasted.

"Thank the gods for that," whispered Torstein in my ear. "I am so hungry I could eat that whole bull raw."

Six large tables, decorated with autumn flowers, had been placed in front of the longhouse. In all there were over a hundred of us present and seated. There were three of us on each table, and every man of our crew was led to his seat by one of the Danes. Turid took my hand and seated me between her and her sister. Helge and Leif sat on the other side of our table next to their grateful hosts – all women of the town. Frida beckoned to one of the serving women and very soon huge trays of food and jugs of ale were brought out and put in front of us. There were steaming trays of seafood, roasted fowl, salted fish and pork as well as mountains of buttered, honeyed bread. There were many different types of cheeses and autumnal fruits of apples, pears, berries and nuts. Every time my plate or my drinking cup was empty Turid would ensure that one of the slaves replenished it, and Frida made a point of visiting each table to personally thank every one of our men for his efforts.

At first, the proceedings had been a little muted for only the day before these people had been in fear of their lives and were still recovering from their ordeal. As the day wore on, and the ale and mead loosened tongues and raised spirits, the atmosphere became more relaxed. Dane and Norwegian grew more comfortable in each other's company. Our own table was, eventually, full of laughter and good humour with stories and jokes swapped and shared in a festive atmosphere.

I turned to Frida, "Your hospitality far exceeds our expectations, Lady," I said.

"Enjoy this small reward, Bjorn. You saved us from great harm and your deeds here will live with us forever."

She raised her drinking cup to us in a toast whilst her sister seated on my other side did the same.

"To the men of Haugesund," said Turid, and kissed me on the cheek.

If I was not quite intoxicated by her before, then I was completely befuddled by now. For the first part of the evening sitting next to her, I had tried to feign a polite indifference, but I had to admit to myself at last that I was bewitched. I turned and met her gaze, and the spell was not to be broken. I could smell the flowers in her hair, and her clothes and skin carried the scent of lavender and fresh pine. She lay her hand gently on top of mine and smiled sweetly, and I was beyond the help of any of my comrades – truly in the lap of the gods.

As the afternoon grew into evening, two young women

appeared in front of our tables, and Frida stood up to call for quiet. The women were joined by three musicians playing the lyre, a flute and some panpipes. They sang and played for us, their music hanging in the evening air, and we were pulled to our feet to dance by our hosts. Turid's eyes sparkled in the reflection of the huge fire that had been built high against the cooling evening, and I whirled her around. The dancing finally slowed down, and the musicians were replaced by a poet who recounted the story of Laeso and its place in history.

Torstein, who had been relatively quiet until then, leapt to his feet displacing the two women perched on each of his knees. He turned to face his audience and declared in a booming voice:

"He is happy, who for himself obtains fame and kind words. Less sure is that which a man must have in another's breast – but you, my friends, are in my heart always. Now I will tell you the story of Ragnar Lodbrok."

He then proceeded to tell the complete saga of Ragnar, the great Norse hero. At the end of his tale, all the guests applauded, and some of the men wept openly at the tale. Torstein bowed low to his enraptured audience and returned to his seat at his table where he restored both the women on his lap. The evening was getting late when Frida turned to me.

"Goodnight Bjorn. I am tired and need to go to bed. I hope you will be staying with us a little while longer before you resume your journey."

"Thank you, Frida, your hospitality has been wonderful, but we will need to be on our way in the next few days while the weather is good."

"Then I will see you tomorrow. You are in good hands," she said, nodding towards her younger sister. I helped her to her feet, and she moved off stiffly.

I turned back to Turid.

"Then I shall do as my big sister wishes me," she said and stood up, wrapped herself in a woollen hooded cloak and held out her hand to me. Without a word, I took it and stood beside her, and we left quietly. Helge, seeing us leave called out, "I don't suppose we shall make the morning tide!" and there was much laughter.

Turid joined in with them and turned back calling: "I am only seeing our guest safely back to his camp."

We walked into the dark and down to the shoreline, walking hand-in-hand by the light of the autumn moon, to where the Raven had been drawn up out of the water. We walked on past our boat and kept walking for another mile or so.

"When do you think you will be leaving us?" she asked.

"We must soon be on our way for I need to reach Jomsborg while the weather is good."

She stopped abruptly and turned to face me. "I am shivering, Bjorn," she said.

She came closer to me, tilting her face up towards mine and kissed me on the mouth. It was a kiss that I was not quite ready for, and it took me completely by surprise, but I kissed her back hard then drew her into my great bearskin cloak. I felt her tremble and press herself against me.

"No, not just from the cold," she said pushing my cloak off my shoulders and onto the dry sand. She took off her own cloak, laid it on top of mine and kissed me again. Then she stood back and removed the clasp on the side of her dress letting the garment fall to the ground, and kicking off her shoes, she stood naked in front of me. Turid took my hand again and beckoned me to lie down on our makeshift bed on the dry, sandy beach. We kissed again, the spell was cast eternally, and I fell deeply under its power.

I have known many women in my life and the simple act of laying with them was nothing new. Since the age of eleven when I was first introduced to our slave girls in Haugesund, I saw the act as nothing more than rutting, like the animals on our farm. Tonight, I lay with Turid beneath the stars feeling her soft skin against my naked body and her sweet breath on my neck, and it was like nothing else I had ever experienced. I

68

was not quite sure of my feelings for her, only that they were stronger than I had ever felt for any woman. She stirred in her sleep, and I watched her beautiful face reflecting silver in the moonlight. Tomorrow we would wake, the dream would be over, and we would have to go our separate ways.

Chapter 11: The Beauty of Byrum

But it was not a dream. I woke early. It had been light for a while, and I reached for Turid but found her gone. The small blue flowers that had been woven into her hair were scattered over the bearskin, but the place where she had lain was still warm to the touch. I sat up in some panic and was relieved to see her coming out of the sea and walking back towards me. She was naked, and her lithe, muscular body was accentuated by the early morning sunshine already casting her short shadow onto the sand. I called to her. She waved and then ran towards me flopping down on our makeshift bed.

"This time I am cold, Bjorn."

I wrapped her cloak around her, pulled her close and embraced her once again. The mighty passion – *inn matki munr* – devoured us both.

Later that morning we talked for some time. She told me of her life growing up on the island, and I sensed a growing feeling of restlessness within her. I told me about Haugesund, my life there, and how and why I left. I told her all about our journey and our quest to join the Jomsvikings. After a while, she stopped asking questions and grew quiet.

"You could stay here with me," she said. "I think the life of a Dane might suit you."

I shook my head. "I cannot stay here … but maybe I'll come back for you one day," I teased.

"And maybe I will have married and have six children by then. Come, let us go back to the town. Frida will be missing me, and she is still in some pain."

We dressed in silence, gathered our things and followed the path of the previous evening. Walking in silence we reached the Raven where a few of my crew were sitting around idly. They looked up at us as we approached, and Helge called to us in greeting.

"I told you we would not make the morning tide," he shouted.

Turid leant into me and said, quietly, "Come and find me later – in the longhouse."

She walked on, past the boat and back into the town.

I called back to Helge, "There's always another tide!" to which he answered, "But perhaps not always such a welcome."

Throughout the remainder of the day, our crew emerged in ones and twos and joined us on the beach. The shepherds left us that day, and after saying their goodbyes we sent them off much the richer for both their experience and their newfound wealth. Torstein finally returned and was in fine, good humour, having been treated royally by one of the women of the town. She was a young widow who had taken him under her roof for the night.

"Will we be so well looked after in Jomsborg?" he asked me.

"I think we will be offered a different kind of hospitality," I replied.

"Still, she is a beautiful girl that Turid, is she not?" he continued elbowing me in the ribs. "I think you may even quite like her?"

"I am surprised you noticed, cousin. You looked like you were quite occupied yourself," I said, and he laughed, clapping me heartily on the back.

We still had a little repair work to do on our boat, which Helge estimated would take us a day and a half. We would leave on the morning tide the day after next. I would go and buy some supplies from the townsfolk later in the day, which gave me an excellent excuse to seek out Turid. I spent the rest of the afternoon with our crew finishing the repairs to the hull and replacing some of the damaged planking. Frida sent some pinewood and tools, carried by a couple of the town's boys, who were full of curiosity to meet their strange new guests. Ulf, having gained something of a reputation amongst his peers as a warrior, talked them through the finer points of the battle. We made good progress with the hull and worked steadily towards evening stopping our labours not long before dusk.

"I have business in the town," I told the men. "Come, Ulf, bring your friends, for I have a job for them."

They put down their tools and scampered after me.

"Me too," added Torstein and fell in beside me. "Do you think you might see that girl?" he asked.

"What girl might that be?" I replied.

"Don't forget cousin – we leave the day after tomorrow. So just have your business done by then?" he said sternly before bursting into laughter yet again.

By the time our little party reached the longhouse, Torstein had left us to look for both ale and the widow. We found Frida sitting outside on her own, and she looked up and smiled.

"Hello, Bjorn. What do think of our island now there are no pirates to look out for?"

"It is a wonderful place – and so beautiful I could be back home in Norway. Thank you for your hospitality again – it was a memorable evening," I replied.

She stood and came towards me. "You are most welcome, and your deeds shall be remembered here for many years. There will always be a warm welcome here for you and your men."

She turned to the boys. "Go to Jan the miller and he will give you supplies for the boat."

I reached inside my tunic for some silver coin to give the boys to pay for our goods, but Frida stayed my hand. "Your silver is no good here, Bjorn, and I am sure you would not wish to insult us." The boys ran off and we were left alone. Her eye had now opened fully, and as the swelling in her face was going down, I could see that she shared her sister's beauty. I thanked her and told her of our plans.

"We shall be sad to see you go so soon,' she said. 'You have been a gift from the gods, but we should let them have you back. But we must make the most of you while you are here – come inside for some food and drink."

She turned and led me through the doors into the longhouse.

The long rectangular building had been thoroughly cleaned since I was last there and it showed no sign of the previous unwelcome occupants. The large wooden building had been restored to its former order, and Frida led me to a chair next to the hearth fire. A couple of dogs, stretched out in front of the blaze, barely noticed my approach.

"We are slowly getting back to normal here," she said. "In a week's time you would not know that we had even been raided."

I nodded but I knew the truth – these people had suffered a good deal at the hands of the pirates. Although the visible wounds would quickly disappear those of the spirit might take a little longer.

"Some ale for our guest," she called loudly to the far end of the hall.

We sat close to the flames, and she put a golden warrior's ring into my hand. "In *Jarl* Eric's absence I am the *ring-giver* here and you have earned this," she said.

Worn on the arms, these warrior rings were often made of silver or bronze, but this one was of heavy gold –it was a very valuable piece. I thanked her and put it on.

She continued: "We hope he will return to us before the winter storms. These seas can be dangerous by then ..." She stopped and looked up over my shoulder to where Turid stood behind me with a tray of drinking cups, ale and food. "... it looks like you have been expected, Bjorn. Come and join us, sister – it is a while since we had a famous warrior in our hall."

The two women sat side-by-side and chattered away while I ate and drank.

Then Frida announced, "I am still a little weary Bjorn, forgive me but I must go and rest." She stood up with some effort, bade us goodnight and hobbled painfully to her rooms. Turid moved in close to me, and I could smell the scent of lavender and pine about her once more.

"Come, drink up Bjorn, I have something to show you," she said.

She took my hand and led me outside into the evening's dying light. We walked for a while, away from the houses until we reached the beach – this time on the other side of Byrum from where the Raven lay.

"Where are we going?" I asked.

"Up there," she said, pointing to the top of the nearby cliffs.

We soon started to climb steeply up a narrow path, and I followed as Turid bounded off ahead of me. We reached the summit after a few hundred paces, and I stopped to catch my breath as she urged me on.

"Come on, old man," she chided, "not much further."

I looked up to see a small stone house close by.

"I thought you might like to sleep in a bed tonight instead of on the sand," she said, pulling me by the hand through the door and into the small house. The fire had been lit, and there was a bed in the middle of the room on which were laid furs and blankets. "I don't want to get cold again," she said. She pulled her dress off over her head, pushed me towards the bed and we kissed.

"I will try hard not to let that happen, Turid," I said, as we sank into the furs. She wrapped herself around me and I was lost to her once more.

This mighty passion was not easily extinguished, and we stayed in that house all night and the following day during which we would occasionally stop to rest and take food and drink before it engulfed us once more. I emerged on the following evening and briefly visited the Raven.

Helge sat with Svein who was still in some pain but they

raised cups of ale and waved me away.

"We must be ready to go in the morning," said Helge. "Just go and make the most of your princess for I have heard there are no women to be had in Jomsborg."

I turned and raced back to our retreat on the cliff tops where Turid drew me eagerly back to our bed. We slept little that night, and as the dawn came up over Byrum, we surfaced into the early light and watched the sun come up. It was cold, and a thin hoar frost covered the grass where we stood. I drew her into the depths of my cloak and we spent the last of our precious time together watching the sunrise in silence. I looked down to see the town was slowly coming to life, and then over to where our crew were gathering slowly around the Raven.

"I will say goodbye here," she said in a hoarse little whisper.

There was an awkward silence between us, for we knew that this was our final parting. I did not know what to say, but I kissed her one last time, and we released one another.

"I will dream of you often," I whispered back.

She turned from me, "You must go now Bjorn, you must go a-viking."

I left her there on the cliff top and trudged down the goat track with a heavy heart to rejoin my shipmates.

Torstein met me with a giant bear hug and bellowed, "Cousin, you have brought me not only fame and fortune but also great love."

He delved into the small but growing crowd on the beach and came back with a woman in his arms.

"This is Anfried," he shouted over her. "When you and I are rich and famous and have carved a huge reputation, I will return and marry this woman – for I love her."

He tossed his captive into the air as though she were a tiny child, then set her on her feet and kissed her ardently on the mouth.

Our men were all assembled and everything we needed

was stowed aboard. A crowd of townsfolk gathered before us and Frida stepped forward and raised her voice above the wind.

"Bjorn and your crew – we wish you the gods' speed and pray that one day the *Norns* will see fit to blow you back to Byrum."

The crowd cheered and pressed gifts of bread and fruit upon us. Ulf shed a tear as we said goodbye but did his best to look like a brave Danish warrior. We pushed the Raven back into the sea, boarded her and backed out. Then we turned, made for the gap in the cliffs one last time and out to the open sea.

As we reached the ocean, I turned and looked up to the point where I left Turid. She had not moved. Her blue cloak and her long, untied yellow hair billowed in the wind as she waved goodbye from on top of the cliffs.

Chapter 12: The Onward Journey

Helge set the course, the sail was rigged, and we pulled away from Laeso heading for Wendland. He reckoned on a six-day trip if the weather held and the wind was good. Today was as much as we could have wished for and the wind blew us steadily southward. We would hug the coast of Sweden until we reached Trelleborg. I had another uncle there, Oyvind, who had settled in Trelleborg some years ago and had ranged into Wendland as a young man. He knew the Jomsvikings well and had fought alongside them in many campaigns. I wanted to see him and talk to him about our plans and how we should approach them.

The men were pleased to be moving again and were well rested after their visit to Laeso. I sat next to Torstein leaning against one of the bulkheads. He was singing aloud as we pitched and rolled gently to the rhythm of the sea.

"I think we can call the Raven's first fight a success," he said. "Ale, booty, beautiful women, sharp axe in a Frisian head. I enjoyed that, Bjorn. It was excellent."

"I think there will be greater challenges ahead of us," I replied, trying to be serious.

"Not all our enemies will die so easily…and the women won't always be so grateful," he said.

"Do you think we will see them again?" I asked.

"No, not the Frisians – they are all dead," he said laughing at his own joke, "but the women – I hope so – one day. First though, we must become famed warriors, and our reputations must go before us – then we can have all the women we want. Unless, of course, you only want one particular woman?"

I avoided his question: "I am told that each new recruit has to defeat a Jomsviking before they are taken in," I said.

"Good," said my cousin. "Then we can show them how

Norwegian warriors acquit themselves in battle. It will be nice to get some proper competition anyway."

The next day passed slowly, but the winds were good to us and took us in a direct line to the coast of Sweden where we stayed in sight of land on our journey south. At the end of each day we searched for a friendly beach, rowed ashore and made our camp for the night. We saw a few people on shore – mostly curious natives – and we also passed a small number of longboats travelling north. Nobody troubled us, nor did we trouble them and our recent adventures on Laeso started to become just a memory.

After four days, the Raven arrived at Trelleborg on the southernmost tip of the land of Denmark. I wanted to see my uncle again before we went to Jomsborg, and hopefully he would be here. Oyvind had left Haugesund seven years before to go raiding into eastern Europe. He made great river voyages with his crew, and they had navigated deep into the river systems of the east where few Norsemen had gone before. Finally, he settled in Trelleborg where he was recruited into the service of the Danish King Harald Bluetooth. The King wanted a fortress built and manned – to protect Denmark and Skåne from Slavic raiders, and he sent his son Svein Forkbeard to take charge. My uncle had sailed with Svein many times, they were good friends and he made Oyvind the Commander of the fortress.

We rowed into the harbour at Trelleborg in good order. The Raven figurehead had been taken down long since leaving Laeso, and we came to rest against the jetty. One of the crew jumped down and secured the Raven fore and aft to the quay with ropes. We moored onto one of several pontoons running out from the town which itself was positioned directly in front of a huge wooden fortress the like of which none of us had seen before. It was circular and dwarfed the town lying in its shadow. On the ramparts of the fortress stood several armed spearmen standing sentinel to the comings and goings of all traffic from the land or sea. Two armed men, dressed in mail, approached the Raven and shouted to me where I stood in the prow.

"Please state your business in Trelleborg," shouted the first.

"The Raven is travelling from Haugesund to Wendland, and we seek harbour for the night. I have come to see my uncle, Oyvind, who I believe is Commander here. The men aboard are his kinsfolk."

The man changed his attitude immediately and replied, "Lord Oyvind commands the fortress here and will be notified of your arrival. If you wait here, we will tell him immediately," to which he added, "you'll still have to pay the harbour fees though – it's two pieces of silver a night."

I tossed the silver to him. He dispatched the other man to the fortress while we waited on board, and he continued his collections from the rest of the ships on the quay.

We did not have to wait long before a third man approached the Raven. He was large, shaven headed with a long beard reaching halfway down his chest and a collection of tattoos over his arms and head. He shouted up to us.

"I am looking for Bjorn of Haugesund."

I stood up, and he continued. "You and your men are invited to the Commander's longhall for supper. You must leave all your arms on your boat and follow me."

I gave orders to our Saxons to stay on board and guard the Raven while the rest of us jumped down and followed the man. We made our way down the quay, through the town and up a muddy path towards the fortress. When we got closer, it was even larger than it looked, with the trunks of whole oak trees reinforcing the outer wall and fixed together around the massive structure.

The thirteen of us followed our guide, walked through the huge open gates and into what looked like a series of longhouses within the fort. I counted four of these rectangular buildings before we stopped in front of yet another long wooden hall. The man turned to me.

"This is Lord Oyvind's hall. He is waiting for you."

I led the men into the building where about a hundred warriors were seated at tables and benches. I had not seen my uncle in the seven years since he had left Haugesund, and I looked around frantically for the man I last saw when I was a thirteen-year-old stripling.

"Bjorn" I heard someone shouting, then once again from a different direction. I heard my name being called from several different directions and sensing my confusion the seated men began to laugh. A man at an empty table near the fire stood and raised his hand – and the laughter ceased. It was my uncle, and he walked towards us.

"That cannot be my nephews Bjorn and Torstein," he shouted. "They were nothing but skin and bone when I last saw them." He came forward and embraced each of us, in turn, with a huge bear hug.

"It is good to see you, Bjorn," he said. "Forgive the small joke, there is little in the way of entertainment in here."

He released me and looked over my men. "There are a few familiar faces among you – a little bit more gnarled and with more whiskers than I remember, but it is very good to see you all. And you Helge – you disreputable old sea dog – you have not changed a bit. Come sit and eat and tell me everything."

We arranged ourselves at Oyvind's table, and the rest of the men in the hall, now bored with the new arrivals, resumed their eating and drinking. We sat down at the table, me on one side of Oyvind and Torstein on the other.

"It is good to see so many of my kinsmen again,' he said. "You are all very welcome."

When we had been given cups of ale he raised his drinking horn to each of us in turn.

"Skal to you all! I shall start with you Bjorn – what have you been up to? We have plenty of time."

Although Oyvind was several years younger than his siblings, Rollo and Halfdan, he still bore a striking resemblance to my father, and I had forgotten how alike they had been in thought, word and deed. He was tall, like me, with his long hair and beard worn loose – which were both more grey than yellow. I told him of Haugesund and events there since he had left. We talked of his brother, my father, and his recent death, and all his friends and relatives back in Norway. I went through the last seven years of the town's history and told him of our recent adventures since we left. Our defeat of the Frisian pirates made him laugh out loud, and he would frequently turn to Torstein as if seeking affirmation that all I told him was true.

"My little nephews have grown into warriors," he said, more than once. "Helge, how have you kept these young men under control?"

"Not me," came the reply. "Bjorn is the leader here – and a great warrior just like his father."

"Just like his father," echoed Oyvind hugging me yet again.

"Now, Uncle it's time for your story," I said.

Oyvind had left to go raiding seven years previously with a band of warriors, like us, seeking reputation and wealth. Much like now, it had been a time of unrest. Many Scandinavian people were looking for new lands to settle in; new kings were trying to unify their territories; the scourge of Christianity continued its inexorable creep through our lands; and the towns in Norway were becoming overcrowded. Oyvind left with forty men and sailed south and then east, joining up with men of a similar persuasion as he went on his way. Eventually, there were over a hundred of them in three longboats in search of plunder. They sailed along the routes of the Swedish traders raiding many coastal lands of the Baltic and Slavic tribes. Although their raids were mostly successful and they took many slaves (later sold further along the coast), the booty they captured was relatively small. Eventually, they reached the lands of the Kievan Norsemen, stopped at the town of Staraya Lagoda and turned inland along the great river system of the Rus. This was a place of great danger, and the tribes became wilder as Oyvind's flotilla sailed down the great Volkov River. They travelled south encountering many hostile tribes and faced fierce resistance as they progressed. If their journey was not dangerous enough, they encountered parts of the river that were impassable, and they had to continually remove their boats carrying them to the next access point in the river. Many months after leaving the shores of the Baltic, they arrived at a huge inland ocean called the Black Sea.

The raiders had acquired a little wealth on their journey but nothing like what they had hoped for when they set out. One day they reached a large trading post called Odessa where they stayed to sell the slaves and skins captured on previous raids. Oyvind and the other captain went into the town to find the marketplace and stopped at a tavern. Inside they met an old friend, Ivar the Red, who had left Norway sometime before them. This man had sailed to Odessa by a different route with a cargo of salt. He was a trader of goods who now plied his wares around Eastern Europe and had given up the life of a raider for a more peaceful existence. Oyvind told him that they had not found the plentiful amount of silver they were looking for in any of the towns they had raided – lots of furs and slaves – but no silver. Ivar told them the silver in the East was now in short supply and had been so for many years since many of the larger mines were exhausted. The mines that had previously supplied the rest of Europe with silver were now empty. However, according to Ivar, a new source of silver had been found in Saxony, to the West, and the new mines there were larger than anything that had been known before.

Ivar gave them a map and Oyvind took his men – there were sixty of them left on two ships – to the kingdom of Frankia where they sought out the mines and the new silver. They travelled to the Hartz mountains by river from the Black Sea to Saxony and spent a profitable year raiding the Franks and taking much of the newfound wealth. My uncle's reputation as a war leader increased with each success and his group of warriors grew as men flocked to his banner. The Franks eventually organised their defences and put up a fierce resistance to the Norseman by which time Oyvind decided to leave the region – a very rich man. He and his band of warriors withdrew to Scandinavia, with a huge haul of silver, in search of new opportunities. He was then forty years old, with a great reputation. Fearing his adverse influence in the region, the King of Denmark, Harold 'Bluetooth', asked Oyvind to build and command a fortress in Trelleborg to protect the reunified country. My uncle accepted the King's offer and settled in Trelleborg building an army of twelve hundred warriors to protect and defend Danish interests in the region.

Oyvind finished his story and looked up at the rest of us who were hanging on his every word.

"That is an impressive story, Uncle," I said.

"Thank you, Bjorn. Now, I seem to remember that Torstein was quite a good storyteller himself."

"I thought you would never ask," said Torstein, who stood and called for quiet from the rest of the warriors in the great hall.

"My friends," he shouted in a large, booming voice, "you all know of Mjollnir, Thor's hammer. Well, this is the story of how it was stolen…"

The babble of conversation in the hall turned down to a murmur and then complete silence. As always when he told a story, Torstein plunged into the telling of it, and there was much drama and emotion imparted to his audience. At the end, his fellow warriors showed their appreciation with much cheering and banging on the tables. Satisfied that he had given a good account of himself, he returned to his seat at our table with his face glowing red with the exertion.

"Now my young kinsmen," said Oyvind to his nephews sitting either side of him, "I want to know how you intend to find employment with the Jomsvikings. Many have tried and many have failed."

I spoke first. "We shall sail down to Jomsborg and seek an audience with Styrbjorn Storki and ask to join them."

My uncle smiled. "You will need more of a plan than that. There are thousands of swords and axes for sale in these times, so why should they take you two – a couple of more mouths to feed from the north? The Jomsvikings have more than enough men flocking to their colours every week eager to join them. Here is what you must do.

"First they must be convinced of your worth as warriors who will follow their stringent rules to the letter. You will then have to prove your worth to them, and if they believe you are worthy, you will be tested severely. If you do pass their test you will have to submit to their rules and follow their code – it is not for every man. I know Styrbjorn well – he and I have sailed together and fought side by side. He also owes me a debt, for I once loaned him a great deal of silver at a time when no one else would help him. He is a very proud man, so you must be very careful with this information." At this point, he cast a conspiratorial glance, first at Torstein, then at me.

"How should we proceed?" asked my cousin.

"You must gain an audience with him. You, Bjorn, will introduce yourself as the son of your father – they will know of his reputation. Then, tell him Oyvind the Silver Giver vouches for you – and he will know you have my backing, as few people know me by that name. Then tell him that you and Torstein are bound by blood, and that you cannot be separated. That will hopefully be enough for them to consider you seriously."

"What then?" I asked.

"If you are successful, they will challenge you – by combat. It will be very hard, but I know you well enough to know that you shall triumph. After that, you might be inducted into their brotherhood, and then there will be no going back; you shall have the life you have chosen." He raised his cup to us in salutation.

"Good luck to both of you, boys, for I know you will make Haugesund proud. Skal!" he said, and the rest of our table joined him in raising their cups to us.

We swapped a few more stories of home, and I asked lots of questions of Oyvind, but gradually the men became tired and slid to the floor where they slept. The rest of the hall emptied, and the other men retired to their barracks close by. In the morning we awoke, returned to the Raven and rowed out into the cold Baltic Sea where we raised the sail. I felt the boat turn off the wind, and we were underway. We would soon be in Jomsborg for whatever the Gods chose to throw at us.

They chose not to make things easy.

Chapter 13: Jomsborg

It took two more days to reach the Baltic coast. With the wind behind us, we sailed directly to Jomsborg but did not need to row until we reached the river mouth. Although the winter storms were not due for another month Helge was keen to be on his way back to Haugesund in the next few days. The Raven would deliver us to the fortress of the Jomsvikings, and Torstein and I would attempt to gain an audience – and employment. We had not considered what would happen if we were unsuccessful, but if we did not appear back at the Raven within two days of our landing, the ship would leave and return home.

Jomsborg comprised of a huge stone fortress built on the southern tip of the island of Wollin at the mouth of the River Oder. The island lay in the strait of Dziwna, in the land of the Wends and could only be reached by sailing up a narrow, defendable channel. Like Trelleborg, it had been built by King Harald Bluetooth but was now commanded by Styrbjorn the Strong. He was a Swedish Prince whose father had been murdered, but when he went to claim the throne, the ruling council of the *Allthing* decided that he was unfit to rule Sweden. In a fit of rage Styrbjorn left the country with his men and for many years ravaged the Baltic shores from his raiding ships until he took the fortress of Jomsborg. Styrbjorn had been a pirate since the age of sixteen and had built up a mighty fleet capable of raiding anywhere along the Baltic coast with great speed and devastation. He and his warriors were the power in the region and wherever they ranged they brought fear and destruction. The Jomsvikings lived by a strict code, and as dedicated pagans, worshipping Thor and *Odin*, they saw Christianity as their nemesis. They lived and prospered through their raiding and shared everything they 'won' among themselves, acquiring great wealth and reputation. Oyvind told us that in time of war they sold themselves to the highest bidder and had absolutely no scruples about which side they followed – provided they received enough gold and silver.

We rowed into the port, and I stood in the prow marvelling at the array of vessels that lay at anchor in a huge harbour beneath an equally imposing stone castle. I counted nearly three hundred ships in all. Fat, broad-beamed traders and sleek longboats bobbed peacefully at anchor or alongside numerous jetties projecting from the shore. The harbour bustled with the activity of fighting men and traders being ferried to and from the town. The Raven took a spare berth on one of the jetties.

Torstein and I busied ourselves getting ready to leave our crew. Our armour had been prepared at sea on the final day of our voyage. Blades had been whetted, mail had been polished, and shield bosses and helms burnished. Even my bearskin cloak had been brushed and cleaned. At Oyvind's suggestion, I carried two solid gold candlesticks bearing the sign of the cross that we had taken from the Frisians as a gift for Styrbjorn.

"Let me take one last look at you boys before you disappear into the hornet's nest," said Helge, casting a fatherly eye over us both as we readied ourselves to leave.

"Not bad," he continued. "Your fathers would be proud of you. Now go and make your shipmates proud." He hugged us both, and the rest of the men wished us luck as we jumped onto the quay.

"Remember, Helge," I shouted back at the boat, "if we are not back in two days, leave us to our fate. Take our possessions back and give them to our families at home."

We made our way down the jetty to the shore and stood at the foot of the path leading up to the great fortress.

"Come on Torstein let's go and see what lives inside this castle and whether it is a fit place for us to lay our heads," I said.

"I want little but loot, fame, significance, wealth and importance – all in that order. If they can provide me with these then they shall have my undying love – and even obedience," he rejoined, and we set off up the hill together.

We stopped talking and approached a huge entrance, as tall as three men, leading into the castle. It was made of solid oak and contained within it was a postern gate. Two heavily armoured spearmen stood guard, dressed in long mail coats, and each carried a large round shield with a red cross on a black background.

One of the men, about my size, moved into my path and demanded, "Where are you going?"

I felt Torstein close at my shoulder and the man looked over my head at the giant standing next to me, resplendent in his newly acquired helmet and visor that covered most of his face.

"I am Bjorn, son of Halfdan Strong Arm from Haugesund," I said, "and this is my cousin Torstein. We seek an audience with Styrbjorn Storki."

"What is your business with the Commander," said the man.

"We have been sent by one of his old comrades with gifts from dead Christians, and we seek employment with the Jomsvikings," I replied.

The guard nodded to the other man who disappeared without a word.

"You will wait over there," he barked, pointing to a place by the castle wall. Sometime later, the other man returned and gave instructions to his comrade. The first guard shouted over to us:

"You two, follow this man."

We walked after the other guard through the postern gate and into a huge courtyard.

Here we saw several hundred men taking part in various martial activities. A group of about fifty men were attacking a shield wall with various manoeuvres, whilst another group were practising sword and axe play. Archers were shooting at targets, and yet another group hurled spears in formation. The noise of this activity was as deafening as it was relentless. I have never seen so many men drilling so hard and continuously.

"Wait in there," said the man leading us, pointing to a small, windowless stone building in the corner of the courtyard. We went inside and waited.

After what seemed like an eternity of listening to the clash of steel outside, the door to our waiting room opened and another man entered. He was much better dressed than either of the last two guards and spoke with the authority of a leader.

"My name is Ubbi, and I am one of the Commander's captains. He does not usually respond to such random requests, but he is familiar with some of your kinfolk and will give you an audience. Please leave all your weapons here and follow me. What is in your sack?"

I showed Ubbi the two gold candlesticks. "A gift for the Commander," I said.

Torstein and I removed our swords, axes, helms and daggers, left them on a nearby table and followed Ubbi. We went through a succession of doors and finally came into a large hall. It could have been a feasting hall but there were no tables or benches, just a huge single hearth fire burning halfway down its length. The walls were hung with spears and shields. I later learned that the shield designs denoted each of the Scandinavian tribes from where the Jomsvikings were drawn. I hoped that my shield would soon join them. The hall was about three hundred paces long, and at regular intervals of ten paces stood a spearman in a full helm and mail shirt. At the far end of the room sat the Commander of the fortress.

Styrbjorn Storki, sat still and silent in a high-backed chair positioned on a raised dais. He did not look up as we entered the room.

Ubbi spoke to us quietly. "You may approach the

Commander."

We both marched up to the seated man. We were about twenty paces away when we were stopped from going any further by two of the spearmen standing in front of us. Styrbjorn looked up and regarded us coldly from his chair.

"Let them pass," he said to the two guards who stood aside and let us approach him.

He was about forty years old and wore his long yellow hair and beard loose, and his bright blue eyes shone with a fierce malevolence. He also wore a highly polished steel breastplate under a grey wolfskin cloak, and at his side was an *Ulfberht* sword sheathed in a bejewelled scabbard. He looked at me for a while and then turned his gaze to Torstein, then back to me again.

"Speak," he commanded.

I spoke first. "Thank you for your audience, Lord. I am Bjorn of Haugesund, son of Halfdan Strong Arm and nephew of Oyvind the Silver Giver of Trelleborg."

"And you giant – who are you," he said, pointing at my cousin.

"I am Torstein, the Bear of Haugesund where my father is *Jarl*…"

Styrbjorn held up a hand to stop him from speaking further. "We care not for family connections here, and I am very familiar with your fathers and uncles. We do, however, put a good deal of importance on reputation. But, alas, I have never heard of you two. So, tell me your story."

I continued, "We are experienced warriors seeking opportunity for wealth and reputation. We have raided and killed our enemies with axe and sword for much of our lives and marched deep into the lands of the Saxons, the Irish and the Slavs where we have won much plunder. We have taken our place in the shield wall and stood beside our brothers scattering our adversaries to the four winds. We are formidable fighters and have defeated many fierce tribes who have been brave enough to stand against us."

"Fine words. And what do you seek from me?" said Styrbjorn, fixing us with a steely glare.

"We seek employment in your service, Lord," I said. "We must live the life of warriors where we can be free of kings and Christianity. We wish to go where the *Norns* cast us and to whatever fate they decide for us."

He turned his attention to my cousin. "And you – what will the Bear of Haugesund give me? For I have many mighty warriors at my disposal."

I heard Torstein take a deep intake of breath and knew he was building up to a big performance.

"Lord, the reputation of Styrbjorn the Strong and his mighty Jomsvikings is legendary. We have a great desire to become part of that legend so that our reputations might live forever. If you take us into your service you will, of course, get our uncompromising loyalty and arms. You will also get something more, for I come from a long line of warrior skalds who will record your deeds and victories in verse that will be remembered for all time. You will have both my words and my axe; the saga of Styrbjorn the Strong will be told in the Halls of Valhalla forever. For animals die, friends die, and I shall die, but the one thing that shall never die is the reputation we leave behind at our death. I shall ensure through my deeds and my words that your reputation will live forever."

Styrbjorn's face was impassive as he listened, but at Torstein's suggestion, he leaned forward in his chair. The Commander said nothing then leaned back again, considering our words. I broke the silence by retrieving the heavy gold candlesticks from my sack.

"We have brought you gold, Lord," I said, proffering our gift. "The Christian priests have much gold and silver, and we are very keen to relieve them of it."

I placed the candlesticks in Styrbjorn's hands, and he inspected them with a casual disinterest before speaking again:

"Very well, men of Haugesund. I know the reputation of your *aett* and am prepared to accept that you may have inherited part of their warrior spirit. But for now, you do not have the reputations of either your fathers or your uncles. However, that may be due to your youth, and mighty reputations often grow with time. I will allow you to join us if you both complete our trials – by battle.

"You will both be required to fight and defeat my warriors before I can think about accepting you into our code. If you accept this challenge you will appear ready for battle at dusk today in the fighting yard outside. If you do not wish this, you may take your leave of us now. Do you accept or reject my offer?"

"We accept the challenge," we both said in unison, and Ubbi led us away back to where we had left our weapons, to prepare for the forthcoming battle trials.

"I listened to your words," he said. "They were well-spoken."

Food and drink were brought for us, and Ubbi asked us if we needed any more weapons. "We will fight with what we have brought with us, but we are without spears. Can you tell us who we will be facing?"

"It will be up to the Commander who you will face, but it will be men from the fortress – at least for the first trial," he said.

"So, there will be more than one trial?" I asked.

"I cannot say too much. But fight as you talk, and you will impress. I will see you very soon."

He left the two of us alone to our thoughts. It was difficult to make a plan because we did not know who or even how many warriors we would be fighting.

"Whoever they put in front of us, Bjorn, we will punish them. Anyway, I think the Commander liked the idea of having his own skald. They are very arrogant these Swedes."

We both laughed.

Ubbi returned for us a little later. We were now fully armed again with weapons, shields and helms. Torstein's new crested helmet made him look even bigger.

"Follow me," Ubbi said. "We are ready for you now. You will have two trials today. The first will be against men of the Jomsvikings – they are of Styrbjorn's personal bodyguard. They will come at you hard, and you will need to defeat them all. You will fight until the first blood is drawn."

Torstein looked at me and winked. "You will also have a second trial if you are successful with the first. You will fight some Slavic warriors captured on a recent raid. They have nothing to lose and everything to gain – be careful."

"And then?" asked Torstein.

"Then we shall be brothers-in-arms," said Ubbi, smiling at us for the first time.

We reached the place where the men had been drilling. Torstein and I stood side by side at one end of the square where Ubbi had left several spears for us. Along each side of the square stood armed spearmen, each man held his shield in one hand and a spear in the other. On a raised platform, about midway along one side, sat Styrbjorn observing the drama unfolding in front of him. He stood, and his warriors beat their shields in a deafening cacophony until he raised his hand. There was silence. At this signal, the doors at the far end were dragged open, and four armed men emerged and advanced towards us. They were all dressed in similar garb and carried the emblem of the Jomsvikings on their shields. They stopped about two hundred paces from us and one of them stepped forward, drew a line in the sand and started to shout at us.

"You two hearthfire idiots who have the temerity to ask to join us are about to receive a mighty lesson. When we have shown our brothers here of your ability to fight only like women, we will bend you both down as *sansorðinn* and sodomise you before sending you home to your mothers." We remained impassive as he continued, "I have a fancy for the smaller effeminate man, but we will all take turns to fuck the bear."

While the rest of the warriors laughed, Torstein, who had been remarkably quiet during the ritual insults, spoke to me quietly.

"I think one or two javelins might be called for, Bjorn," he said.

I picked up the first one and hurled it high towards the group of four. It had good height and distance but fell a couple of paces short of our abuser, and he turned and showed his arse to further insult us. He had not expected the second spear in such quick succession, for it sailed down from the sky going straight through the back of his thigh pinning him securely to the ground. His insults ceased on impact, and I loosed another javelin at the group. They had raised and locked their shields, and the third spear was caught by their 'middle' warrior on his shield.

"Come Torstein – *svinfylking*!" I called out a battle tactic long employed by advancing troops about to attack.

Now, the 'swine array' or 'boar's snout' was a battle tactic that had been beaten into us as young boys training to attack a shield wall. Normally it would be employed by a warrior group of fifty to a hundred fighters who approach an opposing shield wall in a wedge formation to cause a split in the defending line. Long-handled axes would be used to reach over the top of the 'wall' and pull it down. When this occurred, the attackers would exploit the weaknesses and pour through the gap. My cousin and I had perfected a two-man version of this technique – I would act as the apex whilst Torstein would drag any opposing shields down with his long-stemmed double-bladed axe, and then I would 'attack the gap'. We covered the two hundred or so paces quickly in very close formation towards the three locked shields. With me in front, Torstein hard against my back, he propelled me forward. The man I had struck with the first javelin was still pinned to the ground and was no longer in the fight.

"Middle shield," I called to Torstein, who leaned right over the top of my head and the middle shield of the Jomsving in front of me, catching its rim and pulling it down. The man holding the shield was open to attack and I hacked

94

at his head with my sword. His helmet did its job and deflected my blows, although the blade went through a gap between his mail and into his shoulder blade causing him to drop his axe before he could retaliate. Blood gushed through and down his mail, and he stared in disbelief at his useless arm.

Torstein raised his axe again and gave the man on the end of the wall a massive blow on the side of the head – stunning him momentarily. We had delivered rapid, telling blows to three out of four opponents, and my cousin went to work on the one uninjured man. He began hacking down on the last shield-bearer in a flurry of devastating axe blows showering anyone close enough with splinters of wood. I engaged the man whom Torstein had recently knocked senseless but who could still fight back, and we exchanged numerous blows – sword on shield. I felt my opponent weakening until, at last, he lowered his shield and sword in exhaustion and fell to his knees in complete confusion. I dispatched him with a blow to his face with the bronze ridge of my shield, and he fell unconscious to the ground. My cousin had, by then, beaten his opponent to the ground and stood with one foot on his chest, axe raised ready to strike. The beaten man lifted his hand weakly in supplication. Torstein lowered his axe and went over to confront the warrior who had a spear through his upper leg which still pinned him to the ground facedown. This man must have been in absolute agony but still waved his axe around uselessly in front of him. I heard Styrbjorn's voice commanding:

"Enough! Take them to the infirmary."

Several unarmed men came forward and dragged away the wounded men. Then he called us to where he sat.

"Some of my men need better training. You have fought adequately enough, but the battle is not over until the last foe is vanquished."

Styrbjorn nodded to Ubbi who led us back to where we had started.

"Well fought," said the captain. "Now kill these Slavs, and I will get you a drink. The gods need a sacrifice."

The doors at the far end of the square opened and six lightly armed men emerged carrying only swords. They were pushed towards us by spearmen standing behind them. We walked out to meet our next opponents who moved nervously towards us. We were heavily armed, and they were not, but we were outnumbered six to two, and great care would be needed.

We met our opponents in the middle of the square as they approached us apprehensively, encircling us and looking for any point of weakness they might exploit. Torstein and I stood back-to-back as these desperate men attempted to strike. Some of them landed blows on our shields and armour. Then I felt a sharp sting as the point of a blade went into my leg. It was not an incapacitating blow but enough to remind me that these men were dangerous. Torstein must have felt my anxiety, for suddenly he turned berserker, launching himself into the Slavs and scattering the men who opposed him. I went for the two men standing in front of me, stabbing one in the eye and the other through the neck. They collapsed on the ground in front of me, the life bleeding out of them. Looking around I watched Torstein dispatch the last of the Slavs with a crushing axe blow to the head of the only man left standing.

"You are wounded Bjorn," he said to me.

"Only a flesh wound," I replied, "and nothing to what these poor devils have suffered today."

"Better to die with a sword in the hand – we may yet see them in Valhalla," he said, and the broad grin returned to his face as we both breathed hard. I felt a hand on my shoulder and wheeled round quickly, but it was only Ubbi.

"Well fought once again," he said and led us back to where Styrbjorn sat.

As we approached, the Commander rose and took a spear from one of his guards and proceeded to beat the end of its shaft on the wooden platform. The rest of the men arrayed around the square joined in with their leader and beat their spears against their shields until the whole courtyard reverberated with the sound. He raised his hand and the beating stopped.

"Well met, men of Haugesund. Thor and *Odin* will thank us for these sacrifices," said Styrbjorn.

He turned and left the stage.

Ubbi took us to the infirmary to get my wound tended, which was cleaned and bandaged. At the far end of the room lay the Jomsvikings we had fought with earlier.

"They picked the wrong men to fight, I think," said Ubbi.

"I am thinking there will be no sodomy here today," Torstein shouted to the vanquished warriors languishing on their cots.

We took some time to clean ourselves up, and some male slaves brought us ale. Ubbi explained that we had done well and had passed both trials, but the Commander needed to sanction our induction himself.

Later that evening, we were invited back to the Commander's long room where he was dining with his bodyguard and where, we were told, he would speak with us. We were taken back into the room where we first met him which was now filled with benches and tables at which men sat eating. Once again, we approached him where he sat, but this time he rose to meet us.

"You are well and have recovered from your trials of earlier today?" he asked us, and then to the rest of the room, "These men have proved themselves in battle today against everything that was pitted against them. They fought bravely and have proved themselves to be worthy of our brotherhood. Therefore, and on condition of passing the third test, we shall ask them to join us."

I tried, without success, not to look surprised, for we both thought we had completed all the trials.

He continued: "Torstein, I had never met a Warrior Skald until I met you today, so for your last trial I would like to hear you recite Ragnarok: The Doom of the Gods."

97

For the first time that day I saw the Commander's face break into a smile, and he joined in with the men laughing at his joke. My cousin turned to face the rest of the warriors in the hall and then broke into his recital.

"I met a wild woman walking down the road..." he intoned with great resonance, and I knew we had found our new employer.

"Welcome, brother" whispered Ubbi in my ear.

The evening passed quickly. The company was good, and we were made welcome. We were given much ale and praise from our new comrades, and Torstein received great applause for the telling of his story. This was not a feast as we were used to, for there was little drunkenness and no women to be seen. When Styrbjorn and his commanders retired for the evening, the atmosphere became a little more relaxed, but everything was still quite restrained compared to what we might have wished. Ubbi was to be our new captain, and the next day we would be formally inducted into the brotherhood of the Jomsviking when blood oaths would be sworn. For now, I was just happy that we had both come through our ordeal relatively unscathed and were on the first steps of our new path. We were given beds in one of the adjacent longhalls which housed some of Ubbi's warrior band of two hundred men.

"I think we might have found a home now," I said to my cousin in the next bed who, by this time, was snoring loudly, and then I slipped away into my own deep, exhausted sleep.

Chapter 14: New Jomsvikings

The following morning, we were woken by the sound of a ringing bell. I was very stiff and not a little sore from the previous day's exertions, as was Torstein. We walked with the rest of the men back into the longhall to be served bread, porridge and some weak beer. Ubbi came over to us and told us to be in the drill square at noon, fully armed, for we were being taken to the Commander for the oath swearing. This gave us the morning to go back to the Raven to say our goodbyes to our friends and let them know our fate. It seemed like we had been living in the castle for a week with everything that had happened to us but we had only been away for a day.

We brought food and drink for our shipmates in the market on the way to the dock. It would be a sad farewell. So far, we had enjoyed good luck; the gods had been kind to us and had looked on us favourably, bringing adventure, reputation and not a little wealth. We had much to thank our shipmates for, and our parting from the Raven should be celebrated. By the time we reached our ship, the men were stirring, and they hailed us as we walked up the dock to join them for the last time. We stepped aboard and were welcomed like long-lost companions as the men gathered around us to hear our story. Torstein needed no second invitation, and we sat in a loose circle as he recounted the story of the last day or so. At the end of it the men congratulated us, we shared our food and drink, and when everyone was full, I spoke.

"We have faced countless different dangers on this voyage which we have endured, and through which we have prospered together. Now I have thanked you I must pay you what I owe."

I gave each man a bag of silver coins brought from Haugesund.

"I have yet another gift to give and that is to our Saxon friends who, although they came with us as my slaves, have fought as bravely as any of us. To them I give their freedom. From today they are free men."

Athelstan and Godwin looked at me and then at each other in disbelief. When their excitement died down, they both scrambled towards me.

"Thank you, Lord, thank you," they repeated.

"I am no longer Lord to either of you – you are both free men now," I said. "We must say goodbye to you all, and it is with no little sadness. Take our news back to our families at home and tell them the story of the Saviours of Byrum. May Helge and the Raven deliver you safely home. Goodbye brothers."

We embraced each man of the crew in turn and then jumped down onto the quay leaving the Raven and her crew, bound for wherever the *Norns* had planned for us to be taken.

Later that day we stood in front of Styrbjorn and the whole of the Jomsvikings who were currently in the fortress. There were about six hundred men assembled in front of us. I have never before seen so many warriors together – but that would all change in time. Each man was armoured and carried a spear, shield and helm. The Commander addressed us:

"Men of the Jomsvikings, today we welcome two new brothers, Bjorn Spear Arm and Torstein, the Warrior Skald. They have passed our tests and must now swear their oaths before us all so that they may pass into our brotherhood. They must swear complete adherence to our strict code of conduct and live by our laws. They must swear to defend their brothers and, if necessary, to avenge their deaths. They will not speak ill nor quarrel with their brothers. In battle they will not show fear or flee in the face of the enemy and must face death for our cause with their eyes wide open, facing the foe. They will share all spoils of battle and raiding equally with their brothers. They will swear to these rules and more. Should they break them they will face expulsion or death." Then he looked directly at us. "Do you so swear?"

"We do," we both replied.

Ubbi came and exchanged our shields for new ones bearing the insignia of the Jomsvikings, at which point the rest of the assembled men beat their spears against their shields. We were now members of this elite group of warriors and our lives would change forever.

The fortress was home to over a thousand warriors and there was a captain for each group of three hundred and fifty. Each group slept in large barracks and drilled, slept and ate together under one roof. Our group was called the Ravens, and the men came from all over Scandinavia – but under a single banner. We forsook all individual nationalities and clan loyalties. There was a small flotilla of ships attached to our group anchored in the harbour, eight of which were longships used for fighting expeditions. Our purpose was to protect the shoreline from the many bands of pirates who waited along the rocky Baltic Coast, and to take the battle to the dissenting Slavic tribes who objected to our presence. We were sometimes required to go and fight for some king or chieftain who had enough gold to pay for our warriors to fight for them. There was great pride in the Brotherhood of the Jomsvikings, and although we fought for wealth, we also fought for each other. It was very much like being part of our warrior group from home but fighting within a much bigger and more disciplined force. The ties that bound us were strong, and the desire to fight was always fierce, but ultimately, we fought for prosperity and went to the highest bidder.

There was a great deal of discipline instilled in the men by their captains. When we were not sailing out to some conflict or patrolling the seas in a show of strength, we would train and drill for long periods. We trained in holding the *skjaldborg* – locking our shields together against bigger forces of warriors. We trained in defeating the *skjaldborg* – devising and executing new tactics to bring it down. We practised archery and javelin throwing, and we spent days perfecting our skills in close quarter killing. We practised fighting with different weapons – the axe, the sword, the spear – alternating them regularly so we could pick a new weapon up off the ground and quickly use it expertly. Our strength and stamina were built up through constant exercise. Our bodies became stronger and bigger, and even Torstein lost the beer belly of which he was so proud. Our skills as warriors were good before we came here, but now, through constant practice, these talents increased. Above all we learned to control and channel our battle fury, and that a disciplined warrior could fight and win against the most extreme odds.

For all the benefits of living within such a strict regime, there were many regulations that we struggled with. There were no women allowed in the fortress and pleasures had to be taken outside the castle walls. It was even forbidden to take captured women as slaves. Our code forbade any show of fear, and even when facing death, a warrior had to confront it unflinchingly, head-on. It was forbidden to die from a blow that came from anywhere but straight towards you.

Quarrelling amongst comrades was also outlawed as was bringing blood feuds into Jomsborg, and even speaking ill of your fellows was disallowed. As such, any anger was channelled towards our enemies, which made us into an irresistible force. So much so that we relished all approaching conflicts and longed for the next encounter as soon as the previous one finished. Each man became richer and more powerful as his horde of battle spoils grew larger after every conquest.

For the first two weeks of our stay, we trained relentlessly and without much respite. Then Ubbi spoke with us saying that we were to patrol the coastline, staying at sea for about four weeks at a time, always travelling within sight of the coast. In all, there were three longships in our group, with thirty-five men in each vessel, and we constantly yearned for our next fight. We were not raiding or going into battle, but we would attack any force that decided to confront us. The purpose of this display of aggression was to deter pirates and kill any that we found along the way. We spent these days at sea rowing or just cleaning and preparing our weapons.

The King of Denmark was both a friend and an admirer of Styrbjorn and paid him handsomely to pursue and kill the Slavic pirates who preyed on the ships travelling from the east to Denmark in the east. Numerous Wendish nobles also paid him to protect their coast from these outlaws. I had no particular quarrel with the pirates – they were only doing what we Scandinavians had been doing for hundreds of years. As Torstein put it, "I don't care what these fuckers have done. If I am paid to kill them – they will die."

As the days passed into weeks, we waited and grew impatient and bored. All along the Baltic Coast, there were inlets and river mouths where the pirates waited for unsuspecting merchants in their ships. They would strike out, killing or enslaving the crews without mercy, taking the cargoes and burning the ships. When there were no ships to plunder, they would descend on the coastal settlements and take anything of value – disappearing, as quickly as they came, with their loot. Sometimes these fleets would consist of hundreds of men – so we had to patrol in some strength. However, our reputation went before us, and at the sight of our banners, they would melt into their river strongholds long before we could confront them.

Before too long we would get all the action and excitement that we craved. On one particular day at sea, perhaps two weeks after we left Jomsborg, we were still heading towards the east. It was cold, grey and the wind was constantly changing direction, ensuring that we had to row. A shout from the lead boat alerted us to a settlement on the shore, which was burning. Thick black smoke blew off the shore and the smell of burning wood filled the air. All three of our boats turned as one, heading landwards, and were driven hard up onto the sandy beach. Arms were gathered, and men leapt down from their beached craft forming up in two lines facing the settlement – Ubbi standing in front of them. Each line would approach the town from a different direction, trapping any aggressors and crushing them between the two forces. We were very close to the town and could feel the heat of the fire on our faces. Ahead of us were about sixty thatched wooden houses about two hundred paces up on some high ground at the top of the beach. My group moved across the beach and formed up on the other side of the buildings – fifty spearmen in all, standing in line – making ready to engage anything that emerged towards us. When we were ready, Ubbi took his men into the settlement, and they moved through the devastated town. We braced ourselves for whatever might arise, but nothing but our comrades came out from between the empty buildings.

Ubbi was the last to come through the smoke.

"There's no one here," he shouted. "Back to the boats!"

A murmur of disappointment ran through the group, and as we trudged back to our ship, I asked Torstein, who was in the other group, about what he had seen.

"Nothing," he said, dejectedly. "Nothing alive anyway. Whoever was here took everything – people, animals, cooking pots, weapons. They took the lot. I was looking forward to fighting as well."

The ships were all dragged back into the sea and we continued to move eastwards, up the coast of Wendland. Around midday, another burning settlement was spotted, and once again we went ashore and formed up ready for a fight but with the same result. This settlement, about half the size of the first was also burning, but the people here had put up a considerable fight and the ground was strewn with dead Wends, their weapons still in their hands. We looked for anyone still alive who might be able to tell us what had happened. One survivor was found – a woman who had been speared through the stomach and who now lay quietly on the ground waiting for her death. Ubbi and one of the men who spoke the local language went over to question her. We watched as he knelt over her, although he spoke too quietly for most of us to hear him. Then he drew his knife, slit her throat, and she died without any more sound. He stood up to address us, and we crowded around him to listen.

"It would seem we are behind a large group of raiders. They came through here earlier today. They are probably the same group that attacked the first place.

"What we know is that there are several ships and lots of men. The woman said she understood their tongue – so they are probably Slavs or Wends. They will now be heavily laden with booty, and we will catch up with them and engage them. If they are too strong, we will send to Jomsborg for reinforcements. Either way, we shall destroy them and what is theirs shall then be ours. For now, we must row hard and catch them and test them."

The men seemed to like this plan, and we hurried back to our ships and re-launched them. Once in open water, our ships lined up three abreast and the race was on. Each man hauled away hard with such fervour that the vessels seemed to fly effortlessly through the waves. The energy of the men on board our ship, the Short Serpent, was high and we sang as we rowed. Torstein was happier than I had seen him in weeks, and his deep, resonant voice carried on the wind:

On the battlefield
They fought for their homes
And the swords of the Norsemen
Were shining true to the night

The fire is burning
And they celebrate their victory
And they all were singing
Their northern song

Every time the singing died down, he would restart it again with even greater purpose, and the men at the oars would respond with more muscular effort. This affected the men on the other two boats who, not wishing to be left behind, responded to our challenge keeping up the mighty pace we set.

After an *eykt* of frantic rowing, the light in the sky began to fade, and the hopes that we would catch sight of the ships we sought began to fade. Then came a cry from one of the other crews that a mast had been spotted on the horizon. Our lookout ran to the bows and confirmed the sighting, and the men cheered. From his ship, the Sea Eagle, Ubbi signalled that we should all stop rowing and ropes were thrown from one vessel to another as we 'rafted' together. He shouted so all the men could hear him, and they were silent as they strained to hear his instructions above the roar of the wind.

"It looks like they are six ships moving together ahead of us. We shall row until dark and then anchor offshore to rest for the night. At first light, we shall continue our pursuit and run them down. When we catch up, we will disable as many of their ships as we can, go aboard and kill them.

"It will be important that we catch them all, for if they are part of a larger force, we do not want the rest alerted. If any escape, we will run them to shore and kill them there. But before they all die, we need information – we will try to take some prisoners."

Our flotilla disengaged and rowed in single file on the course of the sighting. As the light began to fade, we moved closer to the shore where we anchored and settled down for the night. I sat down next to Torstein and sank deep into my bearskin cloak.

"Do you think we will catch them?" I said.

He smiled at me. "I have asked Aegir for extra wings for the Short Serpent and he has never let me down yet." Then he added, "Do you think they will have women on board?"

We ate and slept under an awning, and the motion of the sea soon rocked me into a deep sleep. Much later, the man next to me shook me awake and everyone went straight to his station at the oars. My arms and shoulders were still sore from yesterday's chase, but I soon felt the welcome exhilaration of impending battle and the calm before the storm. The battle lust had each man in its thrall; the madness would all consuming, and we would fear nothing. At the moment a man races towards his foe, he feels nothing but blood lust, fearing neither axe nor spear nor death itself.

But first, we had to reach them before they saw us. Our ships rowed some way out into the open ocean before turning and raising sail. With a strong wind at our backs, the boats dashed forward in the half-light of early dawn. Lookouts posted in the bows strained their eyes to discern the tell-tale shapes of masts, whilst we prayed they had not caught sight of us and made their escape. Then they were spotted; way, way along the shore lay our quarry, and there would be plenty of time before we reached them. All six vessels had been beached and they were not expecting us, for there was no sign of movement as we sailed closer. Surely, they must see us soon and either meet our attack or turn and run as we were propelled towards them like the sea wolves of ancient legend. Death snapped at the foemen's heels and would scatter them to the four winds.

We were still some distance from the shore before the men on the beach caught sight of our three blue sails heading straight for them. Now they had seen us there was no point in trying to conceal our approach, and our ships moved next to one another as the men on the shore, still no more than tiny figures in the distance, fought to launch their ships. When they finally managed to get all their vessels into the water and through the surf, the rest of their crews scrambled aboard and started to row. Unlike us, they would not be able to use the wind and would have to row out to either meet us or simply turn and run. They chose to meet us and were coming directly towards our ships.

Meanwhile, on the Short Serpent we had plenty of time to prepare. Everyone was fully armed and bristling with nervous energy as spears were rapped against shields and the talking stopped. Our enemy was panicked and although we were outnumbered, we knew they would struggle to match us for ferocity and power. They would have seen our Jomsvikings' banners clearly by now but still decided to make a fight of it, heading directly towards us as their oarsmen fought against the tide. As they hove into view, I could see that the Wendish ships were slightly larger than ours and broader in the beam – allowing them to carry more cargo but making them slower and harder to turn quickly. All their men were at the oars, and they would be vulnerable to attack if they could not come to battle stations quickly. Then came our first battle orders.

"Break their oars before engaging," went up the shout, and the message was passed between our boats. The Short Serpent headed directly towards their lead vessel, and the wind and tide carried us swiftly across the distance, about a thousand paces, between the two craft. When we were almost upon them, our helmsman altered course and we veered sharply to their windward side, sheering a whole bank of oars as we passed them at speed. At the same time, some of our men let go a fusillade of arrows and spears at their hapless rowers. Their ship was now helpless in the water and our helmsman focused on our next target: an even larger vessel than the first and with two banks of oars on each side of her. This time the enemy ship nearly evaded us, but we still managed to shatter most of their oars on one side with a huge rending crack. As our stern passed theirs, we dropped sail and our oarsman brought us back round to engage with our first target – now helpless in the water. By this time their men had gathered on the side of their ship and were ready to meet us as our grappling irons caught hold and we dragged the two vessels closer together.

As the two ships touched sides, our crew launched themselves onto the larger craft, hacking away with sword and axe. I leapt forward and struck a large bearded axeman with my shield, knocking him off balance before cutting through his shoulder with a downward sword stroke. He dropped his axe, fell to the deck, and I finished him with several thrusts to his face. I moved through the gap in their line and took several axe blows from a man on my left, but his part in the fight was short-lived as a Jomsviking axe severed his head from his shoulders. Torstein kicked his victim's head into the growing pile of dead and wounded in the centre of the enemy ship. The red mist was on all of us now, and although outnumbered we swept inexorably past any resistance, pushing their remaining fighters before us as they stumbled backwards towards the far side of their boat. I estimated them to be about sixty or seventy men before we engaged, but now there was only a handful left, falling beneath our relentless onslaught. These last fighters, realising that death was not far away, were pushed into the sea where they sank beneath the waves, carried to the ocean floor by the weight of their armour.

I looked around the deck, which was now slippery with blood and gore. I was breathing deeply after my exertions, but I was able to take a closer look at our vanquished enemy. They had been well armed, and most wore mail shirts and helms. They fought well enough but in a wild undisciplined way that allowed us certain victory; it was exactly as we had expected. There was no time for further thought, for the battle was in full flow. Our crew boarded the Short Serpent, cast off and took the fight to the next ship. We headed to join the Sea Eagle, which was fighting two pirate ships – one on each side of her - and soon all four ships were tied together as our crew entered the fray. I could see Ubbi in the centre of the action with his party, outnumbered by more than three to one, but still bringing his enemies down. Our group joined the fight and caught the pirates in between us, in turn forcing them away from Ubbi's group. The pirates fought well but they were fighting a highly organised force of warriors who were much better trained and motivated. Before long they began to tire, and we moved among them, felling them with sword and axe. Before long, the last Slavs remaining on their feet could see the futility of the situation. They threw down their arms and surrendered, but unfortunately for them we had no time for prisoners just yet, and we gave them to the mercy of the sea.

Our other vessel, the Wave Tamer, was grappled to the large pirate ship that we had disabled while the remaining two vessels, having witnessed the rapid destruction of their fellows, had turned around and rowed for shore.

"Let them go, we will deal with them later," shouted Ubbi above the combined sound of the waves and the men in their death throes.

We went back to our ships and rowed towards the remaining sea battle. The crew of the Wave Tamer were climbing up the steep sides of their intended victim with grappling ropes and were making slow progress. While these men climbed, our archers and spearmen kept the defenders busy and away from our comrades. By the time we joined the fight, there were nine or ten Jomsvikings on board with more following close behind them. The Short Serpent attached herself to the far side of the ship and we started to climb. I was the first to reach the enemy ship from this direction, closely followed by my other shipmates, and when I reached the deck there was a fierce fight already underway. Although I could see two of our number among the fallen, twenty or so defenders had already succumbed to the fierce assault. Both groups of Jomsvikings pushed the remaining men back to the stern of their ship, killing them steadily until, exhausted and depleted, there were no more than seven of them left standing. They lay down their arms and pleaded for mercy, but there was none to be had. Like their comrades, they met their fate at the bottom of the Baltic Sea.

Chapter 15: Blood and Sand

There was barely time to rest for we were ordered back to rejoin our ships and chase the last two fleeing vessels. I climbed back down into the Short Serpent, and we went to our positions at the oars. Both ships that refused to join the fight had turned and fled to shore, and we followed at some distance. I was unsure of the logic of their manoeuvre, but we surmised that they would either be returning to their plunder or that they had reinforcements there and would make a stand on the beach. Either way, we did not have long to wait because we were soon close behind them and followed them to the place they had left earlier, before their forces had been so considerably reduced. We were in no hurry, and we knew they could neither outrun nor outfight us. The mood on our boat was confident, for we had fought very hard in the last *eykt*, and the men treated our next action as just another necessary job. With this confidence, all three of our longships landed on the shore, and our men disembarked and formed up in two orderly lines facing the enemy. This was in direct contrast to the Slavic pirates who had left their boats in some haste and had joined up with the rest of their force about five hundred paces from our lines. I estimated their strength to be about two hundred men, but they had, at least, formed up into an impressive looking *skjaldborg* – three rows of shields banked one on top of the next. Torstein, never far from me when the fighting started, snorted and spat on the ground.

"It is there to be broken," he said, scowling.

On the command from Ubbi, our lines moved up the beach until they stood close to the Slavic shield wall. Our Commander stood out in front of us, spear and shield in hand, and addressed the foe.

"You are all thieves and pirates, and we have shown you

how real warriors fight. Many of your comrades lie dead beneath the waves, and you will shortly join them if you are foolish enough to try and resist us. The idiot who led you into thinking you could defeat the Jomsvikings has led you to certain death, and very soon you will all die on this god-forsaken piece of land where the seagulls will come to feast on your flesh.

"If you decide to lay down your arms, you may yet live and walk away from this killing field."

One of their number stepped forward. A powerfully built man, dressed in mail and leather armour and carrying a huge axe, met the challenge.

"I care nothing for your reputation. You are pirates just like us, and you will fight for anyone who pays you – like simple whores. But you are less honourable than the cheapest whore, dancing around in your fine armour and weapons. Let's see how good you are at fighting on land."

Ubbi turned to us and called *"Svinfylking"*, and we prepared to advance in formation. The largest, strongest of the warriors was placed at the head of the formation while after him came two men, and then four, and so on until the whole group resembled a wedge. The men on the outside of the 'wedge' were there to protect the flanks whilst in the centre stood our archers and javelin throwers. Such was our training that it took only moments for us to get in position, and with Ubbi taking his place in the centre, we moved forward at speed and hurled ourselves at the enemy's shield wall.

It is in moments like these when a man realises his strengths and weaknesses. Standing in a shield wall, just before the impact, is the most frightening moment of a man's life. When I first stood beside my father, it was beyond any terror I could imagine. You could smell men's fear. Some of them could no longer control their bowels, yet they had to stand, shoulder to shoulder, with the next man. Waiting for the enemy to come crashing into you, to hack down at you with his axe or find a gap through the shields to thrust his spear, while you could barely move was beyond any description of fear. You could feel the breath of the man trying to kill you as you waited for his blade to take you at any moment. The only way I was able to conquer the sheer dread of standing in the shield wall was to let the warrior's red mist take me and to elevate me to a different level. My breathing would come rapidly, and my blood pumped madly to my arms and legs. My spirit seemed to leave my body and fly high above the fighting, looking down, like a raven in flight, on the destruction we wrought on our enemies. So it was now, as we prepared to let the *Norns* decide whether they would cut the chords of each man on the field – to let us die here or live for another battle.

The first Jomsviking, a giant veteran and our champion, known in the company as Leif Iron Fist, led our Svinfyking into the massed shields in front of us. With a resounding crash, the line in front of us clove in two as Leif drove his axe through the helm and head of the man in front of him who fell to the ground. The gap in front of us opened and we poured through with our men on the flanks doing great damage to the enemy. The defenders were already in disarray as they were split into two groups of fighters and were picked off one by one. Their leader tried to rally them, but it was too late, and they turned into a frightened, directionless rabble.

When men are frightened in battle, they become very easy to beat. They panic; all semblance of order crumbles, and desperation sets in. Our battle-hardened warriors were heavily armoured and well trained, and with one very simply manoeuvre we had broken their spirit. The Slavs fought on bravely, like their comrades on the ships, but very soon their numbers were halved while we, seemingly, suffered only light casualties. Slowly but surely, we broke our formation and began to surround their remaining fighters who continued to fall.

"Remember – I want prisoners," shouted Ubbi, very close to me, as I dispatched a half-fallen Slav with a single sword blow to the neck. Soon only forty to fifty men were opposing us. They were tired and bloodied, yet they fought on, dying on their feet, often with barely strength enough to lift their shields in defence. It was now a complete rout, and the slaughter continued with the remaining nineteen survivors staggering together in a bloody huddle, swaying drunkenly to avoid the final killing blow.

"Stop," came the order, and we stepped back while our spearmen crowded the last of the Slavs together.

"Throw down your arms," commanded Ubbi, and the last resistance ended with the defeated remnants of the pirates kneeling in front of us, among their dead and dying comrades, in the blood and the sand.

Their leader was among them, and he was dragged in front of our captain.

"Where are you from?" he was asked. The man remained defiantly silent, and Leif stepped forward, beheading the Slavic captain with one mighty blow. The next prisoner was brought forward who proved to be more garrulous than the last, and we gathered around to hear what he had to say.

"We are all from Truso, Lord, and we serve the Prince Otto of Wendland who sent us raiding all along this coast."

The man realised that he was now pleading for his life.

"You mean King Borislav's son? The Christian? Why would he raid his own people?" asked Ubbi.

The man hesitated until Leif tapped him on the side of the head with his axe.

"I am just a humble thief, Lord, and I know not what goes on in the heads of kings and princes," he replied.

Leif raised the axe above his head. "Last chance then, thief."

The man continued: "The Prince seeks to ferment unrest in Wendland, Lord. He believes the King's vassals will rise against their sovereign if they believe they are at the mercy of foreign raiders. Our orders were to raid all the coastal region west of Truso and blame it on the Danes."

"What Danes?" enquired Ubbi.

"You, Lord," the man spluttered, "the Jomsvikings!"

"Do you not mean the pagan Jomsvikings?" said Ubbi, not expecting an answer. At this point, there was much muttering among the men.

"Fucking devious Slavs," shouted one man.

"Just cut off his head, Leif," cried another.

"Bind all the prisoners for the present," said Ubbi. "I believe we have a small victory to celebrate."

All the men cheered, and then, as was the custom, went foraging for any battle spoils. There were plenty to be had and the fruits of the pirates' labours had been unloaded and left onshore before they decided to sail out to meet us. They had stripped the raided communities of all their valuables as they passed through. There was a chest full of looted gold and silver ornaments, jewellery and coins as well as household items like cooking utensils and furs. There was also a group of about a hundred prisoners, mostly women and children, who were on their way to the slave auctions.

We stripped the fallen dead of any weapons and armour of value, as well as any valuables they may have been carrying. These were all neatly stacked in piles on the beach in front of our boats. There was a plentiful quantity of ale, wine and food left behind by the raiders – all stolen from their victims. The vanquished pirates were released from their shackles and ordered to carry the dead far down the beach and leave them there for the wolves and the crows and the gulls. When they had finished, they were told to return, build fires and prepare food for us. At which point we would decide what to do with them. From the height of the sun, I guessed it was around noon, and our party all needed sustenance.

"I can't wait for these Wendish women to finish their chores before I can get a drink," Torstein said to no one in particular.

He marched towards the collection of ale barrels and opened the nearest one with a blow from his axe, removing the lid and causing its contents to gush skywards. Then he picked up a loose helm lying close by, filled it to the brim with ale and drank deeply. Others followed suit, and soon several barrels were opened as thirsty warriors relieved their parched throats.

The atmosphere grew more relaxed as men drank and casks were opened. Men who had been like strangers before the battle were now laughing and joking with one another. There is nothing like fighting side-by-side to get to know a man, and warriors from all the Scandinavian tribes and nations moved and talked freely with one another. Torstein was engaged in lively conversation with our champion, Leif, and I talked with some Swedes with whom I had boarded the last pirate ship. Ubbi moved from man to man bestowing praise and congratulations on each of his charges.

It was felt that the Slavs had put up a good fight, but they were no match for the might of the Jomsvikings and our disciplined fighting techniques. I had never taken part in such a fight when two or three times the number of equally well-armed warriors could be so effortlessly defeated. The fight had taken place over a single morning, and our force of a hundred men had killed over two hundred and fifty opposing warriors for the loss of only twenty-seven Jomsvikings. We destroyed four of their ships at sea – the remains of which could be seen still smoking on the horizon – and had taken all their pillaged loot together with any arms that we could reuse.

"A profitable morning's work," said Ubbi coming over to our group which was now seated on makeshift benches taken from the Slav ship. Then looking at me directly he said: "You fought a good fight, Bjorn. Well met."

"Thank you," I replied. "The gods favoured us today, I think. It was good to be part of such a fine warrior band."

He nodded and continued, "There will be plenty more fights like today, but you have seen that when you combine Norse ferocity with an iron discipline you become almost unbeatable. We are only a thousand men in all Jomsborg, but we fight like a hundred times that number. You told me you came for reputation and wealth, and that is exactly what you will get with the brotherhood. Look after your brothers, and they will look after you."

It was my turn to nod now, and he clapped me on both shoulders and laughed. "Welcome to the brotherhood," he said, before moving on to my fellow warriors.

I surveyed the wreckage of the battleground around me. The bodies of the Slavs had nearly all been dragged off, far down the beach, and a large fire was lit, around which we all sat. The newly freed women prepared food from the plentiful supplies that had been found, and we settled down to enjoy the food and ale. There seemed to be an endless supply of each. Our warriors revelled in their victory. The women were happy with their newly found freedom, and the few men that were released with them carried on their duties in a quiet and subservient manner. Before long Ubbi got up from his seat and addressed us.

"Men of the Ravens," he shouted, "you have today fought bravely and done honour to the reputation of the order." At which the men cheered. "You have also made us all a little richer," he added, and the cheer was even louder.

"Tonight, we must give thanks to the gods for bringing us safely here together, and to Tyr for guiding our swords and axes to such mighty effect on both the land and the sea. We must also thank him for bringing us two new warrior brothers, and he demands a sacrifice from us for their delivery."

He beckoned to Torstein and me to come and stand beside him while two Slav prisoners were dragged out before us. Our men were all on their feet and were banging sword and axe on shields to a slow rhythm, and we knew what was expected of us. Wordlessly, Torstein stood behind one of the kneeling men, pulled his head back and slit his throat while one of our men caught the blood in a large silver bowl. I took out my *seax* and did the same to the prisoner in front of me.

Ubbi spoke again, loudly and into the wind: "We give you

117

thanks, Lord Tyr, for delivering us to victory in our battle with these pirates. For as long as the last Jomsviking remains standing we are at your service." At which point every warrior beat his shield with whatever weapon came to hand. Then Ubbi took the bowl and daubed blood on our foreheads, first Torstein then me, before doing so with each man in our company.

The thanksgiving ceremony over, the two dead men were dragged away to join their comrades down on the beach. The drinking continued at pace. At Ubbi's invitation, Torstein was soon at the centre of things again. Standing before the fire and casting a giant shadow, he began to sing:

"I've been with axe and spear
slick with bright blood
where ravens wheeled. And how well
we violent Norsemen clashed!
As flames ate up men's roofs,
Maddened we killed and killed
And speared bodies sprawled
Lifeless beneath their walls."

The men roared their approval at the rendition of this famous stanza and called for more. Not wishing to disappoint his audience, he continued, "Fellow warriors – I give you Gisli the Outlaw's Last Stand," and began another famous tale.

We all knew the words by heart, but there was something in Torstein's telling that gave the story an extra resonance among these warriors thousands of miles from their homelands. At the end of his story, he accepted the rapturous applause that followed, before hoisting one of the nearby serving women over his shoulder and disappearing into the night. Some followed his example while the rest of us settled down around the fire for the night.

The next day Ubbi gave us our orders. We were to give the released Wends one of the pirate ships in which they could load their belongings and return to their towns along the coast. There were enough men in their number to row all the way home. We would keep the gold, silver and valuables as payment for our services. They did have one more task to complete before they made their way home. They were given axes and told to remove the heads of their former captives and to load them into the other vessel. Once their grisly task had been accomplished, they filled up their ship with the recovered goods, women and children and pushed it through the waves and into the sea. We watched them as they disappeared along the coast.

"Poor bastards," said Torstein, "they need to be very lucky to get home and rebuild what they need before winter."

"At least they have their lives," I said. "But you are right — I don't envy their chances."

Our warriors prepared to leave, and the ships were packed with the recently gained plunder and made ready. We were going to take the last remaining pirate ship and deliver it to Truso, together with the severed heads and the remaining Slavs to tell the story of what happened — as a warning to Prince Otto. Should he or any of his followers be foolish enough to defy the Jomsvikings or try to implicate us in their acts of piracy, they would suffer a similar fate. These seventeen wretched prisoners were now installed at the oars of a ship full of the heads of their dead comrades. I was chosen to helm this vessel, whilst Torstein also came aboard to dissuade our prisoners from any thought of rebellion. We would escort it all the way to the pirate base, apparently not more than three days' sail along the coast, where they would deliver our message together with one hundred and eighty-seven heads.

We set off in good spirits, and our convoy of four ships made steady progress towards the east, reaching our destination in good time thanks to some favourable winds. The prisoners were silent during the journey and were quite terrified of Torstein who stood glowering over them and threatening them whenever he felt the need. It was a quiet voyage and we talked amongst ourselves during the next leg of our trip.

"You were right, cousin," he said to me as we planed through the choppy Baltic waters. "This life suits me down to the ground. We came for wealth and reputation, and it seems like we have made a favourable start. Still, if I could change anything, I think I would prefer a few women in my bed in those draughty old barracks."

"Who needs comfort when you live the life of a warrior, Torstein," I shouted back to him, gripping the tiller in both hands. "Haugesund seems a long way away," I mused.

"And I suppose Byrum is never far from your thoughts either," he replied. I ignored him, but he continued to tease. "What was her name now – Tove, Trude, Tryghild – something like that?" I refused to take the bait, and he stopped tormenting me. "Still she was a rare beauty," he said seriously.

We sailed on, struggling to keep up with the faster, sleeker longboats.

Just before reaching Truso, we came upon a large spit of deserted land that indicated we had nearly reached our destination. Our small fleet took a day to reach the end of this sand bar, and then we sailed into a huge inland lake across which sat the settlement of Truso – the pirate's nest – perhaps another day's sail away. It was getting dark now and our ships stopped and anchored for the night. The next day Torstein walked among the subdued and still terrified prisoners and addressed them.

"You will be set free, and then you will row to join your Christian lord like the dogs of *Hel* are snapping at your heels. If I ever see any of you again, I will kill you. If you ever dare to take arms against us again you will die. Take this message to the rest of the Slavic scum that you sail with and make sure you never raise arms against the Jomsvikings again. You will not be so lucky next time."

He then cut the prisoners' bonds, and we jumped aboard the Short Serpent which lay next to us, our comrades at their stations.

"Now, row!" he called to his charges who hastily organised themselves and pulled for the other side of the lake. We followed them to ensure they obeyed their instructions, and soon, the town came into view dead ahead. I could see Ubbi counting the ships at anchor from his vantage point and taking in the lay of the land. We would not engage anyone else that day, and besides that, there were probably many more ships than we could handle with our present force. We turned around and headed back across the lake, into the open sea and back towards Jomsborg.

Chapter 16: Bjorn Takes Charge

It took us six days to reach Jomsborg. The crew had to row most days, which meant there was no time to get bored. Our helmsman, having been injured during the fighting, was unable to man the tiller, and I was given his job at the helm. I preferred this to rowing which was hard work as most of the time we were heading straight into the wind. We were in mid-autumn now, and the weather was getting colder. When winter arrived, it would bring with it the storms for which the Baltic is well known. There would be no respite from our ranging, and we would still be required to patrol the coast whatever the weather or the season.

Finally, we anchored in the great harbour beneath the castle walls. The men disembarked, and our plunder was taken ashore for safekeeping. It was carried to the great stone keep where it was kept behind massive oak doors that were locked and guarded by armed men at all times. The captured weapons were taken to the armoury where they were assessed and tested for strength and quality. If they were good enough, they were put away for future use or else discarded and melted down. The men of the Ravens were then released from duty for three days and were free to do what they wished, provided they did not stay outside the city walls beyond that time. As was customary, Ubbi was required to give Styrbjorn his report on the patrol along the coast, and the helmsmen of the three longboats, including me, were ordered to accompany him for the meeting.

We found the Commander in his longhall poring over some charts at his table. He looked up and called us over, and his thrall gave us ale. Ubbi gave him the news of our patrol, of our encounter with the pirates, how we had fared and of course the amount of plunder we had returned with. He also told him of the information we received of the raids along the coast, and the blame that had been wrongly placed at the feet of the Jomsvikings. Styrbjorn thought for a moment then spoke.

"Borislav is a decent man for a Christian, but his worm of a son should be punished for this slight on our reputation. We take considerable tribute from the King for his protection, and it would grieve me if this stopped.

"For the moment we shall wait to see if Otto heeds your message, but any further incursions by this whelp should be dealt with severely. What is their strength in Truso?"

"About fifty ships, Commander. Between two to three thousand men I estimate," said Ubbi.

Styrbjorn stroked his beard, then looked directly at me.

"And you, Bjorn Spear Arm, what did you make of the enemy?"

"They fought bravely enough," I replied, "but they were not disciplined and were badly led. Once we had killed their best men they were quickly overcome. From what I heard from the prisoners, they believe they could raise many men, but I am not sure of their quality."

"This puppy must be watched. Nevertheless, if we get more reports of his men raiding the coast, we shall have to pay him a visit."

More ale was brought, and the Commander congratulated us on our success. Then, abruptly, we were dismissed, and I went back to the barracks to find Torstein waiting for me.

"Come, cousin, there is no time to lose – let us go and explore this town," he said.

The town beneath the fortress walls had grown rapidly in its shadow. It was a busy trading post of over a thousand houses and bustled with energy as traders and hawkers plied their wares in Jomsborg's relative peace. We strolled towards the square, through the early evening hustle and bustle, taking in all manner of foreign sounds and smells, for much was new to us. Since we started our service with the Order, we had not

123

set foot outside the castle walls, and from our first days of training, we could only look down from its high walls to observe life beneath. But we were now in the thick of it, savouring each moment of our freedom and three days without training. There were many exotically dressed men and women here in the centre speaking a host of different languages that I could not make out. The market stalls were doing energetic trade in many diverse products. There were skins and pelts of every type and hue – walrus, bear, marten, elk and reindeer. There were feathers, tusks, whalebones and antlers. There were fine textiles, ceramic tableware, precious metals, glass and jewellery such as I had never seen. The smell of roasting meats permeated the evening air, and we found ourselves drawn to a nearby alehouse where the carcass of an ox was turning above a large cooking fire.

We made for an empty table and sat down to order our victuals. I have often marvelled at the huge volume of food and drink that Torstein could consume in one sitting. Tonight, he surpassed himself and did not utter a single word until he had finished. Then he let out an enormous belch before declaring that another day on dried rations would have spelt the end for him, before catching one of the serving girls by the arm and demanding more drinks. While she fetched more ale, two of our shipmates, Einar and Rurik, came over and sat down. They were Norwegians like us but came from Trondheim in the north. They were each about ten or fifteen years older than us and had sailed away to seek fortune and fame many years ago. They left Norway for much the same reason that we had. First, they had gone to Iceland, and then to Greenland where they met local women and settled. They then joined another group of Norwegians and took their families on a long and dangerous journey to a place called Vinland on the other side of the world. I had heard of Vinland but had never met anyone who had been there; nor was I even sure it existed. We ordered more ale as Einar told us their story.

"There were about four hundred of us to start with – men, women and children – together with our animals and herds. The land was rich and fertile, and we knew we could do well there. There were huge fields of wild wheat that grew without any help, plentiful game and massive stocks of fish in the rivers and the sea. It had everything you needed to grow fat and wealthy. But it also had many thousands of hostile locals – we called them skraelings – the screeching ones. At first, they were friendly, and we traded with them. We treated them well, and there was peace. Then one of their number tried to steal a bull from one of the herds at night and was killed for his efforts. After that they tried to attack us whenever they could. We were at least two hundred fighting men, but there were thousands of them, and they attacked us every single day. They would shoot arrows at us from a distance or attack small groups of us when we were away from our people. These attacks went on for years, and gradually our numbers dwindled as more of us were killed. Then, one day there was a huge assault on our community and the skraelings attacked us in their thousands, intent on wiping us out forever. My wife and children were all killed in the first big assault with many others – Rurik's family too. They could not kill us all, and our warriors fought back initially, but there were so many of them it became a battle with no end. The more you killed, the more there were that came on, and they were killing us gradually – family by family, warrior by warrior. They pushed us back to our boats, and we prepared to make our last stand, for we were now down to about a hundred of our folk. We put the remaining women and children behind a defensive line, built a wall of earth and sand in front of us, and waited for the final attack. It never came, and in the morning we saw the skraelings had gone leaving the heads of some of our fallen on stakes in front of our line – dead eyes looking straight at us. And that was it; it didn't need much thought, and we packed up and left that very day."

He touched an amulet around his neck to ward off evil.

"We had ten ships on the beach that were always well stocked with rations in case we had to leave quickly. We gathered all the food and drink in three of the longboats and headed back towards Greenland. It was the start of winter, and very soon we were in the midst of a freezing storm and lost contact with the other two ships. The winds were so strong that we could not raise the sail for fear of capsizing, and so we drifted on the ocean's currents for days. We had plenty of food, but it was so cold aboard that some of the men and all the women and children died. We were left with fifteen men – just enough to row the ship when the weather calmed down. When we were able, we just rowed and rowed until one day – many, many weeks later – we spotted land and came upon the shores of Frankia. Tell them what happened next, Rurik, for all this talking has given me a great thirst."

Rurik continued the tale: "We had been at sea for some thirty days now, and although we had food and drink, we were all exhausted and half dead. But we were also very poor and so there was only one thing we could do."

"Strandhögg?" interjected Torstein, enthralled by the story.

"Exactly, we needed to go a-viking immediately," said the older man. "So, we made a fire on the beach, got some life back into our bodies and climbed up some nearby cliffs. When we got to the top, we saw a small town in the distance. Before the day was out, we had marched in, raided it, and made our way back to the ship with silver, food, wine and slaves. Farmers no longer!

"We launched as soon as we got back to the beach away from the direction of the town, much richer and with a dozen slaves to row us eastward. One of our shipmates recognised the coast and knew of a trading post some three or four days along the Frankish coast. We planned to stop there and sell the slaves in an area known as the land of Northmanni where there were many Norse settlements. A great uncle of Einar, and his *aett*, had once been *Jarl* in this land, and perhaps we could stay and make a plan for the next part of our journey. But what that plan was, we had no idea."

"So, our slaves rowed us to Northmanni, and in four days we reached the trading post called Carusbourg, a large seaport guarded by a stone fort. After cheating the freezing seas and storms, we were at least able to start talking about where we should go next. Some men wanted to settle and farm again, but Einar and I just wanted to go raiding. One of the slaves we had captured was particularly well dressed, and when we were discussing how much we might get for such a poor oarsman he blurted out, in our language, that he was far too grand to be sold as a slave at auction. One of the men took exception and went to beat him to get him to row harder. I stayed the man's hand and asked the Frank what he meant. He said he was related to the King of the Franks and that his name was Louis – the same name as his uncle. If this was true, perhaps our luck was changing.

When we got to Carusbourg, we enquired about Einar's great uncle, Rollo. We must have looked quite a sight – fifteen wild-looking, stinking men with twelve slaves better dressed than their new owners."

Both men looked at each other and laughed at the memory, while we urged them on to continue with their tale. "This man Rollo had been famous in Northmanni and had been given the land by another Frankish King in return for his agreement to stop raiding. Rollo was now dead, but his grandson, Richard, was *Jarl* in this land. He did not live in the place where we landed but in somewhere called Rouen. So, after we cleaned ourselves up, we brought three horses, and me and Einar rode to Rouen with Louis to get an audience with Richard – the Fearless, as he was known in those parts. When we arrived in Rouen, we were directed to Richard's castle, and after much explaining, he met with us. Richard was a very wealthy man, and he told us the story of how the Norsemen here and took the land and became rich and powerful. After much discussion, we discovered that Louis was the Frankish King's nephew – a valuable hostage. Not only that, but the king was childless, and our slave was now the heir to the land of the Franks. A very, very valuable hostage indeed."

We all sat silently for the story to continue.

"So now Duke Richard wanted to buy Louis from us and ransom him to his uncle. He asked us what we wanted for him and to name our price. We told him of our struggle in Vinland and of how some of the men wanted to settle while we just wanted to fight again. The Duke came up with an offer: to those of us who wanted to be farmers he would give land to be farmed, but those who wanted to fight he had an interesting suggestion. He had been asked by the Christian ruler, an Emperor no less, in a far-off place called Miklagard for fierce but loyal Norsemen to form part of his bodyguard. Richard was sending a contingent of men from Northmanni to this place where they would be very well paid for fighting. They would be part of a small army of Norsemen who would protect this Emperor from his enemies. So, we agreed on a price for Louis. Our friends were given land and Einar and me would get two bags of gold and a place on another ship taking us to all sorts of opportunities." Rurik held up his hands. "But please, friends, let me slake my thirst. We will tell you all you need to know."

By this time our table had been joined by six more of our fellow Jomvikings – all Ravens – straining to hear the story of these two grizzled warriors.

Einer took up the story now. He was the more serious of the two, and as the story moved on to their journey from Frankia to Miklagard, he grew more animated, as if revisiting some wonderful part of his life. Maybe it was the ale or even the company, but as he told his tale, many years of pain and hardship seemed to leave his leathery, weather-beaten face. He began to smile at parts of the saga as if remembering things that had long been forgotten.

"After striking a deal with Duke Richard, we sent word to

our old crew of the good fortune that had befallen them. Then we joined thirty new comrades on a sleek longboat called the Warrior of Rouen. It carried us south along the mighty River Seine, past the walls of the city of Paris, eventually on towards the Mediterranean Sea – bound for the ancient capital of Miklagard, the beating heart of the Byzantia. When we encountered waterfalls or rapids, we would carry the Warrior of Rouen by land to where we could relaunch her safely upriver once more.

"After about a month we landed at the gates of the richest city in the world, destined to go into the service of the Emperor, a man called John Tzimiskes, as his personal bodyguards. We were escorted into the Emperor's palace where our rough clothes and armour were exchanged for the uniform of the Varangian Guards. Wearing the Emperor's colours and armed with Frankish swords and Saxon axes, we were known throughout the empire as the Imperial Axemen."

Einar paused in his tale before continuing.

"We thought we had died and were already in Valhalla," said Rurik, breaking the silence. "For there were whorehouses filled with beautiful women on every corner and as much wine and ale as a man could consume every night."

The men from Northmanni were now professional soldiers whose main job was to protect the Emperor from his enemies at all costs. There were three thousand of them in all, from all over Scandinavia, and they were also employed to police the streets of Miklagard as well as being employed in the field when Emperor John went to war – which he did regularly.

"What was the emperor like?" asked Torstein.

"He was dark-skinned and handsome in that Macedonian way – almost pretty." replied Rurik. "But he was cruel and brutal and would execute his enemies by the thousands if the mood took him. We fought by his side against the Rus and crushed them to a man. Twenty-five thousand Rus warriors were killed in one battle alone, their bodies piled high for the crows to eat. But he was also very generous and liked the men of the Norse who protected and fought for him and were never defeated under his generalship."

"Yes," said Einar wistfully, "we grew very rich under Emperor John. But all good things come to an end, and after marching east with a vast army to destroy the Bulgars, he died of a fever. His Christian god could not save him from that."

Einar hawked and spat on the ground, and the men at the table, now around twenty of them, banged their wooden cups on its top.

"We were both on guard duty that night outside our Lord's tent when word reached us of his death. It was a tradition in the bodyguard that when an emperor died his palace was looted and his soldiers disbanded. This was no different and we deserted our posts and raced back to Miklagard to get our share of the loot. We left the city with some of our original group, about forty of us, on a boat loaded to the gunwales with gold and silver. One of our shipmates was Ubbi, who had been a Commander of the guard, and we all headed home back to Northmanni and beyond, now very rich and happy."

The men around our table all cheered but Einar held up his hand and continued.

"But our happiness was short lived, and we were caught in a violent storm in the Mediterranean Sea which drove us onto the rocks in the land of Italia, killing half our crew and shipwrecking the rest of us."

There was murmuring at this point in the story with many of the men cursing the luck of our two comrades. Einar held up his hands for silence, once again, and lifting his cup in a toast he declared, "But we do not bear the gods any ill will for our financial misfortune – after all, our reputations are intact. They brought us here to the Jomsvikings and the Ravens, and we shall be rich and famous once again!'

Now, all the men cheered, and the evening descended

into drunken debauchery as the local whores gathered around us sensing easy custom.

Chapter 17: Astrid

For the next three days we stayed in the town, but after a day or so of drinking, storytelling and local women, I grew bored. And so, leaving my companions to their pleasures, I went to explore. Jomsborg was typical of many such towns: large, smelly, noisy places teeming with incoming life seeking trade and fortune. In the centre of the town was the main market where a man could buy anything he wanted. A woman, a slave, a sword – all were for sale at the right price. There were stalls of smoked fish and meat, sacks full of eastern spices, and tables brimming with trinkets. Women browsed a counter full of bracelets, gold rings and silver necklaces; little pagan gods of carved walrus bone and stone amulets filled another; and yet another overflowed with all manner of charms and tokens. Traders called out to their customers in a variety of languages and dialects. I stopped at the slave market and watched as, one by one, the defeated scraps of humanity were led onto a stage where their pitiful lives were bought and sold. I felt nothing for them, for I knew that one day I could just as easily share their fate and spend the rest of my days chained to an oar under the bitter lash of an overseer. For now, I thanked the gods for my good fortune on my journey so far.

I made my way past the stalls and shops until, at last, the traders' bustle faded, and I came across a quiet tavern in a row of small stone houses. I went inside and found a table where I sat alone, enjoying the solitude, with only my thoughts for company. The voyages, the fighting, Turid, the sea battles – so much had happened since we had left Haugesund. We left to make our fortunes, and our luck had held on our journey so far. Torstein was becoming known throughout the fort and the town as a fine weaver of stories, and our prowess as warriors grew with every fight. But for now, I was enjoying the relative calm of being apart from my noisy cousin, and my thoughts turned back to Turid and our days (and nights) together. I wondered what she was doing and whether she remembered me as I remembered her. I knew that, in all reality, I would never see her again, but the possibility had not faded. I had been touched by the golden warrior ring she gave me in Byrum and thought of her as she had watched us leave from high up on the cliffs.

So deep was I in my thoughts that at first I did not notice the woman who came and sat down opposite me.

"Thinking of home, Jomsviking?" she said, waking me from my daydream. I looked across and nodded to her. "Don't worry," she said. "I am not after your money – just resting after a busy day on the market." She nodded towards a tray of amethyst and garnet inlaid rings that sat on her lap. "I make them myself. Got a sweetheart you want to buy something for?"

I shook my head. She was an old woman of about thirty-five, I guessed, but I could see from her features that she was still a beauty, and she wore her long, braided hair covered with a headscarf. She was well dressed in a long-sleeved woollen pinafore fastened at the shoulders by some expensive-looking broaches.

"I have no such woman here," I said.

"But someone, somewhere?" she quizzed and searched my face as if guessing my thoughts.

I smiled back at her.

"My name is Astrid. Have you been in the brotherhood long?" she asked.

"Not long, and my name is Bjorn," I replied leaning closer to hear her above the tavern's din.

We talked for a while, and she told me that her husband had also been a Jomsviking, a captain of the Thor's Hammer company, who had been killed in a fight at sea with a Rus pirate ship. He had met her in the market, and they were together for four years.

"I would only see him when he was off duty, and he

133

would come and stay with me at my house on the outskirts of town. When he died, the Jomsvikings honoured him as they recognise all their dead warriors and left me with his arms and his war chest."

Her husband, Gunnar, had earned plenty of silver and gold, and it was passed onto her as his nearest family.

"I still like to go to the market to sell my jewelry," she said. "I don't need the money, but it is always good for a widow to get out and meet people." She laughed for the second time in our meeting.

Although Astrid was about the same age as my mother, she had a youthful spirit and an almost girlish countenance. She gently persuaded me to visit her house to finish digging a well for her. I was happy for the change of scenery, and when my labours were complete, she cleaned and mended my clothes which were in dire need of repair after our recent adventures. Her husband had been about the same size as me, and his old clothes fitted me well. Later that day she fed me and made a bed for me near her hearth. I was comfortable, well fed, and I stayed with her until the time came for me to return to the fort.

Like so many Norse people abroad, Astrid had a history of travelling, fighting and constant change. I learned that she and her first husband had left Sweden many years before. With six other women, she had travelled on a longboat with forty warriors going south in search of a land where they could settle. They joined a larger fleet in Frankia of nearly ten ships, and then sailed south again. After several battles along the coasts of Galicia and then Cordoba they finally arrived in a place called Niebla where they stopped and stayed, living peacefully on their farmstead for ten years or so. They had two children and were very happy living in a community of like-minded Norse farmers, and they prospered and grew rich.

"The land was good to us," said Astrid, her eyes glistening at the memory. "We had many cattle, and our children grew strong and healthy. We believed we would never leave that place and that Freya had rewarded us for our courage and hard work. One day, over a hundred longships arrived from the North looking for plunder. We had nothing to fear from them for they were our people. They stayed for a while and then sailed to the land of Murcia where they had been told that great riches were to be had. They found no riches but only a large army of Muslims who defeated them, killing over one thousand Norsemen and destroying most of their ships. We were caught in the wake of this retreat; our farm was burned, and the livestock was killed. My husband and some other farmers banded together and made their stand in the face of this vengeful force. They were killed as were nearly all our neighbours, and our children were enslaved. I escaped on the last boat out with a few of the survivors. My husband and children were gone, and I had only the clothes I stood up in."

Astrid paused, and I watched tears roll down her face before she eventually spoke again. "We were heading back to my home in Gamla Uppsala, but the winds took us to Wendland, and we ended up here in Jomsborg. I met Gunnar, and he persuaded me to stay.

"We set up a home, and when he was not fighting pirates or the wars of anyone who paid the Jomsvikings, Gunnar would stay with me. I was well known by then as a silversmith and jewellery maker and had no more ambition to go travelling or even return to my hometown, Upsalla. Jomsborg is now my home and the place where, one day, I will die."

I liked Astrid; she was very different from the women I had known. She had plenty of friends in the town but did not need the company of others and lived happily on her own. She did not need men, and we did not become lovers until long after I first met her. She was also an accomplished healer who could remedy a variety of ailments, from a child with a cough to a warrior with a septic wound. I would visit her often when I was able to leave the fort, and we became good companions. She was always pleased to see me, content to listen to me babble on about my warrior's boastings, my family in Haugesund, or even the girl I left in Byrum. Torstein, in particular, could not understand the attraction, particularly when there were so many good-looking young whores in the taverns around town willing to take his silver. But he seldom questioned my judgment, and neither did he do so about Astrid who gave me a welcome distraction from life in the fort and our battles along the Baltic Coast.

Our lives in the Jomsvikings were routine but seldom boring; we wanted the warrior's life and that was exactly what we got. We craved the path of the raider and the adventurer, and we had been rewarded. When we were not training hard at breaking shield walls or our skills at arms, we were in search of battle from our longboats or as mercenaries in the pay of some minor Wendish nobleman. When we found battle we were invincible, and our training and readiness proved a match for anyone foolish enough to confront us. Our reputation seemed to go before us and had often done much damage before we even threw the first spear. Each of the three companies of the order vied with each other for battle honours, and although there was always plenty of plunder to be had, it was always honour and glory that were most highly prized.

Torstein and I enhanced our reputations as warriors and we were always shoulder to shoulder when the battle's fury reached our ranks, enveloping us and driving us forward in the frenzied storm of the fight. The more we fought, the more successful and richer we became, and in truth, there was precious little that could withstand us man-for-man. Torstein's skaldic verses also became famous throughout the region, and he was often called upon to recite by his fellows or even by visiting kings to our fortress. His fame as the Warrior Skald of Jomsborg surpassed even his own lofty expectations.

After a few more battles, my status was also enhanced, and I became the captain of the Short Serpent, in command of the longboat. I noticed that the raids, presumably by pirates, on the towns along the coast started to increase again, about three or four months after we destroyed the force of Slavs on the beach. It was just before the onslaught of winter. I saw towns and villages ablaze every time we set sail, but this time the perpetrators made sure they were well ahead of us. We visited Truso again, counting many more ships in the huge natural port by the town – far more than we could take on with our small patrol. Ubbi reported to the Commander on our return, and each of the ship's captains was required to attend the meeting in Styrbjorn's great hall. He was angry and informed us all that we would soon be paying another visit to Truso but this time the whole of the garrison would set sail.

"This puppy, Prince Otto, is now causing me great problems, and some of our friends believe we are responsible for the devastation. Some are even prepared to believe the twisted words of this lying Christian. My spies tell me that his army has been growing in strength and confidence. We shall find our enemies at home when we visit them next. Last time they failed to hear our words, but this time they will have no ears left to hear. Get your crews and ships ready to leave in two days. It is time to teach this upstart a lesson."

Our allies of the *Kievan Rus* would bring a thousand men to join our fleet. We were to be the hammer and they would be the anvil against which we would crush Prince Otto and his men. Their leader, Vladimir was fiercely pagan and very warlike – always looking for a chance to plunder. Truso was a rich trading post, and there would be plenty of valuable booty to be had – by both forces. Ubbi and a group of a hundred Ravens would be sent ahead to meet the Rus.

He spoke to me before leaving: "Bjorn, you will command the rest of the Ravens in my absence, and I will meet you at the mouth of Lake Druzno with our fleet in seven days. Be ready, for this will be like no other action you have experienced so far. I know you will not let me down."

Then he was gone with the advance party, and I went to get the rest of our group prepared for war.

"Ah, the moment I have been waiting for, Bjorn," Torstein said as we prepared to leave. "I have been growing bored with our little skirmishes when the enemy flees before we can even give him a bloody nose. What do you know of these Rus?"

"Not much more than you, cousin," I replied. "I know they are fierce and hungry for gold and silver, for their land is relatively poor, but they prosper by invading their neighbours and taking their wealth."

"Excellent," he beamed. "I think I am ready to create the last piece of my tale of the Devastation of Prince Otto of the Wends. This shall be the ending I have been waiting for."

Then he, like the rest of our legion, went to make ready. Swords and axes were sharpened, arrows and spears were collected, armour and shield bosses were polished until they gleamed. Days later we sailed east out of Jomsborg with almost a thousand men to meet our dour allies – the warriors of the Rus.

Chapter 18: The Battle for Truso

One week later, and we were at the entrance to Lake Druzno. Ubbi had sailed alone within sight of the town and confirmed that there was a large fleet at anchor. We had twenty-five longships and there were thirty belonging to the Rus. We also had ten stout cargo ships that we had confiscated during our patrols. It was a good-sized fleet carrying over two thousand men in all, heavily armed and eager for battle. The Rus would take their force back down the coast and up the river Vistula, beach their fleet and march up behind Truso. Our ships would sail across the huge lagoon, and if the winds were in the right direction, we would send in fireships to the harbour. These ships were filled with pitch, tinder and anything else that would catch fire easily. There was also something else on these boats – Styrbjorn called it 'Greek fire', and it had been stored under guard in the cellars at the fort. He seldom took it on campaign, but when it was used it caused an instant, awe-inspiring conflagration, the flames of which would stick to a man and burn him to a cinder. Each of the ten fire ships had large earthenware jars full of this substance stored in the bows which were to be set aflame, then sailed towards the enemy fleet. When they made contact the jars would shatter, spewing their burning contents and igniting whatever they touched. In two days, at nòn, and provided we had favourable winds, we would send these deadly weapons into their harbour. When they had done their work, we would land and destroy what was left. The retreating enemy, for they would surely be so, would be driven into the arms of the waiting Rus. Ubbi estimated from the number of the ships in the harbour that there would be three to four thousand warriors facing us, but we had no doubt they would be no match for us.

We anchored at the mouth of the lake in full view of any

passing ships, for it was good that they knew we were coming. Spreading panic in the enemy was a tactic we used to our advantage, and there would be many fearful townspeople adding to the confusion. On the morning of the attack, we gathered on the shore in full battle array.

Styrbjorn stood before us in gleaming armour.

"Warriors of the Jomsvikings. Men of the Ravens, Thor's Hammer and *Odin*'s Wrath, we are about to unleash the power of our pagan gods on these wretched Christians. Show them no mercy and send them to meet their god."

A slave was dragged forward and hanged from a tree in a sacrifice to the Norse gods as our spears banged against shields with a noise that must have carried across the lake to Truso. We went to our boats – the slaughter would soon begin.

Every day around nón, the wind gathered in strength and blew across the lake towards the town. Our twenty-five longships lay waiting for this wind to come. The fireships had been prepared and towed into position. We waited for our gods to favour us. We were very close to the harbour, and from my position at the helm of the Short Serpent I watched the drama begin to unfold in front of me.

The town was large, with some two to three hundred wooden houses and buildings protected by an outer palisade. In the centre of the town was a large building, apparently a church, next to a large stone cross – clearly visible from where we were anchored. In front of the town were six jetties coming directly out from the shoreline, packed with vessels. So many were there that most were at anchor in the sea – unable to find a berth in the harbour. I could also see a row of large wooden stakes arrayed in the water in a long line across the shallows forming an obstacle to deter attackers like us. There was a deal of activity on the land itself as men moved up and down the shoreline preparing for our assault which they knew would come at any time. Our boats sat in line facing the frenetic activity ashore with the prow of each ship pointing its fierce carved head towards the town. I watched through a gap in our line as the ten unmanned cargo boats, in full sail and propelled by a stiff south-easterly breeze, headed directly for the enemy fleet. They were released one by one and moved silently towards their target, carrying their smouldering cargoes. The first one missed completely after being taken off course by a freak gust of wind and beached harmlessly some way down the shore. The second ship caught on the defensive line of stakes that protected the entrance to the harbour. The third ship and her deadly sisters followed each other into the harbour crashing into the waiting vessels with the sound of shattering timber. Then, one by one, they each caught aflame and exploded as the Greek Fire was thrown out onto to the water spreading its burning tendrils and igniting everything that it touched. Within minutes, many of the anchored ships were on fire and the flames reached the wooden jetties as they too burned. The signal was given from Styrbjorn's ship to head for the shore, up-wind of the town. Each vessel was beached, and our warriors formed up in their companies, a stone's throw from the gates of the palisade which surrounded the burning town. The palisade was about ten feet high and constructed from the trunks of trees, sharpened to a point at the top. There were a few spearmen on top of these walls who were soon engaged in defending them, for our men brought forward scaling ladders and proceeded to make the short climb. The defenders were few here and were soon outnumbered by our men who dispatched them quickly, dropped to the ground and opened the gates. We poured through, forming up on the other side in a long shield wall bristling with spears, waiting for the counterattack which would surely come soon.

Most of the ships in the harbour had caught fire by now and even the water was alight. Any men who were in the water stood no chance, for once the Greek fire touched any man, he too would burn. All six jetties were alight and anything close to it would soon be ash. We had caught the pirate fleet at anchor, and it was all but destroyed. However, the men who had opposed us were still unharmed and started to gather in front of us in a loose formation of between two to three thousand men.

The main body of their force was camped on the other side of the town, and although they must have known we were coming, the destruction of their fleet by our fireships had taken them completely by surprise. They had recovered from the shock of our attack and ran towards us through the streets of the town, gathering in front of our formation. There they stopped in a long untidy line, about three hundred paces away. This was the moment in battle when two armies would stand looking at each other, waiting for the first movement to come, when the commanders would size up the opposing forces before deciding whether to stand or charge. We were outnumbered three to one but were always better armed and trained than anyone we faced; this would be no different. I knew beyond any doubt that we would hold and repulse them before long.

Our lines parted, and Styrbjorn, spear in hand, strode out to a point midway between the two lines of the opposing armies.

"Who commands here today?" he demanded. In answer, a tall, slender man stepped out. He was dressed in heavy mail armour from head to knee and wore a bejewelled helmet that reflected the afternoon sun.

"Otto of the Wends commands here," shouted the young man. "And he is about to send you and your pagan dogs back to Jomsborg with your tails between your legs. Go now while you still have breath to do so."

Styrbjorn said nothing as if the comment was unworthy of reply – he simply hurled his spear in the young man's direction. This was the sign we had been waiting for, and we advanced slowly towards the enemy host making space to envelop our Commander into our ranks as we did so. Torstein, standing next to me as always, shouted encouragement to me.

"Come, Bjorn, let's us see if we can make another chapter for my song – it is not yet quite complete," he bellowed.

We marched in formation in perfect lines of three companies, one behind the other. Our shields locked together, and the enemy was confronted with a thousand spears. The Ravens were in the front rank and would feel the impact first. The 'red mist' came upon us, and the long wait for battle would soon be over.

I have fought in many shield walls, and many times with Torstein at my side. Before the shields clash, men will crouch behind them, knowing that at the moment of confrontation weapons of all sorts will be thrust at them. Spears, axes and arrows will seek out vulnerable areas to penetrate, and men will be fearful. When the lines charge to meet the other there will be a bellow of anger and fear, and then the two forces will try to hack each other to death. But here in the lines of the Jomsvikings, it was different, as if fear had been banished and replaced by the confident expectation of victory.

The two lines clashed and the Slavs, with their greater numbers, might have felt our line check and take a pace backwards. As our shields met theirs, we absorbed the greater impact and moved back a step before countering their thrust to ensure they were off balance. Our spears lunged forward as holes in their lines were revealed and men began to fall. My spear hit home several times before getting stuck in an enemy shield. I let it go, replacing it with my *seax*, which started to do its work on the man in front of me. I could hear Torstein cursing away at the men opposite him until his spear broke against the endless line of enemy warriors.

"They are tiring, Bjorn – I can feel them tiring," he shouted. But I could not yet feel anything give in their line as we kept up the remorseless hacking and thrusting.

When fighting like this, all you can do is to keep your discipline and remember your training. You cannot see much to the left or right of you, particularly when blood and sweat are dripping into your eyes, but if you keep your discipline

143

and your comrades do the same, you will nearly always succeed. I felt the enemy line finally buckle and bend in front of me. We all felt the same, for suddenly the gap opened and we surged through, hewing and slicing to the left and right. To each side of me, the same thing was happening and the enemy line wavered, splintered and fell back. They were still a long way from capitulation although there was no way back for them now and we continued to beat them back on ground that was soon slick and sticky with blood and entrails. Enraged men become maddened – some return from the madness and some do not. Then comes the moment when you feel the life force draining from the men in front of you – when they no longer have anything to give, and they turn and run. That is what happened as the Slavs turned and fled. They had lost perhaps half their number and still outnumbered us, but the field was ours and the day was won. There were still some small pockets of resistance left fighting, but gradually these were quelled, and some fifteen hundred retreating warriors fled back through the town and made their escape with the remains of their fleet still burning in the harbour. We did not pursue them. They fell to the hammer of the Jomsvikings, but their fate would now be settled on the anvil of the waiting Rus in the marshland to the rear of Truso.

After such an encounter, the aftermath of battle is like the calm that follows a fierce, sudden storm – a storm that comes and then quickly disappears, leaving only the devastation caused by its actions. I looked around at the dead and dying men lying all about us. Torstein had received a spear thrust to his side but insisted it was nothing and waved me away. Several men were wounded, and we had lost about fifty warriors – big losses for us. The battle had been fierce, and the Slavs once again fought bravely, but they were unable to make the superiority of numbers count decisively.

Prince Otto's threat to the Baltic coast and the effect of his raiding pirates on our reputation and our pockets was extinguished in a single action – although his body had not yet been found. All that was left was for us to lick our wounds, take our plunder and go home. That would be a lengthy process, for this was a wealthy town and there was much to loot. Our Commander forbade us to enter the town before Vladimir and his Rus finished their task and joined us in the inevitable plunder of Truso. We moved to the deserted Slav camp and waited for our allies to arrive. Spirits were high, but all three companies had lost good men, and while death was an inevitable consequence of our trade, we were not used to losing so many, so quickly. After a battle like this everybody had some sort of injury but the fifty-one men who carried severe wounds would probably die from them. Men with minor injuries such as severed fingers, head wounds or perhaps a lost eye carried on – some in great pain but all uncomplaining. The most severely disabled could not walk and were carried to the camp by their comrades. These men had a variety of lacerations and damage, many from stab wounds or from lost and crushed limbs; several warriors had their guts hanging out. Back at the camp, damaged limbs were removed, guts were inserted back into bodies, and rent flesh was sewn back up. The severest casualties were to be taken back Jomsborg to be treated there, while the dead Slavs were stripped of weapons and valuables, and their naked bodies simply piled up and burned.

The Slav camp was a collection of tents and huts standing next to Truso. There was even a large wooden hall constructed in the centre of the camp containing tables and benches. Their warriors must have left in a hurry when they saw our fireships coming, for there were still cooking fires burning. They had left plenty of food, ale and wine as well as several slaves. Very soon the drinking had begun and tales of valour and bravery on the field were swapped. Men forgot their wounds as they drank more. The night came down, and we thought ahead to what plunder might be had in nearby Truso. Our Commander called for calm and addressed us.

"Men of the Jomsvikings," he intoned. "Today you

145

fought bravely and destroyed everything in your path. I salute you, the living, and say farewell to the dead as they travel on to Valhalla. Tomorrow, when the men of the Rus arrive, we shall empty this town of everything of value. I drink to your health." He raised a drinking horn to his men, and they saluted him with much noise.

That night we feasted at the expense of our defeated enemies.

Chapter 19: The Sack of Truso

The next morning, we assembled outside the longhall where all the plunder from the camp was placed. We found gold, silver and many weapons, left by the Slavs before they came to meet us. These were deposited in piles on the wooden floor as one warrior after another came and delivered what he had found. Torstein and I had slept in one of the abandoned tents and had discovered small bags of hack silver and some golden crosses which we put in the swelling pile of booty. Einar and Rurik were just behind us carrying their collection of valuables.

"I hear you took a spear in the guts yesterday, Torstein," said Rorik.

My cousin laughed. "Nothing that a few Slav women and more gold can't put right. Anyway, the *Norns* have decreed that I must continue to entertain you with my wonderful poetry."

Our men were now waiting for the sack of Truso to commence, and that would not happen until Vladimir and his Rus arrived. We walked down into the still-smouldering harbour to survey the damage. There was nothing left of the six jetties and the boats that had once been moored there. The fire that had jumped from ship to ship had also destroyed the boats that had been anchored in the harbour.

The burned remains of what had once been men now lay at the edge of the lapping water, and all along the blackened shoreline the bodies were being devoured by packs of dogs. Here and there we found a few survivors, terribly deformed but still alive, and these we dispatched with a spear thrust.

"It's a bad way for a warrior to die," I said, as I put another dying man out of his misery. Torstein nodded. "How is your wound, cousin?" I asked him

"Nothing but a scratch, Bjorn," he replied, but I could

see that he was moving stiffly.

"I will get it patched up when we return to Jomsborg. I believe there are many more battles for us to win yet before I get called. Come, let us return to the others – we don't want to miss anything."

We left this scene of devastation with its stink of death and returned to the others.

When we got back to our camp the men were gathered around a group who had come up from the town. Two of the visitors were priests dressed in the finery of their religion while another man, wearing a dirty, brown woollen robe and with the tonsured hair of a monk, was talking with Styrbjorn. The others from the town were both well dressed and well fed and carried several wooden chests with them. They were speaking in a Wendish dialect I could barely understand, but from what I could tell the Commander was getting angry. Einar, who understood what they were saying, told us that they had come to beg for mercy and had brought up everything they owned to give to us. Their warriors had all departed with the Slavs, and the town was undefended and at our mercy. The captain of Thor's Hammer, a tall man called Thorkill, prodded their leader, the head priest, with his spear.

"There is more than this, there is more than this," he shouted at them.

Then this exchange stopped, the sound of a hunting horn was heard, and we all looked in the direction of the noise. A horn from our camp answered it, and we looked to the marshland on the far side of town where men were emerging from the mist and heading in our direction. As they moved towards us through the fog their dark shapes began to take form. They looked very like us, for the people of the Rus were descended from the Scandinavian raiders who went east and settled, breeding with the local tribes. They had a fierce reputation, and from the look of Vladimir and his warriors, you could imagine how they struck fear into the local tribes.

The Rus were all heavily armed, dressed in a variety of

animal skins, with many bearing swords with curved blades – the scimitars and daggers favoured by the Byzantines. They carried round shields like ours which bore the emblem of a wolf's head. They approached us in silence, driving three wagons ahead of them to which men were yoked. When they were no more than a hundred paces from us, they stopped, and our two equally numbered forces stood to observe each other with curiosity. From out of their ranks strode a bearded giant – who I took to be Vladimir – in a long, hooded bearskin cloak. Styrbjorn walked out to meet him, and the two men met and embraced. Then, with the men of the Rus following behind them, they walked back to our camp. The food and drink recovered from the defeated Wends had been laid out on tables, and the visitors were invited to refresh themselves.

Styrbjorn took Vladimir over to the men from the town who were standing together nervously looking around them. Our Commander spoke in a loud voice so all could hear him.

"Vladimir, my brother. These good Christian men of Truso have offered us four chests of trinkets from their coffers – what is your answer?" he asked.

The other man said nothing but in one action unsheathed a giant scimitar and removed the priest's head from his shoulders.

"I believe you have your answer, Christians – now flee back to your town and tell them that the pagans will soon be visiting them. Go!" said the Commander.

The men ran back the way they had come, stumbling and falling in the mud as they tried to evade the hail of kicks and punches that assailed them from each side as they made their escape. Vladimir then spoke to one of his men.

"Bring forward the captives. I have a gift for the Jomsvikings," he said. Twenty-five dirty and bloodied captives, bound at the neck and in slavers' chains, were pulled forward and beaten to their knees in front of Styrbjorn. One of their number was the young warrior who had stood defiantly before us, only yesterday, but who now knelt dejectedly in the mud.

"Prince Otto," said Styrbjorn in a loud mocking voice that carried on the wind. "Your god seems to have deserted you. All your warriors are now dead or captured, and these are all that are left. Your lies and deceit have brought nothing but destruction to those who follow you. This Christian town that sheltered you will now suffer the same fate, but *Odin* has reserved a special fate for you, and only the blood eagle awaits."

The captives were dragged away, and as the Rus warriors ate and drank, we discovered from one of the prisoners what had happened to Otto's beaten army. After we had defeated them on the field, they retreated west through the marshlands with well under half the force that originally stood against us. Tired and hungry, they dragged themselves towards the sea where they hoped to escape along the coast and get succour from a nearby Christian community – about a day's march away. Instead, they met over one thousand fresh warriors of the Rus and their calamity became worse. They tried in vain to defend themselves, but the bloodthirsty attackers easily shattered their shield wall. They surrendered quickly and pleaded for mercy but received only the end of a spear point and were slaughtered in their hundreds. Prince Otto and some of his bodyguards had been spared, if only for a day, and delivered to the Jomsvikings for justice.

Both forces were making ready for the sacking of Truso which was to serve as a lesson to anyone who thought about transferring their allegiance to the Christian god and taking up arms against us. Shortly after the previous day's battle, warriors had been sent to prevent anyone escaping from the town. Some two thousand warriors were now about to deliver their own form of pagan justice, and the terrified inhabitants were to feel the wrath of our gods. We marched into the defenceless town intent on rewarding ourselves for our victory. It was now almost a day since that victory and the red mist was just a memory. After many fights, we would often punish our fallen foes, still with the heat of battle in our blood, and the revenge would be terrible. But today was just about taking what was ours, and the men went about their task with enthusiasm. In truth, there was very little opposition to us. The streets were deserted of people who now cowered behind barred doors waiting for the inevitable. Resistance was futile, and doors were kicked in and the occupants sent fleeing into the streets to be herded like cattle. Some opposition was made by small numbers of men defending their homes, but these sparks were quickly snuffed out as each house was emptied – firstly of people and then of valuables. Even household items like cooking pots and fuel were removed, all methodically piled outside each dwelling. A few armed men from the town gathered defiantly outside the longhall where they died. The body of the headman, killed in the previous day's fighting, was thrown into the streets and his home torn to pieces in the search for his wealth.

Our progress through the town was almost leisurely as Torstein and I moved slowly and methodically, doing our job. We only had to kill one man during the whole morning who made the mistake of opposing us with an axe inside his home. Torstein seemed quite disappointed by the lack of resistance in the town, but I believe he was quite glad, as I suspected he was carrying a painful wound from the battle. Eventually, we moved through the town and found the church that several of the Rus had reached before us. They had discovered several priests inside and were torturing them over a fire in the middle of a large hall. They had also discovered several women priests in the building, stripped them naked and were taking turns to abuse them. Seeing us enter the church, the Rus looked at us disinterestedly and then returned to their task.

"Carry on friends," encouraged Torstein. "These women priests are too ugly even for me."

We started to look around a huge oak table at the end of the building, but it was so heavy that not even the two of us could move it much. I called for help, but the other men were too occupied with the captives. We waited until more men of the Ravens entered the building and came over to help us. Six of us managed to move the table and topple it over revealing a large pit filled with numerous sacks and chests. Each one contained much of the gold and silver which we had been led to expect to be hidden in the church. Silver candlesticks, gold ornaments and chains, and even women's jewellery were found inside.

"It might have been worth that hole in your belly after all," I called to Torstein, who ignored me, lost in the wonder of our find. All six of us carried out what we could lift into the street and made a pile from the discovered treasure while the Rus continued with their depredations of the captives.

"Booty first, women later," called Torstein to them, as we struggled out with our findings, but they were deaf to his entreaties.

It was soon past nòn, and the six of us sat on the ground and shared some of the food and drink we had found in a nearby house. By this time, wagons dragged by the captured people of Truso were loaded with plunder and taken back to the growing horde in our camp. Many of our men including the Rus had the same idea, and the drinking started for the day. Any of the earlier discipline shown by men of the two armies started to deteriorate. By mid-afternoon, both sides were drunk and started to quarrel with each other before fights broke out. Old blood feuds came to the surface with two Rus warriors dispatched in a fight with the Raven's champion, Leif Iron Fist. It was time to separate the two 'tribes', and our captains were sent out with orders to return us to camp.

The Jomsvikings held the plunder, the Rus guarded the new slaves, and in the morning we would split up the booty and go our separate ways. There were eight hundred and seventy-five slaves taken and mountains of plunder, and we all returned to our camp much the richer.

"I am not sorry to be leaving those stinking Rus," said

Torstein, "for they are a people without honour. They cheat at dice and have sex with animals. Anyway, I have never seen this Blood Eagle performed before."

"It is the most painful way to die that I have ever seen," said another one of the Ravens. "The man is held face down while the shape of an Eagle is carved on his back. The skin is then pulled away, and his ribs are cut and separated from the spine. Then the lungs are pulled out and salt is poured over his wounds. The last time I saw this was many years ago when a man of our village betrayed us to our neighbours, and we lost half our *aett* in a night attack when he let them through our defences."

"So should all traitors die. I am looking forward to this," replied Torstein.

When we got back to camp, the air was filled with the smells of roasting meat, for the slaves had been ordered to slaughter dozens of animals and prepare a feast for our men. The grain stores and food hoards in Truso had been plentiful even this early in the year, for this had been a very wealthy trading post. Huge fires were built around our camp, and the many tables taken from the town were set up to feed us – enough to seat and feast every man amongst us. But first came the Blood Eagle ceremony and we sat to watch the prone body of Prince Otto, bent across a large log, hands and feet bound together and lying face down. He was stripped to the waist and was very still. Styrbjorn came to stand over his prostrate form and spoke to his warriors.

"Yesterday you fought well to destroy a much larger enemy, brought together by this maggot in front of us. He sought to make the Wends and the Slavs blame us for his piracy and to encourage them to rise against us. Ubbi and his men discovered this plot against us, and we were able to destroy the threat. Now we can all concentrate on our reason to be here – that is to become rich in body and spirit – and when our time comes, we will go to Valhalla, sword in hand, and sit at the highest table. All men will admire you and know that you fought with distinction as a Jomsviking.

"But tonight, we must give thanks to *Odin* who gave us a mighty victory and made us rich men. Tonight, we shall feast and drink to him, but first he demands sacrifice, and for that he calls for the Blood Eagle."

All the men were silent as the three captains of the Jomsvikings approached the bound prisoner – each with a knife in his hand. First came Ubbi of the Ravens who delivered an incision to the condemned man's back and cut him, bone and all, from his tailbone through to his ribcage. He then kept cutting until several of Otto's ribs had been separated from his spine, and very deliberately he pulled each bone back to reveal the man's internal organs. Then came Hakon of Odin's Wrath who did the same with his knife until the rest of Otto's ribs had been cut and pulled back from his spine laying bare what was beneath. The last captain stepped forward, Thorkill the Tall, of Thor's Hammer, approached the dying man, reached down and yanked the lungs out of his back to where they resembled wings. We all watched in complete fascination until Torstein announced:

"I do believe Prince Otto has grown wings – perhaps he will now be able to fly away."

Another Jomsviking came forward and threw a bucket of saltwater over the wounds, and at last Otto's resistance was over. He tried to scream but no sound came. Leif Iron Fist was called forward, and with his double-bladed axe removed the man's head. Styrbjorn picked up Otto's head by its long hair and addressed us one more time.

"Death to all Christians who oppose us!" he cried.

The crowd answered with the same phrase in loud resonant voices. The Commander tossed the head towards one of the prisoners who had been brought in with Otto earlier.

"Take this back to your people and tell them what you have seen here," he said to the terrified captives.

The man and his fellow prisoners were freed and ran

from our camp, doubtless feeling that they would suffer a similar fate to their prince if they stayed any longer.

The sacrifice to Odin was over, and it was time for the feasting to begin. The men sat down at huge makeshift tables taken from the town, and food and drink were brought to us. We had taken many prisoners, and they served us now. They were all men, for our code forbade us to take women or children captive. However, the new slaves were followed into our camp by several women – eager to escape the suffering of their town which now burned in earnest. In truth, they would be left behind when we sailed, as we had no use for them – but for now, they served a purpose for which they appeared very grateful.

The feasting went on late into the night, and men quenched the enormous thirst that only hard-fought victories can create. Ale, wine, food and women were all consumed to satisfy ravenous appetites. Songs were sung and stories told. The last story told that night came from Torstein, now well known throughout the order for his reputation as the 'Warrior Skald', and he stood before the glowing embers of a huge bonfire set amid the throng. Striking a dramatic pose, he began to incant his Saga of the Wandering Warriors – the story of two nomads who sought their fortunes with the Jomsvikings.

"South over water we sailed
bearing poetry's waves to new shores
of the war-god's heart
our course was set.
We launched our ship of oak
Agin the breaking of ice,
We loaded our cargo of courage
aboard our longboat astern..."

The story told of an epic journey of sailing through stormy seas, great ice flows, fighting mighty battles, loving beautiful women and hanging Christians. There was much, much more and when he finished, he took his bow in front of us all and the men cheered him for many minutes. Then he looked up, staggered and toppled backwards into the fire, the flames licking at his wolfskin cloak as he lay there motionless. Everyone, expecting him to be drunk, continued to applaud, but I knew he would not have succumbed to drink quite so easily, and I raced forward and dragged him from the fire by his feet. I managed to pull him free, but by then his clothes and hair had caught fire, and it took several of us to douse the flames with ale. His breath was shallow, and he was coughing blood into his beard. We carried him to a tent, laid him down inside and took off his shirt, for I suspected that he had succumbed to his battle wounds. His injuries were easy to find, for he had a deep cut that pierced his ribs, breaking two of them and causing an ugly looking gash in his side. The open cut was still bleeding.

Ubbi, who had helped carry Torstein to the tent, inspected the wounds. "This is a bad cut," he said, "and he will surely die if there is much damage inside his body. Bjorn, you will take him and the other wounded men back to Jomsborg at first light."

The next morning all our wounded men – the forty-three who were still alive – were loaded into the largest vessel, the Storm Rider, along with forty oarsmen. The sun rose in the east as we pulled away from the shoreline across the lake and then into the open sea. An opposing wind meant that we had to row along the coastline back to Jomsborg, but our strongest men manned the vessel and we travelled swiftly. I anticipated the voyage to be around four days at the pace we were setting, but the gods were good to us, and we made it in just over three.

It had been a calm voyage and we had lost only two more men from their injuries – the rest were taken into the fortress as soon as we landed. Here, their wounds were treated, and physicians from the town cared for them. They had already received treatment after the battle, and those who lived would probably survive. Torstein, I believed, was in a bad state, for he had not yet gained consciousness since his collapse, and if he was to live he needed urgent attention. I decided to take him to Astrid for I knew she had great skill in dealing with the sick and was forever treating ailing townsfolk with her medicines and potions. We carried him to her house, and she told us to lay him in front of the fire while she inspected his wounds.

Her face was grave when she looked up at me. "He is very sick, Bjorn. The spear has gone deep into his belly from the side, and the wound is infected. It looks bad and smells even worse. You must pray to the gods."

I sent the other men back to the fort while Astrid stripped Torstein and washed the wound.

"Build up the fire, Bjorn," she said, and I did what I was told, watching her work. She produced a set of instruments in a small leather box and selected a curved bladed knife which she boiled in wine. She took the knife, knelt next to Torstein's body and proceeded to make a cut from his ribs to his thigh bone. Then she took another instrument with which she probed the wound and washed the huge cut with more boiled wine. When she had finished, she cut away a small part of the flesh around the wound before stitching it together with animal sinew. Astrid worked at her task for around half a day before she finally applied a poultice to the deep gash, wrapped a bandage around Torstein's sizable girth, and collapsed into a deep sleep over his body. I too had fallen asleep, and when I woke, she was still lying on top of his giant frame while he snored, unknowingly, beneath her. I picked her up and carried her to the bed and then went back to make up the fire again. Torstein was still snoring as I covered him with my bearskin cloak – which I took to be a good sign. Then I lay down next to him and succumbed to the same deep and exhausted sleep as Astrid.

"You have been asleep for nearly a day," she said.

I woke up to find Astrid looking down at me, "Your friend still lives, although he was close to leaving for the next life. The spear blade had gone deep into him but had missed his organs. I cut away the infection and have packed the wound with medicines that will help him. Although he is strong, Bjorn, we must wait to see what happens next."

I handed her some silver and said, "Thank you, Astrid. I am in your debt – please take this."

She pushed my hand away, but I insisted: "If he recovers, he will take a lot of feeding. I will return tomorrow night."

I left her small house and went back to the castle.

The rest of our fleet had not yet returned, and as a ship's captain, I was one of the senior men at the base while the others were away. There were still sentries posted at the gates, but inside it was quiet with only the occasional movement of the servants taking food to the wounded men in their barracks. The forty men who rowed the Storm Rider home were also in the fort yet were no-where to be seen. I visited each company's barracks and saw that the wounded had been attended to. One of the physicians told me that no one else had died since we returned to Jomsborg. I retired to our barracks and was heartened to see many of my comrades still living.

"We cannot die here, Bjorn," shouted one, as I entered our hall. "No man gets to Valhalla without a weapon in his hand."

"Then you must recover quickly," I shouted back, "and we will seek new battles to die in. Anyway, the Warrior Skald needs more verses for his great story of the Jomsvikings."

Those who were conscious enough to hear me responded with some weak laughter. I had no more duties the next day, and leaving a message for Ubbi of where we were, I left the fort with some food and drink and walked the short journey to Astrid's house on the other side of the town.

Torstein was where I had left him beneath my cloak and

Astrid was sitting at her table watching her patient. Before I could ask her, she said, "His breathing is stronger today and the infection is going."

I touched her hand, and she smiled back at me.

"For a pair of rough Norwegians, I am very fond of both of you." She squeezed my hand.

"I have something for you," I said.

I had taken a brooch from one of the Slavs I killed in Truso. He was carrying it in a leather bag at his belt, along with some gold coins and hack silver, and it was a delicate thing – obviously made for a woman. It was gold with small red and blue stones surrounding the face of a man at its centre.

"Here, this is for you." I pushed the trinket across the table towards her. I had no idea of its worth but from Astrid's sharp intake of breath, I guessed she was pleased with my gift. She rushed outside and held it up to the light.

"It is beautiful, Bjorn," she called. "Come and see!"

I joined her in the sunlight, and she jumped up and down excitedly like a young girl. Then she put her arms around my neck and kissed me on the cheek.

"I am glad you like it," I said, and she brought the brooch between us so we could both look at it.

"The stones are garnets and the blue ones are very precious and this man's face – well – he is the Emperor," she said, still very excited. I shared her joy and we both laughed.

"Then we must toast – to Torstein's full recovery – and to the health of his physician."

Springtime had arrived, and the days were getting brighter and longer. It was still cold, but there was bright sunshine that afternoon, and we sat outside the house, bathing in the dappled light.

"How did the battle go?" asked Astrid.

"We won, of course," I said, "but it was far from easy. These easterners are fierce fighters, and there were many of them. They were tough, but the Jomsvikings are a breed apart.

I have never seen fighters like them. I also saw my first 'blood eagle' – it is a bad way to die."

"Styrbjorn is a hard man and teaches hard lessons to his enemies. You are but few, and your reputation must go before you, to instill terror in those who would defy you. The legend of the Jomsvikings is one of your greatest weapons. You will receive wealth and achieve a great reputation, but the brotherhood is a demanding mistress, and you can take no other," she said.

"I had not intended to. This town is full of Wendish women anyway – too short and fat for me," I replied.

"Still pining for your Danish beauty," she chided.

I said nothing but recharged our cups, and we drank steadily as the shadows lengthened and the day grew colder still.

"I must feed us," said Astrid. "And your cousin will wake up one of these days, and when he does, he will be hungry as well."

We went back into the house, and she prepared some food while I made up the fire. Torstein had not yet moved, but I could see that some colour had returned to his face, and his skin was no longer such a deathly grey pallor.

"I think your magic is working," I told her.

"There is no magic," she said, "just someone who has been mending broken men for as long as she can remember."

I watched my cousin breathing heavily in the light of the fire and thought of all the things we had done together in the short time since we had left Haugesund – and how I would miss him if he died. As if reading my thoughts, Astrid spoke.

"Don't worry, Bjorn. He will live. He is blessed by the gods, that one. They love him, but don't want him just yet. Anyway, you two have many more journeys to make together. The *Norns* still have plans for both of you, for you are *Odin*'s Ravens, *Hugin* and *Munin* – his thought and his memory."

I was thinking about her words when she thrust a bowl of fish stew into my hand.

"You better eat something as well or there will be nothing left but skin and bone."

We were both seated together on a bench by the side of her hearthfire, with Torstein stretched out in front of it – now breathing softly and untroubled.

As we had done many times, we talked about our pasts and our families, and tonight was no different. Except that now she sat much closer to me, with our legs and arms touching.

Then suddenly she stood up.

"I am going to my bed, Bjorn, and you can either sleep on the floor next to your cousin or come with me."

I liked Astrid very much, but I had never thought of her as anything other than a friend, for she was an old woman of thirty-six years – not much younger than my mother. I looked down at Torstein's sleeping form and quickly decided that Astrid's bed was a better option than sleeping next to him. I got up and walked over to the bed and found her under a covering of furs. She reached up and pulled me to her with both hands and then kissed me on the mouth. She was naked, and soon so was I. We 'travelled together' many times that night, and when the darkness began to fade, she finally let me slip into sleep until I came to at around noon.

I opened my eyes and found I was alone in the bed, got up and went to check on my cousin, then went to find Astrid. She was outside at the back of the house feeding her chickens and singing to them as she threw corn. I watched her for a few moments. With her hair long and loose, she looked like a young girl. Despite her age, she had always appeared strong and fit – but now she looked quite different. She was a very striking-looking woman, and men would always watch her as she passed them. I could see why, for in truth she was quite beautiful. She saw me standing watching her and called over to me:

"Still hungry, Bjorn? I am surprised you have any appetite left," she said.

I tried to answer but struggled to find the words, then she came to me and led me back to her bed again. We spent the day there together until our passion was tamed – at least for a little while.

"When my Gunnar returned after a fierce battle he would keep me in bed for days – until the last of the battle embers went cold," she told me, laughing at the memory and adding, "don't look so worried, Bjorn, I am not expecting you to marry me."

We both laughed. There was a brief silence between us that was broken by a noise from the floor.

Torstein had woken and was calling: "Now that you have stopped rutting; I would be very glad of some help in getting up."

I rushed over and knelt beside him.

"Good to see you, cousin," he said, grabbing the back of my head and pulling me close so he could whisper in my ear.

"The old ones are sometimes the best, and Astrid is certainly very spritely."

"You are only jealous, cousin, and she is a good woman," I replied.

"I know, I heard how good she was all through the night."

Torstein made a quick recovery, and after two more days in Astrid's care, he was back on his feet again eating and drinking and making a commotion. He was still quite weak and slept a good deal, during which time I would creep away to Astrid's bed.

"Come to me when you can," she told me. "You owe me nothing, and your clothes will constantly need mending. There is always a place for you here." She took my hand and placed it over her heart.

The next day, Torstein was strong enough to return to the fort, and I helped him struggle through the town, up the slope and back into our barracks where he joined the rest of the men recovering from their injuries. After that, I would visit

Astrid whenever I could, and when my comrades went whoring and drinking, I would slip away from them and stay with her. Torstein knew where I went, but he was always too busy to notice for long. Astrid and I were more than friends now, but we both knew that it would not last forever, for the *Norns* would soon be demanding again, cutting the threads to all our fates.

Chapter 20: Making new friends

"Wake up! Wake up!" Ubbi shook me awake. The cock was crowing, and the light was only just seeping through the windows as the sun rose on a new day over Jomsborg. I reached for my weapons in alarm.

"Don't worry, Bjorn – we are not under attack. The Commander just wants to see us in his hall. Meet me in the yard in ten minutes."

I dressed quickly, washed my face from a communal barrel of freshwater standing in our barracks and prepared myself to meet the Commander.

"What is afoot?" I asked the captain of the Ravens.

"Nothing that I know of," he said, "but you will know Styrbjorn is not one to let the grass grow beneath his feet." as we made the short walk to where we had been ordered.

I had been in the company of the Jomsvikings for two years and had been fortunate to meet with success during many raids and battles since our initiation. We had ranged all along the Baltic coast at the behest of our paymasters, discouraging pirates and generally helping ourselves to what we felt was ours by right. Sometimes we fought at sea, but we were most effective fighting on land where our formations and discipline had never been matched. Since the Battle of Truso, our might had seldom been questioned, and we had recruited many men since then to replace our fallen. Each company's size was increased to a thousand, and the barracks and halls were full of men and their equipment. Torstein had made a full recovery from his spear wound since the battle, and his poetry and stories were gaining fame. He had also established himself as a warrior of some repute, and although Leif Iron Fist was the Commander's undisputed champion, Styrbjorn would often invite Torstein to display his valour when it was needed. He would always be asked to recite his

Saga of the Jomsvikings and other works whenever visiting dignitaries were guests at the castle. We had both prospered during our stay there in reputation and riches. Our lives were full and well rewarded.

Styrbjorn looked up as Ubbi and I approached to join him at his hearthside. He beckoned us over to him, and without any preamble he spoke:

"You both know that I am the rightful heir to the throne of Sweden," he said.

"Yes, Lord." We replied obediently.

We all knew the story of Styrbjorn's banishment from his homeland where his uncle, Eric, ruled as King. At fifteen years old, he had killed a man of the royal court and had been sent away in punishment. He came to Jomsborg after raiding in the East for two years and had challenged the Commander, a man named Palnatoki, to a duel at sea between their two ships. Palnatoki's men defeated Styrbjorn's crew, but their two captains battled on in single combat. They fought each other to a standstill and no victor was declared. So, after that, Styrbjorn and his men were accepted into the Jomsvikings as equal partners. On Palnatoki's demise, Styrbjorn became Commander.

"It is time for us to go and teach King Eric a lesson, for Sweden is my birthright and will be a new home for the Jomsvikings. I am tired of living here among these primitive people and want to go home. Both of you are rich men of reputation, but I would like you to be even richer and more famous than you are now. We must cement our alliances with the Danes and our other friends. We will take a small fleet to visit them, and when we have their support we shall go and take what we are owed," he said.

For the first time, I saw that Styrbjorn was angry, and he stood with clenched fists, staring into the flames. He was, by then, an old man but stood strong and straight and still looked like he was at least a generation younger.

He spoke again: "Ubbi, you shall command while I am

165

away. We will take three of the swiftest longboats and fifty men from each company. Bjorn, you shall command my ship, the Drakes Head. Now go and prepare yourselves and your men, for we shall be gone for at least a season. We leave in two days."

With that he dismissed us, and we left to prepare for our voyage which would take us throughout the lands of the Danes and on to my homeland of Norway.

"I envy you," said Ubbi as we walked out. "You will be treated like royalty throughout Scandinavia. Enjoy your guesting, Prince Bjorn."

We selected our best warriors and oarsman and went to make our plans. It took me a day to get our boat ready for the long voyage, and it needed plenty of provisioning. We were the cream of the Jomsvikings and Styrbjorn's personal bodyguard. After all, we enjoyed a reputation throughout Scandinavia for fierce discipline, and our Commander expected us to live up to it. When all was ready, I slipped off to spend a final night with Astrid before we left the next day.

Two summers had passed since we consummated our relationship. She was still very beautiful, and I swore to her that she was getting younger looking every day. She and I were good companions – she was part mother and part lover – and her bed was always a welcome change from the draughty barracks of our fortress. When I told her that this would be our last night for a while, she became sad but made me promise to come back to her from the sea and straight to her bed.

She touched the brooch that I had given her and said, "It will take more than memories to keep me warm at night, Bjorn."

I thought I had angered her, but she laughed, slapped my rump and said that if I was going away for so long, I had better give her something for her to remember me by. In the morning we parted, and I went back to the fort to collect my belongings and to leave for some time.

It was early in the morning as I left Astrid's house and walked past the harbour to make sure our ships were ready. Sure enough, they were, laying silently bobbing in the water like sleeping ospreys before a hunt. They were in pristine condition, having only been built a summer ago and had been cleaned and provisioned by the castle's thralls. They now needed only the men, and we would be away on the rising tide. It had been a long time since Torstein and I had first come to these shores in our little boat from Haugesund, and I wondered if we would be returning anywhere close to the place of our birth.

I went back through the castle gates to where the men were assembling in the yard with their sea chests and *hudfat*s. When all were there, the boats' captains gave the order to move off, man the boats and make ready to sail. We marched down to the harbour in our companies, and the men stowed their gear, each taking a seat at his oar while we waited for the Commander to arrive. We did not have long to wait, for very soon he too was aboard the Drakes Head looking resplendent in shining mail and armour. Soon, we were cast off and headed back to Trelleborg, Denmark and a meeting with Oyvind, my uncle, who still commanded the garrison there. The voyage had begun.

Our new ships were swift, agile and a joy to sail. The Drakes Head responded to my every touch, and once the sail was rigged and full of wind, we flew across the wave tops as she took us inexorably forward, and back to Scandinavia. We passed few craft on the brief journey to Trelleborg and those we did gave us a wide berth, for everyone knew from our colours that these were the ships of the Jomsvikings. If anyone was in any doubt as to the strength of our purpose they needed only to look to the prow of my ship where the Commander stood tall and erect, daring anyone to cross our path.

After four days we arrived at Trelleborg and rowed in perfect order into the harbour. Compared to our last visit, we were treated with great importance, and waiting on the dock was my uncle with his bodyguard. We berthed, tied up the boats, and Styrbjorn leapt down from the Drakes Head onto the dock where Oyvind greeted him enthusiastically. The two men embraced, and I heard my uncle say, "Lord Styrbjorn, you and your men are very welcome here. Come up to my hall, for we have some serious feasting to do."

The two men led the rest of us back to the fort, and we followed at some pace – after three days at sea we had built up an appetite, and all shared a great thirst. There was none thirstier than Torstein who fell in beside me as we marched to the fort.

"A better welcome this time, eh Bjorn?" he said waving to a couple of young girls on the side of the street who were eying us with interest. "Have you still got that taste for Danish *pikke*?"

"Sometimes I think of our time in Byrum," I said in answer to his indirect question.

"More than sometimes perhaps, cousin?" he teased.

"There are plenty more herring in the ocean," I said, trying to divert him, "and, after all, I quite like older women now."

"But still…" he continued, looking at me with his great head cocked to one side.

We had reached Oyvind's hall and passed through the doors to take our seats at one of the tables with the rest of the men. Oyvind, seeing this came over,

"Come nephews, you will dine at my table tonight. I know you will be well behaved in the company of your Commander," he said.

He pulled us to our feet and over to where he sat with his captains and Styrbjorn.

"So, Styrbjorn," he said to our Commander, "have these two boys been misbehaving themselves?"

"On the contrary, their behaviour has been quite exemplary. They are good fighting men who obey orders –

rare qualities in men from Norway. I drink to their health."

He smiled and raised a drinking horn to us both while Oyvind just beamed.

"Their mothers will be very proud," he added.

Oyvind got to his feet and addressed the seated warriors who by now had been brought food and drink by the serving women.

"Warriors of Trelleborg, please raise your drinking cups to our brothers from Jomsborg and their great leader Styrbjorn the Strong. Their reputation is well known to us, and we welcome them as kindred spirits," he said.

A roar came from the seated warriors, and tables were banged energetically.

"I hear you have both acquitted yourselves well," said Oyvind to Torstein and me. "I shall look forward to hearing about your deeds later." Then he turned to our Commander, and the two of them spoke in conspiratorial tones until the fires burned low.

Styrbjorn eventually bade us all goodnight and retired to his quarters, allowing us to tell Oyvind all that had passed in the three years since we last saw him. We told him of all our adventures, while he nodded sagely and laughed in equal measure.

"You have both gained quite a reputation, and it seems like the life of the Jomsvikings agrees with you. I have heard many stories of your deeds from passing traders. I am often told of the two fearless Norwegians from Jomsborg. The hammer and the anvil of Haugesund, they say."

"Uncle, you toy with us," pleaded Torstein.

"No, it is true. I have heard it from many sources now. I have also heard it from Styrbjorn himself who thanked me for sending you both."

He put his huge arms around us both, pulled us in close and said no more. We drank and talked into the night until Oyvind bade us goodnight and left.

"I think I will sleep here tonight, Bjorn," said Torstein,

laying his head on the beer-sodden table, and fell asleep immediately.

I woke up the morning, beneath my cloak next to the great hearth now filled with cold, grey embers. A large elkhound was licking Torstein's face where he had fallen asleep some time ago, and the great man was starting to rouse himself. All around, men in a similar state of repose were starting to welcome the new day. The early morning sun was throwing its rays through the huge doors which had now been opened by the servants who entered carrying cauldrons full of stewed meats and vegetables. Fires were remade and lit, and vast iron pots hung over them while bread and beer were also brought. The men of our company came to and slowly got to their feet as the smell of food began to waft through the great hall. When all had eaten and drank, Styrbjorn strode into the room and addressed us all.

"Good morning, Jomsvikings," he said. "You have no duties today, so go and enjoy the town of Trelleborg, but remember who you are and what you represent here. We shall be on our journey at first light tomorrow."

Then he looked at me and the two other ships' captains and bade us join him at a table.

"As you know we shall be travelling a good deal over the coming season and our task is to make allies for the conflict against the Svear who threaten our very existence. We have many friends throughout Scandinavia but will need to make many more to be successful. Our journey will take us as far as Dubh Linn, and we must keep our discipline in front of our friends and allies to ensure their respect. When we leave here tomorrow, we will travel to Jelling to meet the Danish king. Make sure all is made ready."

Then he turned and left us.

I crossed the room to where Torstein was waiting and sat down opposite him. After we ate *dagmal*, I gave word to our crew to be ready in the morning and walked down to the harbour to check on the Drakes Head one last time. I satisfied myself all was ready for our departure, and then we strolled into the market town of Trelleborg to amuse ourselves for the rest of the day. Trelleborg was not unlike the town of Jomsborg but considerably bigger. In the town centre there were all manner of tradesmen at work or selling their wares from stalls in the market. We saw blacksmiths, jewellers, potters, bone carvers, bakers, leather workers and bowl makers, all focused on their day's work. There were also numerous taverns in which warriors, whores, hunters and fisherman sat talking and adding to the noise of the busy town. Picking the nearest alehouse to where we stood, Torstein pulled my arm and we found ourselves sitting at a table ordering drinks. He finished his in one easy draft.

"The first one of the day is often the best," he said and called for more beer to be brought. "Where will the winds blow us next, Bjorn?"

"Tomorrow we shall head for Jelling and the court of the Danish king. The Commander needs support for the battle with the Svear and will need many allies. Harold Bluetooth is a big supporter of the Jomsvikings, and we shall need many of his men if we are to take the throne of Sweden. Many more men than we have in Jomsborg."

"You think we can win?" asked Torstein.

"Why not, you have seen what Styrbjorn can do with a thousand men. If he gets ten thousand together, he will be unstoppable," I replied.

His attention was distracted by two women who were keen to get ours, and our silver. I was not interested but Torstein took them both up into a loft above the alehouse where he stayed for some time.

"Didn't like yours, then, Jomsviking?" a woman's voice called across the room to me. I looked over to where it came from and saw two women sitting side by side. Neither whores nor traders, they were both dressed in warrior's garb – leather and mail armour – and armed with axes and daggers. I took in the unusual spectacle then asked them if they wanted to join me. They looked at me, then at each other, and both got up and came over to my table. I ordered more ale, and they sat down opposite and introduced themselves. They were friendly enough, despite their fierce demeanour, but after a few drinks they talked freely. Auslag and Brenna had been travelling to England with a company of Swedish warriors. They had separated from them during the previous summer after their ship was storm driven onto the rocks on the island of Öland. They were all that remained of a crew of sixty men and women; the rest had drowned. Both women were about the same age as me, and the taller one, Brenna, had a livid red scar across her face from temple to jaw – without which she would have been quite beautiful. They dressed and talked like men but were slight in stature, and their bare arms were covered in tattooed images of the Valkyria – the angels of death that served *Odin* and Freya. I asked them from where they came, and Auslag began to tell their story.

The women had left their homes in Birka after Eric, the King of the Sweden, had sent missionaries to convert them to Christianity.

"The Christian God has no room in his heaven for fighting women," said Auslag. "Our leader, the Lady *Gunilla*, hanged a dozen of the priests when they tried to convert us and sent the rest back to Eric in pieces. That gave us all a good reason to leave, and many of us left to look for land in England."

Brenna saw me looking at her scar which she touched absent-mindedly as she spoke.

"After the shipwreck we were found wandering by some of the local *Gotar* who took us in and sheltered us. I got this from one of our hosts one night who tried to invade me, and we killed him and his friends. We took their silver and their boat and made it out to sea. We could not row it with just the two of us, but we got the sail up which took us to the island of Bornholm. We stayed there for a couple of seasons until we got a ship to bring us here."

"It's a curious story," I said, "for I have never seen women like you before. Our women in Norway can defend themselves and handle an axe if they are in danger, but they don't look or sound anything like you two."

"There are many women amongst the Svear who fight just as well as the men. We were taught to fight as young girls. There were over two hundred of us who left Birka with the men," said Auslag.

It was not uncommon for a few women to take up arms and fight alongside the men, but I had never heard of hundreds doing so in a single company.

"It is only the local women who come to fight for us – there are women from many counties who have joined us…," she continued.

Torstein's booming voice interrupted her.

"But can you piss standing up?" he shouted.

He slid his huge frame next to me and put his drinking cup down heavily on the table, spilling half of its contents over the two women. What happened next took us completely by surprise: in a blur of movement, Brenna pulled out a small throwing axe and smashed it on the table rending Torstein's cup and pinning his sleeve to the wood.

Brenna spat in his face. "Why don't you come and take a piss with me and find out? You might come back having to squat for the rest of your life."

There was quiet in the alehouse as the other customers looked over to see how this situation might develop. Torstein broke the silence.

"My apologies ladies," he said, pulling the embedded axe free and returning it to Brenna. "I was forgetting my manners. Please, let me get us some more ale – I seemed to have spilt mine."

We spent the rest of the day with our new companions, swapping stories. They told us much about the land of the Svear, from where Styrbjorn was expelled as a young man and to where we would return in force in the spring. My cousin was fascinated with these two ferocious young women, and they eventually forgave him for his earlier behaviour.

"It is a great shame that you two are not men as I am sure you could be an asset to the Jomsvings," teased Torstein.

"And it is a shame you are not quicker in your movements – for the next time you insult me it will be your hand that you lose. And what would you scratch your arse with then?" replied Brenna.

We all laughed; our little group was growing comfortable in each other's company. I went outside to the back of the building to relieve myself where I met another of the Ravens doing the same thing, and we talked for a while about the mission and where we were heading. Then I went back to find my friends sitting exactly where I had left them.

"That is good to see – no more fighting," I said.

"Bjorn, these women have news of a friend of yours," said Torstein.

"Oh," I said, expecting another foolish prank.

"Go on, Auslag, tell him," he prompted, and the woman continued her story.

"For some time the land around Birka was attacked by Finnish pirates, and one large raiding party had been intercepted by *Gunilla* and her warriors. We killed many of them and pursued the rest to their base in the Åland Islands where we caught and destroyed them. They had amassed much plunder, but there were also slaves in the camp that we learned were to be sold to the Rus. The captured men and women were all Scandinavian, and so we set them free. Three Danish women amongst them asked to stay in Birka with us. One of the women asked *Gunilla* to train her to fight, so she might be able to defend herself. We took her into our company and trained her, and before long she became very good at her new trade and was one of *Gunilla's* favourites. I became great friends with this woman. She told me that she had left her home on the island of Byrum in search of a

174

Norwegian warrior who had saved her family and friends. Her name is Turid."

All three watched my reaction. My jaw dropped, my mouth hung open and I stuttered and blustered like an idiot unable to form words.

Auslag continued.

"She is well, Bjorn, and travels in the company of the Lady *Gunilla* who has taken good care of her. Not that she needs it, for she fights fiercely and is probably now in England bringing her fury down on the heads of the Saxons. If the *Norns* allow me, I hope to catch up with her very soon. Do you have anything you would like her to know?"

Before I could say anything, Torstein interjected. "Careful, Bjorn, for too much ale and a man's heart is open for all to see."

By then I had at least closed my mouth, and from my expression there was little more they needed to know. I posed a thousand questions to both women, and it was past ótta when they finally left the alehouse. They had managed to get passage aboard a merchant ship bound for Hedeby, leaving, like us, in the morning. We wished them luck and remembering my duties as captain of the Drakes Head, I went to find my ship and get some sleep before the next part of our voyage.

I fell into a deep sleep, dreaming of lying on my bearskin cloak beneath the stars with Turid.

Chapter 21: Travelling Towards Home

In three days, we approached the harbour town of Velje. Our ships, rowing in perfect order, one behind the other, swept into the port. They were expecting us, for there was a detachment of Danish warriors waiting when we landed. They accompanied us to the King's Hall in Jelling, a half-day's march away. Crowds came to watch us march into town, and Styrbjorn did not let them down as he led his men through the streets. The town was bigger than anything I had seen before, and there were hundreds of folk in the streets to greet us when we arrived. The hall itself was a huge wooden building with carved statues of *Odin* and Freyer standing guard outside. The Commander called our company to a halt, and Leif Iron Fist and the three captains led the men through the open doors of the great hall.

Inside there were over a hundred people who parted to let our group move forward to where the King of Denmark, Harald Bluetooth, sat with his wife, Gyrid. As we approached, Styrbjorn raised his hand for us to stop, and he walked the last few steps towards the King, alone. Harald then stood up before him, stepping down to meet his guest, and the two men embraced. The King was old – perhaps sixty years of age – but he was an athletic, strong-looking man. His grey hair was braided behind him, and a long beard of the same colour reached down to his waist over a flat stomach. His queen, Gyrid, a stern-looking woman, sat on the throne next to the King's, remaining motionless throughout the proceedings as she looked on.

"Styrbjorn, famous son of Sweden," the King began, "you and your men are welcome here in Jelling. We have heard of your mighty deeds along the Baltic coast. The Jomsvikings seem to be an indefatigable force these days – have you been doing as well as the stories suggest?"

Styrbjorn answered: "We are not so many, but for a small force we have been making our presence felt, keeping the enemies of Denmark in their place." He waved Leif forward who put a chest in front of the king. "A small gift for you Lord," he added.

The chest was opened to reveal a small fortune in gold coin.

"We thank you for your gift, Styrbjorn Storki. The Jomsvings are always welcome in this country. Now, come, we must show you our hospitality. Your men will be fed, and we shall talk," said the King.

We were led to a large table next to the hearthfire and given food and drink. I sat there listening to the two men talk – and ate and drank in silence.

"Come spring we must move against the Swedes who are growing in strength and continue to threaten your borders, Lord. If they are not halted, they will continue to threaten Denmark, and they currently believe they can move about Scandinavia with impunity. They must be taught a lesson before you see their longboats sailing in force towards you across the Kattegat."

The King listened and nodded before answering. "I know that you are keen to claim your birthright Styrbjorn, but that has nothing to do with Denmark. We have no love for the Svear or the Goths, but this will be a large undertaking and will need many hundreds of men and ships."

Styrbjorn replied, "You should also know that the Swedes are killing your Christian missionaries, and they deride you as weak and powerless."

"Yes, I have heard this too," said the King. "But I have also heard that you too have been harsh with some of the Christians along the Baltic Coast. Now, tell me of your deeds since we last met."

Their conversation went along like this until the shadows lengthened. The rest of us listened, explaining or describing the details of actions or events when asked to do so. Then the talking was over for the day.

"I will consider your words, and we shall talk again very soon," said the King, "but for now you and your men should accept our generosity. We have prepared a house for you, and there is food and shelter for your men."

He got up and walked off.

The Commander dismissed us saying he had other matters to attend to, and he too left us. Our company moved into the camp that had been prepared for us next to the town where conditions were comfortable enough. During our time there we made a great show of our martial skills and drilled relentlessly in an endless display for the inhabitants of Jelling. The atmosphere was one of conviviality around the town, and the Jomsvikings were given a friendly welcome wherever we went. For our part, we were on our best behaviour, as the Commander was keen that we should be regarded in the best light. There was no brawling and little drunkenness outside the camp. Games and competitions had been organised between the King's bodyguard and the Jomsvikings – wrestling, archery, javelin throwing and even a game of knattleikr.

Two teams of twenty men were selected to play knattleikr. A familiar game to many, the objective is to strike a solid leather ball with a willow paddle through two posts at the end of a field. Each team must attack and defend their position, and our match that day was played with much enthusiasm by each side. Torstein and I both excelled at the game which we had played since boyhood, and although we played on the ice in Haugesund, it was now the height of the Danish summer and our field of 'combat' was a piece of meadowland to one side of the town. The match was watched by all the townsfolk who came out to cheer the teams on in their pursuits. It was full-blooded, within the few rules of the game, but our team prevailed and was victorious. At the end of the day, we were feasted by our hosts long into the summer's evening on tables and benches that were brought out for the purpose.

I noticed that Styrbjorn was sitting next to the King, but on his other side was a woman I had not seen before. She was much younger than him and sat animatedly talking to those all around her.

"That must be the Commander's wife, Tyra," said Torstein, digging me in the ribs. "I wouldn't mind a bit of that myself."

She was very fair, almost white haired, with her locks braided in an intricate pattern around her head. She was about thirty years old with very striking looks and dressed in an emerald-green woollen dress that clung to her lithe figure. I could see many of our men stealing a glance at the woman who lit up the King's table with her looks and laughter.

"I'll bet he misses her on those lonely winter nights in our draughty old castle," continued Torstein.

"Apparently, he took her as his wife years ago as a reward for leading the Jomsvikings to one victory or another – and her mother, Gyrid, is Styrbjorn's sister. A curious relationship if ever there was one," he mused.

I looked at the two women and then at our Commander who were all remarkably similar in looks, although Tyra was considerably happier in her demeanour than her mother.

"The things we do for love," Torstein said, before his attention was distracted by a particularly buxom serving girl who was pouring his beer.

Before the food was brought to the tables the King got to his feet and gave a toast to the men of the Jomsvikings who, "protected the shores of Denmark with their unflinching vigilance and dedication from dark forces." Styrbjorn then stood and toasted to loyalty and friendship whilst Tyra smiled up at him. The evening wore on, and jugglers, fire-eaters, singers and poets all came out to entertain the audience of some four hundred men and women assembled on this balmy summer's evening. Finally, and inevitably, Torstein was called to stand and recite The Saga of the Wandering Warriors. After rapturous applause, he launched into his popular Story of the Jomsvikings, which now contained several more verses attesting to the 'friendship and love of our Danish cousins'.

Standing before the King's table, he bowed deeply as the seated guests applauded his dramatic rendition, and the audience, including the King and Queen, exhorted him to one last performance. Needing no further invitation, he launched into The Death of Baldr and the Punishment of Loki, a famous Scandinavian tale of the son of *Odin*. At the end of this performance, Torstein took more tumultuous applause. On raising his bowed head, the King beckoned him to the top table and made him a gift of a beautiful bejewelled dagger in a golden sheath. He thanked the King before bowing to the audience one last time and returning to his seat in triumph.

"I am glad that at least someone here can properly reward an artist for his work," he boasted, and he put the gift on the table so we all might admire it.

I felt a hand on my shoulder. It was our Commander, and I jumped to my feet.

"Come, Bjorn, let us talk away from this noise."

We walked away from the happy, drunken hum of voices.

"It seems our visit here has been a success, and we have been promised a hundred and fifty ships from King Harald, but only if we raise the same number from Jomsborg. Tomorrow we will leave here and make our way through Denmark and head up to Norway. We need more strong allies in this fight, and then I feel sure will be able to conquer the Swedish rabble. We have done a good job here cementing our relationship with the Danes, but there is more work to be done. Tell the other captains to be ready for we leave here in two days."

"Yes, Lord. We will be ready," I replied, and he turned and went back to rejoin our hosts.

Two days later we assembled in front of the King's Hall and marched out of Jelling, back to our boats in Vejle, resupplied once more for our ongoing journey. With Styrbjorn on the prow of the Drakes Head, we led the other two ships out of the fjord and into the sea. The next few weeks saw our company stop at various Danish strongholds, and we visited Arhus, Fyrkat and Aggersborg to pay our respects to the local *Jarl*s upon whose shoulders our fate would rest in the coming campaign. During our time onboard, Styrbjorn would often stand next to me at the helm and would occasionally seek out my counsel. One day, as we were nearing the northernmost tip of Denmark, he came to me at the tiller.

"Do you think we can trust the Danes, Bjorn?" he asked.

"I do not know, Lord," I replied honestly. "I have had little to do with them in the past. It would seem that their King has a genuine affection for you, and his support will be vital."

"I would agree with that, and if he is good to his word then we shall prevail." He paused for a moment then continued, "His wife, however, is not one of my closest supporters. My sister has never forgiven me for leaving her daughter with child many years ago."

"But is not that our way, Lord?" I said.

"Indeed, it is. A man must follow his destiny, and when the call of the Jomsvikings came – that way became my destiny. But she is a fair woman, my wife, is she not?"

"Aye, sir," I replied, "she is certainly very fair."

He nodded in agreement. "And with none of her mother's shrew-like qualities," he added before walking back to the bows of our ship to continue his vigil.

During our voyages, we would often have these short, sharp conversations, which was as close as I ever got to him. He was a quiet man, but beneath the surface I always felt there was a fierce, unstoppable resolve that would trample anything and anyone that got in its path.

Torstein and I were two of four men of Norway on our ship. When I told them that we would be sailing back over the Skaggerak Sea to the lands that bore us, there was no little excitement. They asked me where we would be going, and I told them that I had been ordered to steer a course to Trondheim in the north of Norway where we would meet Haakon Sigurdsson, who called himself King there. It was a voyage of some ten days, and the weather was good to us, affording enough wind to sail nearly all the way. The Drakes Head led our small fleet all along the rugged coastline's rocky inlets and fjords. As we passed the island of Røvær, the gateway to my home of Haugesund, Torstein came and stood next to me at the tiller.

"What would our people make of us now, do you think?" he asked.

"Well, we will find out, for on our way back we will be stopping there," I said.

He let out a joyful cry, and I noticed him go a little glassy eyed for a moment before composing himself again.

Trondheim had grown considerably since I had last visited with my father on a trading trip over ten summers before. We approached the town through the mighty Trondheim fjord, and from a distance I could see how the town had changed. There were several huge dragon ships at anchor as we approached, and we moved with sails down, rowing in perfect order to where a growing crowd waited on the quay. Styrbjorn would always stand in the prow of the ship on these occasions – expressionless and clad in his shining steel armour. King Haakon was there in person at the head of the crowd on the harbour, and he stepped forward to greet Styrborn who jumped down from the ship as soon as we had touched the quay. The two men shook hands.

"Welcome, Lord Styrbjorn. You and you men are very welcome here. I am eager to hear news of the Baltic lands. Come to my hall and we shall talk," proclaimed Haakon.

With that, they both walked off into the town while the rest of us carried out our shipboard duties before disembarking ourselves. At that time in Norway, many sea kings claimed the crown. As in the rest of Scandinavia, things here were changing and lands that were once ruled by a local *Jarl* were being swallowed into 'kingdoms' under a single ruler. The Kings of Denmark always considered the Norwegians to be Danish vassals, but this was never an opinion shared in Norway. I noticed that there was now a large church in the centre of Trondheim around which numerous tonsured priests buzzed in and out.

"The nailed god has made it this far north, I see," said Torstein and spat on the ground.

"Careful, Torstein. We are guests here. I am sure that not everyone has forsaken the old gods." I said, touching the amulet around my neck.

We stayed in the harbour for two days before taking our boats out of the water on a nearby beach where we cleaned and repaired the hulls. It was a regular duty that was always necessary, particularly during long voyages, but each man knew his task and many expert hands made light of the work. Einar and Rorik, natives of the town, visited their kin who came down and invited my cousin and me to their homes. On our third day, we were feasted in Haakon's great hall and were treated to some fine hospitality. Business between the two leaders seemed to have reached an amicable conclusion, and we were soon on our way again. This became the general pattern of our voyage around Scandinavia, and we were here to make friends and allies. Our reputation was well known throughout these lands, and folk were only too keen to greet us and listen to our story. So far, we had been treated well without any hint of hostility, and from my brief conversations with the Commander, he was gaining some commitment for his plans. During one such conversation, as the Drakes Head rowed out of Trondheim, he said: "We are doing well, Bjorn. The lands of Scandinavia may be changing under the curse of Christianity, but they still remember the old gods. The people remain the same, and they still desire land and wealth. It is good to see.

"I expect you're looking forward to visiting home again?"

Chapter 22: Home to Haugesund

During our voyage back down the coast, we stopped and visited several of the larger towns in the western part of the country, and Styrbjorn met with the local *jarl*s. The large port of Bergen had changed immeasurably, and now a huge church stood at its centre. We were guests in these towns, and our conduct was very respectful. The locals, who welcomed us unreservedly, returned this behaviour. The day came when we were but a short distance from Haugesund. Torstein could barely contain his excitement as he stood next to me at the tiller of the Drakes Head. The Commander approached us.

"You two must be very keen to see your homeland again? Torstein, I think it is only fitting that our Warrior Skald should take a prominent position so his people can acclaim him. I want you to stand in the prow of the Drakes Head today, as we come in."

"I should be honoured, Lord," said my cousin.

Within a few moments, Torstein had donned his armour, including the impressive helm we had taken from the Frisians, and stood proudly in the prow of the ship. I too was excited, hoping and praying that nothing had changed, that my family were well and that everything was as it had always been.

The three years we had been away felt like a lifetime, but as the Drakes Head pulled through an early morning sea mist towards the shore, the town looked as it always had done the day we rowed away on the Raven those years ago. Torstein stood proudly at our head, hands on hips, as the distance closed between the quayside and us. People started to gather on the dock, and soon we were close enough to make out individuals as more and more folk came to watch us come in. Soon there were hundreds of people, several rows deep, watching our progress, and then we were there, throwing ropes to those onshore. I looked at the crowd anxiously searching for the faces I knew. Torstein, by then, had lost his composure and was shouting greetings to those he recognised. Unable to contain himself any longer he removed his helm and leapt into the throng as people started to recognise him.

Styrbjorn called to me: "Go and join him, Bjorn. Your people are welcoming you back."

I let go of the tiller and jumped down onto the quayside, looking around frantically as my name was called. Smiling faces greeted me at every turn and arms were reaching out to embrace me. I saw Helge first, then Leif and Rolf, and struggled to make my way through the crowd, most of whom were hugging me and clapping me on the back. Then the crowd parted and there was my mother standing in front me, arms wide and tears streaming down her face. She grabbed me in a fierce embrace.

"Welcome home, my boy. I have missed you so much," she repeated over and over.

Finally, she released me, and it was my little sister's turn to lock her arms around me. Sigrid had grown into a striking young woman since I left her as a gangling young girl three summers past. My brother, Geir, no longer the stripling I had left, gave me a warm and muscular welcome of his own. I looked back at our boat where my companions were watching the commotion and smiling down at us. Even Styrbjorn was laughing now at his two warriors, engulfed in a sea of welcoming arms and smiling faces.

"You are released from duties for now. Go, go," he called.

Our families and friends bore us away through the familiar streets of the town. I soon arrived at our family home, no longer the longhall I had grown up in, but nevertheless a large and comfortable house in the centre of the town. With my mother on one side and my sister on the other, both clutching at my arms and asking me questions at the same time, and with Geir following behind in their wake, they dragged me through the door where the babble of noise was joined by the baying of my brother's elkhounds.

"I wish I'd known you were coming," said my mother. "We heard that a prince of Sweden was coming but never dreamed that you were coming too – and as his captain!"

She burst into tears again.

Considering that she was so unprepared for my arrival, food and drink were produced rapidly as her servants scurried around under a bombardment of shouted instructions. The initial excitement calmed down, and I was able to take everything in at last. My mother had changed little, perhaps a few more grey hairs and a little thickening at the waist, but still a very fine-looking woman. My fourteen-year-old sister had grown into an eye-catching young woman. She was tall and lean and had the same straw-coloured hair as our mother, which she wore in a single plait. Geir, now sixteen, was tall and the image of his father, but with only the semblance of a full beard on his face. Together we sat at the long wooden table, and I answered their questions in turn while making my way through the mountain of food and drink in front of me. Friends and neighbours came to visit throughout the morning, and by midday I was exhausted and almost bursting at the sides from the huge amount I had consumed. Suddenly, I felt very tired.

"Your bed is still in the same place, Bjorn," said my mother.

I staggered to my feet and took the few steps towards my bed, flopped down and closed my eyes. As I lay there, I felt Sigrid lay down next to me and put her head on my chest – and then I was gone.

I do not know how long I slept, but it was dark when I awoke, and one of my brother's dogs was licking my face. I felt like I had been asleep for many days, and it took me some moments to remember where I was. If I needed any reminder I was met by the smiling faces of my mother and sister looking down at me.

"You are hungry, Bjorn?" asked Sigrid. I shook my head.

"Then you are wanted in the great hall."

I hurried to get up, but my mother raised her hand.

"Your Uncle Rollo said there is no rush. He said that as it has been three summers since you left, and a little more time will not harm," said my mother.

I got up, and as I washed and then combed my hair and beard, I became aware of Sigrid watching me get ready.

"I see you are more handsome now than when you left. My friend, Utte, is very beautiful, and she is looking for a husband," she teased.

"Then Utte had best look elsewhere, for my duty is to the Jomsvikings," I replied.

She looked a little crestfallen, and so I added, "But maybe I will get a little time off," and the smile returned to her face.

After a final inspection from my mother, I was on my way to the great hall to meet my uncle, with Geir walking alongside me. It took us an age to get there, for I stopped many times to greet old friends and neighbours, but eventually we arrived. The town had grown considerably since we left. The palisade fence had been extended, perhaps a thousand paces to the left and right, and it seemed that the streets were densely packed with a far greater number of people than I could ever remember. Many of the passing faces I recognised, and they hailed me enthusiastically, but there were many strangers. Lots of them were not of our people, and I saw there were many different nationalities. Where once there were only folk of our *aett* there were now Lapps, Goths, Svears, Saxons and Franks in the streets of Haugesund – all come to ply their trade. Geir walked proudly alongside me as we made our way to Rollo's hall, and finally we arrived. I walked through the doors unannounced into the long room where I had spent so much of my youth and smelled the familiar scents of my childhood.

"I thought you would never come, Bjorn," shouted Rollo who threw his arms around my shoulders, lifting me bodily off the ground. "This one has been eating me out of house and home since you arrived."

He pointed at Torstein, seated at a large oaken table in front of a pile of empty plates, who raised his drinking horn in a toast.

"Your Commander has been and gone. You will be happy to learn that you have no more duties for a few days now. Come and sit down and tell me of your adventures. My son here has been too occupied to tell me much," he laughed.

"Nonsense!" shouted Torstein. "I did not want to steal his thunder. Famous warriors must tell their own stories."

Over the next *eykt*, I gave Rollo the details of all our adventures. He nodded appreciatively and applauded regularly. When my tale was concluded he looked at both of us.

"You left as boys and came back as men. I know you are not here for long, but you will always have a home here and will always be welcome under my roof. And don't worry, I have been taking good care of your family, Bjorn, and keeping an eye on that beautiful sister of yours. They are my blood, and until *Ragnorok* I will love and care for them all."

"You have all my thanks, Uncle. Now tell me of the comings and goings of our old hometown," I said.

"Everything changes, but nothing changes," he said and began his story.

Since we left there had been plenty of challenges for the Norwegian kingship, but Haakon had prevailed and now held sway over much of the country. He was a staunchly pagan King but did not oppose the Christianisation of Norway that had been espoused by his predecessors. Indeed, there was much money to be made from this new religion and the missionaries sent throughout Scandinavia were often accompanied by considerable wealth.

"Any god that needs to bribe their converts must have too much money," said Rollo. "These Christians are a pious, noisy lot, but when they preach the tales of their crucified Lord and put silver in folks' hands at the same time, they will always get a willing audience. From the little I know, the Holy

Roman Emperor gives plenty of gold and silver to those who listen. The King of Denmark takes his dues and tells the rest of Scandinavia to listen – and that's what we do. We don't kill these Christians anymore, for it is much more profitable to listen to them tell their stories. Anyway, what's one more god in the firmament? This one forgives us all our sins, so he is certainly very busy around here.

"When our turn comes to go to Valhalla there will be no room for Christians, but while they bring us their weasel words and wealth who am I to discourage them? Anyway, I let them build a church on the edge of town, and those who want to visit and sing their songs with them can do so in peace. I can see no harm in it."

We toasted our old Norse gods, drained the drinking horns again and, wordlessly, one of my uncle's thralls filled them all to the brim. Sharing his son's insatiable appetite for ale he quaffed it in one and continued.

"The town has prospered in the short time since you left and trade has brought much wealth here; but it is still in the hands of the few and there are still many poor to be seen," he said.

We shared a moment's quiet reflection before he continued.

"After the Raven delivered you both to Jomsborg, it returned home with tales of your deeds in Laeso. I knew the *Norns* would answer my prayers and look kindly upon you both. And now you are both delivered home to me here, at least for a little while." Then he shouted gleefully, "More ale! But don't drink it all, for tomorrow you and your company will be feasted."

A good deal later, I staggered from the longhouse needing Geir to help me home and to bed. He was now the head of our house, and at sixteen years of age was now a man who dutifully took care of his mother and sister. He was well respected around the town and, I noticed, drew many an admiring glance from the local women. My sister was a rare

189

beauty like her mother had been, so I am told, and the family was well cared for by my benevolent uncle. My family had a small business buying walrus tusks and furs from the north of Norway, which they traded for amber, and gems from the East. My mother employed a small group of craftsmen who made jewellery, which was sold, all along the west coast of Norway.

"You have made quite an impressive venture, Mor," I said at the breakfast table in the morning.

"It is nothing really," she said, "just a small diversion. Your father left us plenty, and Rollo is a generous man. Anyway, we still have enough coin for Sigrid's dowry. When of course that becomes necessary."

I slid a bag of gold coins over the table to my mother.

"This is a small contribution from Jomsborg."

My sister blushed.

"No one has taken your fancy yet, then?" I asked her. She blushed a deeper shade of red and asked us to stop teasing her. Changing the subject my mother asked,

"How long will you be staying here, son?"

"Until Lord Styrbjorn decrees – which will not be long I am afraid but likely to be a couple of days, so I am told. We must journey to Dubh Linn before summer is over. He needs many ships for the spring and is calling in all his favours."

"Then we must make the most of you while you are here."

"As long as I am not usurping Geir as head of the house, then," I said, reaching over to tousle his hair. "Come let us take a walk," I said to him. "I have eaten so much in the last day I will burst if I don't take some exercise."

We walked down through the town towards the harbour, trailed by his two elkhounds, and along the shoreline where I had spent so much time as a boy.

"So, what is life in Jomsborg like?" he asked.

I thought for a moment. "Well brother, it is very strict but has brought me great rewards. If a man wants to build a great reputation for himself there is no finer place to do so. There are many rules, and if you break them you will be punished. The Commander is a stern man."

"Where will you go next?"

"We have a long journey ahead of us from here – first to the Orkneys, then to Dubh Linn, and then home. Styrbjorn is building an army of allies to fight for him in the spring. It's no secret but we will go to Upsalla and fight to regain the throne he believes is rightfully his. We need at least three hundred ships – four hundred if we are to be sure of victory. Styrbjorn will buy his allies with gold and promises."

A tall wooden church on the edge of our town took my attention. It was over two stories high, taller than most buildings in our town and unlike any other. It was a beautifully carved construction with corner posts and a framework of timber with wall planks standing on sills. I nodded towards it.

"Have you been inside, Geir?"

"Only once," he said. "A strange place. They kneel and pray, and a priest comes around and forgives everyone their sins. I think it is quite harmless really, and they paid Rollo a lot of silver to build it there."

I said nothing, and we walked on talking idly about all manner of things past and present. By the time we returned to my family's home, Torstein was waiting for us.

"Good to be home?" he asked me.

"Yes, I have missed the old place," I said.

"The Commander has sent me to look for you – he is down by the harbour. Time to do our duties, and then the rest of the day is ours," he said.

We went down to where our ships were tied securely to the harbour and saw the Commander in conversation with one of the ships' captains onboard the Drakes Head. When it was finished, he beckoned us aboard the longboat, and we sat down at a couple of the rowing benches.

"You have certainly assured us of a fine welcome here," he said.

He was in good humour, almost jovial, which I had seldom seen before.

"In two days, we will be off again, and we need to be ready for the morning tide."

He continued looking at me for a response.

"All will be ready, Lord."

The boats' hulls had been cleaned and repaired recently as had the sails and spars. Tomorrow the last of the supplies would be brought on board and we would be ready. He nodded absentmindedly, thoughts already in another place. I had never made the journey to Dubh Linn before, and we would need to travel through the Earldom of Orkney, and then on around the wild coast of the Kingdom of the Scots. One of the other captains had sailed this way before, and we would be following his ship, Thor's Hammer, for most of the trip – a journey of about two to three weeks if all went well.

"Then I shall see you both tonight. Torstein, you have prepared something special for your audience," said Styrbjorn, spoken more as a statement than a question. "You are now the memory of the Jomsvikings."

"I am honoured, Lord," replied Torstein, and we were dismissed.

"Have you seen the church, cousin?" he asked me as we walked away. I nodded and Torstein continued. "I went inside. Nothing much to speak of really. A little like the one in Truso, but this one was much grander really. It had some women priests as well – I followed one inside. She really very comely beneath that old woollen robe."

I looked up surprised. "You didn't?"

"No, of course not. I am still on my best behaviour," he said, laughing at my discomfort.

The feast that night was a grand affair, and a visiting King and his retinue would have been treated no better. Tables and benches to seat four hundred guests had been placed outside the *Jarl*'s longhall on this pleasant mid-summer's evening. A huge fire had been lit and torches burned all around the perimeter. Seated next to Rollo were Styrbjorn, Rollo's wife Inge, my mother and a few other local dignitaries, while the rest of us sat at the other tables. I sat with Torstein, some of the Ravens and my brother and sister. People were dressed in their finest clothes, and many wore handsome jewellery, with the unmarried women in particular all trying to look their best. Sigrid drew many admiring glances from the men around our table, which in turn drew the odd scowl from Torstein.

"Anyone who disrespects my little cousin here will have me to answer to," he growled at anyone brave enough to snatch another glance at Sigrid.

There was plenty to drink, and an army of thralls endlessly fetched *bjorr*, wine and mead to the tables. Huge plates of meats, fish, bread, cheese, vegetables, fruits and nuts were all brought forth and devoured. Toasts were made and thanks given to all the Norse gods, as people revelled in the balmy evening weather. There were jugglers, musicians and acrobats. The girls of the town, including my sister, entertained and sang to the flute and lyre, and the revelry went on into the night. Then, it was Torstein's turn, and he launched into The Story of the Jomsvikings, followed by The Saga of the Wandering Warriors. As ever, he milked the applause and needed no second invitation to continue his declamations, and the feasting continued until the fires and oil lamps spluttered and died. Drunk and fit to drop, the weary revellers made their way home or to the homes of others, and the day was done.

My time in Haugesund passed quickly. We had returned once and could return again. The day after our great feast, my mother and sister clucked around me like two hens. I would miss them greatly, but I also missed the sea and the waves that would carry us on to our next adventure. I visited my Uncle Rollo to say our private goodbyes, then returned home for one last meal with my family. We sat together, quietly, for none of us knew when and if we would see one another again. In the morning they accompanied me to our boats, and with a hundred or so townsfolk, watched us sail back out to sea. I waved one last time, turned my back and steered the Drakes Head out to the open ocean and headed west.

Chapter 23: Onward to Ireland

After about ten days under sail, we reached The Earldom of Orkney, a collection of craggy islands that had been raided and settled by Norwegians over many years. Our three ships led by the Thor's Hammer made for the mainland harbour for the night and tied up. The local ruler, Sigurd Eysteinsson, invited us into the town and made us welcome, while he and Styrbjorn talked long into the night. Resupplied and refreshed, our ships left quietly in the morning to resume the onward journey to Dubh Linn.

The following morning, the Commander joined me at the tiller for a while.

"The Earl of Orkney is quite mad, you know. He rules his tiny rocks in the North Sea as if he were the King of Denmark, but he was more than hospitable. Although it is not a place I would choose to go myself. But it is important that we, at least, pay our respects to him – you never know when we might need those men of Orkney."

"Do you expect them to come in the spring?" I asked him.

"I do not think so. They have more than enough to deal with protecting their little islands from the Scots who never give up raiding. But we will see. This will be your first voyage to Dubh Linn, then?"

"Yes, Lord," I said, "but I have heard many stories of our people there."

"I have not been there for many years now," he said. "The Norse folk have always met much resistance there and were completely ejected years ago, but they returned to conquer in the end. The locals are fierce but disorganised – I raided in parts of the country myself many years ago. I understand there is much uncertainty in Dubh Linn now, and I am told their King, Olaf Cuaran, might be looking for pastures new. He has over two hundred ships at his disposal, and we might need his help yet. He has a score to settle with King Erik of Sweden and revenge is always a strong motivator."

Styrbjorn was unusually talkative that morning, which I took as a good sign, and so I ventured a question. "Are you satisfied with our progress, Lord?"

"Satisfied?"

He thought for a moment, before continuing.

"Yes, but am I convinced we will recruit enough allies? Let us see. There is little love for the Svear, and many would like to see Eric cast down. But will they come? Time alone will tell. I have been promised much support from Denmark and Norway, but we will only know surely when their ships drop anchor in Jomsborg. One thing I do know: the Jomsvikings will be ready."

I seldom spoke to the Commander, and some days he would simply stand in the bows of the ship looking forward as we cut through the waves. But he spoke more to me than any of the others, and through our short conversations I learned much of our plans. He said little to anyone in truth, but when he did speak it was always something important. Nearly all my time was at the tiller and as the ship's master. I spent the day keeping our path true and away from the rocks. Within a few days, we approached the shores of the Kingdom of Scotland, land over which the Norse people had fought for hundreds of years. It was largely barren and certainly held neither welcome nor succor for us. When evening came, our boats anchored close to the shore, and we would rest there with no need to risk going ashore. Our movements were always tracked by groups of horsemen following our progress as we made our way along the coast. Occasionally, they would be joined by larger groups of warriors gathering on the shore who would shout at us, waving their weapons harmlessly.

"Not the most welcoming of people, the Scots," said Torstein one evening, as we watched a number of these local warriors shouting out insults and challenges to us. "And I think that is just their womenfolk."

These people were either very brave or very foolish, for one night after we anchored some two hundred paces off the shore, a group of them decided to visit us. A boat full of their warriors crept out to the Drakes Head, and I awoke to the noise of something striking our ship. The planks used to build the hulls of our ships were never very thick – perhaps the width of a man's wrist – and anything that came into heavy contact could be felt. I was woken by such a noise and found about twenty of these people clambering over our gunwales to attack us. My sound of alarm quickly woke the rest of the men, and we easily repulsed the attack, dispatching the invaders, beating them back the way they had come with swift sword and axe. The rest leapt into their boat and made their escape into the darkness leaving ten of their dead and wounded onboard. We threw the bodies into the sea. Torstein accounted for the last of the injured with a mighty axe blow that nearly took off the man's head. I looked down at the dead warrior before he joined his companions. In the torchlight, I could see him lying naked on the deck, like the rest of his comrades, clutching a large rusty sword which he had been flailing around uselessly. He was covered from head to foot in crudely drawn tattoos. Torstein was shaking his head as we looked down at the dead man. "These people must be idiots, what did they think they could achieve here except a quick trip to the afterlife," he said.

They did not return, but after that I made sure there were watchmen set every night when we anchored close to the shore. A few days later, we reached a large island, the Kingdom of Man, again ruled by Norse folk who had once invaded and never left. Two days after that and we were at the mouth of a large river which took us into Dubh Linn. We passed many warships as we drew closer to the estuary, all full of warriors, who did not bother us beyond moving in for a closer look and then retreating. One of them, came close enough for us to hear some of their men shouting to us.

"Go home," cried one man "you do not want to die here".

This was followed by a spear thrown towards our ship which fell pitifully short into the sea.

"Here, take the helm," I said to one of our crew. "Hand me up a javelin," I said to another.

Weapon in hand I took aim and released it with as much force as I could muster. I watched it sail over the space between the two ships, perhaps sixty or seventy paces and hit one of their rowers. The ship, which had been keeping pace with us, changed course and veered away drawing some derisory howling from our crew. I looked towards our Commander standing in his usual position in the prow, and he turned towards me and gave me an approving nod. I took back the tiller, and we were bothered no more. Our three ships continued towards our destination now visible beyond a large sandy bay.

Dubh Linn was a big, heavily fortified town with several hundred stone houses. It was protected by the sea and river on most sides and was defended by large earthworks and a high wooden palisade upon which several spearmen stood guard.

"I wouldn't fancy attacking this place on my own," said one of the men to me as I manoeuvred our craft into a tight berth on the harbour. There were many fighting ships there, and the place was very busy with craft of all sizes coming in and out of the harbour. Some went inland, up the river, and others sailed in the opposite direction back out to sea. We had clearly attracted the attention of the locals, and a small crowd had gathered on the quay who stood watching our small fleet with interest.

Styrbjorn came over to me.

"Bjorn," he said, "take Torstein and inform King Olaf of our arrival. I shall be along in due course. You will find his longhouse in the centre of town."

We jumped onto the quay and made our way through the

gathering crowd. The streets beyond were full of people, with many of the men heavily armed. They spoke a Norwegian dialect which was easy for us to understand when we asked for directions. The King's house was very similar to buildings at home; it was a large rectangular structure made of stone and wood. Two spearmen, standing guard at the front doors, asked us to state our business. Torstein drew himself up to his full height and looked down at one of the guards.

"We are Jomsvikings in the bodyguard of the Lord Styrbjorn Storki who seeks an audience with King Olaf Cuaran."

The man disappeared into the building, and re-emerging shortly, he said. "The King says you are very welcome here. We will…"

He was interrupted by another who pushed through the open door. This one was a giant, perhaps as tall as Torstein and just as heavily muscled, with long, unbraided red hair and beard reaching down to his waist. He had a huge smile on his large, scarred face.

"Ah," he called, "the Jomsvikings are here with the Lord Styrbjorn. You are all very welcome. I shall come with you down to your ships. One King must welcome another, surely."

With that we all set off down back through the town to our ships. On seeing our approach, Styrbjorn jumped down onto the quayside and hailed the King.

"Olaf, it has been many years my friend," said Styrbjorn, before the two men embraced one another enthusiastically.

"Come," said Olaf, "there is food and ale for all of you in my hall."

The men from all three of our ships were beckoned to follow him. Shortly, one hundred and fifty of us were seated in the King's huge hall. He and Styrbjorn sat at their own table, whilst the rest were seated at benches and tables served by an army of slaves.

"This is quite some hospitality,' said Torstein quaffing two cups of ale in quick succession. "They seem mightily happy to

199

see us. The Commander appears to have been made welcome everywhere."

"Perhaps one day we shall have such a reputation," I said. "Imagine that, cousin. Never having to buy a drink wherever we go."

"I would not complain at all…" he replied, his attention taken by two buxom slave girls attending our table.

After a while, one of the women, a dark-haired girl of about sixteen shook me by the arm and pointed to the King's table from where Styrbjorn gestured to me to approach.

"Olaf," he said, "you have already met the captain who commands my ship."

Olaf nodded. "Come, join us, Bjorn. Your father Halfdan Strong Arm was a trusted shipmate of mine some years ago. We shared many raids together."

"Yes, Lord, he talked of you much," I replied, remembering that my father had mentioned this man many times to me as a boy. "The stories of the great Olaf Cuaran in Northumbria were oft told in our house."

He smiled again. "Come sit with us, for I am keen to hear of the ships you saw on your way here."

I sat down opposite him and spoke again. "We passed seven or eight longships in all that did not bear your standard. They carried red banners with a black stag's head and were all heavily armed. Some came close to see who we were but did not bother us overly. I believe they were just weighing us up. Each was full of warriors, all seemingly armed and ready for a fight."

"They are ships from the south of the country," said Olaf, "carrying the men of Munster, and a constant pain in the arse they are. There have been more of them gathering in the last months, but they only attack when our ships are greatly outnumbered. As you may have noticed they respond favourably to a sharp lesson."

The King went on to tell us of a new leader of the Irish who had successfully rallied his people and organised an army which now posed a threat to Dubh Linn and the surrounding country.

"This Máel Sechnaill has managed to rally his people into something more than the rabble that we found here a hundred years ago. When the Norse folk first arrived, there were easy pickings, and we took much wealth and many slaves upon which our people have thrived. But we taught the Irish how good warriors fight, and they seem to have learned their lessons well. Dubh Linn shall never fall, but we have enemies all around us. Now, Styrbjorn, tell us of the plans for your spring adventure?"

The Commander took in a breath, thought for a moment and spoke. "Do you remember when we first met, Olaf? I was sixteen years old and commanding a group of pirates intent on death, destruction or glory."

"Yes," replied Olaf earnestly, "I was one of those pirates – not much older than you."

"Can you remember why you came?" said Styrbjorn.

"I came because of you. Because you were a man we could all follow. Wealth and reputation or an early trip to Valhalla. If I remember rightly, I never went to Valhalla."

"Quite so," said Styrbjorn. "I was seldom wrong even at that tender age. I am not wrong now and come the spring I will be leading an army to Sweden to take back what has been stolen from me. This is my birthright. I am the rightful King of Sweden, and I reward all those who are with me with fame and fortune. Just like I did all those years ago. I do not presume on our friendship, but if you still have a thirst for these things, I will share everything we gain."

"That is an interesting proposition, Styrbjorn, but I have no need for reputation, and as for gold and silver, I have more than enough here. Allow me think on it for a while – fighting these Irish dulls the spirit after all. Let us drink some more for now and consider everything in due course. These are not decisions we can make too quickly."

Their conversation stalled for a moment, and we were

distracted by the sound of laughter coming from one of the other tables. The Commander said, "Bjorn, time to return to your crew. Please let me and King Olaf visit the past while we may – we have much to catch up on."

I excused myself and returned to our table where Torstein and some of the crew were in deep conversation with two of the King's warriors.

"Come, Bjorn," he said placing an arm around my shoulder. "These fellows have been telling us all about Dubh Linn. You know every warrior here is given at least one Irish slave as well as land and silver. I could be very happy here you know."

"Then it would be almost as rewarding as being a Jomsviking," I replied, raising my drinking cup to my comrades. "What do I need with slaves and land when I have everything I need around this table. We are all wealthy and we travel in the company of our brothers who would lay down their lives for each other. What need have I for anything else?"

"True, cousin," said Torstein "a man needs little else." Then, grabbing one of the women who had been serving us and embracing her enthusiastically, he added, "But a small piece of these local beauties would not go amiss either."

Later, out of earshot of the others, he asked conspiratorially, "Did you learn of anything interesting at the top table? I believe we have come at an interesting time. There has been a good deal of commotion here concerning – a woman. Shall I go on?"

"If you wish," I said, feigning disinterest, "I had no idea you were such a gossip."

"The ships we met coming in? They were full of Irish warriors," he continued. "King Olaf will send his ships out now and again to chase them away, but they return, and it starts again. The same happens outside the walls – the Irish come and attack, lose a hundred men or so and get beaten back. The streets outside are full of heavily armed men, always ready to fight at a moment's notice. Dubh Linn is constantly at war with these people and it was all because of a woman."

"All that fighting? I hope the woman was worth it," I said.

Torstein nodded to one of the local warriors with whom he had been drinking and the man took up the tale.

"The Norsemen have been here for many generations," said the man, a large, dark-haired warrior named Hasten who was in his cups and keen to tell the rest of the story, "and, long ago, Dubh Linn was nothing more than a *longphort* – a temporary winter base which we could defend and raid from. The early raids were successful, and our people stayed and settled. The Norse tribes fought among themselves for control, but eventually things settled down until in recent years the Irish began to unify and threaten us. King Olaf decided to put an end to this and led us deep inland, stripping each town we met of all their wealth and making slaves of everyone we found before burning the dwellings to the ground.

Thousands of captives were taken and sent back here with the captured plunder. Many were sold to traders and taken away, but many more were kept and put to work. One of these captives was an Irish princess, a beauty by the name of Gormlaith, who was taken by the King as his concubine and who bore him children, including his son and heir, Sigtryg. Gormlaith had been together with the King for over three summers when one day she simply disappeared while he was asleep. No sign was found of her again until word was brought by a travelling priest that she had appeared in the camp of the King of Ireland, Máel Sechnaill."

He lowered his voice to a gruff whisper, and we all craned forward to hear him.

"Apparently, she was his wife and had been long before her capture by King Olaf. The Irish King was happy to see his wife again, but he swore revenge on Olaf and the rest of us for the wrongs that were inflicted upon his queen and people. He swore that he would not rest until we were defeated and thrown out of Ireland. His warbands are sent to Dubh Linn in increasing numbers, and attacks on the city grow more frequent. They don't seem to care how many men they lose as long as the attacks are kept up."

"Imagine that," said Torstein. "Making war over a woman's lost reputation – such unconscionable folly!"

"It is not the first time a strong man has countenanced war for the sake of a woman's honour," I replied absent-mindedly, looking at our Commander. It was then that I wondered how much his stormy relationship with Queen Siegrid had influenced his decision to fight with the King of Sweden.

Hasten continued. "This woman was well treated here, like the King's wife, but she had the reputation for being an enchantress able to enflame men's senses with her soft words. She caused much trouble here, and I am glad she is gone. Now she is whispering in another man's ear, and he sends his men to die beneath our walls all the time. In truth, we care little about these attacks, but those who live outside the wall's protection need to look over their shoulders every day.

"Did you see their warships in the bay? They come ashore and attack any people they find, then hurl themselves against our walls before we chase them away. We kill many of them, but sometimes they get over the walls and cause damage. They say they will not rest until we are destroyed and every last slave here has regained his or her freedom. They are like berserkers and have no fear for themselves. It seems that every defeat only makes them bolder, and there is an endless number of them."

At that moment our conversation was interrupted by the noise of a hunting horn from somewhere in the town. Hasten put down his cup of ale and got to his feet quite calmly before leaving the hall with the rest of his comrades.

"I shall watch over your ale, Hasten," shouted Torstein after the man as he left the building with the rest of them.

Styrbjorn and Olaf were also on their feet, and the King's

thralls were struggling to get their lord into his armour. Our Commander came over and ordered us to form up in our companies as soon as the local warriors were clear of the hall. "Let us see how these Irishmen acquit themselves in battle," he said, and we filed outside to watch the scene unfold.

The news came that ten enemy ships had landed, and a force of about five hundred warriors had come ashore, burning and looting their way to the town. They had been engaged and stopped by a smaller force of the King's warriors who had been pushed back and were in an orderly retreat towards the west gate at the landward side of the town. This was only a temporary respite, and the greater force of Irishmen was on the move again. By now our small force of Jomsvikings had moved towards the sound of the commotion, and our men stood ready should we be required to join the action. The Commander ordered us to be ready but not to take part until he gave the command to engage. He then joined King Olaf on top of the walls that would shortly come under attack.

"Come with me," he said to half a dozen of his senior men, and we climbed the steps to join the defenders who stood armed and ready on the high walls.

From my vantage point, I could see the retreating Norsemen streaming through the open gates in the walls. Behind them advanced a tightly packed group of howling warriors who stopped about a thousand paces from the deep ditch that ran in front of the earthworks that in turn stood in front of the high defensive walls. On top of the walls were arrayed many hundreds of spearmen and bowmen awaiting orders as the two sides eyed each other warily.

"It is always like this," bellowed King Olaf to us. "They wait for us to come out to meet them, and when we don't, they send their warriors in to try and get through the gate or over the walls. They are seldom successful, but they never tire of trying. When they are bored of waiting, they will rush these walls. Then, when they have taken enough arrows and javelins, we will open the gates and drive them back to their boats once more. If they could organise themselves in battle a little better, we might be in trouble but for now, we will destroy this force. It keeps us sharp."

The heavy gates had now been shut, the drawbridge over the defensive trench lifted, and Olaf's retreating men were safely inside the fortifications. They went and stood to one side of the vanguard of reserve warriors, formed up close to the doors. There was no panic or nervousness in any of these assembled men. It was as if this was just another day's training.

I watched and waited, as the force of Irish warriors stood in front of the earthworks howling abuse at us. They beat their swords against their red shields until a man I took to be their leader held his arm aloft and silenced the mob. Other men brought forward several bound women and children who were forced to kneel in front of him. One by one he reached down and slit their throats in plain view of all of us.

"This happens often," said King Olaf. "They capture some farmers and their families and kill them in front of us. They should know by now that we will show no pity. They will approach our walls, and we shall rain arrows on their heads. Then we shall go and kill the rest of them. It is the same every time they come. I cannot fault their bravery, but it is well matched by their stupidity."

The two sides stood watching each other. The Irish finally started to move towards our positions, scaling ladders in hand. As they got closer, they started to run until they reached the trenches in front of the earthworks not more than a hundred paces from our walls. A fusillade of arrows from Olaf's archers was aimed with deadly precision, and one by one the attackers began to drop into the waist-high water as they crossed the trench. Those who made it across tried to ascend the slippery bank of earth that greeted them while trying to evade the hail of arrows, javelins and rocks from above. One or two ladder bearers made it within reach of the walls before being hit and slid back down the slope into the filthy water. The attackers began to falter as their warriors, realising that fate was about to envelope them, turned and made a hasty retreat, trampling on the bodies of their dead and dying comrades.

Following their flight, the gates were flung open and the drawbridge dropped over a trench, allowing as many as a thousand defenders to storm out and pursue those scattering in front of them. King Olaf's men were on them in a trice, overcoming the exhausted Irish and hacking them down from behind. Many turned and faced the Norsemen for one last furious stand, but they were quickly overcome in a tide of retribution.

I watched this one-sided contest conclude, as stout defenders became aggressive attackers, and my eye was taken to a place off to the left of the action. A group of about two hundred Irish warriors had concealed themselves behind the steep slope of a hill and, seeing the defenders rush out in pursuit of their comrades, revealed themselves and ran towards the unguarded bridge – behind the attacking Norsemen.

Styrbjorn saw the same thing and called to me. "Prepare the men," he shouted, and I, in turn, shouted down to the Jomsvikings standing in readiness by the gates: "*Skjaldborg!*"

Our companies immediately formed up, locked shields to the fore and braced themselves for the onrushing Irishmen who had reached the bridge. The sound of the impact of the two forces clashing was deafening, but our line did not move, and all the momentum of the surprise assault drained from the foe as they were brought to a halt.

"*Svinfylking,*" I called down to our men.

Forming into a wedge they pushed forward, axes, daggers and swords hacking at their opponents. Torstein had wrestled his way to the front of the wedge, and now he and several of the biggest warriors led the men forward, splintering shields and rending helms in an unstoppable flurry of violence. The

Irish were pushed back rapidly, and having no answer to our assault, simply turned and ran. We did not go after them, and I watched their remnants run into the lines of Olaf's men, who by then, were returning from their battle. Some of those left alive surrendered their arms, and a few prisoners were taken whilst any wounded Irishman received a swift spear thrust to end his suffering. All that remained was for the scavengers in the town to come out to strip and loot the corpses.

Up on the wall Olaf turned to our Commander.

"Thank you, Styrbjorn. That was a timely intervention. I have heard much about the reputation of the Jomsvikings, and now I see it is all true. Let us see what the prisoners might tell us," he said.

He led our small party down some narrow steps to where a group of bloodied, bound and defeated Irish warriors had been brought into the town, sitting dejectedly in the mud.

"Ask him who his Lord is?" said the King to one of his men who prodded a captive with his spear before questioning him. The man answered and was rewarded by a blow to the side of the head with a spear butt.

"He said they fight for the rightful King and Queen of Ireland, Lord," said the spearman.

"Tell this dog there is no Queen and that she is, in fact, just another whore who will sell herself for a price that suits her," said Olaf. "Then tell them all that those who stand against me will either die or be taken prisoner and sold to Byzantine slavers who will castrate them and take them east to serve as eunuchs in Miklagard. They will be of no use to their Queen then."

I excused myself and went to join our men.

"That was not much of a contest. You must barely have broken sweat." I said to Torstein who looked remarkably fresh despite his exertions.

"I have worked much harder on the training ground in truth," he said, with customary bravado. "But at least we have earned our ale today. How did it look from your lofty perch with your Lords?"

"It was over so quickly I barely noticed," I countered.

It had been an impressive and disciplined display. Our opponents had no answer to the Jomsvikings, and the many *eyktir* spent training and practising our tactics had been in great evidence. We had not lost a single warrior and neither death nor serious injury blighted our victory today bar minor cuts and bruises – the odd missing eye or finger. The King's voice was heard above the hum of the men talking.

"Back to the hall, men. You must have built up a little thirst today," he commanded and led us and his returning warriors from whence we had come.

The light was leaving the day as we marched back to the hall to resume our drinking. Weapons were left outside, and men slumped back down at the tables they had left in such haste only an *eykt* before. An endless line of slaves brought in huge quantities of food and drink. Toasts were made, and the King made a speech thanking the Jomsvikings for their actions and praising our decisive part in the battle. Hasten resumed his seat opposite me, and I asked him of his part in the vanguard of the battle.

"We harried them as far as their ships, and many of them died there. They were brave but foolish and badly led. When they saw there was no escape, they fought well enough. But desperate men have little to lose, and we put them down without mercy. I would rather be dead than live the life of a slave – and I believe that most of them decided that too."

"Why do they keep coming and attacking you like this then – when all they face is defeat?" I asked him.

"They seem driven by some mad desire to die," he replied. "They hate us and wish us gone forever, but they never seem to learn their lessons. I am told Queen Gormlaith exhorts them with magic to take back Dubh Linn from us and release their people from servitude here."

"I cannot see that happening," said another man. "These

209

walls will not be breached, and their only chance of victory will be if they manage to get us into the open field and crush us with overwhelming numbers."

Torstein got to his feet and raised his drinking cup. "To mad queens everywhere, may they lead our enemies to confusion and destruction."

Styrbjorn, hearing the toast, looked over to our table for a moment or two before turning back to engage with his host.

The next day was spent idly wandering around the huge town. Dubh Linn did not seem to be suffering any ill-effects from the previous day's excitement. The market was full of bustling activity, and the taverns, traders and whores were all doing a brisk trade. I visited the thriving slave market which was full of men looking for bargains as wretched men and women were displayed in chains to be bought and sold. We Jomsvikings were made very welcome everywhere we went. If anyone had not heard the story of the town's deliverance at the hands of Torstein and the men of our *svinfylking*, they were given the full details. Each new version was slightly different from the last. I visited our ships in the harbour to find the King had generously sent plentiful supplies of all sorts that would see us back to Jomsborg ten times over.

On the morning of departure, the King came down to the harbourside with a small retinue and gave a speech of farewell in front of our ships. Together with a group of warriors, he waved us off, and we left, as we had arrived, rowing across flat water and back out into the ocean. We looked around for any of the Irish ships that had been lying in wait only a few days before, but now the sea was empty of ships of any sort. The sun glinted off a calm sea, and we pulled for home and Jomsborg none the worse for our encounter with the Irish.

Chapter 24: Return to Jomsborg

The voyage home took us past the lands of the Welsh, the Saxons and even the Franks, but we sailed without encountering any hostile ships. At night we anchored offshore, stopping briefly for respite before continuing at first light, and we made good progress navigating with the summer breezes behind us. Twenty days later we reached the shores of Wendland, and the welcome sight of the stonewalls of the Jomsborg fortress. Slipping quietly into the huge harbour, we were home. The ships were secured, and I jumped down onto the stone quay, feeling its welcoming solidity beneath my feet. The weary crews of each longship joined me on the dock, and with the Commander at our head, we trooped back up the hill to the castle and returned through its gates where the companies were dismissed.

The next day, at dawn, the company captains and the skippers of the ships were summoned to Styrbjorn's longhall where we joined him at his table.

"A successful voyage?" asked Ubbi.

Never one for a quick reply, the Commander considered the question. "Yes, I believe so. We have much support among our friends and allies, and many fine words were spoken, but come the spring we will find out how true these words are."

He went on to describe in some detail all the support that we were promised and what he expected would happen. He finished by listing all the pledges of support that had been made.

"Come the spring, if all men have spoken the truth to me, we will have three hundred ships to sail against the Swedes," he continued.

Each ship would carry at least fifty men and our forces, numbering fifteen thousand, would make a powerful adversary.

Ubbi was the first to respond. "That number of ships would surely bring us success, Lord," he said.

"Yes, if they all come, we shall doubtless succeed. Now, tell me how the recruitment plans are proceeding."

At least two hundred new men had been selected, and they would soon be ready to be inducted into our order. They came from near and far, from all over Scandinavia, Frankia, Byzantium and places I had never even heard of. We needed a large intake of new men, but it would be a great undertaking to get warriors with the right fighting skills and qualities. The discussions went on for almost an *eykt*.

Eventually, Styrbjorn said, "I have made a decision. We will need another company, and it will be led by Bjorn Spear Arm." Then, looking directly at me, he said, "I shall need you to recruit five hundred men by the spring. Take your cousin, use one of the empty halls across the square and make a new company of Jomsvikings. You know the sort of men we will need. There will be coin and ships at your disposal. Ubbi will spare you a few men to start you off."

With that, he finished his briefing and dismissed us all.

"You look a little surprised," said Ubbi, as we walked back to the Raven's barracks. "That will keep you well occupied for quite some time. Now tell me of your voyage."

I told Ubbi and the two other company captains what had happened on our journey, who we had met and what I believe had transpired. They listened to me for some time, and I answered their questions as best I could.

"The Commander has a great reputation among the Norse folk throughout all Scandinavia and beyond," said Thorkill, "but do you believe they will all come?"

"I do not know," I said, "but Styrbjorn has received the promises of many Kings, from Norway to Dubh Linn. If they do all come, we will have many ships."

The three captains nodded in agreement before we went our separate ways, for there was much to accomplish in not much time, and our thoughts were all on the spring campaign.

A little later I was back in our barracks.

"Then I have the honour of addressing Captain Bjorn Spear Arm, of *Baldrs Wrath*," mocked Torstein when I told him of our new quest. "Where will you start?"

"I believe you meant to say, where will we start, Torstein. For there are now two of us at least in this new company – and you are its champion."

"Then I shall be the greatest champion the Jomsvikings have ever seen. A man of iron and great words. But first, Captain, let us drink to our success, for every great journey starts with a single step – and a cup of ale. We must repair to the alehouse to make a plan. We have travelled far in our little ship, and I need to wash away the salt."

We made the familiar journey down the hill to his favourite tavern where the men of the Drakes Head awaited us.

I did not drink with them for too long, for I had other business in town. Astrid would have seen the ships returning and would be waiting for me.

Come to me when you can, she would always say to me when we parted, for she was long since an impatient young girl fretting on the arrival of her lover. She was her own woman, and I loved her for that. Though she asked little of me – and I of her – my heart was always glad to see her. This time was no different. I had missed her company, and I walked eagerly to her house on the edge of town carrying a small bundle of gifts bought on my travels. I knocked for an age until at long last she threw open the door and stood before me looking as striking as she had when I had left her. Her long yellow hair was untied and hung long and loose to the waist of her pale blue woollen dress.

"My young warrior has returned at last," she said, and we embraced for some moments. "You had better come in," she said taking me by the hand and leading me through the door towards her bed. Releasing the clasp that held her dress together, she stepped nimbly out of the single garment, and, naked, she pulled me down on top of her. "Welcome home," she whispered, and our reunion began.

I awoke a long time later to find she had left our bed and was now fussing around her house preparing a mountain of food. She moved lithely around the room from one task to the next, and I watched, admiring her strong, girlish body, marvelling at her form. She saw me watching her but made no effort to cover her nakedness.

"Come, you must be hungry," she said, beckoning me to a table full of food.

"You should cover yourself," I said. "For if I am to finish all this food, I need no distractions."

"Take your time," she replied, "there is plenty here to satisfy the hungriest of appetites."

For three days, we did not leave her house, and as always, she calmed me, fed me and loved me until I needed nothing else. I told her of our adventures and of the many new places I had seen and experienced. I told her of my family and our town, of the wild places we had visited and of all the new churches that I saw.

"Christianity is coming fast," she mused. "Perhaps not here for a while – but it will come. We cannot stop it, and maybe we don't want to. Is there room in our lives for all our gods? By the way, is there a gift for me in that little bag you brought with you?"

I left the house and was soon striding back up the hill towards the castle, bathed, cleaned and nourished in body and soul. Torstein fell into step beside me as we climbed the hill.

"You look better than you did a few days ago," he said.

"Which is more than I can say for you, but that's what the love of a good woman will do for you," I chided.

"I don't know any good women, Bjorn, only very bad ones," he said.

We marched through the gates and on to our new home – the barracks of the *Baldrs Wrath* Company. Our 'new' recruits – the fifty men of the Ravens who manned the Drakes Head, were now installed. Ubbi had released them into my charge with his blessing but not without a little grumbling, for he would need to replace the men before our campaign next spring. My quarters were set aside from the main barracks, and I had a small room of my own to the rear of the hall where I now sat with my cousin.

"Now Torstein, where are we going to get four hundred and fifty new Jomsvikings from?" I asked him

"Let me think on that one, Captain," he replied, almost, respectfully.

The answer came the next day when four ships from Bergen appeared at the harbour entrance. All suitable men of Norwegian blood would be considered for service in the *Baldrs Wrath* company, as the Commander felt this would give our new unit a shared spirit of comradeship. We devised a system of tests which each recruit needed to pass before his induction was considered. There were tests in weapons skills and proficiency with sword, axe and spear, as well as single and group combat trials. If we were still unsure about any of the recruits, they would have to face Torstein in single combat, and although none could best him, we considered those who proved themselves worthy adversaries. In truth, many men came and fought in our square for the honour of joining us, but few were chosen. Of the boats from Bergen, we chose only the crew of a single ship while telling the others to join our force as auxiliaries in the spring.

It was still late in the summer and ships came into the harbour full of men who wanted to be recruited. Each man, lured by the promise of wealth and reputation, was severely tested. Their skill and prowess with weapons were scrutinised on the training square, and I witnessed many feats of outstanding skill with all manner of weapons. Their tactics in the *skjaldborg* went under the most rigorous of examinations. Many of those fortunate in coming through were rewarded with a bout of axe- or swordplay with our fiercely competitive champion who took not a single backward step.

For the rest of the late summer until the waning of the next moon our fortress rang to the sound of blade on blade, of colliding shields, and of men breaking on the ranks of others. The sound of men training at arms, the noise of the blacksmiths, creating weapons and armour at their forges, added to the din. By the time our trials were over, we had recruited enough men for our Commander's satisfaction.

There was no lull in activity during the winter months that followed. Instead of the customary fallow period for the men, up to and after Yuletide we ranged far along the Baltic Coast, in search of conflicts to test these new warriors in the furnace of battle. Many an unsuspecting nest of pirates felt the heat of these new 'winter Jomsvikings' as they became known. Back in the castle, where once our men had wandered the immense emptiness within its walls, our numbers now exceeded two thousand warriors – double the number earlier in the year.

"Will we be ready, Bjorn Spear Arm?" asked the Commander of me one evening high on the castle walls.

"Lord, we will. With these numbers and those of our allies, we will have more than one hundred and fifty ships, and King Harald has promised to match them with the same number. Yes, Lord, I believe we will be ready."

"Ah, the Danes. So much rests upon the Danes. Let us pray the *Norns* do not cut the King's cords."

In years gone by, the winter months passed slowly with the boats and men laid up for the season. That winter was different, for it became a frenzy of activity with the ceaseless comings and goings, in and around the castle, as we made ready for spring and the voyage to Sweden. The Commander continually monitored preparations from his solitary position high on the battlements, and when things quietened for the night he would remain there, looking out beyond the harbour to the sea as if willing the promised ships to come early. The company of *Baldrs Wrath* gradually grew in strength and although the influx of new recruits slowed as the first frosts came, we soon numbered five hundred men in our barracks alone. Many had come from Norway, but we were also joined by warriors from all over Scandinavia, Fresia, Ireland and even England, all driven by the desire for plunder and reputation. Spending the winter in Jomsborg meant that during much of my free time I could visit Astrid, which was always a comfortable alternative to the drafty barracks in the castle.

"You have done well for yourself, Bjorn," she would say. "I am as proud of you as any woman could be, so let us just enjoy our time together and not share our plans with the gods, for they will only change them."

While I spent my limited spare time with Astrid, Torstein spent most of his – and his silver – drinking in the town's alehouses where he would hold court with our new men. He was always popular among the warriors and the whores, and he was held in ever increasing standing as a fighter and a skald. As our company's champion, he had a reputation to uphold, and although fighting with other Jomsvikings was against our code, he always managed to indulge in healthy competition with the other companies. We were, of course, very close, and he never chided me for spending my time with Astrid rather than joining him at his recreation. He owed her his life, and they shared a healthy regard for one another. When my duties at the fort prevented me from taking her fuel or food, he would always go in my stead. Thankfully, our time in this cold, inhospitable season sped past.

One day, Torstein and I were seated in front of the fire in his favourite tavern.

"How do you think it will go?" he asked, casually, of our coming expedition.

"We are more than prepared, but without the Danes it will be hard," I replied.

"What does the Commander tell you of the forces of King Eric?"

"Not much. Only that they are many in number, perhaps

ten to fifteen thousand, and they have a fierce reputation," I said.

"He said nothing of King Eric's wife, then?" he asked, watching me take the bait.

"No, nothing. What of it?"

I had met Styrbjorn's wife, Tyra, in Denmark, but I knew of no other women in his life. For the three years or so that I had known him, I had never seen him in the company of other women. I had no knowledge on any involvement with the Queen of Denmark! Torstein saw that he had my attention, and I looked up at him, encouraging him to continue.

"I have heard some very interesting news from one of the new men," he said in a low voice. "This man is of the Svear, and his father was in the court of King Eric. After the Commander was banished from Sweden for his violent past he ranged for years as a pirate all around the Baltic achieving a great following."

"Yes, we all know that," I said impatiently.

"So, then he received word that King Eric wanted a reconciliation and had him invited back to court to spend time feasting and drinking with his people. The Commander accepted and sailed his ships back to Sweden where he was welcomed with open arms. In fact, it was rumoured he was to be offered half the kingdom of Sweden. However, the King had a beautiful young wife, Siegrid, who bewitched our Commander, and their friendship grew. One night this woman came to Styrbjorn in his rooms unbidden and lay with him until morning. They were discovered, and Eric, not best pleased, banished Styrbjorn for a second time – this time on pain of death. Queen Siegrid's story is that she was taken by force, but everyone knew that she gave herself willingly. Ever since, this enmity has grown between the two men, and over the years the King never forgave his wife for her part in the matter.

"Anyway, many years later, after Styrbjorn took Tyra as

his wife, the two women met when Siegrid was accompanying her husband on a voyage to Denmark. They clashed as only jealous women can, Siegrid accusing Styrbjorn, who was not there, of being a rapist, while Tyra called her rival a witch. When word reached the Commander, none of these accusations or bad blood were ever heard of again, and here we are about to sail to battle. Still, a man has to protect his reputation, does he not? But why is there always a woman involved?"

"Our people have gone to war for far less than the reputation of a slighted woman," I said. "And after all, the Commander is a man like the rest of us. He is flesh and blood. Small wonder there is a feud between him and the King of Sweden. There is also the small matter of King Eric poisoning Styrbjorn's father, Olaf Bjornson, to steal the Swedish throne. I bet you did not know that?"

Torstein nodded. "Yes, there are a few other minor details, but at least we can look forward to the business of plunder to be picked up along the way."

"Of course. Ours is an army that has been expensively gathered, and its wheels will need oiling," I replied, thinking of all the gold that Styrbjorn had 'gifted' his hosts during our long summer voyage.

Our allies, if and when they came, would come to fulfil their oaths of kinship, but also for the prospect of the booty to be won.

"Let us just pray that *Odin* is still with us then," said Torstein, absent-mindedly, for some whores in the tavern were moving towards him and had just taken his attention. But still, I wondered, was our Commander risking everything for such a minor slight from a spurned woman?

Chapter 25: The Battle of Fyrisvellir

Winter passed and spring arrived. There were two thousand Jomsvikings in the castle, and all the new recruits had been inducted, trained and tested. New ships arrived regularly with men from across Scandinavia, from the Orkneys and Ireland. All were welcomed into Jomsborg, and they would fight as our allies. Ubbi took a ship to Denmark to tell the King that we would sail on the feast of Ostara, and good to his word, a hundred and fifty Danish longboats entered the harbour soon afterwards. They arrived to much cheering from the fortress walls. Styrbjorn went down to meet the King of Denmark and bring him into the castle. I stood with Torstein on the castle walls counting the ships – either anchored or tied up, several abreast against the many quays.

"It looks like we are finally ready, Bjorn," he said. "Are you ready for our next great chapter?"

"Let's hope it is not the last one for the 'Wandering Warriors', for our story is deserving of a happy ending and one which needs telling," I said, touching my amulet and saying a silent prayer to Thor.

We stood, looking out over the harbour in silence, each man lost in his own thoughts. Footsteps behind us broke my reverie. It was Styrbjorn, walking the ramparts with his visitor, the King of Denmark.

"You have met these men before, I believe," said the Commander to his guest.

"Yes of course," said the King. "Who could forget the words of your warrior skald or the throwing skills of this man – Bjorn Spear Arm, I believe."

We bent our heads in the King's direction.

"And who is now captain of the company of *Baldrs Wrath*," said the Commander. "Watch for them in battle, for where they lead, others will follow." Then, turning to me, he said wryly, "Have we enough men, Bjorn, now the Danes are here?"

I seldom heard our Lord Commander make a joke, but today he seemed in fine, good humour, relishing the battle ahead.

"More than enough," I answered. "Seventeen score ships carrying Scandinavia's best warriors should suffice."

"We shall give King Eric's army more than a bloody nose, I suspect," rejoined Torstein.

"Very well, then, until the morning," said Styrbjorn.

He led the King away as we continued to watch the frantic preparations down in the harbour below. There were now three hundred and forty longships lying at anchor or beside the wharf, the sides of each festooned with the shields of Norse warriors from a dozen countries. These men had answered our call and were bound to us by oaths, alliances and the rich promise of plunder. It would be the largest fleet ever to leave Jomsborg – or even Scandinavia – and if we could reach the shores of Sweden in one piece, I felt sure that victory would be ours.

We left our place high on the castle walls, and I went down into the town to bid Astrid farewell, at least, for the present. She said little, but as always when I left her to fight, she was a little withdrawn, but hugged me fiercely and pushed me out of the house. I trudged back to the castle for the last night before we left.

At first light I was on the forecastle of the Drakes Head with Torstein, surveying the other ten ships of Baldrs Wrath, each vessel bristling spears, axes and excited men, each with their private thoughts of what lay ahead. The huge warship Ironbeak, with the Commander in his familiar position on his ship's poop deck, rowed through a narrow channel between the stationary ships to a huge fanfare of cheering and the clashing of weapons against shields. Our journey had begun.

We planned to sail the fleet partway along the Baltic coast

where we would be joined by the ships of several Wendish princelings, and from there sail across the Baltic directly to Sweden with some eighteen thousand warriors. I had been given the Drakes Head to command, from which I would lead the company of *Baldrs Wrath*. The Lord Commander would be leading our host from his great warship, the Ironbeak, the biggest ship in the fleet, some seventy paces long and carrying one hundred and twenty warriors.

On reaching the coast of Sweden we would harry all the lands on our way to Uppsala for our confrontation with King Eric. Raiding these towns along the way would cause panic among the local population who would either flee inland or, more likely, turn north to seek protection from their King. Groups of ships would take it in turn to land and attack the local settlements on the way, fanning the flames of panic and causing a storm of people fleeing north. We would sail north and enter Sweden through the vastness of its lakes and islands to the west, then disembark and march on Uppsala and the enemy host.

The sight of this massive collection of ships bearing along the Swedish coast caused panic ashore. The Ironbeak, in full sail with the image of a raven's wings emblazoned on its sheet, followed by hundreds of longships, created terror in every coastal town and village we passed. The raiding parties went ashore killing and looting almost everything they found, but careful to leave a few survivors to tell the tale. In this fashion, we made our way north. At night the fleet beached, and we made a massive camp that engulfed the shoreline for as far as the eye could see. In the morning we would be back at sea with the Ironbeak leading this devastating procession, stopping at the next town we encountered to dispense death and destruction.

"I'll bet King Eric is looking forward to seeing us," said Torstein, as we passed yet another smoking ruin of a settlement. It gave me little pleasure to wreak Styrbjorn's vengeance on these poor folk, but I knew it was a necessary part of our plan.

On day thirteen of our voyage, we arrived at a place where the shoreline became a series of rocky outcrops with many estuaries, and the Ironbeak led us into a huge expanse of water that I discovered was Lake Mälaren.

"Over there," said one of the men pointing north, "is Uppsala."

It was dusk by the time all our ships made it through the channel leading into the lake, and our host made camp on the far side. The Commander sent word to all the captains of the Jomsvikings, as well as the leaders of our allies, to meet at his camp. That evening we made our way to him to receive our battle orders. Once we had all arrived, he addressed us.

"My friends, we have travelled far for the moment when the upstart King of Sweden is to be downcast," he said to us. "Those of you that know him will know he is a cheat and a liar who has led his people down the dubious path of Christianity only to feather his nest. The haughty bitch Queen, Siegrid, has for too long beckoned his allies to lie between her legs and promise them stolen land. Land that was stolen from me and shall be returned. You, my friends and allies, will receive many grants of land and riches when this battle is done. You may settle your folk in the new land or simply take from it what you wish – but first, we must win it with blood."

The group of commanders murmured their assent and then Styrbjorn revealed his plan. We would row the next day to the other shore. There was a town called Graneburg where we would, at first light, unload our weapons of war and make camp. The next day we would march through a huge forest. On the other side of the forest was a vast plain on which stood the town of Uppsala, and here we would organise and attack. Eric had sent emissaries requesting a meeting, but Styrbjorn had sent them back with another message – that he would burn all of the forests in a blaze that would engulf Uppsala and all the surrounding lands if the King did anything other than meet us on the plain of Fyrisvellir.

The four companies of the Jomsvikings would be in the vanguard of the army with the Danes on one flank and the allied auxiliaries on the other. Our archers and javelin throwers would form up behind the companies of Jomsvikings, and we would then move forward to engage the enemy. Having explained this to his audience, Styrbjorn asked the assembled commanders if they had any questions. There were none, save from that of the King of Denmark.

"I am told that King Eric is expecting a mighty host to join him from the north, perhaps another ten thousand men. We are outnumbered as it is – but if it is the truth then we shall be severely disadvantaged. Have you considered that we might be in danger of losing this battle, and thus the war?" he said.

Styrbjorn was silent for a moment, considering his reply. Finally, he spoke, low and clear, seemingly containing his temper.

"My Lord, King Harold Bluetooth, if your heart fails you, I will not expect to see you on the battlefield. The field is reserved for those who do not fear death and for whom defeat is not an option," answered the Commander.

There was an uncomfortable silence as King Harold turned without deigning to reply and left us. Styrbjorn continued as if nothing had happened.

"Tomorrow, we shall leave at first light. Prepare your men and their weapons, but make no mistake: we shall prevail, for Thor is with us and our cause is just."

He raised his drinking horn and toasted us.

The next morning, we rowed to the other side of the lake and all vessels were beached on the far shore – except those of the Danes. Their ships remained at anchor while the rest of us unloaded and camped in front of the vast and forbidding forest of Mirkwood. Styrbjorn, now in full battle dress and armour, walked among the men encouraging them as he moved. The Danish ships, still in the water merely dropped anchor, their crews remaining on board.

"Fucking Danes," mumbled Torstein, as we unloaded our craft. "I smell a rat."

The Commander, clearly displeased by the Danish tactics, stopped for a moment in front of the Ironbeak that had been pulled clear of the water and called out so all could hear him.

"This is the mightiest army to ever set sail from our shores. You have seen men quail and flee at the mere sight of our ships before so much as an axe was raised. You are all now part of the host of Jomsborg, and your names shall be remembered down the generations for you are about to become part of history. From today I promise you that we shall not take a single step backwards. I will not leave Sweden before we have achieved total victory against the usurper."

Then he took a flaming log from a nearby bonfire and, with great purpose strode up to and threw it into the hold of the Ironbeak. One by one, each of his men took a piece of burning timber and did the same until the flames had taken hold and engulfed the ship. Each of the assembled Jomsvikings watched silently, then I did the same and threw a flaming log into the Drakes Head, as did all of my men, and soon the whole of our fleet was in flames on the sand. Few of the auxiliaries burnt their ships, and neither did I expect them to do so, but we had set down a powerful marker and there could be no doubting our conviction.

"This is going to be a long walk home," said Torstein balefully, and we all looked out to see what the Danes were doing. Some of their ships, about twenty or more, rowed to shore and were dragged up the beach, but most stayed where they were, some one hundred paces away, still anchored in the deep water.

In the morning they were gone.

I reckoned that our fighting strength was still around twelve thousand men, which according to Torstein, should be more than a match for any number of ill-met Goths and Svears.

The departure of most of the Danish fleet was a loss, but it was better that we lost them before the battle than when we reached the field. When the men were fully ready and assembled in their companies, the banners were struck, and the war horns sounded at last. Our army was on the move. Led by Styrbjorn and his bodyguard, all men of the Ironbeak, we followed an ancient path through the dense pine forest to meet the foe.

We marched for most of the day, stopping briefly to eat and rest until I noticed the trees thinning out and we reached open space and the great plain of Fyrisvellir. We were not alone. The great army of King Eric was waiting there, and we stopped some distance away from them in our battle formation. The depleted Danish flank was balanced with a large contingent of warriors from Ireland and the Orkneys. There would be no battle tonight, for the evening was getting late and darkness was coming. Bonfires were lit, sentries posted, and we settled down for the night. The hubbub of the pre-battle chatter eventually died away, and men were left alone with their thoughts, wondering what the morning would bring. I fell into a deeply troubled sleep and dreamed I was alone in the forest of Mirkwood standing sentinel over Torstein's dead body against a pack of howling wolves, moving ever closer to feast on us both.

The morning could not come soon enough, and I awoke under a clear blue sky. We were part of a large encampment stretching out on the left and right. The Jomsvikings all slept out in the open, as did the Commander, but many of the auxiliaries favoured skin tents that resembled a great field of mushrooms stretching away to each side of us. Within the time taken to don our armour, the army was in position. The four Jomsviking companies arrayed in neat little squares of five hundred men apiece, while on each of our flanks were thousands of auxiliaries. On the other side of the field, the Swedish host held a scruffy, undulating line, the end of which I could not see. The two armies regarded each other like two fighting dogs held back by the collar before being let loose to attack. Suddenly, a strong, deep, resonant voice struck up in song from within the ranks of the *Baldrs Wrath*. It was Torstein singing out in a voice that caught on the wind and carried not only to the outer edges of our lines but to the ranks of the enemy, thousands of paces in front of us.

We stand by the mighty Yggdrasil
The biggest and best of all trees
and beneath its spreading branches
We prepare to fight next to our brothers
For to die with a great reputation
Is better than an unknown lifetime

Our war drums picked up the rhythm, and the men started singing the battle song which echoed around and across the plain. The volume grew, and the drums pounded defiantly – then there was silence.

Two men from Eric's army stepped out from their lines and stood in the open ground between the two armies. They were dressed identically, armoured from head to foot, and each wearing long mail shirts and enormous helms that accentuated the men's size. They looked like giants standing in the centre ground, armed with round shields and long swords.

One of them shouted at our lines: "Back to Wendland with you, you sons of whores, before your blood stains our sacred land. We do not want to kill you or your man-loving lord, Styrbjorn, who comes as a barefoot beggar with his buttocks shining through his breeches, eager to be ploughed."

The courage of the Swedish line was visibly lifted, and they whooped with laughter at the insults their champion shouted at us. As the two Swedish warriors took the applause from their own lines, Leif Iron Fist stepped out from Styrbjorn's bodyguard dressed only in a pair of woollen breeches and carrying his huge double-bladed battle axe over his shoulder. Our war drums beat out a steady refrain as Leif walked calmly towards Eric's champions. They, in turn, stood poised to meet him, crouching low behind their shields, long swords held high over the top. Leif looked like a giant, his heavily muscled body tattooed with all manner of wild animals and ancient runes. When he was but a few paces away from Eric's men he whipped the massive axe through the air as if it was a child's toy and smote the nearest one such a blow that it split his shield in two. His other opponent rushed at Leif who stepped aside nimbly, avoiding the man's wildly swinging sword. With the return stroke of his swinging axe, Leif caught his adversary a glancing blow on the side on his helm. The man staggered sideways, lost his footing, and went sprawling to the ground. The first man, now shield-less, and with his arm dangling uselessly at his side, turned to face our champion, like a boy before a grown man. The Swede missed with several hastily delivered strikes, and Leif responded with an enormous swing of his axe, cleaving the man's head from his shoulders. Having recovered his balance, the remaining opponent moved forward to attack. For such a huge man, Leif moved with incredible speed, easily avoiding the Swede's sword thrusts and attempted strikes. Then, as if bored with the contest, he moved forward onto his wounded opponent, crashing his axe down on the man and splitting the helm and head to the shoulders. The Swede crumbled to the ground like a deer speared through the heart. With little effort, Leif retrieved his axe from the man's head before beheading him too. A huge roar went up from our lines as our champion held up both the heads of his defeated enemies before tossing them in the general direction of the now-becalmed Swedish lines. Beside me, Torstein mumbled his appreciation as if to himself.

"Not bad, but he took his time dispatching those two deviants. It seems like one Jomsviking is worth at least two Swedes," he growled.

Styrbjorn then stepped out in front of his army and turned to address them. He was bareheaded and walked up the lines of his men who cheered their war leader and beat on their shields.

"This is the day when we clear the field of these useless Swedes. Follow me into battle men, you will never fight alone. Cry 'onward, onward Styrbjorn's men' and your brothers shall be at hand."

He repeated this message as he moved along the lines stopping occasionally to exhort the men to even greater excitement. Then, as if by some hidden signal, the berserkers of the Orkneys and the Norwegians stepped out from our flanks, and like Leif Iron Fist, naked save for their breeches, they rushed headlong at the enemy line now only a few hundred paces away from us.

This then was the signal for the battle to begin, and on the order of *svinfylking*, my men joined with the company of Ravens next to us and a thousand men formed a moving wedge of warriors that marched steadily towards the heart of the Swedish line. With the strongest warriors to the fore, our 'swines head' hit the centre of the Swedish shield wall, which buckled and gave way under the impact. Our axemen at the front, pulled down opposing shields with long-handled weapons while spearmen behind them exploited the gaps created. Archers and javelin throwers dispensed a deadly fusillade from within the centre of our moving mass. I knew that by now the companies of Thor's Hammer and *Odin*'s Wrath would also be advancing, as would our allies on the flanks, but it was difficult to tell for in the heat of battle a warrior can only concentrate on what is before him. Whenever our advance was checked, the persistent cry of onward, onward Styrbjorn's men echoed along our lines as we fought step-by-step ever closer to Uppsala and whatever fate the *Norns* had decided for us.

Within one *eykt*, the battle horns of the Swedes sounded, and their lines retreated swiftly away from us. Fearing a trap, word passed down the line not to pursue our enemies as they turned and fell back in the direction of Uppsala. Instead we stopped, having no one left to fight, and reformed our companies. It was time to take stock, for the enemy was not yet defeated but resting before we hit them again. The fighting had been intense, and as the battle raged all around us, we inched slowly forward.

"There is plenty more fight to come from those bastards," growled Torstein, beside me. Unscathed, save for a few cuts and bruises, we were alive and both welcomed the lull in the battle. Thralls came amongst us with jugs of ale and carried those who were heavily wounded from the field. Bodies of the Swedes and our own men lay on the ground all around us, and although our advance had been barely a hundred paces, the enemy had paid a high price, their dead littering the battlefield in great profusion. There was no more fighting that day. Although many felt we had gained the upper hand on the first engagement, we knew the greatest fighting was yet to come.

Our camp moved forward to the very point where Eric had stood with his forces at the start of the day. It was a small victory, but we carried the day and our banners flew a little closer to Uppsala. The thralls of the Swedes were allowed on the field to retrieve two thousand of their dead and dying warriors. Our losses were much lower in comparison – some three hundred men. The fighting had been brutal; possibly as hard as I had known, and every step we had taken forward was paid for with buckets of blood and many lives.

After we had broken their shield wall their forces descended into chaos as our order and discipline took over and we slashed and hacked our way into their ranks. The first engagement was won, but there was no rejoicing yet, and the war was far from over. After I accounted for the losses to *Baldrs Wrath* – twenty men dead and eleven unable to continue – I went to sit with my comrades as the thralls brought us food and drink. The evening came on us quickly. Fires were lit and exhausted men stretched out on the ground and slept where they lay next to their weapons. The next morning would arrive all too quickly.

Chapter 26: Death or Glory

Our dead warriors were removed from the field, and we envied them, for their entrance to Valhalla was assured. The huge fires built far behind our lines consumed their earthly bodies and sent their spirits to the hall of the warriors. Here, in *Odin*'s splendid palace, they would sit and drink with their fallen comrades and foes, feasting on wild boar flesh, their bodies made whole again. For us, the living, our task was a simple one: to break the stubborn will of the Swedes and take Uppsala. Yesterday's fighting was hard and uncompromising, and we had pushed them back but without breaking them. I was called to a meeting of the captains just before first light.

Overnight, a band of warriors had come into our makeshift camp led by *Jarl* Wolf, an old friend of Styrbjorn. He led three hundred men and had been in the service of King Eric, but disillusioned by the thought of fighting his kinsman, he switched sides. He marched all night and his clothes carried the dirt and grime from the journey, but he came with news.

"You caused King Eric some pain yesterday," he said, "but he is far from finished. He has men coming from the North, perhaps as many as five thousand. They will be here by nightfall."

"Tell them what else, Wolf," said Styrbjorn, "of the little surprise he has planned for us today."

"Your lines will be attacked by a herd of cattle, driven at you in their thousands," said Jarl Wolf. "The King is terrified of defeat, and another day like yesterday will break his forces. He needs time for more men to come and believes your shield walls will not be able to repel a few thousand Aurochs on the charge."

The captains looked at one another in bemusement for a

few moments, and then Ubbi spoke up.

"I have fought against such a tactic before in Miklagard with the old Emperor's Varangians. We once faced a herd of wild cattle driven at us by Moorish forces. We reckoned there were about five thousand of them all told. So, we formed *svinfylking*s, and the beasts ran between our companies and passed us. Such a charge could cause us problems, but it can easily be countered."

"Then go back to your men, captains," said the Commander. "You have heard what is coming. The beasts will surely be aimed at the vanguard in our centre. Once this little diversion is over, we will continue our advance to victory. Another day or so and the field will surely be ours – especially if Eric is relying on cattle to give him victory! Now let us hurry for they will be on us soon."

The captains returned to their companies, and we prepared our men. As soon as we saw the line move, we would form our 'swine's heads', strongest men to the front, javelin throwers in the centre, and divert the on-rushing animals should they come. Torstein looked at me in disbelief.

"This is some joke surely. I came here to kill Swedes, and you are telling me I now have to fight cows!" he exclaimed loudly.

Some of the men around him laughed, but you could see the concern on the faces of others. The Auroch was a fierce beast, never completely tamed; it was the height of a man at its shoulder with a head that had two sharp and vicious horns. Wealthy men kept them in large roaming herds, for they needed much space in which to live.

"On my order," I told them, "we shall form up into our *svinfylking*, javelins in the centre. When they come, they must be diverted through the lines."

Our forces readied themselves and lined up to face the enemy who were some two thousand paces away. Our banners were snapping in the early morning breeze and we, like our

233

foes, waited for the first engagement of the day. Behind their lines there was movement, and a huge cloud of dust enveloped the Swedish lines, parting in their centre with men rushing to get out of the way of what was coming towards us. It started with a far-off rumble and grew louder and louder until suddenly the gap was filled with thousands of enraged beasts heading straight towards us, driven on by the whips of the enemy thralls.

Our companies rushed to get in formation, no man waiting for a second invitation. Torstein and several of the larger, heavier warriors of *Baldrs Wrath* crouched at the point of the 'nose'. Their spears dug into the ground and their shields held high and slanted. I stood behind the first ranks with the javelin throwers and looked over to the Ravens and Thor's Hammer on each side of us, each with a gap of fifty or more paces between them. The rumble turned to a roar and the ground began to shake as the maddened animals pounded towards us. The javelin throwers hurled their weapons, bringing down some of the Aurochs to the fore and causing those following to fall. Closer and closer they came until at the last moment the herd swerved and headed for the gaps between the companies and away from us. The Ravens were similarly avoided but several beasts ploughed straight into the front ranks of Thor's Hammer where they were brought down and slaughtered by the frenzied work of several axemen. The danger from the charge was over in an instant, and I looked up towards the enemy line which was now advancing at pace.

I prepared to issue the command to advance but before the words passed my lips, the Commander was standing in front of us shouting, "Onward, onward Styrbjorn's men." He raced ahead of his bodyguard, who struggled to keep up with him, and ran headlong into the oncoming enemy line at the point where King Eric's banners flew. We, in turn, raced after him as did every man under his command, and there followed a deafening noise as our twelve thousand shields crashed into the Swedish host.

The companies of the Jomsvikings arrived together, and with our allies on each flank, we battered away at the enemy front. Eric's line bent but having learnt their lessons from yesterday they held firm. The Swedish reinforcements had arrived and their effect in strengthening their battle lines was obvious. It was man against man now, and the hewing and slashing continued through to midday and beyond. Styrbjorn moved relentlessly up and down the line and seemed like a man possessed, striking out to where the fighting was thickest. He fought with undisguised fury and led his men seeking out the standard of King Eric, cleaving his way through the massed ranks of Swedes. I lost sight of the Commander on more than one occasion as I led my men forward, and with Torstein at my shoulder, we took the fight to them. It was way into the afternoon when, finally, I felt the enemy ranks buckle and step back a pace or two. Torstein felt it too, for I heard a triumphal note in his voice. He seemed to redouble his efforts as the vast wall of men and shields visibly fell back, and a gap between the two armies grew. The Swedes did not turn and run, but instead they fell back a little, retreating away as a single unit until there was a gap of about fifty paces between us. Some our warriors continued to beat at the enemy line, but in truth we were exhausted from our efforts, and all around me men sucked in the air, panting and wheezing like blown horses. Thralls ran among our men, carrying drink to the thirsty warriors; thus refreshed, they resumed their battle positions – weary, yet ready to continue.

Styrbjorn, now bareheaded, seemingly unharmed but covered in the blood of the vanquished, strode along our lines speaking to us. He exhorted every man to continue to take the fight forward, picking out friends or singling out warriors for particular acts of bravery. At his side stood his bodyguards, not quite as fresh as the Commander, and suffering the effects of the intense fighting. Our auxiliaries had played their part to the full, and behind us the path of our advance was thick with the bodies of our fallen allies from many different countries.

"Your valour and courage on this field today will live long in the hearts and minds of those who remain. I promised you riches and glory and it is well within our grasp," cried Styrbjorn. He raised his great double-bladed battle axe and pointed to Upsalla in the far distance. "Tomorrow we shall be through their gates and the country will be ours."

Our men responded with cheering, for they knew there was no finer war leader than Styrbjorn, and if anyone was to lead us to victory it was going to be him. He turned his attention to the battered army of his enemy, and after ordering his bodyguard to remain in place, strode out into the space between the two forces, with only Thorkill the Tall for company, and faced them.

"Men of the Svear and the Goths, warriors of Sweden, you have fought us long and hard, but you cannot defeat us. For two days now we have fought, and you have been pushed back. We have captured your baggage and supplies and tonight we will sleep in your tents and drink your ale. If you fight us again tomorrow, we will push you back even further and soon we shall be at the gates of Uppsala. We have killed you in your thousands and shall continue until not one of you stands alive. You have a choice – stand against us and die or lay down your arms and go home."

There was no sound from the lines of the Swedish army, just the snapping of the banners and pennants as they caught in the wind. A gap appeared in front of King Eric's sigil and six men, clad only in breeches, carrying spears and shields, ran out and raced towards the two Jomsvikings. Styrbjorn raised a hand to stay his bodyguard who were running forward to protect him, and raising his axe and shield, he waited calmly to meet the foe. They were Eric's berserkers – men who, when released, rushed fearlessly into the heart of battle with great fury and with no concern for their own safety. Now, howling like animals, they sprinted towards the Commander and his captain. The first one to arrive lunged with his spear at the

Commander who moved aside with great agility. Styrbjorn countered by bringing the steel rim of his shield into the man's face with such force that it shattered bone and teeth, killing him instantly. The second berserker also thrust with his spear, missing wildly, but this one was met with a powerful downward strike of the battle axe splitting the man's skull in two and leaving him in a crumpled heap on the ground. Thorkill now entered the fray and parried his attacker's spear thrusts with his sword, and after a struggle lopped the man's head off with several powerful sweeps. It was two men against three now and the fighting was fierce as spears clashed with axe and sword. Despite the two days of fighting, neither of the Jomsvikings showed any sign of weariness, and their iron discipline soon overcame the naked ferocity of the berserkers; the remaining three succumbing to a brutal, unrelenting attack. They crumpled dead at the feet of our two champions. Styrbjorn tapped Thorkill's shield in acknowledgement of their victory. They were both unharmed save for a cut to the side of Thorkill's face. Then, breathing heavily, they stepped over the dead bodies and moved closer to the Swedish lines.

"Lay down your arms, and return to your homes," Styrbjorn called to them, "or tomorrow you will suffer the same fate as these men." Once again, he was met with a silent response, then he turned and walked back towards his army. There would be no more fighting today. The Swedes retired to lick their wounds, while our captains stood down their army and retired to the captured enemy camp.

The men were completely exhausted. Two days of vicious fighting had produced little in the way of gains. We had captured the enemy camp, which provided sustenance and a little comfort to our war-weary men, but beyond that, and killing perhaps five thousand warriors, there had been little ground gained. However, this did not dampen our spirits overly, and there was little complaining beyond the normal moaning of the 'greybeards'. Torstein revelled in the fighting and was living the role he had been born for, proving quick to revive any flagging spirits he found in our company. The Swedes had lost many men, probably five times our losses, but they were proving to be worthy opponents who were both hardy and obstinate. Not a single man among us was unscathed. Each carried at least one wound from the fighting, although most carried their pain in silence. There was great optimism in the camp, and we felt the enemy would crack before long. Another day would do it.

"If it wasn't for those cowardly Danes, we would be in Uppsala by now," Torstein said spitting on the ground before downing even more captured Swedish ale.

That night a huge fire was built in the middle of the camp and sacrifices to Thor were made. The captured thralls of the Swedes, those that had been driving the cattle, were brought out and hanged from a nearby tree, while Styrbjorn implored Thor to give us victory the next day. His voice was strong and powerful, and it carried on the evening breeze so that men on the outer reaches of our camp could hear him.

"In your name, Thor, we give sacrifice that you shall grant us victory over our enemies tomorrow." Once again, the men roared their approval and banged on their shields with weapons – a sound that would be heard in Uppsala. I held my amulet and gave out a quieter prayer to *Odin* for a swift victory in the morning.

Chapter 27: The Final Day of Battle

The next day was misty on the plain of Fyrisvellir. It was very early morning when I awoke, and I could see little in front of me. I roused Torstein who came to like an angry bear.

"Get the men ready, Torstein. Today we shall have our victory," I said.

"Then, let us hope Thor was listening last night," he grunted, and we both set out to raise our company to arms.

It did not take long, and after a quick meal of bread and ale and a little grumbling, we were ready and in position. The fog was so thick we could not tell who was to our left or right, or even where King Eric's army was. The cooking fires burned some of the fog away, but there was neither sight nor sound from the enemy lines. We sent out scouts, but it seemed as if they had vanished into the fog during the night. Orders were sent out to stand firm until the mist had lifted which it surely would, for the day was getting warm, and there was little point in trying to attack an enemy we could not see. There had been fog on the plain of Fyrisvellir each morning since we arrived there two days before, and each day it had disappeared as the morning wore on. Today was different, and the mist seemed to settle and swirl about us for an age, showing no sign of dispersing. Men shuffled about in their positions as we waited and waited. The creak of leather, the clank of armour or a muffled order were all that could be heard up and down our lines. It was unsettling as we waited, and we were keen to finish the fighting today. That other mist, the 'red mist' of battle, was not something that could be evoked at will.

Much later that morning, the swirling fog lifted, the plain in front of us revealed itself, and all men looked to where King Eric's men had arranged their lines. I expected them to be close to where we had seen them last at nightfall. However, they had fallen further back far across the wide plain to take a position in front of the town of Uppsala in the distance.

"What trick of Floki, is this?" said Torstein to no one in particular.

The Swedish lines had not only moved back to take a defensive position in front of the town, but the size of their host, which we had decimated the day before, now seemed to be much larger.

"Looks like their reinforcements finally arrived," I said quietly.

Torstein turned to me. "It looks like we will just have to walk a little further to kill them today. We must kill them quickly to get the job done."

No one said a word more. The order came to move towards the enemy, and our army walked forward in formation to meet them. The Swedes had retreated further than appeared at first, and it would take some time for us to close with them. We moved forward as a long, unbroken line, the Jomsvikings in the centre and our auxiliaries on the flanks for what I prayed would be the last battle. As we approached the enemy, when we could see the faces of the men who opposed us, their ranks had grown significantly. Yesterday we killed them in their thousands, but now they had been bolstered by many new men. Their line was long, and there were many ranks of warriors waiting for battle, one in front of the next.

"They will still die, as they have done for the last two days," shouted Torstein to his comrades around him, his great booming voice carrying some distance.

Our Lord Commander leading his army across the plain this morning raised his arm, and the advance stopped two hundred paces from our enemies. There was no need for speeches or prayers to Thor this morning, for each man of us knew what had to be done. The four companies of Jomsvikings joined together and formed into the familiar Boar's Head but with a single intention – to splinter the enemy and finish the battle. We moved to close with King Eric's men, and each of us braced himself for the collision, which did not come as I had ever imagined it.

Our allies also rushed forward in their lines to join the assault. Suddenly, the men at the apex of our 'wedge' started to fall. In the confusion of their falling, the men behind them started to fall, until our tight formation began to buckle and falter. We had run, pell-mell, into a concealed trench that had been dug along the length of the enemy line and now men were falling over bodies and equipment as they plunged into the trap before them. All along our line, the moving wall of shields was breaking, and men were going down. Some managed to struggle to their feet, and in their frantic efforts to recover shields and weapons, they were met by the men behind them as they fell too. It was chaos as thousands of men stumbled and fought to recover themselves.

I struggled to prevent myself from falling as the trench, deep as a man's height and wide, took its toll. It was not a deadly obstacle but a simple enough distraction, and its effect on our charge was devastating, stopping us in our tracks. I looked at our enemy, but they had not moved forward to take advantage of the confusion, and I quickly discovered why. I heard the whistling from above as thousands of arrows fell from the sky. I raised my shield to ward off several as they found their target, as did the men around me. Others were not so well prepared, and many, prostrate on the ground and trying to get up, were hit. This hail of arrows continued for some time, and the effect was devastating with hundreds of our men falling around me. By now I had cleared the trench, rallied the men, and we tried to form up once more. The rate of arrows had slowed now to a trickle but was still effective, and I looked over my shield at the enemy. They were advancing towards our disintegrated formations and unleashing a fusillade of javelins, which struck true as they drew closer.

I looked for Styrbjorn and saw him beyond the trench

rallying a hundred or so men around his banner. They gathered themselves together, and he led them in a furious charge at the oncoming Swedes. There were several pockets of us who, emerging from the confusion and devastating volley, banded together in small groups and moved forward again.

"Onward, onward Styrbjorn's men," I shouted, relieved to find Torstein was still at my shoulder. We followed the Commander's banner into the seething mass of men and weapons in front of us. All semblance of order was gone, and our formation was destroyed. Such was our discipline, and despite the odds turning against us, we were still taking the battle to the enemy. We fought on but it was now man against man, and every time an enemy warrior fell in front of me there were ten more to take his place.

The tide of the battle turned irreversibly, and we failed to recover from our earlier setbacks. We were beaten back, and the number of men around me gradually whittled down as Eric's army, sensing the moment of victory was upon them, poured forward in a relentless tide of steel. Thorkill fought his way over to our group.

"Bjorn, there are few of us left now. The Commander and his bodyguard have been killed," he shouted. "I saw them heading towards King Eric's banner, and then they were lost to us. He is gone, and we should leave this place. There is no dishonour, and if we stay we shall all perish."

I nodded and called to those remaining men of *Baldrs Wrath* to follow me. With Torstein and Thorkill to the fore, we turned and left the field. We had to fight hard to get away for there were enemies on each side of us now, and with every thrust of an enemy spear or hack of an axe, more of us fell.

The Jomsvikings who fought on numbered no more than three hundred men, and unless we got away there would soon be none. Our allies had fled the field some time before, and the vanguard of our army, Styrbjorn's four companies, had been left to fight on alone. Desperate men can always find hidden strength from somewhere, and beset by our foes on all sides, we hacked our way clear until the Swedes around us became fewer. A huge roar went up from our enemy and I turned to see Styrbjorn's head being paraded on a stick for the victorious army to cheer.

"It looks like Thor has deserted us today," shouted Torstein. "Come, cousin, we have much work to do. Let us live to fight another day. I am not ready for Valhalla just yet."

All Swedish eyes looked towards the spectacle behind us as we fled the battlefield as fast as we could.

There was little dignity in our flight, and so overjoyed was the triumph of Eric's army that we escaped and were not impeded beyond a few idly flung spears at our backs. It was now a race back the way we had marched so confidently only a few days before. We ran through our deserted camp, scooping up anything we found. Food and drink were our main need, for we had toiled on the plains of Fyrisvellir without sustenance all day. We marched onwards to the forest of Mirkwood which would give us refuge at least for one night. It was getting dark as we entered the trees, three hundred-odd survivors of the great army, in retreat. We were bloodied, battered and defeated, but we were still alive, and Valhalla would have to wait a little longer for us to come.

Chapter 28: The Flight of the Jomsvikings

We moved deeper into the forest, back along the path we had taken four days earlier. Unable to take another step, we settled in the trees away from the main track. Every man carried battle wounds of varying degrees, and we were all utterly exhausted. Those with food and drink shared what they had, and without another word each man fell asleep where he lay on the forest floor.

I woke up early the next day and looked around me. Men lay where they had dropped the night before, their weapons and shields about them. There were a few like me who were on their feet, stretching out and waking their sleeping comrades. I saw Thorkill, a short distance away moving quickly among the men and rousing those around him from their slumber. I went over to him, and he turned towards me.

"We must gather the men and move quickly, Bjorn. Eric will be sending his army after us, and there is no time to lose. Get everyone on their feet, and we will leave," he commanded.

Thorkill looked, as I probably did, filthy and bloodied. His mail shirt was rent in several places, and he carried a deep gash across his face. We were the last two Jomsborg captains left alive. He had been Styrbjorn's right-hand man, and he was now the leader of what was left of us – at least for today.

"We must reach Graneburg by this evening and take what we need there. We will take the remaining boats and leave this accursed place," he said.

It was a simple enough plan, and if we could get to the lake by nightfall, we might yet make our escape. Quietly, men were waking all around us, and those who could, staggered to their feet and prepared to leave. There were a few who had died in their sleep from their wounds; those we left where they had fallen, without ceremony. The rest of us made for the road, and with all haste went as fast as we were able, back the way we had come. I took Torstein to the rear of our bedraggled company ensuring that any stragglers did not fall too far behind, cajoling and encouraging as best we could. We lost several men throughout the day whose wounds simply prevented them from taking another step, leaving them on the side of the road to breathe their last.

Stopping only once that day to share the last of our food, we made surprisingly good progress. We reached the edge of the forest well before nightfall at the small town of Graneburg on the shores of Lake Malaren. It was early evening, and the town lay between us and the remaining longboats – those that Styrbjorn had not burned. When we landed many days ago our army had left the town alone, for it was a small, insignificant place that had been of little interest to us. Now it was a different matter, for we were desperate men who had eaten little for many days, and we would march in and take what we needed.

Summoning up the last of our energy we fell upon Graneburg like wolves. After crushing any resistance and killing the few men who attempted to stop us, we emptied the town of every last morsel of food. It was bitter, cruel work on this small community of perhaps two hundred people, but it was necessary if we were to survive, and no mercy was shown to anyone who put up a fight. Taking what we could carry, we left as quickly as we had arrived and headed towards the boats on the beach and, hopefully, our flight across the lake. The blackened remains of the Jomsborg fleet lay where we had left them, but a little further down the shoreline were many craft that had belonged to some of our allies. They would be more than enough to take us home.

"How far can we get tonight, Bjorn?" asked Thorkill.

"Far enough to take us out of danger," I replied. "Just take the best boats. We should leave without delay, for I sense we will soon have company. But first, we must scuttle the rest of the ships."

I pointed back to the edge of the forest where, even in the twilight, we could see men emerging from the trees in large numbers. Between us, we split the men up into groups of fifty or so, launched the boats into the water and left without delay. We rowed as hard as our battered bodies would allow. Torstein marshalled the men onboard, and I took the helm of our boat, a simple but rugged Wendish craft that I prayed would take us home to safety. In great haste, our little fleet of six ships left the shore, and its beaten crews hauled us away and clear of the danger at our heels. With our ship in the lead, I steered a course out the way we had come, and in the last glimmer of daylight, I watched our pursuers become smaller and smaller figures on the shore until we could no longer see them. By the time it was dark we had reached the far side of the lake where I felt safe enough to drop anchor and wait until morning.

The cry of the seabirds brought me awake, back from a dream in which I was with Turid in the little house on the cliffs above Byrum. I had fallen asleep at the helm, and I opened my eyes to find Torstein standing directly in front of me. The dirt and dried blood encrusted in his hair and face gave him a frightening appearance, but he had a broad smile across his face.

"You were dreaming cousin. I think you must have been somewhere pleasant, for you were sighing like a blacksmiths furnace," he said.

I grinned back, and we started to laugh until the ribs that had been broken by a Swedish axe two days ago brought me back to the present. I had also received a blow to the side of the head and was completely deafened in one ear. Torstein also carried several raw battle scars. He had been hit by two arrows in the shoulder, a spear thrust in the thigh, and his mail shirt was in tatters from the numerous blows. The arrows had been snapped off at the shaft leaving the stubby wooden ends protruding from his shoulder.

"It is good not to be fighting today, eh?" he said.

We surveyed the wreckage of our crew who had all suffered a variety of battle wounds and were now asleep at their oars or in the belly of the boat.

"It seems we live to fight another day, although I shall not be sad if I don't have to raise my axe today," he continued.

He lifted his left hand to reveal two missing fingers.

"That was not as we had expected. Did you see the Commander fall?" I asked him.

"I followed him and his bodyguard towards Eric's banners. It was hard to keep up with him, and he was fighting like a berserker striking down all who stood in his path. Ubbi was at his shoulder with several of the Ravens. Then I lost sight of him, and the Swedes swallowed them up. That was the last I saw of them both."

We were both quiet for a moment as we reflected on our lost leader.

"It was a brave plan," I said, "and but for the Danes, we might have prevailed. For now, we must lick our wounds and try to get back to Jomsborg. Let us return there whole, if the *Norns* allow it. We still have a great deal of water to cross before we can breathe safely again. We should take this time for a little rest."

He grunted and slumped down beside me, and we both dozed a little longer. I was woken a little later by one of our men shaking my shoulder. It was Leif, the Old Norwegian who had fought beside us for so many years. He looked particularly dishevelled and had lost an eye in the fighting.

"We have company, Bjorn," he said and pointed towards the shore of the lake, about five hundred paces away, which was swarming with Swedish warriors.

They watched us from the water's edge but could do little for they had no boats and we were well out of bowshot. Our six ships had been lashed together overnight and now every man aboard was awake at his oars and ready to go. The ropes tying us together were released, and one by one each crew dipped their oars and rowed for all they were worth. We passed out of sight of the men watching us malevolently from the shore.

Days later we reached the open sea where at last we picked up the sea breezes that filled our sails and blew us back across the Baltic. Glad of the break from rowing the men sat, listless, in their positions with the welcome feel of the sun on their backs. It was a quiet crossing and they talked among themselves reflecting on the disaster that had befallen us and probably, like myself, wondering what the *Norns* had in store for them next.

After twenty days of leaving Swedish soil, we reached the shores of Wendland and the welcome sight of the harbour of Jomsborg. It was no triumphal entry this time, and we dragged ourselves off the ships and limped towards the castle. We were no longer an army, just a rag-tag collection of flotsam and jetsam that had miraculously survived a doomed expedition. Although some of the broken bodies had mended a little during the voyage home, we shared a sense of collective failure and loss. Our mighty fleet of ships had left these shores packed with warriors and led by a man we all admired and respected. His headless body, stripped of its armour and weapons, had been left on the plain of Fyrisvellir with over ten thousand of his army. We, the survivors of the great battle, had nothing to console us, for this was a mighty defeat for the Jomsvikings and one that, but for a little good fortune, might have destroyed us completely. Men's bodies would recover in time, but the effect of such a devastating defeat would haunt us for many years to come.

All six ships made it safely home. More men had died from infection during the passage, but the surviving Jomsvikings, led by Thorkill the Tall, climbed the hill and arrived at the castle gates. The small band of warriors who had been left behind to guard the castle looked at us in wonder and disbelief, and few words were spoken. Of the five hundred men of *Baldrs Wrath*, there were only sixty-seven left.

When we reached our barracks, Torstein was the first to speak.

"At least we have plenty of room now," he said, but nobody laughed, and the men staggered back to their bunks to consider what might have been.

It was time for the healers and apothecaries to do their work, and they had much to do. All of those who returned carried a variety of wounds, great or small, and men broken to this degree needed time to mend. My own body had taken a beating. I had broken bones and two large open wounds on my arms that needed tending urgently. In desperate need of Astrid's healing powers, I left my men in the care of others and walked painfully back down the hill and towards her house early the next morning. When she saw me, she was silent and just pulled me inside.

"Don't speak Bjorn. I will make you well," she said and led me to her bed where we had spent so much time.

"I don't think I will be up to much this morning," I said.

"Hush, my boy," she said. "I will need to concentrate, for I have much work to do."

She made me drink one of her concoctions before my head went down, and I fell into a deep sleep that lasted for many days. During this time, she cut the tattered remnants of clothes from my body, bathed me and tended my wounds. She bandaged my ribs, cleaned and sewed up the cuts to my arms and did her best to mend a host of other injuries about my body. When I woke, she fed me, and then I slept again as soon as I had eaten. Each night she would lay down beside me, and the last thing I remember was the warm touch of her skin. It took me many days and nights to start to heal and recover my strength, but eventually I got better. When, finally, I was awake long enough to hold a conversation with her, I learned that we were not alone, for she had sent to the castle for Torstein. He now lay snoring on a cot on the other side of the room.

"They brought him here yesterday," she said. "He was in

249

much the same state as you were, but it seems that you Norwegians are indestructible, and you will soon be able to try and kill yourselves again."

She brought me food and drink, and after I had wolfed it down, she sat on the bed.

"I am guessing that you have brought me no present this time, Bjorn?" She curled up beside me like a cat and put her head on my chest. She slid her hand below my waist and felt a response. "No damage down there," she said, before pulling her dress over her head and climbing on top of me.

In a few more days, I was able to get up and walk around stiffly. Although it was mending, my body was covered in livid cuts and bruises to which Astrid would apply her ointments and salves each day. Torstein took longer to recover, for the arrowheads that were in his body when he arrived were buried deep and had damaged some of his internal organs. I told Astrid our story, and she listened in silence.

"He was always a reckless, headstrong man, the Commander. You were lucky to return at all," she said, at the end of my tale. "But you are here now, and for that I should thank the *Norns*, for they have cut the cords of most of the men who sailed with you."

We were sitting outside her house in front of her little garden where she grew her plants and herbs. It was now midsummer; the days were growing longer, and the evening air still held some of the warmth of the day. I looked at Astrid, her eyes closed in thought, and noticed she was pale and wan. There was little flesh on her anyway, but now she had lost weight; her skin had a waxy pallor to it and there were dark rings under her eyes. She opened her eyes quickly and caught me looking at her.

"Is there something interesting that you see?" she snapped.

"Just looking at what I had been missing on these long voyages," I replied. She gave a small grunt of disapproval.

"Now you are feeling better, I have a few jobs for you to

do." She nodded towards a pile of logs stacked untidily next to her herb garden. "That should keep you occupied for a while. You have to earn your keep somehow."

Over the next few days, Torstein was also able to get to his feet, and together we set about doing many of the chores around the house that had been left undone for so long. The roof needed repair as did some of the walls, and we worked cutting and joining the wood.

"This makes a nice change from being clattered around the head by Swedish axes," said Torstein, as we sat together on the roof nailing some new tiles into place. "What is next for the Jomsvikings, Bjorn. Do you think they will survive this little set-back?"

I shook my head. "I don't know, Torstein. There are so few of us left now. Enough for a decent war band but not enough to do much more. We are also quite vulnerable now; there will be those who have heard of our downfall and will smell our weakness. We have much gold and silver under lock and key in the stone keep. Plenty to offer temptation to many in these lands."

"Our share of the plunder from these past years is all there, and I saw it before we left. It is a king's ransom, Bjorn, enough for anything we need. More than I could spend on ale and whores in a lifetime," he replied.

"I shall speak with Thorkill in the next days, for we need to have a plan," I said.

"But on no account tell the gods of our plans, for when Styrbjorn shared the last one with Thor he realised that the gods have a strange sense of humour."

In a few days, all the chores had been completed, our bodies were slowly mending, and it was time for me to return to the fortress to check on my men and to see Thorkill. Torstein came with me, and we made a slow journey up to the top of the hill and through the castle gates.

"Do you think Astrid is sick?" he asked as we crested the brow and stood before the postern gate.

"Yes, I believe she is. She tries not to cough when I am there, but I have heard and seen her when she thinks I do not notice," I replied.

"You must look after her, cousin, for she is very dear to me as well as you. She is like a sister — an older sister of course — but a sister, nonetheless. After all who will save my life again if she goes?" said Torstein earnestly.

Together we both walked stiffly past the sentries, through the gates and to our barracks. Inside, it was quiet and almost empty as we moved around this large room surveying the empty cots, remembering the faces of the men who had once lain on them. Einar and Rurik, who had joined us from the Ravens, were both there. Einar had lost an eye and Rurik, recovering from a vicious spear wound to the chest, had been unable to rise since our return. Out of the five hundred men of Baldyr's Wrath only a handful remained, and there was not a man of that number who would be fit to fight for some time to come. Torstein, tired from the exertion of climbing the hill, found his bunk and threw himself down on it while I went in search of Thorkill. I found him in the barrack hall of the Thor's Hammer, sitting down with his men while thralls served them ale. Seeing me enter he called to me.

"Come, Bjorn, take some ale with us. We had given you up for dead. You are recovered from your wounds?"

"I am well, Thorkill. Cuts and bruises, but nothing more. And you?"

"Much the same," he replied, but I saw that he was still heavily swathed in bandages around his chest, and he carried a broken arm in a sling.

"Broken bones can always mend," he said raising a cup full of ale with his good arm and making a toast. "Here is to all our fallen brothers," he continued. The men around the table, about twenty in all, raised their cups, drank and fell silent again.

"Let us walk," he said getting to his feet.

Outside, the square where only weeks ago two thousand

Jomsvikings stood, fully armed and ready for the fight was now deserted except for one or two thralls scurrying, heavily laden to and from the barracks.

Chapter 29: Healing and death

"It might take many years, Bjorn," said Thorkill through clenched teeth, "but I swear vengeance on that Danish coward Harald Blue-Tooth whose actions cost us many thousands of lives as well as victory. If it takes me forever, I shall repay him,"

"Vengeance, yes," I said. "But first we must regather our strength, for right now we are a match for no one and would be hard-pressed to fight anyone. We are easy meat for the smallest of forces."

"I agree," said Thorkill. "We have only a hundred or so men able to bear arms, and the rest will take many months to recover. We must be vigilant at all times. Now tell me true, Bjorn, what are your plans? As one of Styrbjorn's captains you have every right to be the next Commander. He put great store in you as a leader, you know."

"I have no desire to lead the Jomsvikings," I said honestly. "You should be the next Commander, for all men look to you in battle. You have their respect, and they will follow you willingly."

"That is good then," said Thorkill, "and with your support, I shall rebuild and lead the men. For now though, we must heal and mend before we can think about doing anything other than defending ourselves. I value your friendship, brother, for we have fought side by side for some three years now, but if you desire to leave I would not hold you back. You would leave a wealthy man."

"You have my support, Thorkill, but these are early days to decide too much, and we should consider all things, for there is a long winter ahead of us."

"I agree. But for now, we shall just be vigilant and mend as quickly as the gods allow broken men to heal. You remember my brother, Sigvaldi?" he asked.

I nodded, Sigvaldi and Thorkill were the sons of the famous Scanean chieftain Strut-Harold and when we first arrived, they fought side-by-side in the company of Thor's Hammer. Sigvaldi was the younger brother by two years, but both men were tall, strong and fine swordsmen. They were held in high esteem by Styrbjorn and all in Jomsborg. He left with the Commander's blessing and a small company to seek his fortune in the Varangian Guard in the service Emporer Bassil of Miklagard.

"He has fared well?" I asked

"I believe he has," said Thorkill, "but you can ask him yourself, for he and his men will be guested here for Yuletide."

"We have plenty of room at least," I said, "and it will be good to have a few more men."

"For now, though, Bjorn, my orders are to recover and get your men back on their feet. There is no other duty than that."

We shook hands to cement the agreement and went our different ways – he back to his barracks, and me to Astrid's house.

The walk down the hill and through the town seemed to take forever. I found her sleeping in a chair outside her house, a shawl wrapped around her shoulders although the summer sun was warm. Normally when I arrived, she would be on her feet to meet me, but I had surprised her today, as, being asleep, she had not noticed my approach. I watched her for a few moments as she slept. She now looked much older than the woman I had left behind when I went to fight the Swedes. I noticed a few strands of grey in her hair, and her face, still beautiful to me, was showing many more lines than I remembered. As I looked down on her she must have felt my presence, for she awoke with a start.

"I was not expecting you back today," she exclaimed and started to cough uncontrollably, her body doubling up as she struggled for breath.

"I think it is time that I looked after you for a change," I told her.

"There is nothing wrong with me," she countered when the coughing had stopped, but I knew this was far from the truth. She let me gently pull her to her feet and lead her into the little house.

As my body mended and my wounds healed, so Astrid became sicker. Summer left us, the weather became cooler, and soon an autumnal wind blew through Jomsborg. As the summer sun faded, so did Astrid. She grew weaker, unable to leave her bed for long. She was popular in her neighbourhood, for she had helped heal many of her community in the past, but now it was their turn to repay the debt. Her neighbours frequently came in and out of the house bringing gifts that might hold some comfort for her. I hired a servant so that she was never alone, and Torstein was a frequent visitor who refused to leave until he had made her laugh. Together we watched over her as, before our eyes, she diminished and became a pale shadow of the strident woman I had met three years before. I shared my time between watching her and my duties at the fort, although there was little enough for me to do there as we moved into winter.

Astrid would often tell me that she felt better, or would be getting up the next day, but we both knew the truth; she was dying. One night, as I sat with her as she slept, she woke suddenly and reached for my hand. She had been in a fever dream, and there was a thin veil of sweat on her forehead. I cooled her by holding a damp rag to her forehead – as she had done so many times for me – and calmed her.

"You were dreaming, Astrid," I said to her quietly. "You are safe. I am here with you and shall never leave."

She raised my hand to her mouth and kissed it. "I never loved my first husband half as much as I have loved you, Bjorn," she said weakly. "Whenever you were away, I would dream of you, and I prayed night and day that Ran would fill your sails and bring you back to me as soon as he could. And when you returned, I would give him thanks until the next time you left."

I could see that her eyes were now glistening with tears, and she gripped my hand even more fiercely.

"The *Norns* are cutting the cords that hold me to you and this life. Soon the last one shall be severed, and I shall be gone to Helgafjell," she continued calmly and clearly. "I want you to leave the Jomsvikings, for Thorkill will lead you all to your deaths. He is not a bad man, but he is headstrong and impulsive, and he will doom you all, just as Styrbjorn did for the others."

"Hush, hush," I told her, "you have just had a bad dream and have a fever."

"Bjorn, I am going on my last journey. When I am gone, I want you to leave this place. Take the small box beneath my bed so you have something to remember me by. You will always be my beautiful Norwegian warrior, and I will see you much later on – but you must leave this place. Now just lie down with me one last time."

I lay down next to her, took her hand and stayed with her through the night.

The next morning, she was gone.

I left her bed for the very last time and opened the front door to let in the morning. It was a bright, frosty day and a weak, early-winter sunlight lit up the front of the little house. As had been my custom during the last months, I went to the place where Astrid stored her firewood and picked up some spare logs to make the fire. It was only when I reached her hearthfire that I realised there was no longer any need for this daily chore, and her days of feeling constantly cold were over. I smiled to myself and dropped the wood on the floor. I went over to her lifeless body and kissed her on the mouth one last time. Then reaching underneath her bed, I retrieved a small wooden box, tucked it under my arm and left the house forever.

That year I lost hundreds of friends and comrades, but

the loss of Astrid was the one I found hardest to bear. In my time here at Jomsborg, she had been the cool voice of calm in a sea of madness. She had been my anchor and the holy place I could visit when I needed quiet and peace. Even in the darkest of times, the knowledge that she would be there, my safe haven, was all I needed to get me back to shore. Now she was gone, and the impact of her passing was starting to sink home.

I found her servant, a woman I had employed from the market, and ordered her to prepare Astrid's body for the funeral. Leaving her some silver, I trudged back up to the fortress with the heaviest of hearts.

I looked for Torstein and shared my news with him.

"Ah, fuck it," he said angrily. "She was a good woman. I grieve for the both of you."

"We shall say goodbye to her tomorrow. Her funeral pyre is being prepared on the edge of town," I said.

He put a hand on my shoulder, no words were needed, and I retired to my small room lost in my grief.

In the morning I carried Astrid's bound and covered body through the town to the pyre that had been prepared for her. I was followed by her friends and neighbours and was gratified to see over two hundred people in our procession. I placed her body on the stack of wood, stood back, and Torstein stepped forward to speak.

"We say goodbye to our dear sister, Astrid, on her way to the Holy Mountain and bid her safe passage. She has touched the lives of all of us here, healing many who were sick and giving us back our strength so we might meet another dawn. We ask Freyr to see her safe to the other side."

He went on to say more, but I could not remember all his words in my grief. I took fire to the wood stack and stood back, watching the flames consume her body. I waited there for some time until all that remained were ashes on the sand.

I felt a hand on my shoulder. "Come, cousin, we need to take her to the sea."

Torstein had been waiting patiently with the survivors of the *Baldrs Wrath* company, and they stepped forward to scoop the ashes into a large iron bucket.

"She healed many of us here who have been wounded and gave us all hope of living another day," said Rurik quietly to me.

We took her remains, and the men rowed a waiting longboat out to the open sea. I said my final goodbye and gave Astrid's remains to the deep water.

Chapter 30: The Winter of Decision

Sigvaldi's fleet came into the harbour a little over one month later as Yuletide approached. There were twenty longships in all, carrying over a thousand men. I watched them dock from on top of the walls of the fortress. It was an impressive fleet, full of long, sleek vessels, all built for battle. It was a windy day with a heavy swell, even within our well-protected harbour walls. This made it difficult for the ships' captains to dock, but eventually all were successful, and they tied up without incident. Thorkill went down to meet his brother and brought him and his men inside the castle walls where they would be our guests over the winter period. We had plenty of room in the barracks for the extra men. Food stocks were high, for the summer had been good, and with our depleted numbers we had far fewer mouths to feed.

In the last weeks, I had busied myself in my duties around the fort. The survivors of Fyrisvellir had largely recovered from our flight from Sweden, and we began to drill and train again. Despite the damage to our reputation, men still came to Jomsborg to try and join us. Their numbers dwindled as winter came on, but there were still a few ships coming into the harbour, their sails and sheets thick with frost. Despite our diminished size, I refused to let our standards drop, and each new man had to pass through the same rigorous tests of arms which Styrbjorn had insisted upon. Torstein always featured last during these trials, and as ever he took not one backward step in his fierce examination of the new recruits. The old companies were disbanded, and all four companies became one, although the men still retained their allegiances to their old comrades.

"It will take us many years to rebuild at this rate," I said to Thorkill after one particular induction where we took in another three men.

"You are right, Bjorn. I believe Sigvaldi and his men desire to join us, but we need to be in no hurry. We must be strong again before we can be a serious threat to any who would stand in our way," he had replied.

Our new Commander was now striding up the hill with his brother at the head of a thousand men, and they entered the castle through the main gates. I went down from the ramparts to greet Sigvaldi, a man who I had fought beside on many of our campaigns along the Baltic coast. He saw me coming towards him and turned to greet me.

"Bjorn Halfdanson, it is good to see you. You are looking better than I feared you would – I heard you were badly wounded in this summer."

"The body mends quickly if the mind is willing," I said, and we embraced. "It looks like Miklagard has been good to you."

Although he was the same height as his older brother, Sigvaldi had always been wiry and nimble. He was now very broad in the chest and full in the face.

"Plenty of the Emperor's fine food and fighting every other day will do that to a man," he laughed. "Bjorn, I would like to introduce you to my very good friend here," he said putting his arm around the fierce looking, finely dressed warrior at his side. "He is one of your countrymen. Let me introduce you to Olaf Trygvasson."

Olaf stuck out a hand to me in greeting. He was a huge man with light, fine, almost white hair who stood a head taller than me. His piercing blue eyes set broad in a heavily scarred and tattooed face were startling. He was a little older than me, perhaps in his thirties, and his powerful demeanour marked him as a leader of men. I liked him from the first moment of our meeting. I had heard of this man, and like many Scandinavian adventurers of our time, his story was spectacular.

Olaf had been born into the Norwegian royal family and

261

was the son of the King of Oslofjord. The King had been killed by a renegade, and Olaf's mother, still carrying her unborn child, had been forced to flee their home to escape the massacre. The baby was born to the Queen during their flight, while they were being pursued by those intent on their death. When the boy was three his mother took him along with their small party of fugitives and boarded a ship that took them east to find her brother, a man of rank among the Rus in Novgorod. They sailed across the Baltic but were captured by Estonian pirates and sold into slavery. Olaf's foster father was killed immediately, as he was deemed too old and useless for work, and the rest of the family were enslaved.

By chance, the boy, who had been a slave all this time in Novgorod, was discovered some six years later by Sigurd, his uncle, who purchased him from Olaf's owner. The boy was cared for by Sigurd who brought him up. Some years later Olaf ran into his former owner and took revenge on his foster father's murderer with an axe, killing the man dead in front of many witnesses. The boy, now almost fully grown, was imprisoned and tried, but after hearing his story, King Valdomir of Kiev – Sigurd's master – released the boy and took him into his employment.

Olaf went on to fight in the ranks of the King's army and grew in importance with every battle he took part in. He became very popular with his fellow warriors, which ultimately displeased the King and caused him to be jealous of his former favourite. Olaf left the royal service and took a small fleet of ships raiding along the Baltic coast. During one stormy night, the fleet was caught at sea. The storm destroyed all but Olaf's ship, which was wind-driven onto the coast of Wendland. King Borislav of the Wends offered him protection and a place at his royal court where he met and married the monarch's daughter, Princess Geira. Olaf once again fought with distinction, this time for the Wends against Harald Bluetooth - the same King who deserted the Jomsvikings at Fyrisvellir. Geira died after three years marriage, and Olaf left and went a-viking once more.

I put my hand into Olaf's bear-like paw and shook it. "Any enemy of Harald Bluetooth is welcome in Jomsborg," I said, and he returned my welcome with a dazzling smile.

"Come," shouted Thorkill from the midst of the throng of warriors. "It is a while since we had visitors, and we are forgetting our manners. Follow me, we have food and drink for all." He led us off into the Commander's feasting hall.

It had been a while since we had feasted anyone in the great hall, and it was good to hear the large room ringing with the sound of men laughing and boasting. I was invited to sit at the Commander's table with Thorkill, and I sat down next to Olaf.

"I hear you can hit a man in the eye with a javelin at a hundred paces," suggested Olaf.

"You may have me mixed up with my father," I countered.

"Ah, yes, Halfdan Strong Arm had a fine reputation with the spear, but his son's has surpassed that of his father I hear," he said.

"I am honoured that you should have heard my name during your voyages, Olaf. You have built something of a reputation yourself. How do you come to be here with Sigvaldi?"

"We are friends of old," he said, "and we met by chance in Grobin where we were settling in for the winter before heading for England in the spring. He persuaded me that I would get a better welcome in Jomsborg, and so far he has been correct. Now brother, if I may call you that, if it is not too painful for you to recall please tell me the story of Fyrisvellir. I am interested to learn of what witchcraft King Eric employed to defeat the colossal Styrbjorn's Jomsvikings. Do not omit a single detail."

I told him every part of the campaign to Sweden, and when I had finished my story Olaf put a hand on my shoulder saying, without a hint of irony, "Sometimes even the mightiest of men must admit defeat in the face of such numbers. Your reputation is not blemished, Bjorn, and without your leadership not a single one of your men would be alive today. Take pride in that thought."

He flashed his stunning smile once more, got to his feet and raised his drinking horn.

"Let us drink to our fallen and curse our enemies. A cowardly man thinks he will ever live if warfare he avoids; but old age will give him no peace, though spears may spare him."

Every man in the hall stood, raised his drink and beat his fists upon the table.

Over the next months, I saw a great deal of Olaf. We hunted and trained together in the snow and ice. When the weather was too bad to venture out, we played *hnefatafl* or shared stories of our past. There were games of knattleikr, on the frozen lake behind the castle at which we both excelled. I had a good deal more in common with the man than I might have thought, and although I did not share his royal blood, we were similar in many ways. Olaf's men respected him greatly, and when he spoke to them, in low regular tones, each one of them listened to him intently hanging on his every word. He still felt the recent loss of his wife Geira as keenly as I missed Astrid, and although we spoke little of our departed women, we both knew something of what the other was feeling.

I suspected Torstein was a little jealous of our friendship, and he would slink off whenever Olaf joined our company with some excuse or other.

"I have heard he is a fine warrior, your cousin," said Olaf to me one day.

"Yes," I said, "he is. We have fought next to one another since we were boys, and I have never seen him fail in a fight. He is not one to wear his deeds or reputation silently either, and he has a thousand stories to tell. If ever you needed a fighting skald then Torstein is your man."

"His reputation is well known to me," said Olaf. "I have

heard the story of the Wandering Warriors told even in Miklagard, and it might surprise you to know that you and your cousin are also known as *Hugin* and *Munin* – Odin's Ravens. Now that really is something – two Norsemen who can fly. Tell me, Bjorn, what are your plans come the spring? Do you intend to stay here and help rebuild the Jomsvikings with Thorkill? I am sailing to England with an army, and you would be welcome to join our company. There is still land and wealth to be had there for an organised army. The Saxons are much more organised than they were since the days of Ragnor and can mobilise their defences quickly enough these days. But they are vulnerable to a large force of Norsemen hitting them quickly. Their king is weak and would rather pay us to go away than engage us in the field. I could use men like you and Torstein," he said.

"We have gold and silver already, Olaf," I said, trying to match his radiant smile. "But I must admit that the thought of some land in a place like England is of great interest. I am sorry to say that we cannot fly though, but I will talk with Torstein,"

"Tell him I need the best skald I can find, for there are great deeds to be done, and the world must remember what Olaf Trygvasson did before he became King of Norway."

He left that thought with me and went away to join his men. Another night of feasting was underway, and ale and mead were already raising the volume of chatter in the vast hall.

I roused Torstein early the next morning from his bed.

"Come, cousin," I said, "let us talk."

He followed me into my rooms and said, "When are we leaving for England, then?"

"You know of Olaf's plans?" I asked, surprised.

"Well, his men certainly do. Come the spring they will leave here and meet up with a fleet of Norwegians before going south to raid in England," he said.

"He has asked us to join him. What do you think?"

265

"I think you would like to go, and where you go so do I. And I must admit to getting a little bored here now I have visited each whore in Jomsborg a hundred times over. I think I would like a little land for my seed to grow in, and England has been good to many of our people. So, yes, I think we should go. But what of Thorkill? Will he not be angry if we leave?"

"I think not. He has his brother with him now – he and Sigvaldi are very close – perhaps too close than is comfortable for those not of their family. I have spoken to him already, and he has given us leave to go should we desire. But what of our other comrades? There are many here I would have join us," I asked, for Torstein was always close to our men.

"What is left of the Ravens would come with us to a man. There may be few others I would pick, but we would make at least one formidable fighting ship," he replied.

"Then I shall speak with Thorkill today, and if he is still content to let us go, we can start to make our plans. I think you would make a fine farmer in England."

Torstein snorted in derision at this last suggestion.

I left my rooms and the barracks and went to look for Thorkill. Crossing the snow-covered drill square, I found him in the great feasting hall sitting alone at a large empty table. He hailed me when he saw me and bade me to join him at a place by the fire.

"What do you think of our guests, Bjorn?" he asked.

"They have brought a much-needed breath of life to the place this Yule time," I answered. "It would have been a dull and quiet winter for all of us without them."

"Yes, I agree with you, Bjorn. You are fully recovered from your wounds now I hope?"

I nodded. "Yes, those of the body have long since mended, but it is the pride that will take a little longer. Thorkill, I must speak with you on a matter of some importance."

"Ah, yes of course. You wish to go a-viking with Olaf in

England," he announced.

I looked up with some surprise again that he had this knowledge.

"The purpose of Olaf's visit here was always to recruit my best men, so it was obvious he would start with you. He will be King of Norway, maybe more one day, so you should be flattered by his attention. He has a good eye for the bravest warriors, but you must promise me one thing; do not take all the Jomsvikings with you. When you are a rich lord in England you must send for me – then I will come a-guesting at your castle. You have my blessing, and for those who wish to go with you, I release them from all their oaths to the order. They have all done their duty on the plain of Fyrisvellir, and I can ask no more of them."

I laughed at his comments but was relieved that he had taken my request so well. I enquired of news of his brother's plans.

"Sigvaldi will stay here with his men who wish to join the Jomsvikings, and I promise you they will not be admitted easily. They will still have to fight their way in. Now let us drink to the success of your new venture."

He called for ale, and we sat drinking and talking for the rest of the day.

Chapter 31: The Continuing Saga of the Wandering Warriors

I told Olaf that we would be joining him with sixty to seventy men in the spring. We would take a new ship, which we renamed Drakes Head, and sail with him to England where we would harry the coastline.

"I have been promised fifty ships full of our countrymen, Bjorn," he said. "And we shall wait for them in Northumbria. My cousin Erik leads them and unless he perishes on the way he will be there. I am expecting others to come, and we shall have some one hundred ships to begin the campaign. We'll head to the Kingdom of East Anglia where there are rich pickings for us. The Saxons there have lost much of their strength since they last saw the backs of the Norsemen and are led badly by a boy of twelve."

I harked back to the words of Styrbjorn who had said similar things of King Erik of Sweden, but that was now history.

"You were born to the life of a warrior, and I shall make you richer than you would ever be staying here in Jomsborg. Now tell me, is Torstein ready to tell my story?" he continued.

One cold, foggy day in spring we left. Olaf, in one of his ten ships, gave the Drakes Head the honour of leading our fleet out of the harbour, and as I had done many times before, I steered us across the huge anchorage and out of the entrance. Our comrades, men who we fought beside for the past three years, lined the dock. We had shared many experiences together, ranged with them for thousands of miles and were now leaving them all behind. Onboard were all the members of my old company, the Ravens, who had decided to a man to follow me to England. I had told them where I was heading and invited them to join me, and all had voted to come.

Fyrisvellir had been a bitter, harsh experience, and this was a chance to make things right again. We were brothers in arms, and our journey in the Jomsvikings had bound us closely together.

We were also very wealthy and carried on board the fortune we had accumulated from our years of raiding. In the days before we left, Thorkill had taken us to the castle's stony keep where each man's treasure had been stored in an iron chest. These chests were now all on the Drakes Head, used by the men as rowing benches on which they sat at the oars and pulled the ship across the flat water. The men on the dock, honouring us in full battle dress, beat on their shields and called to us as we left them.

"Show those Saxons plenty of Jomsborg steel," cried one man.

A small group of women, gathered by the far end of the quay, waved and called to us.

"The whores in Jomsborg will be a lot poorer now," another man shouted.

"Goodbye my beauties, do not get cold at night," called Torstein to them.

As we left the harbour, the morning mist burned away to reveal bright sunshine, and we turned west and made for England. The sails were raised, and we were blown towards our fate.

Torstein joined me at the tiller later that morning.

"Are you sad to be leaving?" he asked.

"No. Our time there was over. We went for wealth and reputation and that has been achieved. I believe we are better men for our journey, and it was everything I wanted it to be. And you?"

"You were right, Bjorn. It was everything you promised it was going to be, but Thorkill will be a different leader to Styrbjorn, and time will tell what happens to the order. As you say, we are wealthy men of some repute now, men who would be invited into a king's court just to tell their story. I really could not have asked for more."

I nodded in agreement and said a silent goodbye to Astrid's ghost.

Our little fleet sailed steadily across the Baltic Sea and up past the Danish headlands. We passed a few merchant ships, but winter had only recently ended, and there was scant traffic in either direction. We stopped and made camp outside the town of Skagen on the tip of Jutland, driving our boats up onto the sandy beach for the night. They were all pulled clear of the water, and fires were built whilst some of our men were dispatched to purchase supplies from the town. They soon returned laden with food and drink that had been loaded onto a large wagon and were accompanied by the local chieftain. This man, a wizened old warrior called Hemming, was brought before Olaf, and the two men exchanged greetings whilst the rest of us looked on with interest.

"Welcome, Lord Olaf, you and your men are welcome to what little hospitality our community can provide," said Hemming. "We bring you food and drink that you and your men might refresh yourselves. I will accept no payment for it is our honour to host you, even if it is only on the shore."

"Thank you for your gesture, Hemming. It is good to set foot back in Jutland once more. Now, tell us your news of Denmark."

"Great news, Lord, for Harald Bluetooth is dead, killed by the hand of his own son, Svein Forkbeard."

"That is indeed momentous news, and few of us here will grieve the death of King Harald, but Svein has always been a good man. How say you, Hemming?"

"We will shed no tears here for the old King either, and my men shall be happy to bend the knee to King Svein."

"Then we shall drink to the health of the new King with your fine Jutland ale," said Olaf.

There were, in truth, only a few barrels of ale on the ox cart, but our boats had been richly supplied in Jomsborg and there was plenty to go around. By the time our thralls had the fires lit and roaring, each man had a drink in his hand. Torstein, by this time, the thirstiest of any man, had consumed at least three cups of ale.

He said to me, "That is at least one traitorous Dane that is safe from my axe. Let us pray that *Odin* has not let him into Valhalla."

"You have little to fear, cousin, for I bet you all the gold in my chest that he did not die with a sword in his hand."

We laughed and joined the rest of the men in toasting the new King of Denmark.

Later in the evening, Thorkill came over to where I was sitting on some rocks, drinking with my men.

"You are be pleased to hear of the death of the traitor Harald Gormson?" he asked.

"I have mixed feelings," I replied. "I did not dislike him as a man, and I think there must be a reason beyond cowardice for him to have deserted us at Fyrisvellir. His actions cost us many good men, and for Styrbjorn, the crown of Sweden and his life. I have much to resent him for, but Harald is gone, and the Gods will punish him in the next life."

"For such a fierce warrior, Bjorn, I suspect you have a kind heart," he teased. "Tomorrow our voyage begins in earnest, and then you shall be leading us across the great North Sea. We will all be in your hands."

"The weather looks fine for the time of year, but the North Sea can be a fickle mistress, and storms can blow up quickly, as you know. We must stay together at all times, for many fleets have foundered on foreign shores when they have been split up and windswept in different directions. I have never been to Northumbria before. What is it like?" I asked.

"It is wild and inhospitable," Thorkill answered, "but where we are going – to a place the Saxons call Bamburgh – the coast is long, sandy and suitable to set up camp. The Norse people landed hundreds of years ago and have settled and prospered, for the land is quite fertile. We shall make camp there while we wait for the others to arrive. The local Saxon lord lives in a castle stronghold, but I do not expect any trouble from him; his army is small, and he seldom ventures out from behind his walls. He will not relish a fight with us, and I expect we can wait without much interference."

"When do you expect the others to arrive?" I asked.

"Within twenty to thirty days," he said without hesitation. "They are mostly from my *aett*, and many have fought with the Saxons before. When we have gathered, we shall first sail south to East Anglia and take what we need. There will be land and silver aplenty. You are a good man, Bjorn, and one to be relied upon. Let us make this voyage a success for all of us."

And with that he was gone, moving among the men with light-hearted purpose.

Astrid's warning was not my only reason for leaving Jomsborg. My men were battle weary after our defeat in Sweden and needed new victories; for a defeated warrior must always raise himself from the ground before it swallows him completely. I trusted Olaf, although I had not known him for long, and was happy to follow his banner. Some of my men were getting old, and they needed land to settle on, a purpose for which the life of a Jomsviking is not well suited. An old man needs a family and land to support him, and such a life in Wendland could not be reckoned for. To go a-viking is the path of young men, for sooner or later warriors get old, wounds take longer to heal, and bones become tired. Torstein or I would need to fight for the land if we were to settle, and hopefully we would find it in England. If the gods willed it, we had years of ranging together left for us, but many of our company desired land, their own hearthfire and a warm, companionable woman at night. That night, I asked the *Norns* for their help and not to cut the cords that bound our fate. At least, not just yet.

Chapter 32: Across the Sea to England

The North Sea can blow up unexpectedly and fiercely, particularly in early spring, but apart from the odd squall, there was little to trouble us. A following wind ensured that we travelled in an almost straight line from Jutland to Northumbria. We sailed every night for there was nowhere to anchor, each ship guiding the next with an oil lamp tied to the masthead. After six days of sailing, I spotted land. One of the crew confirmed it was the Kingdom of the Scots, and from there we followed the coast south, all the way down to our destination. Bamburgh proved to be another day's sailing, and we arrived at midday in a large sandy bay overlooked by a huge stone castle on top of a steep hill. Each ship had fastened their carved figureheads, so there would be no doubting that we were a war party. Rurik, one of the Ravens who had visited here before, joined me on the afterdeck.

"We tried our luck here before, years ago, and lost many men attempting to take that place," he said, nodding towards the castle. "The castle could not be taken, and we left empty-handed."

"No matter," I said, "for we are only to wait here for the rest of the ships to join us and shall not be bothering those in the castle."

Horsemen on the beach watched our progress motionless, but as our ships turned to the shore, they beat a hasty retreat before disappearing towards the fortress.

"All the bravery of rabbits," said Rurik.

Then he directed me to a point where we could beach. Moments later all our ships had landed safely and were being dragged up the sandy shoreline. We unloaded what we needed and made our way beyond the sand and into the dunes to a high point above the beach.

I surveyed the area with Olaf.

"Here is as good a place as any to make camp," he said, and our company of six hundred and twenty men began to prepare the area for our stay. "Bjorn, can you send your men to forage? Don't forget to remind them that there are still many of our kinsfolk living around here."

Many generations before our time, a large army of Norsemen had landed and taken a huge area stretching from here to the south of England. It was occupied and settled by many Scandinavians, and our countrymen once ruled the kingdoms of *Jorvic* and Mercia. When they were defeated, they left, although many settlers remained and took Saxon wives. These people still farmed the land, and we had little desire to harm them unless the need arrived.

"Tell your men to use sound judgement. The locals will be of more use to us alive than dead," he said.

Torstein took half the crew from the Drakes Head and went into the local town for supplies. They were fully armed but under orders not to use force unless provoked. The local population were probably already in a state of terror after seeing our dragon ships drive towards the beaches, and the foragers met no opposition. He returned soon after with a small group of locals carrying everything from fuel to food. He also brought with him the town's headman who stood nervously before Olaf. The man spoke our common language, donsk tunga, and once he recovered from his trembling fear, he managed to answer Olaf's questions.

"What is your name?" commanded Olaf.

"I am Orm, Lord. I am the leader of the townsfolk and a Norse man like you. My father hailed from Rogoland."

"It is good to meet a fellow Norwegian in these foreign lands. Well, Orm, you have been well paid for your goods I trust," said Olaf.

"Yes Lord, your men have been generous."

"Tell me who commands in the castle yonder?"

Words tumbled from Orm's mouth in an effort to provide Olaf with the information he needed.

"The Ealdorman Oswulf is the lord of the castle and all these lands. We seldom see him, for he prefers to remain within its walls. He sends his men out regularly, but at the first sign of trouble they go back and leave us to fend for ourselves."

"And this Oswulf, was his father of the same name?"

"Yes Lord, a very cruel man indeed. They are from a long line of Saxons who have ruled here for generations. It is said that the castle has never been taken, and they can see everything that is happening for miles around from the top of that hill."

Olaf thought on these words. "Ah, then he would be the same Oswulf who murdered Eric Bloodaxe, the last King of Yorvik."

"Yes, Lord, the same," stammered Orm.

"So, the son of my uncle's killer lives right here under our noses," said Olaf to no one in particular before continuing. "An interesting but ultimately irrelevant fact. We are here to meet up with our countrymen, Orm, and we would like your assistance for which you and your people will be well paid."

Then he dismissed the frightened man, and the rest of us continued to prepare our camp. The people of the town helped us build a rough wooden palisade on the top of the dunes within which the camp was built. Olaf's banners were secured at its sides so that they could be seen from some distance, and at its entrance stakes had been driven and sharpened to deter any horsemen from charging up the dunes and into our camp. Orm and his people supplied us with what they had – not enough to completely feed our little army but supplemented by an abundance of fish and game. Every day a company of twenty or so horseman sat watching us from the beach below the dunes and every day we chased them away. They, in turn, would retreat and regard us from a safe distance.

275

After about ten days, Olaf came to me one morning as we sat around our fire preparing to go foraging inland.

"It is time we sent these Saxons back to their castle permanently, Bjorn. Tomorrow I would like you and your men to conceal yourselves in the lower dunes before the horsemen come. When they have passed, we shall chase them off and trap them between us."

It was a simple plan, for the Saxons waited and watched us from the same place every morning, further down the beach where the sweep of the dunes sloped down to a narrow path along which they would gallop before stopping to watch us.

That night, we left our camp and hid in the dunes about a hundred paces from the track the horsemen used. It was a dark, starless night, and Torstein and I led the men, all sixty-five Jomsvikings, into position where we waited until morning. At dawn, we were all awake, alert and armed with spears, axes and swords, waiting for our quarry.

"Here they come," said Torstein, as the muffled sound of horses' hooves on sand broke the silence.

He was in a state of some excitement, and we watched the horsemen make their way from the castle down to the beach. They passed in front of us where we lay looking down on them from the dunes – about a hundred paces away. After they passed, I led the men down to the beach where we formed into a double line of shields with fifteen bowmen taking their positions from on top of the dunes. We watched and waited.

"I have been looking forward to this all night," said Torstein happily.

We heard shouts up ahead, and the horsemen came galloping around the bend pursued by our comrades on foot. Before the Saxons could get close to our line they were met with a shower of arrows, and riders and horses fell on the sand, bringing down those behind them. Their flight halted, they did not even reach our shield wall. We broke the line and raced towards them. It was all over in moments. Torstein, leading our charge, was the first to arrive, his axe coming down on the heads of the unfortunate Saxons struggling to their feet on the sand. Before our comrades from the camp could arrive, we had dispatched the horsemen, leaving none alive.

"An impressive display,' Olaf said to me, as he walked towards the remains of the Saxon troop. "Your men are well trained."

The bodies of the horsemen lay before us, naked on the beach. They had been stripped, and their heads had been removed and collected in sacks. Of the twenty horses, three had been killed in the fight.

"Come, mount up Bjorn. Let us deliver Oswulf a little message."

A small group of us took the captured horses and headed towards the castle. We rode along the beach, around the bay and up a steep slope towards the castle gates. The fortress looked even more formidable as we drew closer, and we stopped before the large ditch running around its perimeter. In a half-hearted display of defiance, a few of the castle's bowmen shot down arrows which we caught easily on our shields. Then they stopped altogether and waited to see what would happen next. Two of our men carrying the sacks emptied their contents in full view of those looking down on us from high on the walls. Olaf shouted up to them.

"Do not sneak like thieves around our camp. If you want to visit us you are welcome to come through the front gate," he shouted.

There was no answer from the castle walls, and we turned and rode our captured horses back to camp. It had been a small victory against those who dared to oppose us, but it felt good. That night our crew sat around the fire in high spirits, and the talk was all about the riches that were awaiting us in East Anglia. Rurik and Einar, who had both raided there a generation ago, told us stories of their victories under Olaf

Guthfrithson and their battles with the armies of Wessex. Torstein was persuaded to tell The Tale of Grettir the Strong, a man after his own heart who slew mountain trolls and defeated bad spirits. Olaf came and took ale with us and toasted my men.

"They seem to have got over their flight from Sweden," he said to me.

"It was a ghost that needed chasing away, nothing more, Olaf," I said, and we raised our drinking cups and toasted the Jomsvikings and our new company.

Some twenty days later, the sails of the ships we had been waiting for, hove into view one morning. Eighty ships carrying over four thousand Norwegian warriors landed and were pulled up the beach next to ours.

"I'll bet those Saxons in the castle are shitting themselves thinking we are coming for them," said Torstein as we watched the men on the beach gathering. Olaf was already amongst the new arrivals, warriors of his *aett* and their allies. They were men just like us going a-viking for fame and fortune. That night huge fires were built on the beach, and there was a simple feast given in honour of the new arrivals. Olaf spoke of the riches that awaited us but warned that this new breed of Saxons was tougher than their predecessors.

"Not that we have seen much evidence from the ones skulking in that castle," shouted Torstein to the merriment of all.

We left the day after the next. Olaf was about to unleash a storm on the Saxons which they had not seen in twenty-six years.

Chapter 33: A Storm of Norsemen

In five days, we reached the coast of East Anglia where the raiding began in earnest. We landed and attacked the small coastal communities, taking whatever was there before moving on. Olaf planned to draw the English King's army out to meet us by the continual raiding of his towns. We heard that King Aethelred had built a fleet of ships, but we seldom saw any evidence of this. There was little resistance to our army in those early days.

We would land and march against one town or another, defeat the local defenders with relative ease, and after taking as much as we could carry, simply put it to the flame. We were only interested in gold and silver, and once we had loaded as much as we could onto our ships we moved along the coast for the next attack. We travelled along the coast of East Anglia like a plague, striking down all who opposed us. When we could not find enough big towns, we moved inland and attacked the larger communities. The towns of Norwich, Ipswich and Folkstone soon fell to Olaf's army. We quickly advanced south into Wessex attacking Thanet, Sandwich and even Southampton. Although we were sometimes made to fight a little harder, we always prevailed against the defenders who melted away and retreated inland. The news of our success spread, and the towns in our path capitulated even before the first blow was struck. We captured all the holy people, nobles and leaders we could find and then ransomed them back to their own people. Scandinavians from Ireland, Frankia and England itself – all keen to share in the plunder – joined us. Indeed, we amassed so much wealth that we had to bury it secretly at places known only to Olaf, myself and one or two other trusted leaders. As summer approached, we became bolder, marching further inland, and although the men of Kent proved hardy fighters, they also fell to our lightning assaults. We attacked the town of Canterbury one bright morning and quickly overcame the city's defenders after a brief struggle of less than a day. The hostages we deemed valuable were captured and held in their holy place – a huge church in the centre of the town.

I sat with Olaf after the day's fighting, waiting for the ransom to turn up for our prisoners who had been herded together at one end of the building. They were far more valuable to us alive than dead, and their people seemed only too willing to pay vast amounts of gold and silver for their safe return.

"I think the priests are more valuable than their nobles sometimes," said Olaf, as we sat together away from the babble of the tormented hostages, marvelling at the sheer amount of wealth on display in this huge church.

"Their gods seem to be far richer than ours," I suggested as we took in the high painted ceilings, richly adorned walls and golden artefacts on display. "Just look at this place."

"Yes, I think their gods are much richer, but for all their wealth they don't seem to help their believers in the fighting very much. Did you know I have been to a Christian service in Miklagard – with priests and singing and everything," he said.

"And did anything happen to you?" I asked.

"No, absolutely nothing, apart from getting sore knees. But I was impressed by the amount of wealth on display. I believe this Christianity is just another way of getting rich. Perhaps, this Jesus is just another god – but his people get rich and fat on the story. When I am King in Norway, I will embrace all the gods – particularly the rich ones like this one." He pointed to a golden cross with a man nailed to it. I laughed at his suggestion, but his tone was serious.

"I am telling you, Bjorn, a man could get rich through this religion. There are churches throughout Norway now, and by the time we get home I am not sure the old gods will even recognise us."

"Maybe you are right, Olaf, but as long as they do not

desert us, fighting here in England, I will have much to thank them for," I said.

"Yes, it is pleasing to continue like this, but I fear that before the winter we will meet greater opposition from the Saxons. Aethelred must show his hand before too long, and he cannot neglect his people like this forever," he said.

"Do you think he is gathering his army inland?" I asked.

"If so, he is doing it very quietly for there is no news of his host. I hear many things – that he has built a mighty fleet or that he has an army marching on us from the north. But until he confronts us with something more than an army of priests, we will never know."

We were interrupted by news that men had arrived outside carrying chests.

"Ah, the ransom for our hostages. They took little time to gather it. I'll warrant there is much more where that came from. Come, Bjorn, let us see what they think their priests are worth."

We got up from our seats in the church and headed into the sunlight outside. There was a small delegation of men, three priests and two finely dressed gentlemen, who I took to be local nobles. There was also another man, a tall strong-looking warrior, who stood to the back of this little group. He was unarmed, save for a coat of mail over a black leather tunic and breeches, and his thick, dark hair was plaited in a single ponytail that reached his waist. Unlike the rest of the group, he showed no fear but stood with his head unbowed before a horse and cart. On the cart were three wooden chests that I took to be the ransom valuables.

The fighting earlier that day had been fast and furious. Our army had landed on the nearby coast the previous day and marched overnight to reach Canterbury by dawn. We split into two groups and approached the town from two sides. Half our forces remained in a static position while Olaf advanced with his men from the other side. The Saxons, with a defending force of around a thousand men, were struck with speed and surprise at sunset and their men driven back into two thousand spearmen. Between this hammer and anvil, they were crushed without pity, and the town of Canterbury was ours by early afternoon. The town was looted, its people left to the predations of our men who tormented them for the rest of the day. The group standing nervously before us, with the exception of the man in black, had been captured and sent off with instructions to fetch as much gold and silver as quickly as they could. Two of our men were now on top of the cart rooting through the booty that lay in the chests.

"Just how do simple men of God accumulate so much treasure?" said Olaf to the dejected group in front of us. The three priests, all dressed in long dirty robes, said nothing, and Olaf turned his attention to the Saxon warrior behind them.

"And you," he said, pointing at the man, "I recognise you from earlier. You were leading your men, I think. What is your name?"

The man stepped forward unafraid. "My name is Edmund of Rochester, and I am in the service of King Aethelred."

"Ah, your young King," said Olaf to the man. "And where might he be found while his men give up their lives for him so easily?"

"The King stays in London, Lord, I believe. But I have not heard of him for some while."

"I am thinking that I should sail to London to meet him," said Olaf in mocking tones. "Do you think he might find time to see me?"

"I do not know," replied Edmund, "for my acquaintance with him has been but brief. But I am sure he would be pleased to meet such a famous warrior as yourself, Lord Olaf."

"You know who I am then?" said Olaf, who now stood close to Edmund, the two men regarding one another face to face.

"I am very familiar with the reputation of Olaf Trygvasson. Your fame goes before you," replied Edmund.

"Then when might your King put his army in the field that we might be tested?" Olaf asked.

"I cannot say, Lord, for we men of Kent have little to do with the King, and he keeps his own counsel. If it is a worthy battle you seek then I believe the army of Essex might yet answer your call."

"Another Saxon rabble?" probed Olaf.

"It is not for me to say, Lord, but the Ealdorman Byrhtnoth leads many men in that part of the country, and you may find his appetite for a fight well matched."

"Are you sure you are not telling me this so I will just go away and leave you in peace?" said Olaf.

"I will answer your questions, Lord. Sadly, my men could not offer you a challenge today, but Byrhtnoth is a mighty warrior and leads a sizable army – if it is a challenge that you seek, you may find one there."

"Then I shall seek him out, and you shall come with me to show me the way. I believe we have your wife and family in the church," said Olaf, and for the first time, Edmund appeared flustered and no longer certain of himself.

"They shall be safe for as long as I have your assistance, Lord Edmund. Now let us get these valuables moved to a place of safety, and if you will excuse me, I have an army to feed and keep amused."

We stayed in Canterbury for a few days while our men roamed freely around the town taking what they wanted from the local population. This was a familiar pattern now; following a victory, our men would plunder whatever they could find, most often in a drunken flurry of activity with the townsfolk at their mercy. They helped themselves to the local women, whose men could no longer protect them, and the contents of their homes until, weary of this sport, they readied themselves for our next attack which was never long in coming.

Olaf was relentless in his drive for the next assault on the Saxons and would not rest until he had defeated and humiliated their King. We were amassing a fortune in plundered Saxon valuables with which he was attracting a considerable following of well-paid and motivated warriors from many different Scandinavian strongholds. When his army had 'taxed' the Saxons sufficiently, he would turn his attentions towards our homeland in Norway where he planned to return and take back his father's throne. He was an unyielding leader whose men were very loyal and would follow him anywhere. I believed we were good friends, and he would share many of his plans with me, but he was never a man to allow even his closest of allies to be too close. He had my complete support, for he was a generous leader and never proved to be anything but the most loyal of friends.

In two days, we marched back to the sea, loaded our ships and went in search of the army of Byrhtnoth. Olaf sent scouts out on horseback along the shoreline to check for any sign of this host that he believed was heading towards East Anglia. After two days no sightings had been made, but on the third day word of a large Saxon force coming south and heading towards the town of Maldon was received. Olaf was delighted with the news and was beaming at the meeting of his captains that evening.

"I was beginning to give up any hope of confronting a Saxon army of any size," he told me when the meeting was over. "But this one seems quite large, perhaps six thousand men. Let us pray we can close with them in the next day or so and finish them there."

The *Norns* were about to send me on a fateful journey.

Chapter 34: The Battle of Maldon

At dawn the next day, our fleet, numbering over a hundred ships, entered an inlet on the River Pante. There were so many of our vessels in the channel, now shallow at low tide, that it was almost blocked with our longships making their way upriver. We came upon a small island where we beached our ships and went ashore. Our numbers were swelled by many new arrivals. Men and their weapons were unloaded, and soon the whole island was full of Norsemen and their equipment. It was uninhabited, save for a few hundred seabirds, and I walked with Olaf to its far side. We turned along some barren mud banks which were drying in the morning sun and at last caught sight of the Saxon army which had made their camp on the mainland. Our island was joined to the opposite shore by a narrow causeway across the mud which, although wide enough for two or three men walking abreast to cross at low tide, would be submerged again at high tide.

It was now low tide, and a vast expanse of mud was exposed, across which a shale path ran. Beyond this stood the vast force of the Saxon army waiting on high ground looking out towards us. They did not move, for there was no way that either army could close with each other quickly.

I stood beside Olaf watching them as more and more of our men drew up behind us. The Saxons looked to be in good order, most of their men wore armour and helms, and a forest of spear tips reflected in the morning sunshine. The two forces gathered on either side of the mudflats watching each other warily, and as was customary, each side hurled abuse at the other. However, we understood little of the other's language and the insults fell on deaf ears. Olaf held up his hand, and our men fell silent as he strode forward, motioning to a man in our ranks to follow him. This man, Thorgil, could speak some English, having been captured and kept as a slave in Wessex for many years. He now spoke for Olaf and called to the Saxons on the other side of the mudflats.

"Saxons," shouted Thorgil towards the opposing army, "in the next days you will harvest the wrath of the Norsemen, and you will all fall here in this barren place. The animals and seabirds will come and gnaw at your bones until there is no trace of you. You can die here or leave in peace. If you wish to die, come and fight us, but if you wish to live you may leave with your weapons, unchallenged. The price of your lives will be gold and silver. What shall your answer be?"

A tall, bareheaded man dressed in gleaming armour and carrying a spear stepped forward to answer. He was old but stood straight and tall and shouted back in a loud, resonant voice that boomed across the mud towards us.

"Listen to me you rabble of sea pirates. You ask me for tribute and this tribute we will give you," he shouted, raising his spear towards Olaf. "We will give you poison-tipped javelins and ancient swords. You will win nothing here – just death in a foreign land. Your lifeless bodies will sink beneath this stinking mud. We are only a part of the King's army which grows stronger every day, so it is to you that I make this offer: go now and do not return, for only death awaits you."

"That's fighting talk – but how do we even get to them from here," said Torstein in my ear as he moved up to stand next to me.

Olaf's man returned the challenge.

"Then you shall die here in your thousands," he cried. He flung a spear over the narrow channel towards the Saxon army which fell short of its target and stuck in the mud between the two bodies of men. By this time our army had all assembled behind Olaf, fanned out along the mud bank of our island, each man looking for a way to cross the sticky bog but only seeing the narrow causeway. Unable to wait any longer, two of our number raced out of the ranks and on to the narrow, raised path still slippery with mud and slime from the falling tide. They were Frisians who had joined our company a few days ago on our way to Canterbury and now in a frenzy of battle-lust they were running across the causeway towards the Saxon lines two hundred paces away. The Frisians made slow progress slipping and stumbling on the wet rocks of the path until eventually both men, carrying axe and shield, reached the other side. A group of six Saxon spearmen moved forward to meet them and there was a flurry of hacking axes and spear thrusts as the men of two armies looked on. Ultimately, the spearmen prevailed for there was no way through them, and the axemen, mortally wounded from several spear wounds, fell dying before the defenders. The Saxons, cheering this small victory, beat their weapons against their shields.

"What do you think?" said Olaf to me when the noise had died.

"We cannot engage them in enough numbers across the causeway, and if we approach through the mud and water, we shall get stuck and die here. If we can get to the other side intact before we fight, we might best them," I said.

"Perhaps they will let us cross? Why don't we ask them?" he said.

Thinking he had made a joke, I smiled, but he was serious and moved to the edge of the mudbank with his spokesman.

"I would speak with Lord Byrhtnoth once more, for I believe it was he whom I spoke to before," said Olaf, speaking directly now to the Saxons.

"I am Byrhtnoth," called the tall man who had answered us earlier. "Will you be taking your leave of Northey Island now?"

"We shall not leave before we have destroyed your army," returned Olaf, "but if we cannot meet you, there is no way of knowing what the outcome should be. Will you let us cross before battle?"

There was silence from both sides of the narrow channel now, and I wondered if Olaf had indeed been joking, but he continued.

"If you truly want to rid your country of us, you should allow us to cross and meet you in battle. If your warriors are as fierce as you say they are, then let us put that boast to the test! Let us meet you in yonder meadow and see who is the stronger."

The other man did not answer immediately, as he considered Olaf's words, then he called back.

"There is some merit in this suggestion. Two men shouting at one another is less than dignified. If you are in agreement, Olaf Trygvasson, I shall meet you on the causeway, and we can talk."

Olaf, needing no second invitation, handed his shield and spear to one of the men and strode out onto the causeway. Byrhtnoth appeared to do the same and both walked out to a midway point and began to talk. A little while later after some discussion, they returned to their armies.

Olaf addressed his men:

"The Saxons will let us cross, and we shall meet them later in the day in the meadow that sits behind their forces. They will withdraw for the moment so that we might cross unhindered. We will meet them on their side of the water today."

All eyes went to the Saxons, and sure enough, their lines were breaking up, their men turning around and marching off.

"You look surprised, Bjorn," he said to me shortly, "but there is sense in the decision for both of us. Byrhtnoth wishes us gone forever which he can only achieve through our defeat. This is his best opportunity, and he probably has some reinforcements on the way. But we shall defeat him on that field today, and the road to this country shall open up before us. There will be blood."

Then, calling his captains around him, he gave us our battle orders. When the way was clear we crossed. Using the causeway was slow, and to increase the pace men leapt into the shallow water and waded through the mud to reach the other side. It was filthy and laborious work, which took some time before we were all across. Eventually, the men made it through and marched into the huge meadow nearby to form up into battle lines. This time there would be no surprise, and we stood patiently facing a well-disciplined army only a hundred paces in front of us. My Jomsvikings stood around Olaf beneath his battle standard, a double-headed raven, for we were now his personal bodyguard. His Norwegians stood on our left with the remainder of our army, about two thousand warriors from many different kingdoms, on our right.

Our men on each flank formed quickly into two wedges – *svinfylking*s – and we marched forward together. There was none of the normal preamble, no champions sent out to fight, none of the ritual insults hurled by each side – we simply attacked swiftly and brutally. The 'boar's snouts' arrived at almost the same time and struck the men in front with great fury for the red mist was descending on us all now. I felt the Saxon line give under the impact and saw both their flanks waiver, but they held and did not break. Our little group made its way forward and we headed for Byrhtnoth's standard in the centre of his troops – stabbing, cutting and thrusting at the men in front.

Our left wing met the Saxon right and broke through the line, butchering their way through the enemy. However, our right flank met great resistance from the enemy's left, and they had not only been checked but were now being pushed back. The whole Saxon line was wheeling as the opposing forces drove at each other in a series of drives and counter drives. As it did so, the locked shields of both armies broke apart and men fought one on one. Our company around Olaf was deep within the Saxon army, which was finally wilting under the force of our attack, and we bludgeoned our way towards Byrhtnoth and his men.

"Let us hope Thor does not desert us today, Bjorn," Torstein shouted, felling yet another Saxon spearman with his axe.

"He is with us today, cousin, for surely we do not deserve to be punished again," I returned and heard Torstein laugh.

Then, as suddenly as we had been moving forward, we were retreating. Olaf ordered the horns sounded and called us all to withdraw from the field. The two groups of warriors on both sides of us simply turned and fled. The speed with which our advance stopped and reversed into flight took the Saxons by surprise, and many of them were slow to pursue us. Once they realised that the enemy was on the run, they seized the opportunity and gave chase, their packed defensive formations disintegrating as they surged forward to attack our backs.

Another horn sounded and our warriors stopped, turned and came together as one. Thousands of Norsemen formed into a single wedge in one fluid, preordained movement. For the first time Torstein left my side, and together with our strongest warriors, took his position in the apex of the boar's snout. It was a bold manoeuvre and fraught with danger, for many things could have gone awry. On this day though, the gods did not fail us, and we drove back into the Saxon host with redoubled fury, splintering the bedraggled lines in front of us. The boar's snout bit deep into the enemy, and although they tried hard to reform, they could not check us. Their discipline held, and once again they were saved, at least for a little while longer.

Olaf's voice could be heard above the sound of clashing metal and splintering shields.

"Onward Norsemen, the day is ours!" he cried. "Leave no man of these Saxons alive today, for they have doubted your courage and must learn their lessons."

Still we moved forward, but our progress had been slowed by our enemy who reformed quickly, and I realised we were taking casualties on either side of the wedge as the enemy fought to counter our progress. As the battle raged and boiled around me, I caught sight once more of Byrhtnoth's standard and saw him standing close beneath it. I could clearly see him about fifty paces from me, a head taller than the men of his bodyguard. I snatched a javelin from one of my men and hurled it, without a second thought, at his head. I watched the spear fly in a shallow arc towards the Saxon leader. I thought it had missed and then I lost sight of him for the battle was still in full fury around us.

Olaf's voice could be heard again: "His standard has fallen! Byrhtnoth has fallen! The battle is ours!"

At these words, the men around me found that hidden strength that men discover when victory is within their grasp. Our wedge, having served its purpose, splintered, and the men fought individual battles with the ever more desperate Saxon defenders. The fighting in front of me cleared for a moment, long enough to see the prostrate figure of the Ealdorman of Essex with my spear through his neck. He was bleeding to death in the churned-up mud, surrounded by the *thane*s of his bodyguard standing over him. He struggled to stand, for the spear had struck true; its barbed head protruded his neck by an arms span. His men stood in a tight defensive formation about him, and it was clear that whether their lord lived or died they would not leave him there. On each side of this tight little group, the battle began to die, as the Saxons, realising the day was lost, fell back and retreated, presenting their backs to the spears and arrows of our men whose turn it was to become their pursuers.

Above the noise and the confusion, I shouted for my men to form up on me, but there was no need for they were all at my shoulder to a man. The slaughter wolves of the Jomsvikings fell with renewed fury upon Byrhtnoth's defenders who dropped, one by one, dead or exhausted from mortal wounds. Soon, the last man fell, dispatched by Rurik's spear to his face, and we stood panting like hunting dogs amongst the carnage. One of the men dragged Byrhtnoth's body out, cut off his head and mounted it on a spear for all to see. The battle was over, and after half a day of the most intense fighting I have endured on the field, we triumphed.

291

It had been won but at some cost, for many of our men had fallen. Over a third of our army lay dead on the battlefield, and many more were to die of their wounds by the next day. My Jomsvikings had fared better, losing only three men, and neither Torstein nor I suffered anything other than scratches and bruises. The Saxons had fled the field and had been completely routed. Their Lord's body now lay naked and headless in the company of three thousand of his countrymen's corpses.

We had many wounds to lick but nothing like those of the Saxon army. They were defeated and shattered, and Aethelred's army of Essex were scattered to the winds. The dead Norsemen were taken from the field by our thralls and placed in rows with their weapons and shields. Huge funeral pyres were built from wood taken from a nearby forest, on which the dead were laid together in their aetts. It was an enormous task for there were many bodies, and the work continued long into the night. The next day the fires would be lit, the flames would consume the corpses and the smoke would transport their spirits to Valhalla.

Meanwhile, the rest of Olaf's army took their spoils from the battlefield and moved into the deserted Saxon camp. Finding it well supplied, there was more than enough ale and mead to slake even Torstein's enormous thirst, and the sack of Maldon would have to wait until the following day. But the visit to the town did not happen, for in the morning we received visitors carrying a message for Olaf.

Three riders approached the entrance to the camp as the day was breaking. They were Saxon nobles and they waited, standing at the gates of the rough wooden palisade that ran around the camp. Armed men streamed out to meet them and surrounded the little party. Olaf soon appeared and waited for the commotion to die down before he spoke to the visitors who were now completely encircled by spearmen. They looked like they had ridden all night, for their horses were lathered with sweat, and both men and animals were caked in mud. Edmund, our ennobled Saxon prisoner, was brought forward to translate, although by now I had picked up enough words to understand what was being said. The men were in the service of King Aethelred, and they had ridden from his camp with a message for Olaf.

"You have ridden hard through the night, my Lords, but I am afraid you have missed the battle." called Olaf to them. "But we will be happy to fight again with the King's army. Are you here to tell us where this might be?"

This drew much mirth from our men who were straining forward to hear the conversation. The horsemen were led by a man of about forty years old who dismounted and approached Olaf. He announced himself as Thoren, the Ealdorman of East Anglia, who had been sent by the King with an offer of *Danegeld*, a bribe that would be paid in exchange for the cessation of our raiding.

"Then you should have been here yesterday before we routed the mighty Saxon army. I asked Lord Byrhtnoth for *Danegeld* then, and he refused me. His head is now on that stick over there," said Olaf.

Thoren ignored the hoots of derision and continued his entreaty.

"The King offers you a payment of ten thousand pounds of silver for you and your army to cease all hostilities towards him and his people. Should you wish to accept this offer, he invites you to *Lundenburgh* to hear his terms," said Thoren.

There was complete silence as each man who heard these words considered the enormity of the sum that was being offered, for this amount of silver would fill the bellies of several of our largest ships.

Olaf observed Thoren briefly before declaring, "That is a great deal of wealth. We must be causing your King a great many problems. I shall come and listen to his terms – we shall be in *Lundenburgh* in five days."

"Then we shall expect you, but please, Lord Olaf, you are asked to stop your raids, at least until you have met with the

King," replied Thoren.

"Of course," replied Olaf, his hands spread in an open gesture, "we shall stay our hands for now.'

Thoren bowed, mounted his horse, and the Saxons left the way they had come in.

Yesterday's victory had taken its toll on our army. We had lost many men, almost fifteen hundred, and more would die of their wounds before long. The army had been raiding for most of the long summer, and we needed some respite. Olaf wanted the people of *Lundenburgh* to see his army in the best possible light – fierce, well-disciplined Norsemen sailing their dragon ships up the River Thames, gunwales bristling with spears and shields. He wanted them to see his army and quake. Our army this morning was exhausted and filthy. We were drained and battered and needed a few days to restore our bodies, weapons and ships.

Olaf beckoned me and several of his captains to him.

"We shall stay here for three days," he said. "We have more than enough supplies without the need to find more. I want you to prepare your men for the trip. They should rest first and then make ready. The boats need mending, as do armour and weapons. There will be no more raiding for now, and I want Maldon left in peace – at least until we have Aethelred's silver."

The captured camp was as good a place as any to recuperate from the battle. There was a large freshwater lake nearby where men washed and cleaned their equipment. The Saxons had brought blacksmiths with them and although they had departed, all the equipment had been left behind together with their forges, hammers and anvils. Men returned to their boats and repaired hulls and sails.

"It is a shame," Torstein said to me later, as he sat combing his hair. "I was looking forward to visiting Maldon, but there will be plenty of time for that later. Let us collect our winnings, Bjorn, for it would appear that we are now men of even greater reputation and wealth. How much do you think we have amassed?"

I rubbed my chin. "We were wealthy men when we left Jomsborg," I said, "but now we are even more wealthy. The raiding has produced much plunder and with our share of the *Danegeld* there is enough to keep you in ale and whores for a hundred years. Why do you ask?"

He put down his combs and looked at me.

"I have no desire to risk changing our good fortune, and we have indeed enjoyed much since we left Haugesund, but surely it cannot last forever. Our crew is not in such fine fettle as we younger fellows, and they often talk of settling. I find the land of the Saxons quite agreeable, and I can think of worse places to stop and take stock."

"I thought we would have to range for another ten years before we talked of this time," I said, "and I had not put you down for a farmer just yet."

Torstein was right, for a few of the Jomsvikings were now carrying their years more heavily than others, and I knew many of them would welcome the idea of settling. Since Astrid's death, I had busied myself with fighting, and this was the first time I had even thought of giving up my warrior's life.

"You would not get bored then, staying in one place? Wives, children, working the land?" I asked him.

"I have thought long and hard of this, Bjorn. I cannot say I will not get bored, but I believe that even as farmers there would still be a little fighting to be done. Our world is changing now – faster than even you promised it would five years ago. Remember? On the beach outside our home? Perhaps we should count our blessings and consider a different path."

"True, there is some wisdom in your words. Let us call the men and talk together. You might be right, and it may well be time to consider what might happen next," I said.

That night my men sat together in front of the fire after we had spent the day making repairs to the Drakes Head. We left the main camp and walked back to the far side of the island of Northey. It was the first time I had appreciated the wild beauty of the place, a trackless island of dark pools and twisting muddy gullies where the huge rise and fall of the tides quickly flooded the land. We joined several other crews on the beach, men recovering from the trauma of the fierce battle, having exchanged their spears and shields for hammers and nails, at least for the day. We worked diligently throughout the morning and into the afternoon, painstakingly caulking the outer planking, joining damaged woodwork or mending torn sails. In the evening we built a fire, and while the other crews returned to the camp, we sat on the ground drinking and talking while our thralls prepared food.

I stood up and called for quiet and when the talking had stopped, I began:

"We have stood together against the spears and axes of many of our foes for over four years now. We have watched our friends and comrades fall beside us whilst the *Norns* have seen fit to spare us for another day. Four years is not so long, and I know many of you have sailed together for much longer. I also know that many of you have thoughts of settling – which has its own merits. You have earned considerable wealth as Jomsvikings, and you will now earn more plunder from Olaf's success. If anyone wishes to leave this army – when its task is complete – no man here will think badly of you. We agreed to come to England and fight for Olaf, and ourselves, but this work will not last forever, and it is always good to hear your thoughts."

Einar, the old Norwegian, a man who had seen more and travelled further than the rest of us got to his feet.

"It is true, Bjorn," he said, "we cannot fight forever. The gods have blessed me by bringing me so far and in such good company. I would hate to think that I had fought my last battle, but each fight is getting much harder than the last. If *Odin* sees fit for me not to die with a sword in my hand, then I shall respect his wishes and be happy to take up the plough.

The land here in England is fertile, and hopefully the same goes for my seed, so I for one would not object to staying."

Several of the younger men got to their feet and took their turn to speak. Most wanted to settle, but there were a few who wanted to continue to go a-viking and take their chances raiding. Now it was Torstein's turn, and he lumbered to his feet.

"It is true we are all brothers in arms," he said. "It is also true that we have shared triumph and disaster, and without our brotherhood we would be but bones on the plains of Fyrisvellir. Just because we should want to settle in one place does not mean we become lesser men. Our strength is in our bond, and I would rather we stay together whether we are warriors or farmers. If we stay here, we will have enemies on all sides of us, and we will need every spear just to survive."

A man shouted from the back of the group, "as long as you don't want us to become priests, Torstein!"

When each man who wanted to speak had done so, it was time for me to take my turn again,

"I left Norway five years ago with this fine young warrior here," I said, touching the seated Torstein on the shoulder. "We left our homes and families, like many of you, to gain wealth and reputation, and now we have both. We also left because the old ways were changing. New kings were taxing us, Christianity was creeping through our land, and the days when a man could raid at will were coming to end. We have achieved much, but our greatest achievement is to have sailed and fought beside you, the warriors of the Jomsvikings." I saw Torstein nodding his great shaggy head. "If you want to stay here in England, I will stay with you, but if you wish to keep ranging with or without Olaf's army, then I shall come with you too."

As was our custom when such a momentous decision was to be made, every man took a vote. Sixty of us voted to stay in England, while only four wanted to keep raiding.

"That is settled," I said. "I will talk to Olaf of our

decision, and when he releases us from his service, we shall seek land here in Essex. Let us toast to England's new farmers."

"Warrior-farmers!" shouted Torstein jumping to his feet spilling ale over those close to him.

Our company stayed on the beach until dawn, and at first light we returned to join the rest of the camp. This would be our last day here, for tomorrow the army would leave and sail for *Lundenburgh*. The rest had been good, and the men were refreshed.

We left on the high tide. Some of the crews had been so depleted that there were not enough men to fully man all the ships, many of which had to be either abandoned or towed. There was little wind today, and progress was slow as we rowed along the coast until we found the mouth of the River Thames. Turning into the estuary, we sailed up the course of the river before anchoring the fleet offshore near a place the locals called Flete.

We were now a day's journey from *Lundenburgh*. It was an uneventful voyage the next day, but as we made our way upriver, we passed many settlements on the shoreline, increasing in size and number as we drew closer to the city. There was little river traffic going in the other direction, for news had travelled of our impending arrival, and the people of *Lundenburgh* would be wondering what to expect from this vast fleet of Norsemen. There was little to fear from us now, for we thought of only one thing: the *Danegeld* that would bring the Saxons relief from our army.

Chapter 35: Lundenburgh and the King of England

The Drakes Head rowed behind Olaf's dragon ship, the Norse Spear, and when we were in sight of the city on the south shore, we made our way, as planned, to the opposite bank. Here the fleet would anchor while we waited for a message from the Saxons. Some of our ships tied up, where they could find room, in the small harbour of Southwark. I joined Olaf on the quay, and we made our way into the nearby town where we were the subject of keen interest from the locals.

"They don't know whether to welcome us or to flee," Olaf said, "but we shall wait here for a while until we receive word. Come, Bjorn, let us see what our unwitting hosts can provide us with."

Our little party walked through the streets of the town, eventually finding a tavern where we sat and waited. The fleet, either anchored or berthed in the harbour, was in full view of the people of *Lundenburgh* on the opposite shore. We were an impressive sight – nearly one hundred ships full of warriors, all preparing to land. An enormous wooden bridge that spanned the water joined the two shorelines of the river. Numerous shafts driven into the riverbed secured the bridge, and at the feet of each were huge piles of rocks, which held them firm against the strong currents of the Thames. There were large gaps between each pile, but with the river surging through them with some ferocity, it would be difficult to navigate if we decided to go further upstream.

As if reading my thoughts, Olaf called across the table: "That will be an interesting voyage if we need to go upriver. Look, the locals seem to have rediscovered their courage."

We both looked up to the top of the bridge, about two thousand paces away, which was filling up with people coming to gawp at the new arrivals. There were now hundreds of them ranged across the bridge silently looking down on us.

"They are not unlike us, the Saxons," he said. "They came from Germania many years ago after the Romans left this place and took the country from the Britons. We have much in common with these people really. They threw us out a few years ago, so it is good to come back and teach them a lesson. Now, I believe you have something to discuss with me, Bjorn. A good leader should know the minds of all his best men."

I marvelled at Olaf's ability to know everything that was going on in his army, and after recovering from the surprise I laughed, a little nervously, and told of the meeting with my men. When I had finished the story of last night's events he thought for a moment, as he always did before there was something important to say.

"I shall miss you at my side, Bjorn, and I shall miss my Jomsviking bodyguard. You are right, though. Our world is changing, and every man must change with it if he is to prosper. You are sure you want to settle in Essex, though, for you will have plenty of enemies on all sides? You will be a foreign Lord deep in Saxon territory."

"Yes, it will be a little hostile I am sure at first, but our people have survived and prospered in harsher places than Essex. We will be sixty warriors, some a little old, but fierce warriors nonetheless," I said.

"Well, I give you my blessing, but you are still in my service until I dismiss you," he said with a sly wink, "and as my bodyguard you shall all accompany me into *Lundenburgh* to see what this Saxon King has to say for himself."

We called for more ale and talked until a commotion further down the way caused us to pause and look up.

"We have visitors. Time to get your men up here," he said.

I called to Torstein seated at another table and he went back to get the men ready. The three Saxon nobles who had visited our camp only five days ago stood before us. They were accompanied by a troop of about twenty men carrying spears and shields.

"Greetings, Lord Olaf. I trust you had an uneventful journey to *Lundenburgh*," said their leader, speaking in fluent *Donsk tunga*.

"And greetings to you also, Thoren," replied Olaf, in English. "Now, I have come a long way to meet your King. He is ready for me?"

"Yes, Lord. He awaits you in the King's Hall on the far side of the city. We have brought horses for you."

"No need for them, thank you, for we prefer to walk, and you probably have not brought enough animals to seat my bodyguard," said Olaf.

He nodded to where Torstein was marching at the head of the troop of men.

"You have heard of the mighty Jomsvikings? Well, they now protect me in all places, and I am seldom separated from them," he continued.

The men of Baldyr's Wrath looked as fierce as ever. Each man was dressed in full-length mail and helm. They also carried their spears and the round wooden shields that bore a black raven on a red background. Torstein marched at their head carrying his huge double-headed battle axe, casually slung over one shoulder. To complete his impressive appearance, he wore the full-faced silver and gold helm that he had taken from the dead Frisian pirate on Laeso.

Torstein halted in front of us with much ceremony.

"Your bodyguard awaits your pleasure, Lord Olaf," he said, crisply.

Olaf nodded to Torstein.

"And this man is Bjorn Halfdanson, the Spear Arm and slayer of Byrhtnoth," he said to Thoren. I nodded curtly in the Saxon's direction.

"We shall go on foot then," said Thoren. "If you will come with me, King Aethelred awaits us."

Our procession commenced – Olaf, Thoren and me at the head of a column of more than sixty Norsemen and twenty Saxon spearmen. We marched through the burgh of Southwark and up to a large wooden door on the bridge that opened as we approached. Two spearmen pushed the heavy oaken doors wide and we marched through. A huge crowd of people, waiting on the bridge, parted silently to let us pass. They observed us with a mixture of fear and fascination, for it was the first time that many of these people had been so close to a Norse warrior. The bridge was longer than it looked, and I counted two hundred paces, yet we were still on it.

"An impressive structure," said Olaf to me.

Thoren interjected, "We built it on top of the old bridge the Romans constructed. It took over twenty years in all to build, but it serves as an effective defence against anyone wishing to visit us from the sea. It is easy to defend, and the current deters most uninvited visitors from getting through unharmed."

"Then we shall take care not to go upriver uninvited," said Olaf.

As the two of them talked, my attention was drawn to the huge walls on the north side of the river to which we were heading. They were made of stone and wood; the stone looking very old against the newer wood that had been built on top of it. These were the remains of the Roman walls, constructed many years before, which the Saxons now used to defend their city. A high wooden palisade had been built on top of the solid stone base. There was another gate on the far side of the bridge which was open, and we marched straight through. I looked around at Torstein, proudly marching at the head of our men, and smiled knowing he would be playing up to the young women in the crowds who thronged either side of the street watching us. They were no longer silent now but there was little noise from their conversation, and they whispered to each other as we passed. We left the bridge and entered the city's streets filled with crowds standing outside tightly packed wooden houses and shops. Thoren led the procession through a number of winding streets before the road widened, and we marched into the courtyard of a grand looking stone building. Outside this construction were stationed twenty spearmen standing guard.

"The King waits for you inside," said Thoren to Olaf, "but you must leave your weapons outside the palace, and your men must stay here too. We shall fetch them food and drink."

"I have no problem with this," said Olaf, removing his sword belt, "but Lord Bjorn must come with me."

I was stunned, for I had never been called 'Lord' before, but Olaf winked at me and motioned for me to remove my sword and *seax*. Unarmed, we were led up the stairs to the palace and through the open front doors into a large empty room where Thoren asked us to wait before going to announce our arrival.

"What do you think of *Lundenburgh*, Lord Bjorn?" Olaf asked.

"It is a little bigger than I was expecting," I said, "and some of their buildings are quite fine."

"There are a few impressive buildings, but the finest ones are only the remains that the Romans left behind. This place for example looks very grand but scratch beneath the surface and most of it is no more than you might expect in any large Scandinavian town. We are not the barbarians they think we are. Now the city of Miklagard, that is truly something to behold."

Thoren reappeared.

"The King is ready for you. Follow me," he said.

He led us to another door into a huge well-lit room lined with men on each side. We followed him through the room towards a man seated at the end who rose to his feet as we approached. King Aethelred was a little younger than me, perhaps eighteen or nineteen, and wore a gold crown. He was also much shorter than me and looked more like a priest than a warrior. He wore no weapons and had on a long, black woollen coat. His hair was cut short, and his large round face betrayed signs of nervousness as he met Olaf's gaze.

"You must be Lord Olaf Trygvasson," he said, turning then to me. "And this is…?"

"This is Lord Bjorn Halfdanson, Commander of my bodyguard and leader of my fleet," announced Olaf.

"Ah, the slayer of Byrhtnoth," said the King, "and how did he die? Bravely?" he asked, staring at me.

"With a sword in his hand in front of his men," I said.

"Yes of course. You Norsemen prefer to die in battle, I am told."

"It is true," I said looking him in the eye. "A warrior's journey to Valhalla can only be made with a weapon in his hand."

The King smiled nervously at me then returned his gaze to Olaf when he spoke.

"You have an offer for me, I believe," he said.

"I have," said the King. "Now come let us sit and talk civilly."

He pointed to a long oak table at the side of the room to which we were led by Thoren. Olaf and I stood at one side and waited for the King to be seated at the other side, flanked by his nobles. We sat down opposite England's King to hear his terms.

"These men are my advisors, part of the *Witan*," explained the King. "They have counselled me on the problems that your invasion has caused us. But first I am curious to understand something – why do you attack us with such fury?"

Olaf thought for a moment before answering. "Your land is rich, and ours is not. You have much fertile land while ours is mostly harsh and barren. We are strong and hungry for land and wealth. We will be content when we have taken what we need."

"If we give you what you need will you leave us in peace?" said the King.

"I shall give every consideration," replied Olaf.

"Then here is my offer. We shall pay you ten thousand pounds of silver to leave these shores forever. You shall cease to attack our towns and cities and will attack neither our ships nor the ships of merchants coming to or from the ports around my kingdom."

Olaf considered these words and spoke. "That is a considerable amount of money. But why should I not stay and continue to plunder your land? If I stay and keep making war on you, I will keep getting richer."

"Because, as we both know, this will not happen. You have destroyed Lord Byrhtnoth's army of Essex, but that is but one army of the many I can raise in my kingdom. You have suffered many losses also, and those men cannot be easily replaced. We have many more men than you do, and in the end we will triumph. You should take our offer and go while it is here."

"The offer is a generous one, but some of my men like the land around Maldon, where we fought, and rather than laying waste to it would prefer to stay, as many Scandinavian people have done before us in the *Danelaw*. They would prefer to settle and farm the land than take it by force, and if they had your royal protection they could live in peace.

The King said nothing as he contemplated Olaf's request.

"And how many of these 'settlers' might there be?"

"They are but sixty men – and their families, and they have a liking for Essex. They will be ruled by Lord Bjorn here."

The King once again, thought for a moment and looked at me as he considered his answer.

"This is a small number of men to consider, but I would ask this. If I give you this land you must protect it against our enemies and repel all invaders, including any of your hostile kinsman."

Olaf said nothing but looked at me. I nodded in agreement.

"And they must convert to Christianity," continued the

King.

"I am sure that they would embrace this religion with open arms," said Olaf enthusiastically.

"Then I agree to your terms," said King Aethelred.

We stayed for a little while longer while the two men engaged in conversation, and then the meeting was over. There would be a written agreement, and we would return in one day for Olaf and the king to sign it. We left the King's Hall and rejoined our men who were standing around in the courtyard outside. Torstein and his troop were in one corner of the tiled square casually regarding the Saxon spearmen who were standing guard.

"We have concluded our business for the day," I told the men. "We will go back to join the others now."

Thoren and his men escorted us back through the city to the gates at the far side of the bridge. The crowds had grown bigger on our return journey, and they stood in great numbers at the sides of the roads. They had discovered their voices and although no-one dared to call to any of us directly, they were less subdued now. Thoren saw us through the gates. He would meet us tomorrow morning and take us back to see the King for the agreements to be signed.

"That all seemed easier than I expected," I said to Olaf a little later as we sat outside an alehouse in Southwark.

"Never underestimate the fear that these people have for us, Bjorn. The fear that makes it hard for them to defeat us. It is easier for them to pay us off than to fight us and they do not lose a single man. This Aethelred is a weak King who would give us gold and silver to make us go away when he should be spending it on making his army strong. He knows it will only be temporary and we will be back next year. Tomorrow I shall sign his parchment, and we will wait for our silver and gold. No one will die, and we will all be wealthy men.

"Now have you told your men they are to be Christian

farmers yet?" He laughed, clapped me on the back, calling for more ale.

Later that day I gathered my men together in our rough camp outside the burgh of Southwark. It was on high ground just up from the river away from the foreshore where we could observe the bridge into *Lundenburgh* with all its comings and goings. I told them what had happened, of the huge sum of silver that we had extorted from the Saxons, and of how we would be given a large tract of land in Essex on which to settle. There was great excitement at the news and the babble of voices grew, but I raised my hand and called for quiet.

"There is one condition though. We are all to be baptised as Christians," I said and waited for a reaction from the hushed company. No one spoke, and each man considered what I had just said as my gaze passed from face to face looking for a reaction.

Torstein broke the silence. "I understand that there is a little bit of getting wet, and then their god will forgive us our actions against the Saxons, and then we can get on with things again. For this small indignity I am prepared to say I am a Christian."

"Think of it as just another god to join the ones we have already. I don't think Thor and *Odin* would have brought us here in the first place if they were displeased," I said.

There was a lot more discussion as men asked questions which I tried to answer, but in the end, there was no dissension. For the small chore of our baptism, we would have land aplenty. Our gods had sent us favourable winds to bring us here and make us wealthy men, and we would not turn from them completely. Eventually, when there were no more questions our group broke up, and Torstein took me and some of the other men to an alehouse that he had discovered in the town where we spent the rest of the day contemplating our good fortune.

Southwark was quite a large town, not as big or grand as

Lundenburgh on the other side of the river, but still a substantial settlement of perhaps five hundred people or more. There were many Norse folk – some of whom lived there, and others just passing through. There were also people of many different nationalities – merchants, tradesmen, shop owners – all living in relative peace. The news of the victories of Olaf's army was well known by the time we arrived, and although the welcome we were given by the local people was a little cautious at first, we were well received. The men behaved boisterously as only a victorious army could, and the keepers of the well-stocked local taverns were delighted to receive our coin. It felt good for the fighting to be over, at least for the moment, and to be drinking in the company of trusted friends with whom I had travelled so far and shared so much. I was happy and content, but very soon my world would be changed forever.

"Will we have to go to church?" called Torstein to me across the table.

"Only if we have committed many sins against our fellow Christians," I called back.

Torstein was on his feet again calling for yet another toast to the victorious army of Norsemen. As he held his drinking cup high, toasting the roomful of seated warriors, he looked over my head, eyes wide, and his jaw dropped. I turned to follow his gaze and saw her coming towards me.

Chapter 36: A Ghost from the Past

She wore black woollen stockings, a thick leather tunic, and at her waist hung two small throwing axes and a short *seax*. Her bare, tattooed arms bore the symbols of wolves and ravens, and her long hair was pulled back in a single plait. It was Turid. She strode towards our table with purpose. I was on my feet and facing her in a single movement.

"Too famous now to seek out an old friend?" she called across the room.

I opened my mouth to reply, stuttered and stammered like an idiot, but finally got a few words out.

"Turid? Is that you?"

"Of course, it's me. Are you going to give me ale? I have something of a thirst having spent the last five years looking for you. Come, old friends are allowed to embrace, you know."

She was smiling now, and her arms were held wide inviting my response. I reached for her and wrapped my arms tightly around her, lifting her off the ground as we embraced.

"It is so very good to see you," I finally mumbled in her ear. She said nothing, just held me in a fierce embrace. I eventually put her down and looked into her eyes. It was quite a few years since I had watched her on the cliffs as we sailed away from Byrum on the Raven. She had changed – as, no doubt, had I – but she was still the beautiful girl I left five years before. Her face was shining with tears that rolled down in a constant stream which she tried wiping away with the backs of her hands.

Torstein broke the spell and thrust a cup of ale into her hands. "You cannot expect a lady to ask twice for a drink," he said. "Come, sit with us, and I will introduce you to our friends here while my cousin regains his senses."

The men made room for her at our table, and she

squeezed into a seat between Torstein and another man while I returned to the bench opposite her.

"To old friends," said Torstein, raising his cup to Turid. "Better to fight and fall than to live without hope or love. This woman, despite her girlish fair looks, is a very old friend, and I hope she can be persuaded to tell her tale."

My comrades raised their cups to her. With such encouragement, Turid began her story while I looked on like a lovelorn youth. She told us of her journey to Sweden where she went into the service of Gunnila, a warrior queen from Birka. She served the Queen until her death and then sailed to England to raid the coastline with a small company of Swedish warriors, men and women. They settled in the Isle of Man, but Turid left in the spring in the hope of joining Olaf's army on the south coast where it was rumoured to be heading. She was on a boat full of Danes that followed our progress along the coast until they found our fleet sailing away from Northey Island.

"But, alas, by the time we caught up with you the fighting was over. We did hear of the exploits of some mighty warriors of Norway, one of whom sounded like the man I had been searching for these past few years," she said, looking in my direction.

I had not taken my eyes off her since she sat down at our table, and I watched in awe at how boldly she spoke in the company of these grizzled warriors. She would be twenty-two years old now, and her tanned, youthful face betrayed little of the perils she had sailed through to get here. Her frame was still slight, and she carried not a morsel of spare flesh, but it was her startling blue eyes that held my gaze as I listened to her words. Then, finishing her story and her ale, she turned to me, fixing me with a determined look that I had forgotten.

"Come now, Bjorn," she said, "I have not travelled these five years to sit here drinking all night, even if your comrades are very fine fellows. We have much to catch up on."

She got up and came around to my side of the table, took

my hand, and led me out of the tavern. The night had fallen, but the evening was still warm and balmy. She said nothing, but she turned to me and kissed me with great passion.

"I said we have much to catch up on, Bjorn. If you still have that bearskin cloak fetch it now, for we will have need of it."

We walked out beyond the town, past the beached ships on the foreshore and up onto the high grassy bank where we made our camp for the evening. I laid my cloak on the ground, and there we stayed until dawn.

The morning light broke gently over our little camp, and I woke to the sound of the river fowl and Turid's gentle breathing. She clung to me fiercely, even in sleep, and I carefully prised her arms from around my neck. She did not wake but rolled over, and I watched her sleeping for a few moments lying naked beside me. It had been almost five years since we had lain together on this same cloak, and her body had changed a little. The soft curves were as I remembered, but her limbs were now sinewy and muscular from her years of training at arms. She moved in her sleep and curled into a ball revealing the curve of her naked back on which she wore the tattoo of a raven in flight. I dressed as quietly as I could, thinking she was still deep in sleep, but as I buckled on my weapons she spoke.

"You are not leaving me again so soon, Bjorn," she declared – a statement, not a question.

I put my weapons on the ground and lay down beside her. Then I put my arms around her and pulled her close into me.

"Only death shall part us again, my love," I whispered in her ear. "Now though I have business and must meet Olaf, for today we will secure our future. I will come and find you later when we are done."

"Do not make me come and find you again," she said sleepily, her eyes still closed, "for you know there is no place for you to hide." I kissed her neck, covered her with her coat and left her there.

It was a short walk along the foreshore back to the Drakes Head where I washed and combed my hair and beard. There were a few men sleeping under an awning, but most were still in the town or staying in the makeshift camp just outside. I readied myself and stepped off the boat onto the harbour. One of our men called down to me; it was Rurik the Norwegian.

"You look fit for a King's company, Lord Bjorn." he said. "I wish you luck today for you have all our fates in your hands."

"Lord Bjorn? I think not, but I will see you a little later at the feast, for I believe even humble farmers must have a plan. Now, where can I find Olaf?"

I found him outside the tavern where we had been the day before. He was waiting there with Torstein and three horses which had been saddled up ready for us.

"What do you think of these beasts, Bjorn? Handsome enough for Norwegian nobles? I do not think we need the bodyguard today – the Saxons are fearful enough. If there is any trouble, I expect we three can be a match for anything."

The three chestnut stallions, brought from a local stable in the town, were huge, strong animals, but we were all experienced horsemen who had learned to ride from an early age. We mounted up and rode off towards the gate at the bridge to meet Thoren. He was there waiting for us with his men.

"A smaller company today, Lord Olaf?" he called as we approached.

"I thought the three of us would suffice, this morning," replied Olaf.

Thoren called for his own horses, and once mounted, led us through the gate and back over the bridge to the King's Hall. There were fewer bystanders to witness our procession this morning as we filed through the streets of Lundenburg, followed by Thoren's troop of men. Once in the hall, we were shown through to the King who waited for us at his table in the long room. We were invited to sit opposite, and with Torstein standing at our backs, the meeting began without ceremony.

A man seated next to the King spoke. Finely dressed and about thirty years old, I discovered later that he was Leofwine, the son of Byrhtnoth. He pushed a large piece of parchment towards Olaf.

"In return for your guarantees of peace to our land, rivers and shorelines we shall deliver to your camp ten thousand pounds of silver or gold equivalent in ten days' time. You will be required to disperse your camp and return home. You read the Latin script, Lord Olaf?"

"Well enough. It is what we agreed," Olaf replied, looking at the document, reading the words and nodding his head.

"And the provision for my men who will remain in Essex?"

"They shall receive a tract of two hundred and fifty hides of land which they shall be given on their baptism. The land shall be theirs in perpetuity, and they shall be required to guard and protect it and any people that dwell on it. They will also be required to repel any invaders."

Leofwine pushed another parchment towards Olaf who pushed it to me. I pretended to read it.

"You are satisfied with this offer, Lord Bjorn?" asked Olaf.

"I am," I said, nodding.

The priest sitting on the right of Aethelred then addressed us in a high pitched, reedy voice.

"You must have your men ready for baptism this Sunday. We shall meet you on the riverbank in two days' time." Then, turning to me, he added sniffily, "We shall be sending a priest with you to Maldon, Lord Bjorn. We have recently built a new church, and after the disturbances the town is empty. Perhaps

313

once people see a benevolent new leader they will return."

I nodded but understood little of what he said. Another priest hurried in with a goose quill and some ink. He gave it to King Aethelred who took both parchments back and signed each before pushing them to Olaf who did the same.

The King then spoke for the first time.

"Your ransom shall be brought to your boats, my Lords. Then, praise God, you shall leave our shores and let the people of this land enjoy His blessings. He celebrates each and every new Christian, and there will be joy in heaven at the conversion of your men." Then, looking directly at me, he said, "You will find our Lord Jesus very forgiving. Please obey the laws of men and God, and I pray you will find peace."

The King rose and left the room, followed by the group of attendant priests and advisors, leaving Thoren to see us back to our horses.

"You know your way back to the gates by now," he said. "I shall bring your ransom to you once it has been collected. Until then the freedom of Southwark is yours, but I must ask you to stay beyond the walls of the city of Lundenburg. The people are fearful of your army camping under their noses, and frightened men and women can be both foolish and unreasonable."

We mounted, left the courtyard and were soon clattering our way across the wooden bridge towards the city gates which the guards opened to let us out.

"They seemed quite glad to see the back of us for some reason," shouted Torstein as we rode three abreast through the open gates and along the riverbank towards Southwark.

"A good morning's work, all the same. You are now landed English nobles it would seem. What will your first act to your local people be?" shouted Olaf to us both.

"I believe Torstein is keen on repopulating Maldon with Norse blood. That should account for his activities for the next year or so," I answered.

"Perhaps I should start practising tonight," said Torstein.

"The sight of so much silver in a man's hand is enough to turn any maid's head."

"Let us wait until Aethelred delivers the ransom before we start spending it," said Olaf. "Anyway, I have organised a feast for us for the next few days, so that should give you plenty of opportunities to spread your favours. We have brought all the spare ale in both towns so let us hope you have a thirst."

He spurred on his horse to where his army, two thousand strong, waited patiently for his return, gathered on the riverbank in the gap between Southwark and the gates to London Bridge. Each warrior knew the outcome of the morning's meeting, for the ransom amount was well known, but they gathered anyway to welcome back the man who would give them gold and silver aplenty. Then there came the thunderous sound of spears beaten against shields and men cheering as Olaf approached his troops and stopped in front of them. When the cheering died down, he spoke:

"Today is a good day for England, for we have agreed to stop waging war against them, and they have promised us a king's ransom to leave these shores. When you have all been paid your battle shares, I will release you from service. You may join me, for I have some unsettled business in my homeland and shall return to settle it. There will also be a new settlement here in England, in the place where we shed much blood not so long ago, and we will say goodbye to many of our brothers who will be staying. Our good friend here – *Jarl* Bjorn of Maldon – who has fought at my side this summer and deserves his reward, shall rule there. Now enough of this sentiment, for we have much feasting to do."

He leapt down from his horse and lead the host of Norsemen back into the town to where mountains of food and drink had been prepared for the feast. Torstein and I were left alone on our horses.

"First a Lord, now a *Jarl*. I feel I should at least bow my head, cousin," he said mockingly.

"You know very well, Torstein, that what is mine is yours – so we shall each be half a *Jarl*."

"No, that does not sound like it will work very well, so I reject your offer. I will be happy to be the *Jarl*'s champion and head farmer."

"Then I gratefully accept your offer," I said. "Now, come, you must be thirsty after all that standing around."

We turned to follow the others but stopped in our tracks as a slight figure came striding towards us. It was Turid. I dismounted and led my horse to meet her.

Torstein called to me as I passed him, "She has been waiting a long time for you, Bjorn. I will keep you a seat at the hearthfire." He kicked his horse forward to follow the others.

Although she had the build of a boy, she walked with the confidence of a warrior. After all, that was what she had become in the past few years, and her many arm rings testified to the battle honours she had won. It took me a long time to understand that the young girl I had left behind had now turned into such an accomplished fighter.

"So, it is *Jarl* Bjorn now? I had better treat you with a little more respect," she said.

I felt myself blush slightly.

"Don't worry Bjorn. You are still that callow Norwegian boy I remember." She reached up and kissed me on the lips before I could utter a word. "Now let us get up on that fine stallion of yours and take a closer look at this country so that I might decide whether to stay or not."

I mounted the horse again and pulled Turid up behind me.

"Which way do you want to go?" I asked her.

"It is of no consequence. I do not care as long as we are not parted again," she said.

I turned the stallion towards the east and the sea. Giving the animal his head, we raced away from *Lundenburgh* and Southwark, following the road beside the river. The dwellings became fewer and fewer until there were none at all, and we stopped by a shady clump of trees. We dropped to the ground and let the horse drink from a brook nearby.

"I am a little hot and dusty," said Turid, unbuckling her weapons and removing her clothes before running headlong into the river. I needed no invitation and followed her. Soon the two of us, naked in the cool water, were oblivious to everything but each other. We left the river and threw ourselves down onto the shady patch where the passionate hunger of our years apart boiled to the surface. Finally, exhausted, we slept, arms and legs entwined.

I woke sometime later and looked up to see her staring down at me, still naked, hands on hips. Her long, slim limbs were perfectly defined, and her flat stomach was taut and muscular. She stood above me with her legs slightly apart, watching me.

"Now, that is a fine sight to greet a waking man," I said.

"It's getting late. Time to go," she said, "let's hope the horse knows his way home."

We dressed quickly, mounted up and traced our path back to Southwark. For the first time since our reunion, we found time to talk. I told her of my journey, and she shared hers again with me. Not all at once, for I sensed she had suffered, at least for some of the time, and I did not press her for the details. On the way back there were moments of quiet, but the silences were easy between us, and I prayed that we would have a lifetime together to share our stories. It was getting dark, and the lights of Southwark twinkled away far in the distance. Turid had her arms wrapped around my waist, her head resting against my back as the horse picked his way through the night along the riverbank.

The town was quiet, and we skirted around it to find the camp and the place where the feasting was taking place. There were two spearmen guarding the entrance to the camp, but both were drunk and paid us little attention. We made our way to where the fires were burning and huge tables and benches had been set up. The army was seated all around, but they were completely quiet as all eyes looked to where Torstein's easily recognisable frame cast a long shadow in front of one of the fires. His words, caught on the night breeze coming off the river, held the rapt attention of each man and woman in the audience. I recognised the words of his story: The Saga of the Wandering Warriors. The tale, once begun, drew rapturous applause and words of praise from the crowd. We took a seat at a nearby table and people moved up to make space for us.

Whether Torstein saw us I do not know, for he was in full flow. He recounted our deeds along the Baltic Coast, the battle of Truso, the treachery of Harald Bluetooth, the flight from Fyrisvellir and our recent adventures in England – including the death of Byrhtnoth at my own hands. He went on for some time and had many new verses, but by the time he was finished he was bathed in sweat and milked the applause from over two thousand men and women.

"You are indeed famous now Jarl Bjorn, I should treat you with more respect," said Turid, above the noise.

I was about to reply but cups of ale were thrust into our hands and men drank to my health.

"To the hero of Maldon," she shouted, before quaffing the first of many ales.

Torstein had seen us come in and came over to join us.

"What do think of our tale?" he said to her, and before waiting for the answer he continued, "What have you done to my cousin? I have seldom seen him so happy and carefree. Is it some Danish witch's spell?"

She said nothing even as Torstein winked at her suggestively.

"But whatever it is," he continued, "please do not stop, for I could get used to this version of my cousin."

The feasting continued long into the night until the fires burned down and men dropped to the ground in drunken exhaustion or went off with the local women. Turid finally prised me out the heartfelt embrace of my brother Jomsvikings.

"It is time for us to leave as well," she commanded, and we retrieved the horse and my bearskin cloak from the Drakes Head before retiring to a secluded place, a distance away, where we spent the remainder of the night.

The sun was high in the sky when we awoke.

"I could get used to living in this land," she said, as we watched the flight of a pair of noisy geese flying downriver.

"Now tell me of where we are going, where we are to settle."

I told her what I could remember, which was not much, for we had left only a few days after the battle and had not even entered the town of Maldon.

"It is green and fertile," I said, "and the fields were full of ripening crops. If I were a farmer, which I am about to become again, I would pick no other place."

In truth, I could really only remember the piles of bodies after the battle, the stench of blood and the carrion descending to feast on the corpses, but I made no mention of these memories.

"And I shall be a farmer's wife," she announced, "and a Christian one too. Now tell me what you know of this baptism ceremony we must take part in."

I was surprised at her words but pleased, for although she had agreed to come with me to Essex, she had said nothing about becoming a Christian.

"What is it?" she continued. "Another god to have in the house I suppose," she said.

"Yes," I said, "just one more god."

There was another day of feasting. It followed the same pattern as the day before, and there was plenty of eating and drinking. In the evening Torstein performed once again. This time he told The Saga of Olaf Trygvasson at the end of which he bowed low in front of our table.

"To the new King of Norway," he shouted to the crowd howling their appreciation for his story. Olaf, sitting next to me, was clearly moved and bade Torstein come close to him to receive the gift of a gold warrior ring. His army was drunk and happy in the knowledge that within eight days the ransom would be at their feet, and they would be rich men.

The excitement died down, and Torstein was replaced by a troupe of musicians who sang and played for us.

Olaf turned to me. "So tomorrow you will be baptised. I am curious – does this Holy Spirit actually come down and enter your body?"

I shook my head. "I do not know, for there is not one of us who has even seen a baptism before. I am told it is painless, but after tomorrow we will all know something different," I said.

"Then let us celebrate your last night as a Pagan – just in case this new god decides to take you off to his heaven."

The next morning all the Ravens gathered about the Drakes Head and we waited for the Saxon priests from Lundenburg. They finally arrived in a great procession from the gates of the bridge, followed by Thoren and a troop of about fifty spearmen. We watched the group approach, the priests in a long line behind their bishop who was dressed all in white. He wore a tall mitred hat, and beside him walked a boy of twelve or thirteen carrying a long pole on top of which was a large golden cross. Torstein shuffled about nervously muttering of magic and witchcraft. The rest of our group observed them silently, whilst other members of the camp came out of their tents to watch the unfolding events. Soon there were hundreds of our men watching. The bishop, a man called Aethelstan, who had sat at the King's right hand at our meeting, approached me directly. The rest of his attendant priests looked nervously about them at the growing number of armed warriors on either side.

"Good morning, Lord Bjorn," he said confidently. "You and your people are ready?"

"We are," I said, "what would you have us do? "

"I shall go into the water," he said, pointing towards the

river, now at high tide, not fifty paces away, "and you shall join me, one by one, to receive God's blessing."

He turned and led his retinue, all ten of them, into the water, waded up to his waist and beckoned us to follow him. I was unsure of what to do next and had no desire to look foolish in front of the camp. I looked to Thoren for guidance, but he simply nodded in the direction of the waiting priests.

Turid, standing next to me, said impatiently, "I have seen this done before. Just follow me."

She unbuckled her weapons, removed her leather tunic and walked into the water while we watched. The bishop said some words, and she let herself fall back into the arms of the other priests who submerged her completely before raising her back to her feet. I followed her lead, removed my weapons and armour and waded out. The bishop spoke words of Latin and made the sign of the cross as I was lowered into the water. The priests brought me to my feet again and the bishop spoke to me – this time in a few halting words of *donska tunga*.

"Welcome to the Kingdom of God," he said.

I walked back to shore and passed Torstein, who was the next to be baptised, and he looked at me as if trying to see if I had changed in any way. I smiled at him, which seemed to put him at ease, and he took his turn. One by one all my men entered the water and were baptised until none were left. The priests waded back out, and then the whole group of Saxons moved off as quickly as they had arrived.

"So now we are Christians?" asked Torstein.

"Now we are Christians," I confirmed, and the rest of the army, bored by the baptism ceremony, resumed the third day of feasting.

Chapter 37: Norse Warriors, Christian Farmers

The next week passed quickly, for there was much to organise and prepare. During our baptism, Olaf met with Thoren who confirmed that the danegelt was being collected and would be delivered as planned. The feasting eventually came to an end after a few more days, and my thoughts turned to our new life in Essex. Turid was happy, Torstein grew restless and my Jomsvikings prepared themselves for the next part of our journey.

"Becoming Christians was as nothing, but the conversion from Jomsviking to farmer is a far greater leap of faith," said Torstein one morning as our departure grew nearer.

The day the ransom was delivered, five carts drawn by oxen were pulled into our camp loaded with our gold and silver. There was more silver coin than I had ever seen before, and one cart was almost overflowing with silverware including candlesticks, cups, jewellery and plates. There was a separate cart carrying the gold, and a hundred Saxon warriors guarded the whole precious cargo, once again with Thoren at their head. There was so much gold and silver that it took an age for us to calculate its value and assess whether the ransom was complete. The gold caused more problems because we seldom used it to buy or sell anything, and although highly prized it was never easy to attach a value. However, after a great deal of counting and weighing the huge fortune, Olaf decided that the ransom had been paid in full. He called to Thoren after the final count.

"Give your King our thanks. Tell him we shall be gone in the next few days. We shall send the wagons back in the morning."

Thoren nodded curtly and led his men away without saying any more.

The silver was shared out according to the agreements Olaf had made with the individual ships' captains or the sea kings who had come with their warriors. The Saxon ransom, added to the loot plundered along the way, meant that most men would be returning home very wealthy. My crew had buried their treasure on Northey Island before we left, for it was simply too much to carry with us.

The next day, ships began to leave the beach. Some men would stay with Olaf and follow him back to Norway; others would drift off, but under oath not to raid the shores of England, at least for one year. The crew of the Drakes Head split into two when we purchased one of the longboats that had been towed from Essex. There were more ships than crews now, for we had lost so many men in the last battle they would have been scuttled and left where they lay.

We also brought several animals that would be making the journey to Maldon with us including a pair of milch cows, a breeding sow and boar and several chickens. With the animals in one boat and our valuables in the other, we prepared for our journey, and once the priest who would guide us to Maldon came, we left. Several of the men, led by Torstein, had by now persuaded some of the local women of Southwark to join us in Essex, and they too would be coming on our journey.

Olaf came down to see us as we made our final preparations. He took one look at the men struggling to get all the animals aboard and tethered and started to laugh.

"You know you can always forget about farming and join me. You are all brave and skilful warriors who will be much missed," he said.

"Thank you, but no," I said. "The die is cast, and the decision made. We shall try our luck on this fine piece of land that you have found for us. We are decided, we are of one mind."

"Then I wish you luck, Bjorn Spear Arm," he called to us all, "and all your men – and your women." Then, taking me to one side, he said, "Ah, I nearly forgot, this is for your service. You may be a *Jarl* now, but you are still my warrior. I give you this." He handed me a heavy gold warrior ring engraved with all manner of ancient runes. "Do not lose it when you are behind your plough, for there is not another one like it. It was given to me by the Emperor in Miklagard."

"Do not worry on that count. I shall take good care of it," I said.

"I have no doubt you will, Bjorn, and should you change your mind, you and your people will always be welcome in my longhouse. There will always be a special place at my hearthfire for you," he said.

He embraced me in a bear hug and turned and left us. I watched him walk back up the beach towards the camp, then turned to catch Turid looking at me.

"He won't be able to keep you warm at night as I can," she called over, before turning back to gather up a clutch of escaped piglets.

The priest did not arrive until the next morning. His name was Leofrith, and he hurried towards our boats wearing a dirty brown woollen habit and carrying a small bundle of belongings and a long wooden staff. He was small and weasel-like and wrung his hands nervously as he stood before me. He seemed a humble fellow unlike his master, the Bishop Aethelstan.

"I am sorry to keep you waiting, Lord Bjorn, but the Bishop was keen to give me final instructions," said Leofrith, scuttling to a stop in front of me.

"You are welcome, priest, but get in the boat quickly and we shall go before we lose the tide," I said.

He went to the Drakes Head and scrambled in, up over the side. With Torstein taking command of the other vessel, we pushed both craft into the river and rowed for the estuary and the sea, joining the busy traffic of departing ships on the river.

It took us two days to reach Maldon, and once again I took the helm of the Drakes Head. I invited Leofrith to join me at the tiller, and I questioned him about his life and his religion. He had been taken into the service of King Aethelred as a young boy where he was schooled as a priest and taught to read and write the Latin script.

"So, this Jesus Christ, he died and then came back to life before rising to the clouds to meet his father? He died so that we would be forgiven all our sins?" I asked.

"Yes, that is correct," said Leofrith, "and if you follow his path you shall join him in heaven as well."

"It is not so fanciful a notion," I said, for the Norse gods also have many strange and different provenances. "But will he forgive me for taking the lives of so many men."

"If you follow his path, he will forgive you everything."

"I will think on this, Leofrith. Now tell what you know of this place, Maldon."

"It is a town of farmers and fishermen and was where I was born. I was overjoyed when I heard that your Norsemen have not sacked it. The church was built in the time of the great King Alfred and had many followers. I served the priest there as a boy. I am happy to be returning, but I fear that the local people will flee when they see your ships arrive at Northey Island. It would be well that you have their support as the new Lord."

"And what of the old Lord. What happened to him?" I asked.

"Lord Eadred. He fell beside Lord Byrhtnoth some three weeks ago," he replied.

I cast my mind back to the recent events when I felled the Saxon leader with a spear through his throat. The battle had been at its height, and men were screaming and shouting all around me when I let go the javelin that changed the day.

"You knew him?" I asked

"Not well, but I knew him to be a pious and respected man, and he looked after his people well. You might do well to keep the local folk on your side, for their support might be a blessing to you in time. The land is vast, and it will take more than your men to farm it all."

"I will try and remember that, Father Leofrith," I said.

I had known him for less than two days, but I could not help but like the man. He had been given a difficult task in guiding two boatloads of heavily armed Norsemen to the place of his birth – a place that the same Norsemen had nearly destroyed only twenty days before. Yet, despite the odds, he took his duties very seriously and carried on cheerfully and helpfully. In due course, we arrived at Northey Island once more where we stopped and retrieved our plunder, and there was a great deal of it. In our time raiding along the English coast we had built up a considerable haul of captured silver coins, jewellery, plates, candlesticks and a good deal more. After this, we arrived heavily laden in the harbour at Maldon where we landed, tied up and started to unload. With our crew of sixty-three men of Baldyr's Wrath, ten thralls and five women we stood on the land which was now ours – or at least until someone took it away from us. We unloaded our goods and animals on the deserted quayside to prepare for a new life.

"Does this feel like home?" shouted Torstein.

"Not yet," I replied, "but it will not take long before it does. Now, let's see if the locals are friendly."

Leofrith bade us follow him through the town's empty streets, and Turid, Torstein and I walked after him. None of us knew what might happen next. In fact, nothing happened at all. Nothing stirred besides a stray dog who barked at us as we approached the church in the centre of the small town.

Leofrith turned to us with a look of triumph on his face. "And now I am home," he declared.

He walked up to the barred front door of the stone building. We helped him lift the large, wooded bar that kept the doors closed, and he pulled them open enthusiastically.

Leofrith plunged into the darkness inside leaving the three of us looking anxiously in.

"Come, there is nothing to fear. You are Christians now," he called out.

Torstein spat, and I felt for the amulet around my neck. Turid, a throwing axe in each hand, was already inside. We followed her into the darkness and looked around. The room was big enough for about a hundred people to sit on long wooden benches arranged in rows in front of a large, raised table upon which stood a silver cross.

"No one has been in here for some time," called the priest looking around. "I will have my work cut out for me."

We heard footsteps behind us and span round to see a woman and a small child silhouetted against the daylight by the open doorway. The woman clutched the child to her in alarm, and Leofrith called out to her. They clearly knew one another, and the woman was pleased to see the priest. She hurried towards him and they embraced as she gabbled away, throwing us nervous glances. Leofrith asked her many questions, and after some time he dismissed her gently and she left the church. He turned back to speak to us.

"That was my sister. She said that many of the people here left the town before the battle and have not returned. Many of the men died fighting in the *fyrd* for Lord Byrhtnoth, and those that remain are mainly widowed women and orphaned children with nowhere to go. The crops in the fields have not been gathered, and the cattle have gone untended for many weeks. They will starve this winter without food. I told her to tell them that we have a new Lord, a benevolent Norseman who will protect and feed them."

Turid raised her eyebrows at this last remark, but I answered him.

"We have been promised land here and will take what is ours," I said. "Any local people who desire our protection will need to work for me, the *Jarl*, as they would in our homeland. Please inform these people of my wishes."

"You can inform them yourself after worship on Sunday. I will ensure they are all gathered here. Now I will need to show you to Eadred's hall. You will find it comfortable enough and may wish to take it for your quarters. Please follow me."

The dead Lord's hall was indeed comfortable, but it had been left in a hurry, and there were signs of a panicked departure; food and drink, abandoned weeks earlier, lay untouched at the table.

"These people were in some haste to leave," said Turid.

"Can you blame them? They thought they were about to get a visit from Olaf and three thousand Norsemen," replied Torstein.

"And Norse women," she scolded.

I said nothing, and Leofrith carried on, fretfully tutting away to himself. The Lord's 'hall' was part of a large farm with several outbuildings and a huge stone hall at its centre – not unlike one of our longhouses at home. Inside was a great deal of furniture, and it looked like Eadred had a large family for there were clothes and possessions everywhere. Weapons and armour were hanging from the walls. Several hunting dogs roamed free around the land and buildings, and there was a plentiful stock of swine rooting through a nearby copse. We found a grain store that was still half full and barns that were well stocked with food. The surrounding fields contained several horses and cattle although there were also a few dead cows lying around.

"No one to milk them, of course," said Torstein sadly when he saw the rotting carcasses. "That is a shame."

"We looked after the cows together in Haugesund, as boys," I explained to Turid.

"You were farmers?" she asked.

"A lifetime ago," I said, remembering our boyhood. "And now, we are once again, so it would seem. They did not want for much here."

"Only an army of warriors strong enough to hold onto

all this wealth," she said.

I nodded in agreement, for these were rich lands indeed. The Lord and family lived in considerable wealth, and there was food in abundance.

"I would not have given all this up without a fight," said Torstein, "and I wager that somewhere in this hall is a hoard of hidden silver."

"Plenty of time for treasure hunting," I said. "But for now, I shall be happy enough just to have a roof over our heads for a few nights. Now, let us fetch the others, for we have much to discuss and plan."

The rest of our crew soon came to join us, and we settled into our new surroundings for the night. In the morning I took a group of men out to look over our new land. I rode my stallion, whom I named Dragons Breath, and the others found mounts in the nearby fields. With Leofrith as our guide, we explored these new lands which were green, fertile and full of all manner of unharvested crops. Fields were full of ripened wheat and corn, the trees in the orchards were heavy with fruit, and there was much game for the hunt.

"A man could grow happy and fat in these lands," I said to Turid who rode a frisky little roan mare beside me.

"He could also raise many children and keep a happy wife," she said, kicking her horse on to race ahead.

We had been riding for over half the day before Leofrith pointed out the boundaries of our land. We passed quite a few farms, many deserted now. There were a handful that were still inhabited, and the priest insisted we stop at each and greet the frightened farmers and their families, introducing them to their new lord.

We stopped at the borders of the land and rested for a while to eat.

"You approve of your new realm, *Jarl* Bjorn?" asked Torstein with a bow.

"I will if you stop calling me that," I snapped.

"Well, you had better get used to it, for it seems you have

a few more dependents now," he said, referring to the farmers and their families we had seen.

"And you, cousin, have you chosen a woman to be your farmer's wife yet?"

"I am in no hurry, for it seems that there are a good deal of women to choose from here," he said.

I knew he had already grown weary of the women who had come with us from Southwark, and they had already found willing new partners amongst the men. He was right, we had seen few Saxon men in evidence, for those who had fought against us were dead or gone. There would be many young women in search of a man. The battle of Maldon had claimed many lives on both sides, but the effect on the local people had been particularly harsh.

We returned to Maldon by nightfall to find that some order had been restored to Eadred's farm where a few of the local people had been persuaded to come out from hiding and volunteer their labour. All our men knew the wisdom of respecting our new neighbours, and the local people were treated with deference. Leofrith had taken great pains to instruct me that Saxons responded better to fair treatment rather than to the abuse with which we might treat a vanquished people. I, in turn, had passed this on to the men, but this had been a needless message, for each man could see a long and prosperous future here. Before winter came, most of them would take local women as spouses, and a union made in free will would make a better partnership than one made by force.

We decided to form secure farmsteads in groups of ten to twelve men. These farmsteads would be fortified and peopled by the men and their partners, and they would collectively settle their chosen area and make it their own. Each man would take a parcel of land, and he would farm and protect all those who dwelled on it and any land to which it was attached. We also agreed to offer protection to all the local Saxons, and unless they rose up against us, we would treat them kindly. In the fullness of time, we would create our own governing council, or Allthing, but for the present, I would be the sole arbitrator for any disputes.

As *Jarl*, I took Eadred's Hall with Turid. I chose ten men who would own land close to me, and we fortified the ground around the hall to ensure it was secure against the threat of any invaders. Torstein did the same with a group of men who moved close by and created their own fortified farmstead. In all, there were six such communities – all within a day's march of each other. The men took over the deserted farms and buildings where they settled, and there was no need to eject any Saxons. We had reached what the Christians referred to as their 'chosen land', and we were prepared to hold it at the cost of our blood and lives.

In those early days, there was a great deal to do and with the assistance of the local people, we restored some order. The dead animals were dragged from the fields and burnt, while the living ones were gathered and put back in their rightful place. The hunting dogs, not yet feral, were rounded up and returned to the kennels in one of the outbuildings. We learned there were hounds for hunting, each breed to its own quarry – deer, boar and otter. It was clear that Lord Eadred was fond of the hunt and spared no expense to indulge these pursuits.

The crops in the fields were also in need of attention, for they would soon go to ruin if left unattended. Leofrith was dispatched to bring all the remaining farmers to the church on Sunday to meet their new Lord, and after the service they would be feasted at the hall with all the rest of the people. Leofrith advised me that the people should be invited to work in the fields to bring in the crops for which they would be paid a wage. It was a far cry from our normal practice of enslaving a beaten population, but the priest was insistent that this gentle treatment of the Saxons would be far more productive. This would, of course, require at least a few of us to go to church on Sunday.

"Obviously you and the Lady Turid should come to address the people, and as many of your men as wish to come," he said to me earnestly. We argued which of us should attend.

In the end, at least twenty of the men decided that they wanted to 'practice' their Christianity and the following Sunday we were quickly schooled in the ways of the church service. The 'Lady' Turid found a dress to wear among those left behind by the womenfolk who had fled the hall. After bathing and grooming herself for an age, she emerged into the sunlight that morning in a plain woollen dress. I was immediately taken back five years to the beach in Byrum where I first saw her. She wore no warrior's rings nor any weapon now, and her only adornment was a plain gold necklace around her neck and some summer flowers woven into her hair.

I stared at her in some surprise.

"You look like you have seen a ghost," whispered Torstein to me, who had himself spent a good deal of time grooming and combing his hair and beard.

"I have," I said, moving towards Turid to get a closer look. She smelled of crushed lavender and thyme.

"Do you think I might pass for a Saxon lady?" she asked me.

"Every bit of you," I said. "That is until someone makes you angry. Now, come let us meet our new neighbours before I get distracted."

Leofrith interjected, "It is time to leave."

He led our party out of the courtyard and up the street to the church. As we approached the building, I could see more people outside than I thought were left in the town. They bowed their heads, and the crowd parted to let us through. We were mostly unarmed, although every man carried a concealed blade, out of caution, despite the priest's assurances that a show of weapons would be unnecessary.

In the throng were mostly women, although there were a few men among them, not warriors but farmers and tradesmen. We passed through and then went inside. There were many more people in the church, and they got to their feet as we entered and followed Leofrith up the centre aisle to an empty bench at the front of the large room.

The priest, now cleaned and scrubbed, with a glowing countenance, took his place on a raised platform and addressed us all in a loud voice that could be heard by all. I had no idea what he said, for he spoke to the Saxons in their native tongue, and we Norse-folk sat sheepishly pretending to listen. At his request the people kneeled to pray, and as he had instructed, so did we. He mumbled more incantations to the assembly, then mercifully the service was over, and I heard him say my name as he beckoned me to join him on the dais to speak to the people.

I left my seat and went to stand next to him looking into a sea of faces before me. Beyond the first bench where we sat, over a hundred Saxons looked expectantly towards me, waiting to hear their new Lord speak. I cleared my throat and addressed them, stopping from time to time for Leofrith to translate my rehearsed speech.

"My name is Bjorn Halfdanson, and I have been given this land by your King to live in peace with my people. We have promised him to protect you and your families and to defend you against invaders. You will live under our protection. You may see us as invaders and think we are here to steal what is rightfully yours. But your King has seen fit to grant us a new home, and you will come to see us as just and righteous people who will work and fight alongside you."

I continued in this vein and noticed one or two heads nodding in assent, but the reality was that we had taken this land by force and all the honeyed words in the world would not disguise that fact. Eventually, I came to the end of my address and concluded by inviting them all to a feast outside our new hall. Leofrith said a final prayer and dismissed us. I walked back through the church, Turid at my side, and led us back home to feast with our new neighbours.

"That was complete bullshit," said Torstein, as we walked together. "Still, we can at least show these people how Norse folk entertain their guests."

"We treat these people respectfully, Torstein. Remember they are not our slaves, so just keep an eye on the men to make sure they behave themselves."

He gave me a quizzical look and then dropped back to make himself known to a group of women who he been watching since we left the church.

It was around midday and the late summer sunshine bathed the courtyard in light where wooden tables and benches had been neatly laid out. An ox had been slaughtered and was roasting nearby. The Saxons had left us with plentiful food and drink – more than enough to provide for our gathering of two hundred people or so. The locals shuffled in and took their seats without talking and Turid took charge of proceedings, ordering our thralls to start serving ale. Leofrith blessed the food, which I learned he would do before each of our communal meals, and the food was brought to the hungry guests.

"Keep bringing out drink until they start talking," she ordered the thralls.

There was great activity as men and women went from table to table dispensing ale as quickly as they could. Torstein and some of the men went to sit with the Saxons, and I watched them encouraging the local people to eat and drink. It was a slow start, but eventually the speed at which cups were emptied and refilled increased. The level of talk also increased as Saxon and Scandinavian voices mixed in the afternoon sunshine. We could not understand them, nor they us, but as the day wore on more drink was consumed, tongues loosened, and no one cared what was said. Toasts were made, speeches were given, songs were sung, and as the afternoon moved into evening, our warrior skald got to his feet and gave stirring renditions of our favourite stories. The Saxon men and women had little idea of what he spoke about, but such was the drama of his performance as he capered and pranced in front of the fire, that it mattered not.

Turid had busied herself throughout the day talking and drinking with as many of the people as she could and making herself known to them. As the evening wore on, she returned to my side.

"It is time for us to go now, Bjorn." she said, "I hope you can lay your hands on that bearskin cloak again, for I have found us the perfect spot."

She took my hand and led me off into the night.

Chapter 38: A New Start

In the morning the work of gathering in the crops began. Leofrith had arranged for the locals to meet in the first of many fields which needed tending. They were very well organised and knew exactly what to do. Teams of men and women worked the field scything through the corn before collecting it and stacking it in neat sheaves. Soon over a hundred people were labouring, and we watched them as they went about their tasks with great enthusiasm, moving through each field before going on to the next. Our men tried to join them and help, but the work needed skill, and the clumsy warriors only hampered their efforts. Leofrith fussed away, cajoling and encouraging the men and women in equal measure.

"There will be plenty of opportunities for your men to learn to become farmers," he shouted to me, "but for now let these people get on and complete their work."

We watched them and learned as they worked. Even Torstein had to admit defeat and threw down the scythe with which he had been trying to cut some wheat to no great effect. By the end of the day, several areas had been harvested and over the next few days, the remaining fields were worked with the same efficiency. We fed the workers at the end of their daily toil, and each new dawn they returned and started again with the same enthusiasm.

After five days, the harvest from all the fields had been collected. The women tied the wheat into sheaves which dried quickly in the late summer sunshine. The bundles were then thrown into a cart, and one of the men would take it away to store it in an empty barn. We had no such fields at home in Norway, and I was amazed by the abundance of both wheat and corn which was piled high onto the ox-drawn cart. One of the Saxons took Turid and some of our people and showed them how to thresh and winnow the grain. Before long the grain had been stored, the hay had been stacked, fruits picked from the orchards, fences mended, and sheep shorn.

"Do you still think you can turn your warriors into farmers?" asked Leofrith as we sat in a field at the end of another busy day.

"Father, these men have had their fill of facing death in the shield wall, and it was their choice to take another path. It was not an easy decision for them to settle. They may not enjoy the fame they had as warriors, but they will all make stout farmers," I said.

"Then may you all enjoy God's blessing and live in peace," he said, making the sign of the cross for what may have been the hundredth time that day. I looked over and watched Turid still hard at work with her little group. She had found more dresses in the hall and had now chosen to wear them in preference to her own warrior's garb. She caught me watching her, and I called over, "You look much better than you did when you dressed as a man."

"I will show you what a woman can do with one of these," she called back waving a flail in my direction, and we both laughed.

Since being reunited, my life seemed to have taken a new direction. We spoke little of our pasts to each other and asked nothing of one another. She told me she had been searching for me for years, and now she had found me I was hers for eternity – there was no going back. I accepted this willingly, for although I had never expected to see her again, I was overjoyed to get her back, and the more time we spent together, the more inseparable we became.

Once the harvest had been brought in it was time for each group of Norsemen to go and start their own settlements. They took provisions, animals and some willing local women, and set out to find suitable land where they could plant their seed and set down roots. Torstein's group was the last to leave Maldon, and I went with them to a large, deserted farmhouse not far away from mine. His farmstead had been occupied until very recently, and there were sheep and goats in the fields. It was not as grand as the buildings and lands that I now considered home but more than sufficient to provide them with shelter and a good living. He had attracted the favours of a young Saxon widow from the town, and she had accepted his offer to join him in his new life. She was both bright and pretty, and they made a good match. Her name was Hild. She was from good farming stock, and Torstein would need her skills in his new life on the land. When the time came to leave, he took me aside and looked me in the face earnestly.

"Cousin, when you first told me of your plan to leave Haugesund I did not believe we would make it to Jomsborg. For me, it was just another adventure, and I knew that whatever happened you would not let me down. Now look at us – wealthy landed warriors of reputation with our own *aett*. Thank you, Bjorn, for without your foresight I might still be at home scratching my arse."

"You have nothing to thank me for. Your presence at my shoulder has always been its own reward. Maybe this will be our home forever – but only the *Norns* can tell that. I will give thanks every day for our good fortune and pray that the old gods can still hear us," I said, touching my amulet.

"Pray that our seeds will take in this ground, for I feel truly at home," he said.

He caught me in a powerful bear hug that crushed the breath from my body.

"Now go and make up for your lost time with Turid – she is not a woman to be kept waiting – and take that bloody priest with you," he said.

He let go of me, and I mounted Dragons Breath, shouted farewell to the rest of the men and left for Maldon. Leofrith followed on a small brown mare he had found abandoned in a field, and we rode home.

The town slowly came back to life. The people, despite the recent slaughter of so many of their menfolk, began to trust us. Although they were not yet comfortable in our company, they gave us no trouble, worked diligently and kept their word when they gave it. Much of this was due to the high regard in which the Saxons held Leofrith who was always busy among them, and they looked to him for advice and guidance. The harvest had been brought in, but there was still much to do before the summer ended. We needed to fortify the town, and so we built earthworks, a moat and a wooden palisade to deter any invaders from attacking us.

When our daily work was finished, we trained with arms as we had always done, and taught some of the local men and women how to fight with weapons. Turid was happy in her new home and was forever busy organising people and events. We attended church every Sunday, which we saw as our duty, listening to Leofrith drone on in endless speeches. The men nearly all took up with local women, many of whom fell pregnant before long. The first half-breed babies were expected in the early summer of the following year. Turid, too, became pregnant, putting away her armour and weapons for the time being. Torstein visited often but refused to come with us to church and was forever chided by Leofrith for remaining a pagan despite his baptism. In later years he would consent to a Christian marriage, but only to stop Hild from scolding him for creating "a tribe of bastards". Our men gladly embraced their new lives (if not Christianity), and I seldom heard a grumble from the ageing warriors. Even in their cups, during the long winter nights in my hall, I never heard anyone expressing a longing for Jomsborg. However, in secret, I sometimes yearned to be back at the tiller of my longship steering the crew towards the beach and into the fight, the fierce wooden carving on the prow guiding us towards our fates.

As summer left us and the first frosts of winter covered the fields, we removed both of our ships from the water to dry land where they would over-winter. They would not be used again until next summer, but I was keen to keep them in good repair should we need to use them. We had more than enough food to sustain us through the dark winter months, supplemented by the slaughter of the hogs and the spoils of regular hunting trips for deer and boar. As the days grew shorter and many of the women's bellies began to swell, we settled in for the winter.

By the time the snows came, I had visited every farm on my land. In addition to our six farmsteads, which by then had been repaired and fortified, there were another twenty-six Saxon farms on our land which I visited before Yuletide. The farmers were now my tenants and paid rent to their new landlord. After each trip, Leofrith carefully documented what each farm was worth and what rents would be due. In all, he counted seven hundred and sixty-five men, women and children who lived on our land, and come the next year these numbers would be swollen by the progeny of the unions made between my men and the local women. There was enough land to support many times this number of people, it was so rich and fertile, and although the work was hard, our people could profit through their labours. Over the cold, short days Leofrith toiled to teach me latin letters and promised me that one day I would be able to read and write as good as any Saxon Lord. He also schooled me in speaking his language, which I found far easier than the written word, and I was able to converse with the local people before too long.

When Yuletide arrived, our people came to my hall, and our expanded company gathered with their women to feast. It was good to be in the company of my Jomsvikings once more, and we ate and drank before my hearthfire, happy in the comfort of our new land and home. There were songs and storytelling, and during the short daylight period, games of endurance would be played outside. These were happy times for all of us, but we knew only too well that our fates could turn on the throw of the gods' dice. We counted our blessings all too easily, and I prayed for our continued good fortune.

Winter eventually departed, and the frozen fields were replaced with the green shoots that heralded early summer. Our herds of sheep delivered their yearly bounty of lambs that filled the pastures with new life, and shortly after this season departed, the first of our babies began to arrive all around the farmsteads. The Saxon midwives were busy, and by the time summer arrived in earnest there were twelve new mouths to feed. They were sired by the same men who only the year before came to plunder and desolate the land that now supported their families. Turid gave birth to our first child, a boy we called Halfdan, and he grew stronger each day. Torstein and Hild also had their first child, a boy who they named after his father. The young Torstein was a lusty child with a huge appetite who regularly drained the Saxon wet nurse of both her milk and her energy. One day, his proud father brought him to our settlement on horseback to be paraded around. That day we sat outside drinking ale together as we had done so many times before, comfortable with the occasional silences between us.

"This Saxon beer is quite good," he declared after swallowing his first huge draught.

"….and it was made by one of us," I said.

One of my men, Svein, a Vestlander from Norway who had once delighted in slaughtering Saxons, had now been taught by them how to brew beer.

"It is true," said Torstein swallowing another mighty draught of ale, "we have learned much from these people. I never thought the day would come when I had my first child by one, though. When do you think they might be big enough to fight?"

"It will be a few years before the women release them to our care, cousin. For now, though, I am happy to watch them from afar – they are not very productive at this age. Although it seems that you might have bred a giant," I said, looking over to where Turid and Hild sat with some other women cooing and clucking over the new babies. "Drink up," I said. "It is time to go. The men are waiting for us."

We left to welcome six of our comrades who had just ridden in to join us for a day's hunting.

We picked up our spears, mounted the horses and rode out to meet the new arrivals, our dogs chasing noisily after us. The hunt was a productive one with the dogs running down a huge male pig in the woods. They picked up his scent almost as soon as we entered the forest and pursued him for some time before catching him, exhausted, in a thick briar patch. He turned to face the baying pack who snapped and snarled at him. The animal had already been speared in the shoulder and stood facing us defiantly, waiting for the moment to charge his tormentors. While the dogs kept him at bay, I dismounted and walked carefully towards the wounded animal carrying a short hunting spear. The boar panted heavily, his head down, his small beady eyes following my every move. This huge beast, about three times my own weight, suddenly charged at me, shrugging off the attention of the dogs who tried to hang on to his flanks as he knocked them aside. He headed straight at me sending out a series of high pitched, piercing cries in his charge forward. There was no time to hurl my spear at the beast, and I waited for the impact.

Holding the spear in two hands I aimed it at his chest and felt the full force of this massive animal as he impaled himself on the steel tip and drove me backwards. I was knocked the ground by the force of his charge, and the blunt end of my weapon was driven into the rocky earth. The 'wings' of the sharp end preventing the weapon from going too deep into the dying beast as he thrashed about. His forelegs were in the air, and as he drove himself forward on his powerful hind legs, each frantic move brought us both closer to death. I watched the head of this massive animal whipping from side to side with his enormous tusks only an arm's length from my face. The short shaft of the spear was the only thing between the dying beast and me, and in that moment, I prayed hard that it would not snap before he departed this life. I was close enough to smell the pig's fetid breath as he grunted in his death throes. The boar died suddenly when one of the men smote it a mighty axe blow on its neck and it stopped moving, dripping blood and spit on me lying beneath it. The dead beast fell to the ground with the spear still deep in its chest, and I scrambled up to my feet. I was unwounded and my legs were saved from any damage from the battering of the boar's hind legs by thick leather greaves that I always wore for hunting.

"You look like you need a drink," called Torstein throwing me a leather wine flask. I drank deeply, and still breathing heavily from my efforts, struggled to regain my composure.

"We will eat well tonight," I said in as light-hearted a manner as I could manage, for the tussle with the beast had been fierce.

"It will taste all the better for dying so bravely," said Auden, the man who had finished it with his axe.

Boar hunting was always a dangerous pastime and one which we had all taken part in since boyhood. The hunting was good training for young warriors and the animals, particularly the males, generally put up a good fight. The beast we killed today had been no different and had fought and died with admirable ferocity. Still, it had been a close-run thing and one which might have turned out very differently had fate decided otherwise.

The boar was too big to carry on the spare horse we had brought along for the purpose, and so it was butchered where it fell. After the dogs were rewarded with some of the offal, we took our prize home to feed our little farmstead community. In truth, the community was growing bigger all the time, and all told we numbered thirty-three including the three new babies and ten thralls, making us the biggest of the six farmsteads. The other communities each had their new additions, and although two of the Saxon women had died in childbirth, the folk were otherwise healthy.

It was soon time for the annual Thing, our community assembly where each freeman and woman met to speak to discuss the major issues deciding our lives. As the *Jarl*, I had the last word when making decisions, but where possible I was keen to let the people decide for themselves. The Saxons were all invited, and although they were quiet initially, they became more vocal as the first meeting progressed. The matters discussed were many and included deciding boundaries of new farms, the amount of military training that was required of each man and the scale of fines that transgressions of the law required. In all, it was a relatively quiet affair but gave all the people, Saxon and Scandinavian, the chance to speak and give air to their opinions. Father Leofrith was very keen to raise the matter of a tithe to the Christian church at our meeting, which drew little interest. Sensing defeat he moved onto to his next favourite subject, which was to encourage our new couples to be "blessed by the sanctity of God's wishes in holy marriage". The gathering, in all, was good natured and, if nothing else, drew the Saxon and Scandinavian communities closer together.

Over the next year our lives settled down to an existence far removed from anything we could have possibly contemplated. In one year, we had exchanged one life for another; we would surely take up arms once more to protect our lives and land, but I could not see the time when I would ever go a-viking again. I was now a father, a landowner and the leader of a group of people who were once deadly enemies. My new responsibilities were many, but I was in control of my destiny and that of a great many others, and I resolved to lead our people as justly and wisely as I could. Turid was always there with her unwavering support, which never, ever faltered.

Chapter 39: At Peace in Maldon

When the yellow and gold of spring burst into life all around us, the people and animals began to overcome their winter sluggishness. The gorse, the trees and the hedgerows each took on a buttery hue as winter was left far behind. The maids wore thinner clothing now, and the few Norsemen who had been reluctant to take up with a local woman, found a rekindled interest in the Saxon girls. In full bloom, these pretty flowers turned many a Scandinavian head. As had been Leofrith's wish at the Thing, we followed the rules of the Christian faith and pledged to marry our women. Leofrith wanted me to be the first to set a good example, and so shortly after the first of the season's seeds were sown, I married Turid. The church in Maldon was packed with over six hundred townsfolk. We said our vows and made promises – to each other and to Jesus Christ – then feasted our guests in the open air in a celebration that lasted for days and where I suspected many new babies were conceived. More weddings followed ours, dowries were produced, bride prices paid, and the crops started to grow along with the bellies of the womenfolk. It was a time of contentment and peace, and even the bitterest memories of our retreat from the plains of Fyrisvellir began to fade.

Merchant ships arrived in greater numbers at our little harbour, and as the year wore on we had more and more visitors from the sea bringing in all sorts of exotic goods to trade with us for the vast quantities of excess grain we had amassed over the winter. Our local craftsmen were also skilled in the production of all sorts of farming tools with which we produced such a bountiful harvest, and these became a draw to many of the merchants who came from not only the Saxon kingdoms but further afield. Traders visited us from Normannia, Frankia and Scandinavia with merchandise to sell or barter. Such was the demand for our goods that I was able to levy taxes and tariffs on produce coming in from foreign ports, and we began to create wealth from new sources. It was all gathered in and accounted for by Father Leofrith who duly taxed me, on behalf of the church, on our profits. The wealth of the freemen of Maldon accumulated and Turid bedecked our longhall and farmhouse with all sorts of extravagant adornments.

Not all the visitors to Maldon were friendly, and now and again we caught wind that longships had appeared further along the coastline and were raiding. By the time these ships were spotted near our land, we were ready for them. We assembled our warriors and those Saxons who now stood in our shield wall. This always proved deterrent enough for the raiders to seek their fortune elsewhere. In the summer of my wedding, three Danish dragon ships sailed into our harbour bearing fierce wooden carvings on the prow of each vessel, looking for a fight. They headed for the shallow water of the beach, and the first ship was met with a hail of arrows and javelins that cut down many of their number as they tried to land and wade ashore. Those who made it onto dry land died on the sand beneath the axes of a hundred men of Maldon lying in wait for them. The other two crews decided against landing and turned around and rowed back out to the open sea in search of easier pickings. We burned the beached ship, which served as a reminder to other raiders who might be tempted to invade our rich new homeland.

After this attack was repulsed, we received a visit from Thoren and a troop of the King's guard. Word of this minor skirmish in which the raiders lost fifty men and a ship had spread and grown into a story considerably bigger than the actual event. Thoren was sent by the King to learn the events of the fight, but more importantly to learn about the Saxons and Norsemen fighting side by side. I asked Torstein to provide the Saxon Commander with details of the encounter, and with his typical enthusiasm, he elevated our limited actions on the day into a major event. Duly impressed, Thoren returned to London and the King to report on the success of the "united men of Maldon".

A little later that summer, Leofrith's masters called him to London, and he left in an open wagon with a troop of horsemen I sent to look after him and to protect the tithes he had exacted from us. I had to admit to missing his company, fussing around the place, providing me with advice. He lived close to my longhouse and was a constant presence in my life having succeeded in teaching me to read and write some rudimentary Latin. He had much more success in teaching me Saxon, although Turid was far more accomplished in the native tongue, presumably from chattering endlessly with her group of women servants and companions. She was still a man's woman first and foremost, but the women folk admired and adored her, and she kept them amused and entertained, doubtless with stories of her time as a shieldmaiden.

Throughout the summer months we harvested our crops of grain. Barley, wheat, rye and oats were all plentiful in our fields, and we Norsemen proved to be good students. One year of relative peace meant that the land rewarded us with an increased yield, and our barns were overflowing with the harvest. Leofrith returned from London to inform us that "God had smiled on us again and repaid our peaceful ways with his favours". I could not help smiling at his pious outpourings as I thought back to Torstein's savage dispatch of the recent Danish invaders. My cousin's ferocious display had impressed the Saxons in our ranks after he led them into combat with his double-handed axe and showed them how to defend their land with blood and steel. I was glad to see the priest; his masters were apparently pleased with the 'progress' he was making with the pagan converts. I suspected it had everything to do with the tithes he had delivered rather than the number of souls he was saving. I was pleased for him that he had been recognised by his masters for the work he had done and agreed that there should be a religious festival to give thanks for the harvest. In any case, I thought, we had a similar celebration at home in Norway and what harm would thanking another god do?

Our second summer in Maldon was soon coming to an end and we had much to give thanks for. Each of my men had settled, and all but a few had taken local women. Our first year had been a prosperous one, and my large collection of gold and silver had grown considerably by peaceful means. I had land and wealth, and so did Torstein, which he had managed to keep now he was free of the temptation of the alehouse whores. Turid had slipped effortlessly into her role as the Lady of the burgh, and she took her responsibilities very seriously. Although heavy with our second child, she made sure that our food stores were full, that our servants and their families were healthy, and that sickness and hunger were kept in check wherever they showed themselves.

Yuletide came around quickly once more, and guests arrived from Norway to stay. They were three of Olaf Trygvasson's captains who were sailing home to Normannia with a crew of thirty men. Olaf had triumphed in his quest for the crown of Norway and was now King. We gave thanks to the old gods for his victory. He had ordered these men, three brothers who had fought for him, to visit us on their way home to ensure that his friends in the new Scandinavian settlement did not need aid. They and their men were made welcome and stayed with us until the wild winter weather subsided and they were able to continue home. They told us of Olaf and his battles for the Norwegian throne. My old friend had built a mighty army with the proceeds of his plunder of England and had defeated all his rivals. Our guests were distant cousins of Olaf's and they had led a force of one thousand men from Normannia to support him. After he had been crowned, they were returning home much the richer, following the rest of their group who had left for home ahead of them. The eldest of the brothers was Rolf, a man of about forty who was a Count in the service of the Duke of

Normannia. Rolf had reluctantly taken his younger brothers William and Richard along after much pleading to accompany him.

The younger man, William, who was fifteen, and the older one, a nineteen-year-old called Richard, had begged their brother to take them to gain experience. Rolf had eventually relented.

"It does a young man the world of good to stand next to his countrymen in a shield wall facing thousands of angry Norwegians," he told me as we sat drinking by my hearthfire one evening.

"Is that true?" I asked, turning to both the brothers who sat on my other side.

"Up until one of the enemy's berserkers broke through our lines and killed the two men I was standing next to," said William, "...before turning his attention to me."

"I saw my little brother was in trouble," said Richard, "and I was fortunate enough to dispatch the attackers when they were occupied. Otherwise, it is highly likely we would be taking home some very bad news to our mother."

I liked all our Norman guests but grew very fond of Richard who had a wicked sense of humour and was always keen to learn new things. He was particularly fond of hearing Torstein perform The Saga of the Two Wandering Warriors and would always call upon him to recite the work. There were obviously more verses now since we had made England our home, although Torstein had embellished the story of our brief fight with Danish invaders. At the end of another rendition, while Torstein was milking the applause, Richard asked me, "Do you think you might have been victorious at Fyrisvellir but for the treachery of the Danes?"

"That is a good question, Richard," I said, "and yes, I think we would have overcome the Swedish host."

"Thorkill the Tall told me that but for their betrayal you would have been a nobleman in Sweden by now. He told me you were Styrbjorn Storki's chosen man and destined for greatness."

I laughed kindly at this remark but offered no reply. Thorkill had taken his Jomsvikings to the aid of Olaf in Norway and had been part of his victorious army. I felt sure that Thorkill would have been thirsting for revenge after the disaster in Sweden and Olaf's campaign in Norway would have suited him perfectly.

"Thorkill said that you and he had saved the Jomsvikings from being wiped out and that you killed at least two hundred Swedes with your *Ulfberht*," piped up William, "and that you could shape-shift into a raven, like *Odin*'s *Hugin*, and fly high over your enemies to learn of their plans."

"Perhaps that is a little over-exaggeration," I said, "but I am sure that Torstein probably accounted for something like that number," I said, prompting the younger man to badger my cousin who had taken his seat next to us.

"Do you ever think of returning to Norway?" asked Richard.

"I think not now. We are settled here, and the land has been good to us. My family were all healthy and settled when I saw them a few years ago. I will send for them in the summer again, but I doubt that I can persuade my mother to make the journey," I replied.

"I am sure she will be proud of you whatever she decides, for you have become wealthy and wise – many have told me this – and she would surely be delighted to see her grandchildren. Your former comrades speak highly of you and with much admiration," said Richard.

I smiled and changed the subject.

"Now, tell me, Richard. How does a yellow-haired, blue-eyed Norseman come to speak Frankish?"

"Ah, now that is quite a story," he replied, and he began his tale.

The brothers' great-grandfather was a famous sea king called Rollo the Walker who once raided Paris, the great city of the

Franks. Such was the fear of Rollo's Norsemen that the King of the Franks promised him and his men a vast tract of land in Normannia in return for leaving Paris alone. Rollo accepted and settled his people who protected the land against invaders. The King rewarded him further and gave him even more land. Rollo's people continued to prosper and repel all invaders, mixing with the local Franks. Eventually, they started to speak Frankish, stopped building longships, took up Christ as their Lord and became a power in the land. They became known as Normans, started to use horses in battle and became skilled at mounted warfare. They even travelled to new countries where they met even more success. They fought in many foreign lands and built a great reputation for themselves in distant battlefields.

William could remain silent no longer. "Rollo was just like you are here in England, Bjorn. First, he frightened his enemies into giving him land then he showed them how to use it properly. You are building a new kingdom here in England, and I think the land is even richer than Frankia. Your line will prosper even more than Rollo's, I think."

"I do not think so," I said. "We are only warriors, some even older than me, who got tired of wandering the world and fighting. Even Torstein got tired of the killing."

"He looked quite capable of lopping off a few more heads with that battle axe in the summer," joined in one of the men of my cousin's community. "He saw off those Danes practically single-handed."

"When a man tires of killing Danes, he is surely tired of life. Now let us have a story. Who would like to hear The Tale of Anvari's Ring?" shouted Torstein. Without waiting for an answer, he began another performance before a crowd of a hundred men and women in the longhouse. We settled in for a night of raucous drinking and storytelling.

The brothers were finally ready to leave us for Normannia when the weather improved, and we went down to the harbour to see them off. Rolf asked me to visit them in

Normannia, in a place called Pirou. He wanted me to bring some of my Saxon farmers to show them how they made such impressive yields come harvest time. He also made me promise to send Olaf news of our settlement to Norway to ensure that they had completed their final act of fealty to him. We wished them good fortune on their journey, and they sailed away from Maldon and back to their homeland.

"I have never set foot in Frankia," I said to Turid as we walked back to our hall.

It was a day in late winter, and she was wrapped in a thick woollen cloak with the hood pulled over her head. Despite the bright morning sun, there was a chill wind blowing off the sea.

"You forget Bjorn, I am no longer a shield-maiden with whom you can indulge your manly adventures. I have my work here running the estates and delivering your children. Although I daresay Hild will be glad to see the back of Torstein if you want to relive old times. But I will know if you so much as look at those grand Norman women and your life will not be worth living. By the way, would you like to feel your handiwork?" she said, grabbing my hand and putting it on her belly. "It is a girl, you know."

Hild was indeed pleased to be set free of Torstein, at least for a little while. I sent word to Rolf and his brothers that we would come to guest with them once the harvest was over. The crops were even more plentiful than they had been in either of the previous years, and we had to build new barns to house the grain. We took five of the farmers together with their ploughs and tools and sailed our ship across the sea to Normannia. It felt good to be at the helm of the Drakes Head again. It was the first time I had sailed her on anything other than a short coastal journey since we had raided the English coasts three years before. We carried only a small crew of thirty men and were loaded with farming tools. Torstein was probably as excited as me as we stood at the tiller together on the first day, laughing like madmen each time the salty spray hit our faces.

"I have missed this life, cousin," he shouted above the noise of the wind. "The two of us and our crew sailing to new lands. I love my new life, my home and my family but by Thor's Hammer I swear that I shall never tire of riding the wave tops in the company of these good fellows. We may not be going a-viking this time, Bjorn, and that life may now be behind us, but the sea will always be in my blood."

We arrived in Normannia three days later after an uneventful voyage. We had passed a few merchant ships but nothing that appeared remotely threatening, all the same, we sailed armed and fully prepared to meet any threat to our journey.

The sun was setting behind us in the west and a gentle breeze pushed the Drakes Head towards her journey's end. The fortress of Pirou stood overlooking a shallow, rocky coastline protected on all sides by marshlands. The castle had immensely thick wood and stone walls and was as tall a building that I had ever seen. It had watchtowers on all sides, and our approach would have been seen from some distance away. We docked on the quayside on which sat half a dozen plain-looking cogs, and as we tied up I looked up to see the brothers Richard and William riding down the beach towards the harbour. William arrived first and leapt off his horse in one fluid movement, calling a greeting.

"Bjorn, Torstein, you are here! We saw you coming earlier in the day. Come, we have been waiting for you."

"Forgive my brother's excitement," said Richard, "but he has been watching for you for many days now, and I thought he would burst when he finally saw your sail this morning."

"It is good to see you both again. We have brought the best farmers and warriors from England. If you just tell them where they should take themselves, we can join you."

"Nonsense," said the older brother. "Leave everything where it is. My men will take care of it. Now, let's go up to the castle. Rolf is looking forward to giving you a proper Norman welcome."

The two brothers led us all up to the castle where Rolf and his wife, Poppa, met us on the bridge that led from the main gate over the moat.

"*Jarl* Bjorn," Rolf said, "you are as good as your word. Welcome to our home. You and your men should make yourself comfortable. But first we must offer you some hospitality. Come and refresh yourselves in my hall."

Turning, he took us through the gates of the castle where his uniformed guards saluted us smartly.

The hall of the castle was a grand affair. It was about the same size as Styrbjorn's hall in Jomsborg, but the walls were furnished with a great variety of decorations including sigils, paintings and crosses. Rolf was dressed very finely, and with his hair cut short and beard trimmed since I last saw him, he scarcely looked like the Norse warrior I remembered.

"I hope you don't mind, but many of my friends have heard your story and wanted to meet you," he said, and I looked around to see several men and women, also finely dressed, looking towards us. "After all," he added, "my friends are your friends. Now come join me at my table."

He stood before the gathering and toasted us all.

"We welcome *Jarl* Bjorn of Maldon and his men. They have journeyed far at my invitation, and they are to be given every hospitality during their stay with us. The *Jarl*'s people have prospered in England and are now wealthy landlords who have brought their farmers with them to share their secrets with us. It is hoped they can help make Normannian soil every bit as gainful as in their homeland."

The room was laid out in a similar style to my hall with tables and benches, but there the similarity ended, for everything was laden with gold and silver ornaments. Our Saxon farmers were wide-eyed at the splendour of the place and confessed to having "never seen the like". The tables were heavy with all manner of food – there were roasted meats of all sorts with all the fruits and vegetables of the summer.

Drink was also in great abundance served by liveried servants, and the supply of ale and wine was never ending. There was entertainment from minstrels, acrobats and jugglers from all over the world, and the people were in high spirits. There were many women seated at the tables in their finery. Rolf's wife and three daughters sat at our table, all tall women of Scandinavian stock with blond hair and blue eyes. Torstein had already made himself at home, having introduced himself to the women. He appeared to be at his most appealing, for I could see they were all laughing at his jokes. I prayed that his good behaviour would continue as he became drunker, but I had nothing to fear, and he sustained a polite if raucous manner for the rest of the night. At one point, Richard incited the seated guests to call for The Saga of the Warrior Skald. Answering their requests, Torstein rose to his feet and gave one of his renditions, to the delight of all.

Rolf and his brothers were fine hosts, and we hunted for many of the days of our stay. I could see they had prospered here for they owned huge areas of farming and woodland. They had over three hundred men-at-arms, all of them expert horsemen, who drilled and practiced remorselessly. They would train on foot every day, and the Captain of Guards invited us to join them at arms. Although I declined, Torstein and the rest of the men accepted the offer of some exercise and vigorously set about showing our hosts how to attack a shield wall. They were not asked again so readily.

The castle was busy with the comings and goings of all sorts of merchants, soldiers, farmers and local people. Rolf and his brothers were vassals to Duke Richard, their liege lord, who ruled all over Normannia, and whose men were frequent visitors. We stayed for six weeks in Pirou during which time our farmers worked with theirs and schooled them in the ways of Saxon farming. They had brought ploughs and tools with them, and they spent much time teaching them in their usage. The head of our little group, a Saxon called Aldred, came to me one day and explained the Normans' problem to me.

"Lord Bjorn, the farmers here work hard and the soil is good. It is much the same as ours, but their ways are very wasteful. Their ploughs and tools have not changed for a hundred years, and their methods belong to a different age."

"What should they do," I asked.

"They need to make a new plan and start to use new methods and ways. They should be getting harvests of three and four times what they yield. They must learn new skills and employ a modern way of doing things."

I liked Aldred. He was a very serious man of some forty years and had always been forthright and honest in his dealings with me. When we had first arrived in Maldon, he had taken the responsibility for teaching my men about farming and what needed to be done. I thanked him and told him to continue his work while I relayed everything back to Rolf.

I spoke to him later that day. "After many years of being taught the Saxon ways, I am still no farmer, but your problem seems clear to me. It is no wonder your land is not producing enough. It seems that your farmers are using the ways that our great, great grandfathers used hundreds of years ago in Scandinavia to scratch a living from the poor, rocky ground. If they change what they are doing things can be much improved."

Rolf thanked me for the efforts of my men and promised to reward them for their work. He was very keen for his farmers to change their ways and suggested to me that if he were to offer me some land here, I might employ some of my people here to tend it and teach his Norman farmers.

"This seems like a good idea," I told him. "But I want no gifts from you, Rolf. Instead, I would rather buy an estate here in Normannia on which I could settle with my people to farm. They could then show your folk our ways, in the same way the Saxons did with us when we arrived in Maldon."

"Then it is settled, Bjorn. We shall find you some good land that will suit this purpose. I shall get Richard to find something suitable. How much longer can you stay with us?"

"We need to be back to England before the weather starts to turn. Let's say another two weeks until we should set sail for home."

Rolf was as good as his word. He gave me silver to reward my men and found me a tract of good, fertile land further along the coast. We agreed on a fair price, and it was mine. We also agreed that come the spring I would send several folk to the area to settle in Normannia under his protection, and they, in turn, would teach the local farmers some of their skills. I charged Aldred with finding these people from our community when we returned home. We left one early morning on the high tide, and the brothers came to see us off. It was a cold, grey, morning and the rain was blowing in from the sea meaning that the wind was against us. Rolf had feasted us well the previous evening, and we had settled on a price for the supply of some farmers and their families who would be sent in the new year before the fields were ploughed. Aldred would run my estate here. My Saxon farmers had been well rewarded and were keen to return, but the rest of the men just wanted to go home to their families to prepare for the coming winter.

We waved farewell to our hosts, and the Drakes Head, now unburdened from her heavy load of ploughs and tools, sped out of the harbour and made for England, home and our families. The voyage was rough and stormy, but once the winds changed and became favourable, we sailed quickly and safely making the crossing without any bad luck befalling us.

Winter at home had come almost as soon as our return, and the men went back to their homes and farms to prepare for the cold, dark months ahead. While I was away Turid had delivered another child, a tiny girl we named Sigrid. She was so small that she was not expected to survive, but she inherited her mother's fierce instincts to live and grew stronger each day. Most of the other babies born to our settlement were not so lucky. As Yuletide approached many grew sick with a fever and died within days. The sickness took Saxon and Scandinavian babies alike, with no favourites, and the bereaved families grieved for their lost children. Like the previous winter, there was plenty of food and drink to see us all through the long season, but the loss of so many small children made for a subdued festive period. Father Leofrith prayed with all his might but to little effect. I stood next to Torstein and his anguished wife, Hild, when we buried their child. Torstein turned to me with a voice raw with emotion.

"It seems this Christ does not hear our prayers after all. I have given up raiding and even freed my thralls, but it seems he has not forgiven me after all and continues to mete out his punishment."

I had never seen him so sad and careworn, and I bade them both join us in our longhall where Torstein tried to drink his sorrow away. It was a long, dark winter, and although we were all used to losing our children to the gods, the loss of so many, so quickly, was a bitter blow.

As fast as it had settled on us, winter was gone, and the shoots of growth arrived. Aldred's farmers and their families made ready to leave, and together with some of my old unmarried warriors who had no families, they set sail in our second ship, heavily laden, for Normannia. Leofrith prayed on the harbour for their safe delivery, and much to his disgust, some of my men slaughtered a goat as a sacrifice to *Odin*. Torstein, who by now had recovered some of his humour, tried to calm the little priest. "You cannot be too careful on a dangerous voyage, you know Leofrith. Best to keep all the gods happy!"

A month later we received word from a passing merchant ship of their safe arrival, together with a request from Aldred for more ploughs and tools. It seemed that the Norman farmers had been impressed by what they were seeing and needed us to make much more equipment. There were so many needed that I ordered the construction of a new forge, and the blacksmiths were kept busy well into the summer months. Having deserted us in winter, the gods seemed to favour us once more in the summer, and many of our women, including Hild, were heavy with child again. I prayed that this new crop of babies would grow strong. Mostly they did, and each of our farmsteads was soon full of lusty little voices crying for their mothers' milk.

"You see," said Leofrith, "God sees everything. He sees you turning your swords into ploughshares and rewards us all."

I nodded and smiled, while Torstein, who was within earshot spat on the ground. Turning his back, he mumbled that our swords and axes were doing nothing except waiting to smite the next group of invaders foolish enough to come ashore at Maldon.

Babies were born healthy and strong, the crops provided a bountiful harvest, and no one dared set foot on our land. We sold our entire grain surplus to Rolf's people, and there was a great demand for our blacksmiths to produce more heavy ploughs from all over Frankia, which we sold for great profit.

King Aethelred of the Saxons had recovered from his defeat at our hands and was building a strong army and navy which patrolled the shores of southern England, discouraging pirates and raiders. He sent Ealderman Thoren to visit once a year, probably just to spy on us. This year Thoren came with a company of twenty men at the end of the summer, and we guested him in our longhouse.

"You have settled here well, *Jarl* Bjorn," he said, as we sat by my hearth fire one evening. "You have made a good match here – your people and ours seem to have become one."

"It is true. There are many children here of mixed blood. And my men have made good farmers."

"Still warriors at heart though, I'll warrant," he suggested.

"I think not. They no longer crave to die with a sword in hand and no longer need to make war on peaceful folk." I said, with some deception. I had learned through one of his drunken men that the King desired to have my Jomsvikings in his army. "They are now simple farmers and are content to farm their land and father their children."

"That is a shame, for the King would surely appreciate your arms if he were in need."

"For my part, I would gladly fight for him, but my men are getting old, and our wounds still haunt us. We cannot fight as we once did. We are Jomsvikings no longer and only wish to live in peace. In any case, I do not think the Norsemen will bother these shores again, and King Olaf has other things on his mind these days," I said, telling another lie.

Thoren accepted my answer, at least for the time being, and did not ask me again. We were at the end of our third year in England, and I could not have expected a better outcome. Three years quickly became five, and our community numbered over eight hundred people throughout the borough. In all, there were twenty-five farms including the fortified farmsteads we set up when first we arrived. Each of these farms was on the fertile land that was ploughed or grazed by cattle, and although the work was hard the bounty was plentiful. Aside from the sickness that had taken so many children, we were not blighted by further pestilence, and as the folk prospered so did I.

My estates in Normannia also prospered, and Aldred and his people created something of a reputation increasing the farmers' yields. Rolf showed his gratitude by giving me more land around Pirou. Turid had now given birth to twins, Eigil and Freya, and they and their brother and sister grew sturdy and tall. I thanked the gods for my good fortune. And as for my growing horde of gold and silver, Turid would hide it beneath the earth. I always tried to be generous with the profits we made, always sure to give Torstein a share and reward our men. After our first five years we had lost only two of the Jomsvikings, one from a hunting accident and the other from the winter coughing sickness. My family never came to join us from Norway despite my pleas, but I heard that they were prospering as merchants. My mother was old and had remarried. Like me, my sister and brother now had their own families. Although I was sad that they did not come, I was glad for them and thought of them often.

Five years became ten years and my eldest son was now nine years old. Turid was thirty years old and I was thirty-three. She wished for no more children but said she loved me as fiercely as she had when we first lay together so many years before. I had no reason to disbelieve her. Come summer, she would carry my old bearskin cloak to the beach, and although we did not need to rekindle our passion, it was something she liked to do each year. Torstein and Hild overcame the loss of their first two children and now had a family of five enormous boys who were all the image of their father.

The town of Maldon grew in size and population, and there was a small fleet of merchant ships that traded our goods from the harbour. The Drakes Head kept a prominent position on the quay during the summer months from where I would occasionally take her out with her crew. She no longer carried a company of warriors going a-viking. We always made sure that we never ventured too far from home without being fully armed, although we seldom had cause to fight. Leofrith's church became bigger and contained more gold and silver than it deserved. He became ever more pious which did not stop him from taking a fifteen-year-old girl to his bed. We were no longer Saxon or Scandinavian folk but one group of people whose roots made little difference to the way we lived.

Then one summer's day something happened that would change our lives forever.

Chapter 40: The Treachery of Saint Brice's Day

It happened after the harvest in the tenth year of our settlement. It had been customary during the short history of our lives in Maldon to celebrate the end of the harvest with a festival of thanksgiving, which was part Christian and part pagan. This was followed a week later by a meeting of the Thing during which all manner of local matters were discussed and which signified the coming of winter for the people of our borough.

The day after the last sheaf of wheat had been winnowed and the grain stored in our barns, Father Leofrith came to my longhouse in a complete panic.

"Bjorn, I must speak to you without delay," he said gripping my arm. I knew that this was urgent because he had dropped the title of Lord by which he normally addressed me in public.

"Come, Leofrith, calm yourself. Tell me what excites you so much." I replied, ushering him through the front door to a nearby bench.

"I have bad tidings indeed," he said, the words tumbling out of his mouth as he looked around nervously for anyone else in earshot.

"Don't tell me your new wife has already grown tired of you," I joked.

"This is no laughing matter. I have news from London. King Aethelred believes there is a plot to kill him, that you are planning to have him murdered."

"Me?" I said, "that is complete madness."

"There is more," he replied. "The King has ordered the deaths of every Norseman and woman in the country. His agents are now travelling the land fomenting trouble between Saxon and Dane. His people are inciting every Saxon to rise up and kill their neighbours when they least expect it – on the feast of Saint Brice's Day."

"When is that?" I asked.

"It is forty-one days from today," he said.

"And how do you know this?"

"The Bishop sent a priest to warn me."

"Worried that he will lose the plentiful tithes that I have been sending him no doubt," I said, my mind racing to take all this in.

"Your people will be murdered in their beds," he said.

"Your people? That's an interesting choice of words," I snapped at him.

Leofrith checked himself, "I am sorry, Lord, I only meant that the families of the Scandinavian settlers will be in danger," he said apologetically.

"Then we shall defend ourselves and all those who stand with us," I said angrily. "I have been good to all the Saxons in this borough and we have over two hundred children of mixed blood here. Will the King kill them as well?"

"I am told that all men, women and children with Scandinavian blood must die," he said. "Let me remind you that my wife is also one of your people, and she is with child," he said, still smarting from the sharpness of my tone earlier.

"Then we shall defend ourselves as we have done so often before. This land has been paid for in blood and no one shall take it from us."

"Or we might flee?" suggested Leofrith.

"Flee from a few disaffected Saxons?" I asked him incredulously.

"There is more news, Lord. The King is sending an army of Northumbrian mercenaries to aid the slaughter, and anyone who stands with you shall fall. There will be one thousand men at our border by Saint Brice's day."

This last comment caused me to pause, and then I understood. "Ah, so Thoren wants my land then as well as our blood."

Leofrith said nothing, just hung his head like a beaten dog

and nodded.

"Then I will give him nothing but steel and six fot of English soil – or however much it will take to bury him in," I continued, my voice raised in anger.

Turid, some distance away with our children, heard these exchanges and looked in our direction.

Later, when Leofrith had gone and she had put our children to bed, I went to her and relayed my conversation with the priest.

"What will we do?" she asked.

"We have few real choices. We can stand and fight or flee. I can send to Norway for help, and Olaf would surely come, but who would crew the ship? I cannot spare a single man. The winter storms have come early this year, and there is no guarantee that help will get here in time."

"What about Rolf and the men of Normannia?" she said.

"His hands are tied, for his Lord, Duke Robert, and Aethelred have a pact. Robert has been paid a king's ransom not to involve himself in the affairs of England."

"Then we are alone?"

"I will send word to Olaf when the next merchant ship passes through heading for Norway and pray he hears us. But for now, we must prepare to defend ourselves. Now tell me, how many of our Saxons neighbours do you think we can count on?"

"A good many, husband, but let me think on this and you shall have an answer in the two days it will take me to find out from the womenfolk of the borough. For now, though I will start practising with my throwing axes once more." she said. "Now come, husband, it is time for bed."

At first light the next day I rode to Torstein's farmstead to seek his counsel.

"We are sixty-five Jomsvikings and have maybe another two or three hundred Saxon men who might stand by us in a fight. I say we should make a stand, for how will we send away all the families and the little ones? Have we even got the ships to take all our people? I have not fought and killed so many foemen to leave this place to our enemies. Anyway, we are happy here, we are part of the land now. If these cowards are coming for us, thinking they can kill us meekly in our beds. I would like to give them something to think about," said Torstein.

"If the Saxons of this borough stand with us here, we have a chance. If not, we will be overrun, and we will all be killed. Even if I could reach Olaf, I think he will not get here in time. If we stay, we must rely on the support of the Saxons. Let's not forget we killed their Lord and his army only ten years ago," I said.

"Then let us hope they do not have long memories. Anyway, you are now *Jarl* and must decide for all your folk, but for my part, I will follow you whatever your decision."

"I will call a meeting of all the *Baldrs Wrath* in two days and talk further," I said, but I knew the die was cast, that we would be staying and standing. But it was the fate of our families that concerned me most.

The day after next, all sixty-five of the old Jomsvikings arrived at my longhouse. They may have been ten years older than when we last fought over this land, but their spirit was the same as it had always been. Their rugged, defiant faces were more lined, and there was now more than a little grey in their hair, but I could see there was no way they would leave this land without making a stand. Like me, their concern was for their families, and like me, they wanted to fight for their homes. If we could get enough support from our neighbours, we might stand a chance of success. We talked long into the day, and each man had his turn to speak and say his piece. All were for staying. When everybody had spoken, I got up to say mine.

"You have all spoken well and I have listened to what you have said. We all want to stay and fight for what we hold, but we cannot win without help. I have sent to Norway for aid, and King Olaf will surely answer our plea when he hears it, but I fear he will not get here in time. I have sent to Normannia for enough ships to take our families should we be unsuccessful in our battle. We may have to fight two enemies here, the King's men and also our neighbours if they decide to turn against us."

I asked Turid, who had been sitting quietly, to come and speak. She was very popular with our people and when she came to address us there was complete silence as we all listened to her words.

"We came here as enemies of these Saxons, but I believe that many are now friends. I have toiled beside the women of this borough, and we have worked in the fields together; we have born our babies with each other's help, and we have wept for the loss of each other's children. They tell me their men respect us and do not fear us. And why should they? We have never abused them or stolen from them, despite what they may have thought when we first came. Some of their men have stood with you in the shield wall when we needed them, and they tell me that they will not betray us and turn against us. I say that this is true, but if the time comes, and there is the opportunity of silver and land, then some of them may turn their backs. How many? I cannot say, but I believe that the strongest amongst them will stay true while the weak will see how the wind blows before deciding. If you know how many such strong Saxon men there are in this borough then you will have your answer."

There was some murmuring as the men discussed which of the Saxons we could trust or, more importantly, mistrust.

Torstein got to his feet again.

"I have trained many of these men, and I think I know those I can trust with my life. I count about a hundred of them."

"Maybe a few more," said Leif, the veteran Norwegian warrior, "but I would agree."

There were more murmurings, this time of assent.

"So, that is the sixty-five of us here," I said. "The thralls who we have now made freemen will count for another fifty, and the Saxons in our ranks will make our little army over two hundred men. The enemy in front of us will number five hundred of Aethelred's men, probably more if the reports are correct, and we do not know how many Saxons will oppose us here in Maldon if things go badly."

"Then we shall have to make sure that things go well." said Torstein good-humouredly. "After all, they did not appear that fearsome in London. Leofrith have you anything to add?"

The priest shook his head and cast his eyes down, for since he had delivered the news to me, he had been very quiet. I could feel his shame, and despite our predicament, I felt uneasy for him, for I believed him to be a good man, undeserving of such treachery from his King.

"Then we shall stay and fight, and from today we shall prepare to meet our enemy as we have often done before. We shall raise the matter at the Thing in ten days and allow our Saxon neighbours to respond, for there are many good men amongst them. For now though, be vigilant, and do not allow mistrust to make you blind, for we may yet come to rely on them."

We all stayed together in the longhall until the next morning, drinking into the night and reflecting on what we must do. Leofrith came to me when the speaking was over and said he needed to see his wife who was heavily pregnant.

"Lord Bjorn," he said formally, "I think you should consider taking your leave of Maldon once and for all. The King is coming for you and your people and God may not be able to protect them when they do."

I became irked at his manner and dismissed him without listening further before returning to my warriors.

The Thing was held ten days later when the whole community gathered together. There were over five hundred folk including all the women and each freeman of our community. Everyone would be able to speak and have their say. As the 'lawgiver' I presided over the proceedings and I had the final say. It was always a good social gathering and afterwards, there was drinking and feasting. But this year I noticed there was a slightly sombre mood within the group. Since we had met in the longhouse my men had started to prepare for the battle, but we had not spoken to any of the Saxon men of the borough yet. There were the normal grievances – a stolen pig, a wronged woman, disputed borders – which were all discussed and resolved. At the end of the meeting I rose to make the final address as was customary.

"Men and women of Maldon, for ten years I have presided over this meeting, and for ten years we have settled our differences amicably. Like all neighbours we had our differences but never so great that we should fall out. I have been your Lord since we arrived, and you have made decent farmers of us. But now I have some serious news that I must share with you all. For reasons I do not understand, King Aethelred believes that I am plotting to kill him."

There were some sounds of surprise, and I held up a piece of rolled parchment.

"This contract was signed and given to me by King Aethelred ten years ago making me Lord over this land in return for fair protection and justice for all its people. I am now told there will be an uprising on Saint Brice's Day when the King's army will come and kill every person with Scandinavian blood in their veins, which includes nearly two hundred children. It may be that some of you here agree with the King. If this is the case, you have no place here, and for the safety of us all I would ask these people to leave now. You may take everything you own and will be given safe passage. If you decide to stay, I will ask you to swear to Jesus Christ that I have your allegiance. I will not ask you to fight for me unless you desire it, but you must swear to do us no harm. Now, it is the manner of the Thing that all men can speak freely, and I invite you to do so here."

The first man to speak had been the first Saxon to train and fight for us when we arrived. Tostig was a farmer who had come to me and offered his services as a fighter. He also brought with him over a hundred young Saxon men who we had turned into decent warriors.

"Lord Bjorn, I speak for the men who joined you and defended our homeland against the invader. You have always been as good as your word, and I know of no reason why these men should not join you in battle once more. I was one of the first men here to stand with you in the shield wall, and it would be my honour to do say again. My first loyalty is to my people, Kings must come second."

"Well said, Tostig," shouted Torstein, "I shall be proud to stand with you once again."

Those gathered murmured their approval. Another Saxon stood, Cynewulf, the miller, who shifted about nervously before speaking. "I am with Tostig, but if we fight for you will we not be denounced as traitors, should, may the Lord prevent it, you fall in battle?"

"Honestly spoken, Cynewulf," I said, "and it is true that should we fall, the victors might not look too kindly on those left living who opposed them. I say this. No man has to fight for us, but nor must any fight against us. They must swear this on the blood of Christ."

"Then I say we must all swear this thing," declared Cynewulf.

"Father Leofrith," I said turning to the little priest. "Will you arrange such a thing in your church next Sunday.

"Yes of course," said Leofrith, looking nervously around and refusing to return my gaze. "It shall be done, Lord."

"Then unless there is any more to say I declare this Thing closed, and it is the time to seal our friendship with food and drink from yet another bountiful harvest."

The men and women sat down around benches and tables for the customary feasting. Compared to previous years this event was a much quieter affair, and although the people mixed freely, there was much furtive talking amongst the Saxons which ceased every time I drew near.

"Is it me," said Torstein, surveying those gathered before us, "or is this a little quieter than we are used to?"

"Perhaps they will also drink a little less than last year then," I replied. "I am sure you can find a home for more ale."

"Not if I want to get back into my old mail shirt again. Hild is saying that I am crushing her every time I lie with her – I think she might prefer me better as a warrior than a farmer," he said.

"Tell her she will soon have her wish then. As long as you can still cleave heads with your axe there is hope."

"There is always hope, cousin. Now let us show these nervous Saxons how to drink properly."

The next day I sent spies to *Lundenburgh*. Two of my servants were sent off at dawn on horseback. They were to stay in the city and keep watch on any movement of warriors. As soon as there was any news, one would report back to me leaving the other one to return when the King's army were on their way towards us.

All our fighting men started to prepare for the battle. We worked on the fortifications; the earthworks around the town were heightened and the ditch deepened and filled with sharpened stakes. All the gates to the town were blocked save two, and we watched them keenly to ensure no strangers came in. The harbour and the river leading to the sea behind the town were guarded by natural barriers of sand bars and hidden channels. I did not fear an assault from the sea, particularly at this time of year; any boats coming would need to be guided in. Our blacksmiths worked tirelessly to get us ready. Mail armour was repaired, spears made, and weapons sharpened. We trained every day, well away from the town and the prying eyes that I suspected were watching us from within. None of the local people left town, but I had my doubts about their loyalty when the time came, although I did not voice it to anyone. Many fine words were spoken at the Thing and oaths were sworn to me on the Christian's Holy Bible, but

I knew that when the moment came to stand and fight, we could rely on but a few.

If we were to prevail, we would need every fighting man to do his work relentlessly. When you close with the enemy and see into their eyes, you must reach into that place of death where swords and axes do their worst. I could trust the men around us now, but I knew in my heart it might not be enough, and I had every expectation that we would face overwhelming numbers.

Nobody came or left the town, and the borders of our borough were watched continuously for any movement. It was a strange time, for we knew that a storm was coming but could do little about it except to prepare for its arrival. Father Leofrith eventually gave up trying to persuade me to leave, and his once frequent visits to my longhouse became fewer. He now spent much of his time praying in the church or visiting his flock.

"He has a faint heart, that one, and perhaps a deceitful one," said Turid, after one particular visit. "You can trust yourself, your family and your men, but there is little comfort to be had from the weasel words of this priest."

We watched him trudge away, head bowed, shoulders stooped.

"He does little to inspire confidence in his church," I replied. "I do not think we can rely on the intervention of Jesus Christ to help us."

We both laughed.

Leofrith walked out into the street beyond my courtyard and was passed by the rider of a huge bay stallion coming towards the longhouse. I did not recognise the horseman at first, but as he drew closer I saw it was William from Normannia. He hailed me from a distance and rode up to me at a trot.

"Three days sailing, and no welcome? It took me an age to get past the guards at your gate as well," he shouted down to me before dismounting.

"It is good to see you as always, William, but we are not making any more ploughs this year," I said.

"I thought you called for ships," he said. "Now, tell me exactly what is going on here, for I am hearing many strange rumours."

"Some refreshment first, I think."

He followed me into the longhouse, and Turid hurried across to greet him. Of the three brothers from Normannia who we had first guested years ago, William was probably the most likeable. He had lost none of the enthusiasm he had as a boy but had now grown into a strapping and confident young man.

He sat while servants brought him food and drink, and as he ate, I told him of the King's plot and of his anticipated, imminent attack. He listened intently, and when I had finished, he spoke.

"Truly, King Aethelred is a treacherous dog, and he has probably been plotting to retrieve his land ever since he gave it to you. These Saxons can scarcely be trusted. Did you know he has paid Duke Robert a king's ransom not to aid or support his enemies? But I do not think we need worry about that too much," he said winking conspiratorially. "Now, I have brought your ships, and as you requested, they wait for you at Northey Island. Saddle up your horse for there is something I wish to show you. Do you still have your stallion, Dragons Breath? I think I may have a horse that could finally best him, and he could do with a gallop."

My horse was saddled and stood waiting next to William's and together we left the town making our way to the banks of the estuary where we galloped off. Northey Island had not changed since we first landed with Olaf ten years ago and we crossed the narrow causeway in single file to get onto the deserted marshland.

"You could hide an army here and nobody would know," shouted William to me.

"I know. We did that too," I replied, as we picked our way

across the dry scrubland to where his ships lay.

"So what do you think?" asked William as we rounded the corner and found his camp.

For a moment I was speechless, as in front of us on the beach lay twelve large longships having been dragged free of the water. William's men had landed, disembarked and built their camp on the high ground overlooking the beach where the vessels rested, and their tents lay in neat rows. What took my breath away were the fifty tethered horses, tied up in lines beside the tents. But they were not ordinary horses, they were Norman warhorses specially bred for their speed, stamina and ferocity in battle. These destriers could carry heavily armoured warriors into battle and would terrify any hapless foot soldiers who had the misfortune to confront them. I had seen them train in Normannia where the riders would practice endlessly, riding in close-knit groups and aiming their spears at the enemy. I had ridden with William when his men had repelled a group of Breton raiders who had crossed into Normannia to pillage some of the farms on their borders. William and a troop of twenty riders had caught fifty or so of these raiders and charged at them. The Bretons had formed a defensive shield wall, which shattered under the impact of William's charge. Those who were not speared or trampled beneath the ironclad hooves ran in all directions only to be ridden down by these enormous beasts. The horses themselves joined in the slaughter, biting and stamping the fleeing men.

"Let's go and meet your new guests," said William, and we dismounted and walked towards the line of horses. Their size was even more impressive up close. Each of the stallions was enormous; their huge shoulders matched the height of our tallest men, and their front and rear flanks were thickly muscled.

I smiled at William with some bemusement, for I knew that he had probably been forbidden to come to our aid.

"We seek permission to hunt on your land, Lord Bjorn."

"Granted, but what do you wish to hunt?"

"Aethelred's warriors," said William.

He went on to explain that the Duke of Normannia had some sympathy for our plight, and despite an agreement with King Aethelred, we should be offered a small assistance. This assistance came in the form of fifty Norman warriors who would stand with us on Saint Brice's day and, regardless of the outcome, would disappear as quietly as they had arrived. The boats that had been sent were also sufficient to carry all our wives and children away should things go badly for us.

The gods had answered my prayers, in a small way at least, and although William's horses would not be the same as a hundred of Olaf's ships, they were a welcome addition to our little army. Until Saint Brice's Day, they would stay out of sight appearing only when the time came to confront whatever the King sent to destroy us. The day of reckoning was but ten days away, and we needed to defend ourselves by all available means.

Later that day, one of my spies returned from Lundenburg with news. My servants had stayed in an alehouse within the city walls, saying they were Frisian traders looking for a place to over-winter. The talk in the city was that the King was terrified of all the Scandinavian folk who had settled, and that there was a plot, led by me, to kill him. Many warriors were arriving in London, and a good number of them were Irish. According to the rumours, the King had a spy in Maldon who reported that I was gathering an army of my countrymen to destroy him. The King's army would destroy me first, and when they struck on Saint Brice's Day, the rest of England would rise up and do the same to anyone of Norse blood in the country. I rewarded the man with silver and dismissed him.

"Aethelred has clearly gone mad," said Torstein later in the day as we sat together eating the evening meal.

"He just wants his land back and thinks if he kills us all before Yuletide he will no longer be threatened by any more Norsemen."

"We should have finished him off ten years ago when we had the chance," snorted Torstein.

"I doubt whether we will have that chance again, for you can be sure he will not accompany his troops. In ten days, we shall march out to meet whatever is coming our way and will have to let the *Norns* decide. How are the fortifications of the town progressing?" I asked.

"All is finished," said Torstein. "The palisade and earthworks are as high and strong as we could make them. There is but one way in and another way out, along the river. If the Saxons here stand up as they would have us believe, we can give anyone a fight."

"And our two hundred men under arms?" I asked him.

"More than ready. They will all fight to the last man."

"But can the Saxons amongst them be relied upon?"

"They are not in doubt, and their men can be relied upon. It all depends on the size of the force Aethelred sends against us," he replied.

I turned to Turid.

"You must take all the women and children to the boats on Northey Island. There are plenty of ships for everyone. If we fail, you must be ready to leave. Tell the women they should be packed and onboard the ships if the signal comes. If we have to leave there will be no coming back."

"They will all be ready," she said. "In the days before you meet the Saxon army, they will leave their farms and come to town. Now, Bjorn, we are forgetting our manners, this young man has probably not eaten well for days. We must make sure he has food and drink if we are to expect him to lead his horsemen against our enemies."

Turning to William, she raised her drinking horn to him in a toast, to which he smiled in acknowledgement.

"Thank you, Lady Turid. Let us drink to your victory over your enemies," he said, raising his cup in turn. "It is good to spend at least one night away from the men and our flatulent horses. If you ask me, the King has overstepped his mark and will stir up a hornet's nest. Your people may have come here uninvited, but they settled here peaceably enough, and you have brought the Saxons stability and wealth."

"True enough," she replied, "but men are greedy and unforgiving. Maybe in a hundred years we will be welcome. But not, I fear, as long as this King lives and remembers the shame we once heaped upon him."

We were all deep in silent thought until Torstein could bear the quietness no longer.

"We shall just have to bloody his nose once more," he said defiantly.

One by one, the families came into town over the coming days. They left the six farmsteads, put their children and valuables into carts and drove into Maldon with all their livestock. The town was full of people, and in the days leading up to the expected battle, Turid led the women and children away to Northey Island to the boats that would carry them away. The Drakes Head and the rest of our little fleet in the harbour were taken on the same short journey to join the waiting Norman ships. The Saxons of the town carried on with their normal lives although there was obvious tension. Everyone knew we were waiting for the arrival of the King's army from *Lundenburgh*. It came the day before Saint Brice's Day, when my servant, who had been sent to the city to spy, rode in on an exhausted horse. He had ridden through the night and was covered in mud.

"They are coming, Lord," he said excitedly. "There are many of them."

"Come," I said, "tell me exactly what you have learned."

Betlic and Eadig had lodged in an alehouse in *Lundenburgh* near the gates of the city for nearly forty days. After Eadig had returned with news ten days earlier, Betlic remained with orders to ride ahead to warn us of any force of men leaving the city in our direction. He watched around fifteen hundred men leave the city led by Ealderman Thoren and a Saxon Lord called Leofwine.

"Leofwine?" said Torstein standing behind me as he also listened to Beltic's news. "Is that not the son of the Saxon Lord you killed many years ago?"

"It is," I replied. "He has waited a long time for his vengeance. Come, we have little time left. Now, get the men ready for we must act with speed."

"The men have been ready for some time, Bjorn. Say the word and we shall march. We are ready," he said.

Torstein was correct. We had been ready for some days, and the men were waiting for us outside the longhouse. We numbered just over two hundred warriors fully armed with a variety of weapons, and each man carrying a freshly painted shield bearing the sign of the raven. We marched from the town leaving only a few armed men, and after barking final orders to them, I led the rest out to meet our fate.

Chapter 41: The Second Battle of Maldon

I decided to camp on a small hill, on the boundary of our land, that gave me a clear view of the road from *Lundenburgh*. We left Maldon in good time and were joined outside the town by William's horsemen. Together we marched for over several *eyktir* until we reached the place. It was the start of the winter, and I gave orders for huge fires to be built on the top of the hill to keep the men warm – and so that Thoren's men would see our position from wherever they were. We could watch their approach from miles away when it was light, and the small steep hill would give a well-needed advantage. Two hundred and fifty against fifteen hundred was a daunting ratio, but although the men were aware of the odds against us, they did not let it show as we settled in for the night.

"I have missed this life, cousin," Torstein confided as we sat before one of the great fires. He handed me a goatskin bag filled with wine. "The life of a farmer is a decent one but a little tame," he continued. "Now, this really is the life for me."

"You did not once tell me of this before," I said.

"I am not saying I disliked sleeping in a soft bed with the same woman every night, and I am very proud of all my sons. But this," he said, waving his flask around, "waiting with my brothers on the eve of battle for whatever comes our way. Now, this is the life for me. To fight beside you once again was always my heart's desire, and here we are, once more about to take death and destruction to those who would defy us. For me this is truly living."

"You do not fear the odds then?" I asked.

"Never, and not with you at my side, cousin. There is no other place I would rather be. Now please hand me back the wine for I feel the night is getting colder."

Torstein's courage and optimism were as infectious as

ever and seemed to inspire all the men around us. We might be heavily outnumbered but come the dawn we would meet our enemy head-on, without fear. The battle's fury would descend upon us all at least one more time.

The next morning, we stood on top of our hill: two hundred spearmen, arrayed in a single line, looking across at the opposite hillside. In the valley between the two hills ran a muddy road by which we had come. This was the main road to and from *Lundenburgh*, and from our vantage point I could see Thoren's army camped a little way in the distance. They had arrived late in the night, long after we took our position yesterday, for I had seen no sign of them during daylight. The morning was cold, the first early-winter frost dusted the hard ground, but the rising sun was warm on our backs. The Saxons had lit no fires, and for them it must have been a freezing night with no shelter on the open ground. After a day and half of marching, they would be cold and hungry. However, there was a vast number of them which I estimated to be around two thousand men, many more than I expected.

I turned to address my men.

"What you see down there is a cold and hungry army who want nothing more than to go home. We stand here, not as Saxons and Scandinavians, but as men defending our homes and families. We are all that stands between what is rightfully ours and these outlaws, and today we shall make our stand and send them home. I count many men down there but do not overrate their thirst for battle. They are men with little to fight for, whereas we have everything to lose. You know what to do, and we shall fight as we have trained to do. You all know our plan, and if your hearts quail during this battle, look for me, for I will be where the fighting is thickest."

They beat their weapons against their shields, the noise echoing through the hills.

"That should wake those bastards up properly down there," said Torstein who, as he had done so often before, stood at my shoulder.

He was dressed in a long mail coat and the massive helm he had taken many years ago on Laeso. It was gleaming in the early morning sunlight, and its burnished bronze and gold had lost none of their lustre over the years. He swung his huge battle axe easily with one arm, relishing the coming conflict and eager for what lay ahead.

"Let's hope they make a fight of it," I said to him.

I knew our chances of victory were thin. I hoped, at best, that by striking an early blow we might encourage the enemy to turn and go home. Our fate was with the gods now, but if we played our part as I knew we could, they might yet favour us.

"Look, Bjorn. There is movement," he said.

We watched a force of about five hundred men move away from the main Saxon army towards the bottom of the hill on which we stood. They arranged themselves in a loose formation at the foot of the slope, five or six hundred paces from us. They carried round shields painted black and were armed with an assortment of spears and axes. Some wore helms and mail, but most were dressed in leather armour spattered with the mud from their march. They carried a single banner, a simple black flag that gave no clue from where they came.

"They do not look like Saxons to me," I said to Torstein as we looked from one group to the other.

"Those over there do," he said pointing his axe towards the main group, "but these in front of us I do not recognise."

Two men stepped out from the group beneath the black flag and walked a little way up the hill, stopping halfway between the two lines of standing warriors.

"Looks like they want to talk," I said. "Come, Torstein, let us see what nonsense they have to say."

We set off down the slope to meet them. As we got closer to the men, I could still not make out their origin.

"Speak," I commanded them.

They were both tall men and their leader, a wiry, red-headed warrior spoke first.

"You will not remember me Norsemen, but you killed my brothers many years ago, and I seek vengeance."

"I have killed many men, and they mostly deserved it, but what was the crime of your brothers for which they died?"

"My name is Tagdh, and I lead these Irish warriors. You saved the Finngail Olaf and his people at the gates of Dubh Linn many years ago and killed my brothers."

"Ah, I remember your rabble on that day. I believe those of your people who were left standing turned and fled. Now, what are you doing on my land? Do you wish to join your brothers? You look cold and hungry, Irishmen, perhaps you would like to come to my camp and get some food and warmth before returning home. Or you can just die here."

"Lord Thoren has promised me your head, and before this day is done I shall have it. He has sent me to say that he will spare the lives of your families if you lay down your arms to us. We know you are but few and will be overrun and dead long before this day ends, so why not spare your people?" said Tadgh.

I looked over to where Thoren sat motionless on his horse in front of his men. What I saw took me by surprise, for there, sitting on his old brown mare, was the little priest, Leofrith, looking towards us. Tadgh saw my shock, for I could not conceal it.

"You have been betrayed," he said.

I could feel Torstein moving restlessly beside me, like a hunting dog scenting his prey.

"You can tell your paymaster, Thoren, that if he does not have the balls to speak with me in person he can only expect to die with the rest of you this very day. Have you anything else to say?" I said, recovering from the truth of Leofrith's treachery.

Before the man could speak Torstein interrupted.

"I shall look for you both today," he said, with huge menace pointing his axe at them as if it were but a small stick.

We were both taller than either of the two men before us, and our position on the slope enabled us to tower over them. Tagdh smiled and turned away, and taking the other man with him, returned to his warriors. We did the same, but when we were halfway back up the slope, I felt an arrow whistle close by my head and land in the ground in front of us.

Torstein looked at me quizzically. "You can never trust Irishmen," he said.

I said nothing but handed him my shield and hurled a javelin towards the two Irishmen walking down the hill. It was a mighty throw; the spear sailed through the air and caught Tadhg's companion in the back, felling him in an instant.

Torstein nodded his approval. "That is a good start to proceedings," he laughed, and the rest of our men once again beat weapons against shields.

The Irish warriors, clearly incensed by what had happened, grew very noisy, and I watched Tadgh exhort them to further fury before they started their rush towards our lines. They began their charge at full speed, but to reach us, at pace, on the top of the hill carrying shields and weapons was a task beyond most men. At the halfway point their pace slowed, and their lines spread out. They met a hail of arrows, shot by our archers with deadly accuracy. By the time the Irish got to within fifty paces of our lines, I ordered a volley of javelins released which had a similar effect to the fusillade of arrows. The advance staggered, and their men fell all the way along the line. Some of the Irishmen reached us only to meet their deaths at the end of a spear. I watched as Tagdh and a dozen of his men reeled into our shield wall. This little knot of men had managed to get within an axe strike of our double line of warriors standing behind locked shields. There they stood, heavy limbed, trying to hack away at the solid wall before them.

Despite the recklessness of their charge, I admired the bravery of these men who had run up a steep slope against a deadly shower of arrows and javelins. I saw our wall part, not because it had given way, but to allow Torstein and his men through the gap. He advanced like Thor come to earth, and in a heartbeat, he was amongst the enemy leading a spearhead of men through their drained ranks. He was like the warrior I long remembered, reaping his opponents like so much ripe corn. The cream of the Jomsvikings were in full flow, doing their deadly work, and in a moment our lines had broken as the men seized the opportunity to finish off any resistance. Tagdh's group was quickly splintered and finished off, and the rest of his men retreated down the slopes, leaping over their fallen comrades to escape our hacking blades. I ordered the hunting horn to be sounded and called our men back. There were hundreds of Irish bodies lying on the slope in front of us, and the dead and dying covered the ground. I looked towards the army of Thoren who had stood motionless as the carnage in front of them unfolded. They had not made a single effort to aid Tagdh's men and had been content to see their comrades slaughtered in front of them. The survivors of the hilltop ascent fled towards their lines.

Torstein appeared in front of me grinning from ear to ear.

"That should give that fat bastard, Thoren, something to think about," he shouted, dragging a man who was more dead than alive towards me by his remaining leg. It was Tagdh, who earlier that morning had promised to behead me. His leg was severed at the knee and he had been slashed heavily about the head and body.

"Hello, Tagdh," I said cheerfully. "You are about to join your dead brothers. This you can do quickly, or we can make you last for days. Just tell me what Thoren's plans are, and we will deliver you to the next world before you know it."

The wounded man was clearly in a great deal of pain, but as he looked at me, I knew that he understood.

"He promised us land for my people and gold for your head," he spluttered through bloodied lips and shattered teeth. "The King has put an enormous bounty on you. Thoren will kill you all here and then take your town and farms. Your neighbours are probably helping themselves to your women and your silver right now. All over Aethelred's kingdom, your people are being put to the sword. You will soon be dead, and your wives and children will be taken away and sold into slavery."

I said nothing but nodded to Torstein who took off the man's head in one mighty sweep of his axe before kicking the lifeless corpse down the slope, Tagdh's detached head bouncing carelessly before it.

"We will deal with Leofrith and his treacherous Saxons in due course, cousin. For now, let the men refresh themselves before we march down to meet Thoren and his army and see what they are made of. Now, how many men have we lost?"

"Precious few, cousin. Three dead warriors only," he called as a man pressed a wooden flagon of ale into his hand. All around men were drinking silently and re-gathering their strength. There was little celebration, for we all knew that our greatest test was yet to come.

The hunting horn sounded again, and my men reformed their two lines. We moved down the slope to where the ground levelled out and wheeled around to face the enemy five hundred paces away. We were still outnumbered by about seven to one, but the display against the Irish had given Thoren's men plenty to think about as they waited to see what we would do next. Our decisive movements had forced them into forming their own shield wall, which dwarfed our own, but we marched purposefully towards them and stopped on my command. The shield wall in front of us now stretched way beyond our own flanks. We were close enough to see the faces hiding behind locked shields.

"*Svinfylking!*" I called, and the men formed into the wedge that we had practised and executed so many times before. We did not run but walked forward towards the Saxon shields in a tightly knit group, Torstein and our strong men at the apex, the rest providing the wood behind the spear. I called for the group to halt only fifty feet from the enemy lines. We waited there, each man silently contemplating his task ahead. It was a moment the like of which I have never experienced, nor ever would again. It was a moment when time stood still, and we waited and watched the anxious looks from the men opposite, bracing themselves for whatever was to come. It was Thoren, who broke the silence.

"Do not fear the crow fodder that stands before you. Look how few they are. These are nothing but bastard Norsemen and their traitorous companions who are all about to die. They will not be able to withstand us. Give me Bjorn Halfdanson's head, and I will pay the man who kills him with its weight in silver."

On my command, from within the boar's head, our hunting horn sounded thrice and we moved forward. We closed to near where Thoren sat on his horse beneath his banner, behind the shield wall. I believe he was as surprised as his men were to see us advancing on their greater numbers. We were almost upon them when I felt tremors run from the ground and up through my legs. Then the sound of galloping horses, the noise of their hooves growing louder and louder. It swept past us like rolling thunder and what followed was the almighty clash of armoured horses and men driven hard against the far flank of Thoren's line. With the screams of the Saxons and the sound of splintering shields as our signals, we charged at the line before us, which rapidly lost its shape.

William's men had arrived exactly as planned, and I looked over briefly to see him and his men wheel away from their shaken quarry to reform before returning to fight. We closed with the line in front of us and punched a hole straight through the front ranks, striking out to the left and right. The battle's fever coursed through my blood, and I was filled with a strength and anger that no man who opposed me could match. Warrior opposed warrior in frenzied combat, and we hacked and cut our way through everything in front of us for what seemed like an eternity. I watched old comrades fall beside me as we continued our progress through the mass of confused men towards Thoren's standard, and I could sense that perhaps we might have turned the day.

The *Norns* are known to play with the hearts of men, and sometimes when it seems as if they have decided a man's fate, they cut the cords and send him spinning in the opposite direction. This was such a time, for the skies opened and it began to rain. Not just a winter shower but a deluge that poured down without mercy, soaking each man with a freezing, driving torrent of hail and rain. Our progress was checked and the ground, which had been firm, turned to mud beneath our feet and slowed our progress. The clash of steel on steel was replaced with thunder and lightning. The enemy ahead melted away and for one heart-lifting instant, I thought we had bested them. Then I looked up and saw them gathering around their leader a hundred paces or more away, bloodied and shocked perhaps, but not ready to show us their backs. I looked for William, now dismounted, who was walking leaden footed towards me. I could barely hear what he was saying, for the noise of the storm was deafening.

"The horses are getting bogged down, Bjorn. It is no good – they are struggling in the mud as much as your men are."

I swore and cursed the gods for betraying us.

"We can do no more like this," I shouted.

The men gathered around me waiting for my decision, and as suddenly as it had arrived the storm ceased and the clouds parted, through which the sun shone on a sodden, bloody battlefield covered with the dead of each side. As it did so, I looked towards our foes and saw they were moving off the field, led by their Lord and the traitorous priest who rode at his side. They were not going back to *Lundenburgh* – they were heading towards Maldon, and if they arrived before we did, all would be lost.

"That treacherous bastard Leofrith knows that the town is guarded by women and a few farmers," I said to our men.

"If Thoren gets there ahead of us he will likely meet little resistance."

"Then we will get there first," said Torstein calmly.

"I will go with William, and we shall slow them down. Torstein, take the men back to the town by the hunters' trail. It is a day's march to get there, and you will reach the town by morning if you do not stop. Go now and we shall meet you tomorrow," I said, and one of the men went to fetch Dragons Breath who had been waiting patiently in last night's camp.

The hunters' trail was a path leading through the hills and into the forest which stood between us and Maldon. We had discovered it some years ago when we had caught poachers coming to take our deer. It was a single-tracked path that hunters used to get in and out of the dense forest that stood on one side of our town. Torstein gathered his men around him and led them off as fast as they could go.

It looked like we had lost about a quarter of the original number of warriors, and our men were tired and battered. They had given a good account of themselves and had left hundreds of enemy warriors dead on the field. But for the rain, we might have carried the day, but we would never know. All that mattered was that we reached our town first, for even if the Saxons of Maldon resisted the invaders, which I doubted, they would surely not be able to withstand a force that numbered over a thousand men. William and I were left standing together, and we walked over to where his men stood by their mounts grazing the same grass on which they had recently trampled Thoren's men to their death.

"Do you think we can do enough to give Torstein and his men some time?" I asked him.

"It might have stopped raining, but we will still struggle to make many charges in this mud. But it is good that the Saxons do not know this. Mounted warriors strike fear into the enemy well before the first spear hits home. Terror shall be our weapon of choice until we reach Maldon," called William cheerfully back to me.

He spoke with his men and told them what our tactics were to be. There was still an *eykt* of daylight before sunset and the horses, now refreshed and fed, were mounted and steered in the direction of Thoren's men who were making slow progress along the road. The way they had chosen was across open country, and we watched them as their army of a thousand men trudged through thick mud. I learned from William that his men – he called them cavalry – feared arrows more than anything else but that the wet weather and the cold conditions rendered archers useless. Although the going was heavy, our horses were still able to ride close to the enemy vanguard causing panic and uncertainty whenever we got close enough. Each time we did so they would stop and make a defensive shield wall, and we would wait and simply ride off again. We also picked off the men at the rear of their column – the stragglers who could not keep up with the rest. The alarm that these forays raised caused the whole column to continually stop and restart, and the pace of their march slowed to a crawl. Eventually, Thoren and his captains decided to camp for the night, and his exhausted men lay down on the side of the road to rest. In the day's remaining half-light, William led our company off to some nearby high ground to rest men and horses before we continued our game of cat-and-mouse at dawn.

"Don't worry, Bjorn. Torstein will get there in good time," said William, as we sat around the fire later that night.

"Oh, I believe he will get there, but I think we will need to leave this land in the end. There are just too many of them for us."

"It is unlike you to talk in such terms," said William.

"When we fought as single men we had no thought for anyone except ourselves. We fought for reputation and riches and nothing else. But we have families now and our thoughts are with them. Wait, it will come to you one day."

"And tomorrow, what shall our plans be then?" he asked.

"If the town's Saxons are steadfast, we may have a

chance, but if they desert, which they may have done already, we must leave. You will take your men back to the boats and see our women and children safely away from these shores. I cannot ask any more of you, for this is our fight not yours."

"Of course, I understand. But you, *Jarl* Bjorn, what shall you do then if all is lost?" he asked.

"We shall have to see what tomorrow brings," I said.

I was tired and quickly fell into a deep sleep. I dreamt I was back in Haugesund with my family. They were all there, my father, my mother, my siblings. Turid was also there with our four children, and we were on the sand by the sea outside the town. Standing beside me was Torstein and Hild with their five strapping sons. It was a summer's day, and we were smiling at the children playing at our feet. Suddenly, a mighty sea creature rose out of the ocean, a Kraken with a huge raven's beak, which snapped at us. With one peck it picked up Torstein and swallowed him whole and then started to peck at our screaming children. Turid leapt at it and grabbed hold of its neck, gripping with her knees behind its huge head, while she hacked away with an axe in each hand. The creature bled black blood which soaked us all. It screamed and retreated, back into the sea taking Turid with it.

A hand on my shoulder rescued me, waking me from sleep.

"Wake up Bjorn, Dragons Breath is calling you. There is work to be done," said William, handing me a piece of hard bread. "Let's wake these Saxons up shall we."

The morning was cold but dry, and at first light William led our troop down a slope to the flat land where the long column of Saxons waited. Their men, many still asleep were alerted by sentries, and the clatter of men getting to their feet resounded along the length of the road.

We stopped and watched them as panic, caused by our approach, spread like wildfire through their ranks.

"Fifty horsemen against a thousand foot soldiers and see the effect! Now just imagine if there were five hundred of us.

This would all be over by now," shouted William. The Saxon line started its slow movement into life and continued on its journey. "Let's see what's happening at the front."

He wheeled away and led us to the head of the column to feign a charge. Thoren and his captains were seated on their mounts behind a wall of rapidly assembled shields, but before we got to within thirty paces our flying column wheeled and turned away.

The previous day, I had marvelled at the effect that William's small group of cavalry had on so many warriors. Not only did they inspire terror as they approached but the impact of these armoured beasts hitting a line of shields had been equally devastating, knocking defenders senseless before their riders skewered them with spear work. We lost only one horse and rider after they had become bogged down in the heavy rain-soaked ground. Although the Saxons became used to our tactics of charge-and-feint, the manoeuvres still caused panic, for every time we got close to their line they were forced to stop and defend. I looked to the line of trees far away that marked the start of the forest through which Torstein and his men had travelled.

"Keep this up a little longer and – the gods willing – he will be there in time," I shouted to William.

"He will be there, Bjorn. Nothing will stop him," replied William.

"Come, let us hit the back of this line properly this time. Twenty silver pennies for the first man to spear a Saxon," he shouted, and we raced away with his men bringing down their spears, couching them under one arm.

We continued harrying Thoren's men for half the day until I saw the town in the far distance. I pointed it out to William who nodded and turned his troop towards Maldon, cantering off, away from the line of marching men. There was little movement from the top of the town's palisade, neither did I see any movement from the huge earthworks in front of it. The gates were closed, but as we came closer my heart leapt

390

to see our Raven standard hoisted above them.

Chapter 42: The Retreat of the Wandering Warriors

"There you are, I told you he would make it," said William.

As he spoke, so the wooden gates swung open, and Torstein's unmistakable frame walked out to meet us. He was followed by a smaller, slighter figure that I first took to be a boy, but as we approached them, I saw it was my wife. She was dressed in her old fighting clothes and carried a shield and spear.

"What kept you?" called Torstein. "Turid has been entertaining us with her axe throwing while we have been waiting."

"Where are the town's people," I asked them.

"All gone," Turid called. "Disappeared with everything they could carry."

"But not before she reminded them of where their loyalties should lie," said Torstein nodding in the direction of two dead men lying inside the gates.

"Let's get in and close the gates," she said. "We have little time."

She turned and we followed her back through the gates into the town. Turid told us that when we left to meet Thoren, the townspeople gathered and started to raid the empty houses. The six men we had left there ordered them to stop. But the mob refused and turned on the men, killing two of them. Turid, who had just returned from Northey Island after conveying the last of the women and children there, joined the four remaining men. The mob of several hundred were encouraged by their success and came to my longhouse to attack Turid and the men inside. She went out to talk to the people but was attacked and knocked to the ground. Our men came to her aid and speared two of her attackers to death which quieted the mob who then turned and went in search of easier pickings. As they turned and left, a Saxon woman – one of Turid's servants – told her they had been promised a silver shilling for each dead Scandinavian settler – man, woman or child.

"They are looking for all the women and children now," Turid told me, "but they are safe on the island, at least until low tide when they can be reached from the mainland."

"And who was to pay them this money?" I asked.

"King Aethelred has promised the bounty – but Leofrith the priest was to give them the money when he returned."

There was silence. I swore, and Torstein spat.

"We took the hunting bows and shot a few arrows, then set the dogs on them and chased them out of town. There was a little resistance at the gates, but I put an end to that with these," said Turid tapping the little throwing axes at her belt. "I sent the men back to the causeway to guard it until you got here."

"You did well," I told her, "but as soon as Thoren gets here they will be back."

"Then do we fight or flee?" asked Torstein.

I stood in the middle of the circle of warriors and went from each man searching their faces to fathom their thoughts. They were friends, family, neighbours and allies, and I had led many of them for fifteen years, from Jomsborg to this place where we now stood. Our lives and those of our children and wives were in the balance. They were dirty, disheveled and streaked with blood – from the men they had killed or from their own wounds. There was still some fight left in them and if I asked them, they would fight with me until the last man dropped. The Saxons who had stood beside us so stoically, particularly over the last day and night, looked bewildered and lost. I knew what must be done.

"We will give them nothing but ashes. They are coming for our heads and will soon be here, but there will be nothing for them but dust. We are not Saxons or Normans or

Norsemen here. We are warriors-in-arms of the same *aett*. Any man who wishes to stay will do so with my blessing and my silver. For me the place is accursed and all those who wish to leave with me may do so. We shall put the town to the flame before making for the boats." I looked to Edgar, a Saxon who always spoke for their group.

"We have spoken, *Jarl* Bjorn," he said, "and we wish to come with you, but…"

"Your families are all safe, Edgar," said Turid interrupting. "They are waiting with the ships with the rest of our people."

"Then let us make haste. William, please take your men to the island and get them ready to leave on the high tide. The rest of us will not be far behind you, all the ships must leave as soon as we get to you."

"As you say, *Jarl* Bjorn," he replied

I then turned to Turid. "Take Dragons Breath and go with William. Make sure that everyone is ready to leave."

I bent over her and kissed her, whispering in her ear, "you have fought well, my love, I need you to protect our people until I get back."

"Just don't be late then,' she said and mounted the horse before joining the Normans to ride off.

"It will take them a while to get all the horses over the causeway, so we must give them a little time," I said to the men. "Now, let us set some of these buildings aflame."

We torched the first houses in the centre of town and then my longhouse. The buildings were all made of wood and thatch, and despite the recent rains, they soon caught, and the wind fanned the flames which leapt from house to house. The church was the next to go up, and the tall wooden structure was ablaze, blowing glowing embers onto the thatched roofs of all the town's houses and before long everything was alight. Above the heat and the crackle of the flames, one of the men on the ramparts called out a warning. The enemy host was here and would soon be upon us. We carried all the bows,

394

arrows and spears from the longhouse and stood on top of the ramparts watching Thoren's men, no more than five hundred paces away from the earthworks.

"When the last arrow and spear leaves these walls," I shouted, "we go! Thoren can have his town but not a single one of our heads. We shall make them pay for their folly once more, but by the time they climb these walls we shall be gone."

"That is a shame, for I would love to see the look on the face of that little shit, Leofrith, when he sees his church. Now to arms," Torstein shouted back before releasing the first of many javelins. It did not reach the priest, who had positioned himself well out of harm's way, but it did find a target, killing a man who was racing towards the gates. A shower of arrows and spears followed, and when these were exhausted, our enemies had reached the gates and were trying to batter their way in. We picked up our shields and climbed down from the walls to make our escape. We ran as fast and hard as our weary legs could carry us, the heat of the fires scorching our clothes and hair as we made for the small gate behind the town. Then we were out and running, along the riverbank towards the island. It seemed like an age until we finally reached the causeway, all of us gasping from the effects of the smoke and our flight. The last of the horsemen had only just reached the island over the causeway, and I saw from the level of water that high tide was still some time away. We could not follow them yet, for the enemy would be in pursuit and would soon be here. This is where we would make our last stand, for our people needed more time to make good their escape.

"Three lines, fifty men each and lock those shield tighter than you have ever done before," I ordered.

We turned and the men took up their positions in the shield wall that we had practised so many times before, forming a tight crescent shape around the entrance to the causeway. Torstein was at my shoulder as ever, and we waited for an eternity for our killers to arrive. When they did, they came like an angry storm of hornets.

Through the smallest of gaps in our shield wall, I watched them approach as we waited and braced ourselves. The moment of impact, when it came, was shattering. There were so few of us and so many of them that they were unable to use the full force of their numbers against us. Our little half-moon of resistance held firm at first, but slowly the spears and swords that came stabbing through the gaps started to take their toll, and my men began to fall, one by one. The more of our men that fell, the harder we fought, and an inexhaustible spirit carried us way beyond the limits that any normal man could endure. Still, we fought on until each man carried a wound of some sort, and each blow we suffered reduced our lines. Soon, only half of us remained standing while we fought on, struggling against wave after wave of attack. I heard Torstein bellow his defiance as a spear thrust caught him deep in the chest. I stabbed his attacker in the throat, dropping him with my *seax*. Our men fought for an age, long after the last of our energy expired. I tried to raise my voice above the din of weapon upon shield.

"It is time, brothers! To the boats," I cried.

One by one, as we had planned, the rear ranks withdrew and retreated in single file over the flooding causeway. Each man followed the next until only the remnants of the front ranks stood, before they too retreated towards the island. There were just the four of us left now - Torstein, the two old Norwegian warriors, Einar, Rurik and me.

"The last men of *Baldrs Wrath* should leave together," shouted Torstein.

He charged our attackers once again and halted their progress for an instant making the most of the newfound space about him. Despite his wounds, he whirled his battle -axe about his head bringing destruction to all who stood in his way. We backed over the causeway as best we could, and it took the remainder of my strength to pull Torstein with me before he descended into the mass of warriors in front of us again. The water level on the causeway reached to our knees, but we backed across blindly, each man guiding the one in front by a hand on the shoulder. Some of our attackers tried to get into the water and take us from the sides but were sucked down by the mud and then covered by the rushing tide.

"Come Torstein we are nearly there. We shall beat death together one more time," I encouraged him.

Painstakingly we reached the far side of the causeway but not yet to safety. Saxon warriors were still coming after us even as we reached the banks of the island to scramble ashore to higher ground. The causeway could only take two men standing close together, and although the tide raced in and covered it, there were still Saxon warriors wading across the deepening water to get to us. There must have been at least a hundred warriors, in line, trying to reach us on the causeway, and we had to stop them here. We stood together, a small knot of resistance holding against the rising tide of enemy warriors who would surely engulf us at any time. I looked at Torstein and saw the extent of his injuries. His mail shirt was torn open from neck to waist, and he was bleeding profusely from his spear wound. His helm had gone, and he had a deep cut than ran from his chin to his forehead exposing the bone. His left arm dangled uselessly by one side from an axe wound he had received as we retreated. The onrushing Saxons paused on the flooding causeway wondering what we would do next, and in that moment of hesitation, Torstein looked back at me.

"I can go no further, Bjorn, for I was not built to go backwards. You will not come with me on this occasion for you have to lead our folk to their new home. You also have my five sons to feed, and if you should find yourself in bed with Hild, I must warn you that she is a woman of enormous appetites," he said, laughing. "Now go, I have a feeling that Valhalla is finally calling me. I shall keep a seat for you next to me."

He launched himself back onto the causeway to close

with the enemy. Einar and Rurik pushed their way past me, to follow him, scattering anyone who stood in their path. I hesitated and then turned to hear my name being called; it was Turid, waiting on a mud bank up ahead.

"Come quick Bjorn, the boats are leaving," she called. I ran towards her and then looked back. The tide had risen to chest height over the causeway and many of the Saxons had been swept away. I could no longer see Einar or Rurik, but Torstein, his axe gone, was grappling with two of the remaining Saxons on the land bridge. He roared defiantly, then toppled over, taking them down into the muddy water with him. They disappeared from sight only for Torstein to rise back to the surface, and with his *seax* in hand, he stabbed down at the men in a frenzy of thrashing and churning water. Then there was silence and all three sank beneath the swirling waters, not to resurface again. Time stood still for the length of a few heartbeats. I was deaf and blind to everything around me save only the vision of black feathers carried on the sea breeze. *Munin*, one of Odin's ravens, was falling to earth from his home in Asgard, and I could do nothing to save him.

I felt Turid take my hand and pull me after her. I walked along the mud bank in a stupor, the rest of my men some way ahead of us. I cast a glance at the far bank, separated by the thin channel of rushing seawater that had just taken my cousin. Thoren's men stood in a long line watching our escape, jeering and waving their weapons as if they had won some great victory. Thoren himself sitting there among them, impassively, astride his horse. Leofrith was next to him on his small, brown mare – a disconsolate figure in a dirty brown robe.

"Wait," said Turid, bidding me to stop, and she walked to the edge of the water that moved swiftly between the two banks of the mudflats. She stood there facing the foe until the jeering stopped. Then she raised her voice above the noise of the wind and roaring water so all could hear her. She cursed them. This small, fierce woman, her bare, blood-covered fists clenched in rage, roared her vengeance and cursed them. She cursed their families, their kings and their god and promised them all their crops would fail and their unborn children would wither in the womb. She cursed them first in her own language and then in Saxon.

"You are all cursed and will once again reap the wind from the north. My people will return here again, and your homes, your wives and your children will be put to the axe and the flame. Your land will be burned, those of your families who live will be enslaved, and your god will desert you. This is the price for your treachery. You will long for the time when we offered you peace instead of death and destruction. This curse you have brought on yourselves shall not be lifted for generations." She pointed a single finger at them as she spoke, before her gaze settled on the priest. She spat her wrath at him, and he seemed to recoil as if burned. Then she returned to my side, and we carried on walking as our enemies on the far bank fell into a stunned silence.

My men ahead disappeared from view as they took the path to the far side of the island, and we followed until we reached the others waiting patiently for us. There were fourteen ships in all, full of our people and belongings. William's men and horses had been loaded onto their stout merchant ships which waited at anchor offshore for us. The Drakes Head lay in shallow water as the last of my men climbed aboard her taking their positions at the oars.

"Your people are waiting for you, Bjorn," said Turid.

"Are they all ready?" I asked.

"They are. Our children are with Hild in another ship. Come, it is time to go."

We walked to the water's edge and waded into the sea to the Drakes Head. Many hands reached down to pull us aboard and with a huge effort, I got to my feet and went to the back of the ship to take the tiller. The large rock of an anchor was hauled in, oars dipped, and we pulled away leading our little fleet out along the Blackwater River and into the open sea.

To be continued …

Cast of Characters

Aethelred: King of the Saxons

Aldred: One of Bjorn's Saxon farmers

Astrid: Bjorn's partner in Jomsborg

Athelstan & Godwin: Saxon brothers and Bjorn's slaves

Bjorn Halfdanson: the Spear Arm, Son of Halfdan Strong Arm, leader of Baldyr's Wrath, Jarl of Maldon, husband to Turid

Borislav: King of the Wends, under Styrbjorn's protection

Ealderman Byrhtnoth: Lord and leader of the army of Essex

Eric of the Svear: King of Sweden

Frida: Jarl Eric's wife, Turid's elder sister

Geir: Bjorn's brother

Gormlaith: Concubine to King Olaf of Dubh Linn, wife of Máel Sechnaill

Gyrid: Wife of King Harald Bluetooth

Haakon Sigurdson: King of Norway

Hakon: Jomsviking Captain of Odin's Wrath

Halfdan Strong Arm: Bjorn's father

Harald Bluetooth: King of the Danes

Helge: Captain of the Raven

Hemming: Headman in the village of Bamburgh

Hild: Torstein's wife

Leif Iron Fist: Champion of the Ravens

Leif: A Norwegian member of the Ravens

Leofwine: The son of Byrhtnoth

Liv: Bjorn's mother

Máel Sechnaill: King of the Irish

Olaf Cuaran: King of Dubh Linn

Olaf Guthfrithson: Old King of Dubh Linn and Jorvik (York)

Oswulf: Saxon elderman and Lord of Bamburg

Otto: Son of King Borislav

Oyvind: Bjorn's uncle, Commander of Trelleborg

Ragnar: Ulf's Grandfather

Richard & William: Rolf's younger brothers

Rolf: A Norman count

Rollo: Bjorn's uncle, Torstein's father

Rurik: Leif's fellow adventurer and Raven

Siegrid: King Eric's wife

Sigrid: Bjorn's sister

Sigurd Eysteinsson: Jarl of the Orkneys

Sigvaldi: Thorkill's brother, son of Strut-Harald

Styrbjorn Storki, the Strong: Sea King and Lord of the Jomsvikings

Svein Forkbeard: Son of Harald Bluetooth

Svein: Rolf's brother, one of two identical twins from Haugesund

Thoren: Aethelred's general and advisor

Thorkill the Tall: Jomsviking Captain of Thors Hammer

Torstein: Bjorn's cousin, fellow warrior, warrior skald

Tostig: A shepherd from Byrum

Turid: Young sister of Frida

Tyra: Wife of Styrbjorn the strong, daughter of the King and Queen of Denmark

Ubbi: Captain of Jomsvikings & the Ravens

Ulf: Boy from Byrum

Vladimir: Leader of a band of Kievan Rus

G lossary & Terminology

Aett: Clan

Allthing: A democratic, open meeting held annually by the community

Baldrs Wrath: Bjorn's company of Jomsvikings named after the Son of Odin & Fryr

Bjorr: Beer

Dagmal: Breakfast

Danegeld: A bribe to that would be paid in exchange for the cessation of our raiding

Danelaw: Part of England in which the laws of the Danes held sway

Donsk tunga: The common tongue of Scandinavian folk

Eykt (plural Eyktir): A period of approximately 3 hours or one eighth of a single day

Fot: Term of measurement equivalent to one foot

Fyrd: Saxon army made up of the local populace

Gotar: (Geats) People of a certain Swedish tribe

Gunilla: Female Chieftan of a Swedish tribe

Gunnlogi: Bjorn's Ulberht sword

Hel: A hell-like existence in the afterlife

Hnefatafl: A board game, like chess

Hudfat: Large skin bags used as sleeping bags and for carrying

Hugin: One of two mythical ravens that sat on Odin's shoulders, flying out each day to gather news for his master. He represented Odin's knowledge

Inn matki munr: Old Norse meaning - in the throes of passion

Jarl: A lord, local ruler

Jorvic: York

Kievan Rus: People of Swedish descent who settled in the East

Longphort: A temporary winter base

Lundenburgh: London

Munin: One of two mythical ravens that sat on Odin's shoulders, flying out each day to gather news for his master. He represented Odin's memory

Nón: Noon

Norns: Female deities who rule the destiny of gods and men - roughly corresponding to other controllers of humans' destiny

Odin: The oldest and most important of Norse gods, father of Thor

Ótta: 3:00 a.m.

Pikke: Young women

Ragnorok: The legendary "end of days"

Ring-giver: King or overlord

Sansorðinn: Homosexuals

Sea Jotun: Sea God

Seax: Short, Saxon stabbing sword

Skåne: Part of the Kingdom of Denmark

Skeid: Classic longboat design

Skjaldborg: Shield wall

Strandhewing: Raiding for supplies

Strandhogg: A raid onshore for supplies

Svinfylking: Boar's Snout – an offensive battle tactic

Thane: Saxon Nobleman

Ulfberht: Frankish sword of great value and reputation

Witan: The Saxon King's advisory council

Printed in Great Britain
by Amazon